THE TOLL

THE TOLL

MICHAEL MEWSHAW

THE BODLEY HEAD

LONDON   SYDNEY

TORONTO

The quotation from Ernest Hemingway's For Whom the Bell Tolls
is reprinted by kind permission of Jonathan Cape Ltd.

Copyright © 1973 by Michael Mewshaw
ISBN 0 370 01455 3
Printed in Great Britain for
The Bodley Head Ltd
9 Bow Street, London WC2E 7AL
by W & J Mackay Ltd, Chatham
First published in Great Britain 1974

For Philip Moulton Mayer,
a friend generous with hospitality and advice

"He had the feeling of something that had started normally and had then brought great, outsized, giant repercussions. It was as though you had thrown a stone and the stone made a ripple and the ripple returned roaring and toppling as a tidal wave. Or as though you shouted and the echo came back in rolls and peals of thunder, and the thunder was deadly. Or as though you struck one man and he fell and as far as you could see other men rose up all armed and armoured."

Ernest Hemingway, *For Whom the Bell Tolls*

I

STRETCHED on his stomach, Ted Kuyler stared over
the edge of the rock down the length of a shallow canyon.
Lined by giant red boulders like the one he was lying on,
the canyon narrowed but didn't close at the opposite end.
As Ted waited, watching this corridor, the sun burned his
shoulders through a faded flannel shirt, and he felt his
heart beating steadily against the warm stone.

He was a big man whose body had gone slightly soft and
spread out in the middle. It wasn't fat. Just stomach muscles which had given in grudgingly over the years, so that
around his hips he had what people call "love handles."
But he didn't call them that and didn't find it the least bit
funny to show signs of age. In his business when you lost
your body, you didn't last long.

The rest of him looked lean and hard. His shirt-sleeves
were rolled, and a thick net of veins webbed his rawboned
arms. There was a tattoo on his right bicep, the rose petals
pale against his sunburn. Ruddy rather than tanned from

wind and sun, he had permanent crowsfeet at the corners of his mouth and grey eyes, but though he appeared older, Kuyler wasn't quite forty.

Beside him, resting her chin on her folded wrists, lay a huge blond girl, the one they called Puff, who wore a flowered tent dress that couldn't disguise her exaggerated, overweight curves. Yet, curiously, her face wasn't fat. Chiseled, fair, and striking, it had a kind of Nordic fierceness, and her blue eyes closed to slits as she suddenly lifted her head.

By reflex, Ted lowered his when he heard footsteps near the corridor. A dark, stocky man darted in, crouching low as he sprinted toward them, carrying a rifle at his chest. Two men with pistols followed a few steps behind him. One of them, a lanky redhead, was lame and had a metal crutch clamped to his elbow to compensate for his limp. He fell behind the others who moved toward Puff and Ted.

A small girl in a dungaree shirt came into the canyon after them with a coiled rope over her shoulder. When a breeze blew a lock of long black hair across her face, she started to push it back, tripped, and would have fallen if the crippled fellow hadn't caught her.

Ted shot to his feet, shouting, "That's enough."

The burly man raised his eyes and the rifle. Both were aimed at Ted. "What?" The word echoed in the rocks.

"I said I've seen enough."

"What the hell, we haven't . . ."

Ted stepped to the far side of the flat-topped boulder, leaving Puff to watch the puzzled quartet in the canyon. She looked unhappy. Well, so am I, thought Ted, wondering whether the money was worth it. Hot and tired, he tried to control his temper. He had to be calm when they climbed up to confront him.

As he squatted on his haunches, he reflected, at least I learned a new expression. They'd promised to show him their plan like a piece of "guerrilla theatre," which he now assumed was the same as what used to be called Amateur Night in Dixie when he was a boy in Clifton Forge, Virginia. Too bad I can't tell them that. Somehow, without angering or insulting anybody too much, he had to convince them it wouldn't work. Not their way.

His forehead felt tight and stinging, the inside of his head dry and enormous after a day of surprising February heat. He ran a hand through his short reddish-blond hair. The fine pink dust that had covered his skin and clothes seemed to sift into his brain, and Ted had a tough time thinking straight. What could he tell them except the truth?

When he shifted his back to the sun, his shoulders began to burn again. The weather here was one-sided. There was no other way to describe it. A short step into, or out of, the shade instantly changed the season, for Morocco was a cold country that just happened to have a warm sun.

Across the valley, near the tiny town of Sidi-Abd-ej-Jebar, a truck took the unpaved track toward Tafraoute, spraying red dust above the tallest palm trees. For a moment he weakened and wished he were in it, headed for the Grand Hôtel du Sud and a cold shower, a couple of drinks, then dinner and a bottle of the inky local wine. All I want is to be in bed drunk, and to be able to pay the bill in the morning. I won't even ask for a woman. Is that too much? I'm too old for this bullshit.

But he'd be sleeping on the ground tonight. Hearing the group labor up the cliff, their breathing loud and hoarse, Ted thrust the thought from his mind. He refused to fool himself. If he wanted the money, he knew he faced a lot of hard work and more cold nights in the open.

Polo, the dark, stocky man in his mid-twenties, was the first one over the top. Puff offered him a hand, but he brushed by her and rushed at Ted, whose instinct was to stand and meet him. The slightest nudge would have sent Ted sailing off the rock. But he stayed down, bouncing lightly on the balls of his feet.

Halting to catch his breath, Polo held the rifle in both hands and threw back his head, bunching up a roll of muscle at his neck. Short, blunt arms, bristling with black hairs, flexed from the chopped-off sleeves of a fatigue shirt. His khaki pants and boots, too, were army issue and though he wore long hair and a bushy moustache, he had the bearing of a military man.

"What's this shit?" he said. "You didn't give us a chance."

"We'll wait on the others," Ted quietly answered. "Go help Phil."

The metal crutch clattered against the rock until Puff grabbed it. Polo, who wouldn't put down the rifle, gave her a hand and together they pulled up the thin crippled fellow. Though embarrassed and perhaps in pain, he smiled, thanked them, and sat next to Ted. His cheeks were flushed from exhaustion or the heat. It was hard to tell which, since Phil Powell had a pasty complexion, flecked with freckles, that registered every change in temperature and mood. He obviously had questions, but this was the wrong time to talk.

Ants Lyons, small, wiry, and nimble, made it up on his own. He was the youngest, in his late teens at most, and a page-boy haircut and sparse blond goatee didn't add any years to his face. Grinning broadly at the ease of this climb which his friends had found difficult, he said, "Hey, what's with you people? Sounds like a TB ward up here. Been smoking too much, right? I thought . . ." But at a look from Polo, he turned to catch the rope which the girl tossed him.

They called her Bert for some reason. Ted couldn't figure this, or why she dressed like a field hand. A pity. She might have been a pretty girl. But her long black hair was the only part of her appearance she seemed to care about, and it *was* beautiful.

Once she'd scrambled onto the stone, she nervously combed it out of her face with her fingers. Despite the name, the sloppy dungaree shirt, and patched Levis, she didn't look like any boy, and the way she walked, the way her high breasts pressed against the denim, suggested someone much taller. Though she wore no make-up, her mouth was dark and full, her brown eyes huge. Ted wished he'd see her one time in a dress. But in a few days it wasn't likely he'd see her at all. No great loss, he thought. She hadn't so much as glanced at him.

"Why don't you all sit down and rest," he said, and everyone, except Polo, settled in front of him. "You, too, Polo."

Lowering himself on one knee like a defensive lineman, Polo rested the rifle on his thigh. "How about an explanation? You asked for the plan. Why did you stop us half-way?"

"From what I saw, my friend, you don't have a plan. You've signed a suicide pact."

"Meaning?"

"You heard me. What's that rifle, an M-16?"

Polo nodded.

Ted took it from him for a closer look, surprised to find the automatic off the battlefield in civilian hands. It was light and compact, constructed of alloys and plastic. A few veteran soldiers, when they'd first handled it, thought it was a plaything. Then they'd shot it and changed their minds. It was a sweet weapon—for war, though, not what they were planning.

"Where'd you get it?"

"Don't worry. I got it."

"Okay, since you were so good at getting it, I suppose you know you lug it into that jail and squeeze off a few rounds, there'll be bullets bouncing all around the cellblock. You'll shoot every light bulb and brick in the building before you hit anyone. Then it'll probably be your own men. And how're you going to carry it in there without someone spotting it?"

"I'll work on that."

"Yeah. You do that, old buddy. And while you're at it, tell me, why the girl with the rope?"

"She'll tie up the guards while we're freeing Gypsy."

"Jeezus." Ted shut his eyes an instant, exaggerating his amazement and irritation. He wanted to emphasize the differences between Polo and him from the start. "You really think she could tie a knot that'd hold a man?"

When no one answered, Bert bowed her head, staring at her feet.

"Let's level with each other." Ted passed his eyes over the group and brought them to rest on Bert, who didn't look back at him. "As it stands now, you don't have a chicken's chance in a foxhole."

"That's your opinion," said Polo. "I'd like to know why the fuck . . ."

"I'll tell you why the fuck. You want me to draw you a picture? I'll draw you one. Like where'd the getaway car be?"

"Puff would have it outside the jail."

"Great! That means after you'd shot your way into the

cellblock and out again, you'd have to drive across that big-ass square—assuming any of you were left—and go through the medina or the souq. Either way, it'd take just one donkey cart or truck or even a beggar in a wheelchair to bottle you up until the cops came and blew your brains out. Man, you have to be crazy or something."

"Hold it. What the hell gives you the right to talk to us like this?" Polo had lowered his voice, and it sounded more menacing than if he'd shouted.

Ted intended to let this pass, but Phil said, "For Christ's sake, Polo, be reasonable. He's had experience and . . ."

"And what did he learn except how to napalm villages and torture prisoners?"

"I learned to keep my mouth shut when I didn't know what I was talking about."

The rifle butt struck the stone as Polo pitched to his feet. "Look, jack, I don't have to swallow this shit."

"Neither do I." Ted rose slowly and carefully, conscious once more of how little it would take to tumble him off the rock. Though shorter, Polo outweighed him by a good thirty pounds and had the M-16. Ted knew he couldn't let him make the first move. "You people asked for help getting your friend out of jail. If you've changed your mind and don't think you need me, that's fine. We'll forget it."

"No, wait." Phil stood between the two men. "We need you. Come on, Polo, calm down and listen."

"Okay, but lemme say something first. There may be a few facts you're forgetting," he shouted over Phil's shoulder at Ted. "You tell me not to take the rifle, but if you were here after the attempted coup last summer, you remember these pigs love nothing better than pulling the trigger. They don't give a good goddamn who you are. A lot of people got burned. More than the newspapers ever admitted. Gypsy's lucky to be alive, and so's Bert. The point is, he's a political prisoner, in with other political prisoners, and we aim to liberate him. You think you can do that unarmed, you're . . ."

"Gimme a break, friend." Sinking on his haunches, Ted wearily waved a hand. "Spare us the propaganda and crap. Gypsy's in jail for possession of hash and an unregistered pistol. I don't care whether he's guilty or not."

"You don't understand." As he crouched awkwardly with the rifle across his lap, Polo's voice was tinged with genuine anguish and regret. "It wasn't his gun. It was mine. As for the hash, they couldn't even find a roach. The cops had to vacuum his pockets to pick up shreds. For that he drew an unreal sentence. Five years! It had to be political. They must have thought he was part of the coup."

"Stop. I've heard this before." Though he hadn't heard it about Gypsy, Ted had listened to much the same story in several languages and on four continents. The hysteria, the hyped-up paranoia about oppression and political prisoners, the slogans, the rhetoric—he detested all of it no matter who was right or which side he was on, because in the end it meant more killing, and he knew who would have to do that, as well as the dying. "It's simple. Gypsy's your friend. He's in jail and you want to get him out. Why pretend you're doing it for political reasons?"

"Probably you think money's a better reason."

"He's not my friend. For me it's the only reason." He could tell none of them liked this, but he didn't take it back. Did they expect he'd risk his ass for nothing, for a man he'd never met?

Polo was smiling as he gnawed at his moustache. "Okay, you win. Why argue? You don't like politics, I don't care about money. So we'll spring Gypsy for the hell of it. To show the bastards who put him there we don't rattle."

"Hey, I don't like that," said Phil.

"Neither do I," said Puff who, for her size, spoke in a startlingly high-pitched voice. "Where does it leave Gypsy? I mean he's not just some excuse for you to play Pancho Villa."

"Look," said Ants, "the best reason is obvious, right? We're doing this because it's better for him to be free."

"We all agree on that," said Phil. "The question is, how?"

"By using our brains and betting on a long string of good luck. Guns won't help," said Ted. "They spook people—the ones who're carrying them and the ones they're aimed at. On a job like this the thing is to keep cool—right now while we're discussing it and later when we're doing it. We have to go at it strictly nonviolent so we . . ."

"Don't gimme any more bullshit about political clichés," snapped Polo. "That's the shaggiest one of the bunch, and I'm sick of hearing it. Nonviolence *is* violence, man, by another means. When it works—which isn't too damn often —it's because you've backed the other guy up against the wall and badgered him into busting your ass. You force him to do the dirty work, then claim you won. Well, I don't need that. I'm tired of lying down and being beaten. I'm not afraid to mix it up." He turned from Ted to the group. "Why not fight for what's right and what we want?"

"I told you," said Ted, "it doesn't matter what's right or what you want. Your politics give me a pain in the ass. All's I'm saying is, you use those guns, somebody's going to get hurt. No matter how careful you are, you could screw up, and if it comes to that, I'd rather be in jail than dead."

"You wouldn't think that if you'd done time in a Moroccan jail. Five years is like a life sentence," said Bert, her voice flat and matter-of-fact. Her hands held her bare ankles, and she seemed to be studying her sandals.

"Or a death sentence," Puff put in anxiously. "We have to break Gypsy before they send him to Casablanca. Here we have a chance. Up there he'll be lost. He won't last five years. Wait till you see him after six months at Tazenzit."

"Okay, okay, I'm with you." Ted swallowed to smooth the rough edges from his voice. Dust grated between his teeth, and when he drew a deep breath, his nostrils burned and the inside of his head ballooned larger. Unlike in any army he'd known, you couldn't give an unquestioned order to these people, and it was wearing him down. "We gotta spring him quick. But we also gotta have a good plan so no one gets shot or slapped in jail."

"Do you have one?" asked Phil.

"Yeah, and it's not much different from Polo's. First, we oughta be on foot. We could leave someone with the cars outside the city walls and walk through the souq to that square. But before we go in the jail, we need a diversion to draw out the guards and switch attention from what we're doing. An explosion or something. Then we could take our time freeing Gypsy, recrossing the square, slipping into the souq, and blending in with the crowd while we hustle back to the cars."

"Then what?" Phil pressed him, tightening his grip on the metal crutch which lay over his lap, a pathetic parody of Polo's M-16.

"What did you plan?" Ted asked Polo.

"There's only one thing to do. Drive over the mountains to Marrakech, travel north, and take the ferry from Tangier to Algeciras."

"Which is exactly what they'd expect. That's the first border they'd close. Without papers, you'd never get Gypsy

past customs, and if they didn't nab you then or on the road
north, they'd have three hours on the boat to try again. And
say you somehow sneaked by, where would you be? Spain!
Which isn't what you'd call famous for welcoming fugi-
tives."

"What country is?"

"You tell me."

When Polo didn't answer, Ants said, "The road's good
to Tan-Tan. From there it's a short trip to the southern
border."

"Not a bad idea. They wouldn't figure we'd head in that
direction. But that'd bring us to the Spanish Sahara. We
can do better."

"You mean Algeria?"

"That's what I mean."

"Christ, Polo, why didn't you think of it?" asked Ants.
"You've been there. What's it like? Would they grant us
political asylum?"

Polo looked extremely uneasy. Brushing his moustache
with the back of his thumb, he ignored Ant's puppy-like
enthusiasm and kept his voice level, his face blank. "It's a
long trip to Oujda. They could close that border too."

"That's why we wouldn't go north. From Tazenzit we'd
drive to Ouarzazate, then south down the Dra Valley past
Zagora to Mhamid. From there it's a few miles to Algeria.
There's no official crossing point, no customs authorities,
and the border's long and disputed. They can't patrol all
of it."

"They don't have to," said Polo. "Look at a map. That's
where the desert starts. Real desert. It's nothing but sand
dunes and rocks from there to the Sudan."

"There are trails. Pretty good ones, in fact. Camel caravans cross the area all the time. And if we head east, we'll

reach a road on the Algerian side that runs north from Tindouf to Béchar, and up to the coast. In Oran or Algiers we could catch a boat."

"I'm not worried about me. The Land-Rover'll make it. I don't know about your Renault."

"It's a good machine. I'm willing to chance it."

"Are you willing to chance your life?"

"Easy, friend. It won't come to that. The Renault breaks down, we'll pile into the Land-Rover."

"Fine, but it'd be a tight squeeze." Though he shrugged nonchalantly, Polo still appeared to be upset.

"What's the matter?" asked Puff. "You act like you don't want to go to Algeria. I thought you had contacts there."

"I don't dig this. None of it. We had it worked out."

"The man showed you we didn't."

"Back up a bit. His plan has risks, too."

"Fewer than yours," said Ted.

"You haven't proved that to me. How can it be safer without guns? You'd better have a hell of a diversion to pull those cops away from the jail."

"I'll have one. That's what you're paying me for."

"Look, you could set off an H-bomb in that square and at least a couple of guards are bound to stay in the cell-block. They're not about to hand Gypsy over to us without a fight, and how are we going to force them to?"

"Ever think of bribery?"

"Shit. Don't tell me that's what you've been leading up to. Phil and his family laid bread on half the big honchos in the country, and it didn't do a damn bit of good."

"It's true," said Phil. "A lot of them took money, but it didn't help at the trial, and they turned down our appeal."

"I'm not saying we should waste time or money on government officials. A few hundred bucks would go farther with one or two guards. There has to be a man in that jail who'd like to make a quick buck. Think a minute. Has anyone been specially friendly, willing to do favors?"

"You're just jacking yourself off."

"Wait, Polo. There's the guy who pats us down and checks our packages. The one with the bad eye. They let us bring Gypsy food and cigarettes once a week," Phil told Ted. "The same guard always searches us. Over the months he's gotten friendly. We don't speak much French, but he knows a little English and cracks a few jokes. He's careful, but never hassles us."

"That's because he swipes half the stuff we bring."

"Good," said Ted. "He's our man."

"I'd never trust him," said Polo. "He'd pocket the money, then turn us in."

"Maybe," Ted muttered, his mind elsewhere, trying to decide how they could protect themselves.

"Maybe, hell! We'd walk in empty-handed and never get out."

"You're wrong. We'd cover ourselves so they couldn't prove a thing."

"Yeah, but if we blew it that'd be the last chance. We've got a week at most. One shot and that's it. Once Gypsy's in maximum security at Casablanca, you can kiss him good-bye."

"Look, a bullet through the head would blow our chances, too," said Ted. "It boils down to this. We use guns, somebody's liable to be killed. My way, no one gets hurt."

Polo nodded. "A nice safe compromise. A straight business deal. Minimum risk, high return for you."

"Not a compromise," Ted shot back. "A sensible plan instead of a half-ass scheme."

"I think he's right," said Phil.

"Oh, you do?"

"I've thought that all along."

"So have I," said Puff.

When Ants and Bert agreed, Polo stood up. "Well, fuck you one and all."

"Don't be an ass," said Puff. "Sit down. If it weren't for you and your goddamn guns, Gypsy wouldn't be in jail in the first place."

"So that's how it is. I should have known." His chunky shoulders were churning inside the fatigue shirt. "Lemme ask one question. What do you plan to do about the other prisoners?"

"Nothing," said Ted.

"That's what I thought."

"I don't understand." Bewildered, Phil appealed to either man for an explanation.

"No, you wouldn't," Polo said. "You have a big, bleeding heart, but not enough guts for anything more than selective indignation. You pick up on the little problems and pretend the big ones don't exist."

"I still don't get it."

"Gypsy's not alone in that jail. There are at least thirty men—three in the same cell with him. So what you'll have to do after breaking loose your brother is shove his buddies back into the slam and leave the poor bastards stewing in that shithole. You people make me sick.

"When Gypsy was busted, you got steamed up and agreed things had to be changed. But it doesn't take much to turn you around. Your friend'll be free, The Gravy Train'll roll again, and as far as you're concerned the rest of the country can rot."

His words sank in. Their heads were down, and they

wore embarrassed, pained expressions. But Ted wasn't
worried. He knew it wouldn't work. They were as tired as
he was, and what Polo urged on them called for an army,
not this passel of amateurs.

Even an idiot should have seen how impossible his plan
was. But blinded by anger, Polo couldn't be—he refused to
be—reasonable. He's gone about it ass-backward, Ted
thought. Starting with a notion that everybody ought to be
free, he believed he couldn't fail. That was the way to make
trouble, nothing more. You couldn't liberate anybody until
you freed yourself from this delusion. Maybe it worked like
that in books, but when you played for keeps, you didn't
stand a chance unless conditions were right and you had
organization and men who were willing to follow orders.
Then you needed luck, because once it began, you never
knew how it might end. But Polo had nothing except a bad
temper and too many ideas he hadn't thought through.

"I'm splitting," said Polo, yet hesitated before backing to
the edge of the rock.

From the corner of his eye, Ted watched the others. Puff
stared at Polo unblinking as he shouldered the rifle and
started down. Phil, clearly uncomfortable, was inclined to
accept the blame for trouble he hadn't caused, while Ants,
amazed that the argument had ended with Polo in retreat,
looked to Ted. Bert alone seemed to notice nothing. Her
eyes were fixed on her hands, which clung to her feet.

When Ted heard footsteps on the stones below, he said,
"Last chance. Anyone want to go with Polo?"

No one spoke, no one stirred. The Land-Rover grumbled, and a plume of red dust pursued it as Polo sped
toward the falling sun. On the west side of the valley, in the
shadow of a rock wall, it was already dusk, but on the
eastern slope, daylight lingered, and the houses, mosques,

minarets, and casbahs, all hand-molded from orange mud, were burnished a deeper, richer gold. Then as the gold was slowly transmuted to baser metals and the villages lost the sun, a muezzin called. Ted shivered in the suddenly cold air. He didn't care for this hour. Lately for him each evening had been like the end of an age, each change in the season like the end of everything.

"Let's go down," he said, "before it's dark."

2

THE campsite, at the base of a steep, sandstone ledge, had been barricaded on three sides by their automobiles, and now that Polo had left with his Land-Rover, one end was unprotected. Faced by that broad space of darkness, Ted felt exposed and vulnerable, but didn't have them rearrange the VW bus and his blue Renault. He had to prove he didn't suffer from the same paranoia which turned Polo's smallest actions into army maneuvers. There's nothing to be afraid of here, he told himself. Yet these kids, the whole situation, made him jumpy.

They built a big fire of cedar branches, and the three men sat between it and the cliff, savoring the warm, spicy scent, while the women went to fetch the food and cooking equipment from the bus. Everyone except Ted had pulled on a hooded, woolen djellabah, a brown, ankle-length robe worn for warmth. In a red ski parka, Ted looked more out of place among them than usual, a bright ember in a bed of ashes.

He was no skier. He'd bought the coat cheap last spring in Switzerland when a freak snowstorm had caught him in a cotton shirt. He'd gone to Geneva to collect some money that was owed him, but he hadn't gotten it then and wasn't likely to ever.

"Think Polo'll cause trouble?" asked Ted.

"Hard to tell," said Phil.

"Nothing he did would surprise me," said Ants.

"Would he tip off the Moroccans?"

"I doubt it," said Phil. "You saw him at a bad moment. He's a much better man than that. Besides, he hates cops. I think he's wanted in the States."

"That right? You sure?"

"As sure as you can be about anything with Polo. He told us—I should say he implied—he was one of the Weathermen who went underground after the Days of Rage in Chicago."

"Yeah, but he also claimed he'd lived in Algeria, and you saw how he acted when that came up—like a man in church with his fly unzipped. I wouldn't believe anything he said." Then Ants added, chuckling nervously, "Unless he told me he was going to whip my ass."

"Don't overdo it. You're giving Ted the wrong impression."

"Just joking."

"He always goes a mile too far and tramples on people's toes, but Polo's not a bad guy. And he's as anxious as I am to free Gypsy. In fact he's the one who talked me into this, this . . ." After groping a moment, Phil gave up. Though usually articulate, he either couldn't, or didn't wish to, put a name on what they were doing. "Can we swing it without him?"

"We'll see," said Ted. "I have to think it over."

Much as he had hoped against it and taken care until today not to cross Polo, Ted had expected something like this to happen. He'd known his type in the army—the best sort of soldier when you had time to break him down and guide him as he built himself back up. But Ted didn't have the time, and Polo didn't have the desire or the patience.

So his frustration and anger had fed upon themselves and finally backlashed on him and the plan.

You could tell at a glance, Ted thought, that Polo knew next to nothing about himself. He had no idea of his abilities, much less his mental and physical limits. Even his body with its pumped-up muscles had been nurtured in the hothouse atmosphere of a gymnasium, not by hard work, and since he couldn't seem to gauge the volume of his voice, he shouted and swore to emphasize his points, but the words sounded overblown and hollow. The man was forcing himself badly, thrashing around to find his boundaries, and worst of all, in Ted's opinion, he'd stuck political labels on his personal problems.

A few days ago, when Polo and Phil arrived in the little town of Diabat, down the coast from Essaouira, Ted had noticed the new faces at once, for they didn't fit in with the hippies and hashheads who hung out on the beach. Both of them were better dressed, and clearly had a sense of purpose. The beefy, moustachioed man looked too healthy to crash among the people who stumbled from their huts each morning to lie stoned on the sand. And the crippled guy appeared to be put off by what he saw as he limped around the wasted bodies stranded like flotsam at the water's edge. Later, when Ted learned they were graduate students, he believed it about Phil, but thought in Polo's case there had been a mistake.

He himself had been living for months in a mud house near the ocean. When the wind didn't blow, the place was fine and the fishing good, but when the weather turned foul and wet, this coast could be the most miserable on earth. Then he slammed the doors and shutters, wrapped himself in an army blanket, and inched closer to the fireplace, wondering why he stayed.

Ted had first come to Morocco to meet a man in Casablanca about a job as a security advisor for a diamond mine in South Africa. But when he learned he'd be working harder to keep black workers *in* the compound than burglars *out,* he told the guy to forget it and in desperation drove to Safi to talk to some soldiers about the situation in the Sudan. That war was falling apart, they said. He'd no sooner get there than there'd be a truce. But they put him in touch with a rebel recruiter from Chad. Chad? He had a drunken uncle named Chad. He wasn't going to fight in any country called Chad, not if it meant he'd have the French Foreign Legion against him.

As word got around he was looking for work, strangers started to seek him out—two Tanzanians with tribal scars on their cheeks, a rich, displaced Pakistani from Zambia, an earnest Angolan, who seemed like Ted's best bet until two Portuguese undercover agents called the next day to warn him not to get involved in that one. So he wasn't surprised to have Polo and Phil show up. At that point he wouldn't have been surprised to receive an emissary of the Eskimo Liberation Front.

They went outside to talk in the sun, where it was warmer. Above the high-tide mark, dry sand eddied around their shoes, for there was enough wind to whip the saw grass and send up a low wailing sound. Much louder were the shrill cries of gulls and the choppy surf beating the shore. Ted sat cross-legged. Phil lowered himself beside him, while Polo stayed on his feet.

"We hear you were in the army," said Polo.

"For fifteen years."

"And you fought in Nigeria?"

He'd never made a secret of this. In Essaouira and Diabat any number of people knew about it, but Polo grinned as if he had Ted by the short hairs. "We've been asking a few questions."

"You don't say? Yeah, I was in Nigeria. Why?"

"We're not prying," said Phil. "We just wondered whether . . ."

"Out of work now?"

Polo's self-assurance and his questions that sounded like accusations annoyed Ted. "I'm retired."

"Like a job?"

"I told you I'm retired. Matter of fact, I was about to go fishing. See you fellas around." He got up and ambled along the beach.

"Hey, wait," called Polo.

He didn't slow down. Polo had to run to catch him. But looking back, he saw Phil following them at a painful, hobbling pace, the tip of his crutch sinking into the sand, and Ted stopped. "What's on your mind?"

"Business."

"I'm not interested in my old line of work."

"Would money change that?"

"Probably not." But he didn't leave.

When Phil joined them, Polo said, "Suppose a friend of yours was in a Moroccan jail, what would you do?"

"Hire him a good lawyer."

"He's already convicted."

"Get him a good doctor."

"We're serious," said Phil.

"So am I. But I'm not a doctor or a lawyer," Ted drawled in a down-home accent. "How can I help you?"

Polo grabbed him before he could go. "Suppose you'd decided to spring him?"

"Don't go doing that."

"What?"

"Grabbing at my arm."

Polo pulled back. "You're very cute. I ought to . . ."

"That's enough, Polo. Sorry, mister. Our mistake. We thought you might be interested."

"We don't need him," said Polo.

But judging by the crippled man's eyes, Ted guessed they had more problems than they'd admit and that it was Phil who'd suggested they hire help. "What's the matter?" he asked.

"Like we said, what would you do if you wanted to spring someone from a Moroccan jail?"

"I'd give it a hell of a lot of hard thought. You'd have to have two plans—one to bust him out of jail, a second to get him out of the country. It'd be stupid to do one and not the other."

"How would you go about it?"

"You fellas looking for conversation or help?"

"Help," said Phil. "It's my brother in jail."

"You mentioned money. I'd have to have a bundle."

"How much?"

Ted paused, trying to estimate what they were worth. But the way people dressed nowadays, it was difficult to tell. So he wondered, instead, what it was worth to him and decided it was silly to ask for anything less than a jackpot. "Five thousand."

"Jesus Christ!" Polo exploded.

Phil seemed more disappointed than shocked. "I haven't got it."

"How high can you go?"

"How do you put a price on your brother's life? Naturally I'd give every cent I have."

Ted felt greedy and rotten. This was one of the worst parts of the business—haggling over dollars and lives. He was about to drop his price when Polo said, "Four thousand. That's the limit."

This time Phil did seem shocked. "That's too . . ."

"No, no," said Polo. "I realize how you feel, but I'm not letting you pay a penny more."

"I'd want it in advance."

"Polo, you don't understand. I . . ."

"Not on your life," said Polo. "And have you skip off on us? A thousand down and the balance later."

"Forget it," said Ted. "You don't trust me, there's no sense talking."

Phil had something to say to Polo, but spoke to Ted first. "Wait. We trust you."

"It doesn't look like it."

"That goes both ways. How about you trusting us?" asked Polo. "We could pay two thousand in advance, two afterward."

"Sounds fair to me."

Phil still had something to say, but turning his worried, red-rimmed eyes to Ted, he asked, "Then you'll do it?"

"The price is right. I'll think about it. Who are you, anyway?"

As they talked, he had less and less fear that they were from the government—any government—and intended to trap him. They were too inept for that. Nor did he have any reason to suspect that they were joking. The big, bristly one didn't have much of a sense of humor, and the crippled guy was genuinely upset. Yet Ted found it hard to believe they were serious. They seemed so young, fumbling, and naïve.

The worst kind to deal with. Ted knew that, for he'd had ample experience in losing causes, having fought in Korea, twice in Vietnam, and in Nigeria. A tie, no decision, and a loss. At thirty-nine Ted Kuyler was searching for his first win.

These two didn't look like winners, but he didn't have much choice. He'd run out of money and almost out of places. After the army, he'd tried settling in the States and hadn't succeeded. Too many things had changed, so that even Clifton Forge, Virginia, which had changed less than most towns, had struck him as more alien and unlivable than Morocco.

From what he gathered, others gravitated here, especially to Diabat, for the same reasons he stayed on. Living was cheap, the authorities generally indifferent, and anonymity guaranteed. Yet Ted didn't understand why, in a place where they should have had no problems, people created difficulties for themselves. By buying more hashish than they could smoke and less food than they needed. By not burying their garbage, which attracted rats and wild, noisy dogs. By neglecting their houses and huts, which blew down in bad weather. And by stealing from each other. When he asked a few of them who had lived in Diabat day to day, meal to meal, for years, they said it was because everybody was just passing through.

Finally this was what made Ted want to leave. Much as he liked Morocco, nothing in Diabat belonged to him, and he certainly didn't belong to it. For him, as for the ones on the beach, the town was a throwaway, like a gum wrapper or beer bottle, one more spot to be used up and discarded. What he longed for was a place he could stay, a place that owned *him,* and a way to break cleanly with the kind of work he'd been doing half his life.

So although Polo and Phil didn't look like winners, he hoped the job wouldn't be much of a contest. If it could be done quickly and safely, and he could earn four thousand bucks to get started somewhere else, it might be worth it. But he had to be careful. For the one thing he wanted more than the money and the new start was not to do or see any killing. He'd had enough of that.

"How many people are in on this?" he asked.

"Just us and three others."

"Where are they?"

"Down south. We thought it'd be better if we came alone."

"You were right. Will they keep their mouths shut?"

"Of course."

"I'll have to meet them." Careless and callow as these two were, Ted had to be certain there wasn't a loose, live wire or dangerous connection in the crew. "When you asked around about me, did you let on why?"

"Hell, no," said Polo. "What kind of fools do you think we are?"

"We'll talk about that later. Did you offer anyone else the job?"

"No. You were our first choice."

"I'm flattered."

"Having fun?" asked Polo.

"Less and less as I get older, and I feel like I've put on a few years since you showed up. Say I turn you down, what'll you do?"

"Find someone else."

"You're not afraid I'd blow the whistle on you?"

Phil looked at Polo, and he stared back like the idea had never occurred to them.

"You fellas are just plain fearless, aren't you? Tell you what, do me a favor. I decide not to take the job, gimme time to leave the country before you try it on your own. When the shit hits the fan, I'd rather not be around."

They both bobbed their heads, beginning to see problems where they'd noticed none before. That might teach them caution, Ted thought. Or panic.

"Where's this jail at?" he asked. "I'd like to have a look at it."

"We'll stop on the way south."

Tazenzit, a village in the Souss valley, cradled by the High Atlas and Anti-Atlas Mountains, had twenty thousand people crowded within the three-mile circle of its walls. The entire town's a prison, Ted had first thought as they walked through the winding streets. Escaping from here is going to be like busting out of a barrel of eels.

Since it wasn't visiting day, he couldn't see the inside of the jail, but he stood in the main square, studying the Sûreté Nationale, and computed their few advantages. Though it would be hard to flee through the maze-like medina, it would be even harder for anyone to follow them, especially if they dressed in djellabahs. The element of surprise was in their favor and once they were in the cars, the odds would improve. Since the countryside east of Tazenzit was sparsely settled and the border poorly patrolled, leaving the country would take more luck than courage, skill, or brains. They'd simply head south, pray for no roadblocks, and keep driving until they reached Algeria. If they had inside help and weren't hurt by mistakes, they could make it before the Moroccans organized a manhunt.

Ted was beginning to feel better about the deal until he met the other members of the group—Bert, Puff, and Ants. That had set him back badly, destroying his illusion that they had any advantages. He couldn't believe this crew—a cripple, a girl, a fat woman, a young boy with bangs, and a belligerent, bull-headed, bad-mouthing punk, who was the best man he had. If it weren't for the money, he'd have snickered to himself and stalked away from this side show and, for years afterward, cracked jokes about it. But four thousand dollars . . . he couldn't laugh that off.

So despite his doubts and his uneasiness about Polo, Ted had almost decided to do it, for in the tiniest, darkest corner of his mind, he knew if things fell apart and it looked like they'd be captured, he could abandon them and go off on his own. Alone, with two thousand in cash, he'd squeak through somehow.

But now that that bastard Polo had beat him to the punch and bugged out first, he wasn't sure what he'd do. True, Polo's leaving meant one less problem at the moment, yet also one less man. And to make the plan foolproof, Ted needed more men, more money, and more time. For an instant he imagined the impossible—a plane or helicopter to carry them across the border. But it was useless to daydream. He had to go with what he had. Or fold his hand, flat broke, having wasted a week.

While Bert passed paper plates, paper napkins, and plastic knives and forks, Puff put an old copper pot on a stick over the fire and emptied a can of Dinty Moore Beef Stew into it. On her broad lap rested a loaf of vitamin-enriched Wonder Bread and half a dozen Hostess Twinkies wrapped in sparkling cellophane.

"Where'd you buy this stuff?" Ted asked Bert as she handed him his utensils.

She cringed slightly, as if he was angry at her, rather than amazed. "From the Navy base at Kénitra. We used to trade hash to some sailors who shopped at the PX for us."

"Very nice, no? A picnic lunch every night," said Ants.

"You'd have done better buying camping supplies," said Phil.

"Dull. Very dull. Like, who needs them?"

"Is that how Polo got his guns?" asked Ted.

After glancing at Ants and Puff for approval, Bert nodded. "But we haven't gone there since Gypsy was busted."

"Christ, no. No more dope dealing or smoking for us. We have to be clean in case the cops come down on us. So scarf up these goodies, lads," said Ants. "The larder's running low. Won't be long before we're reduced to a diet of lizard tongues, bat wings, roach antennas, and rat nipples."

"You don't care for Moroccan food?"

"Care for it? You have to be kidding. I hate it. They have this horrible habit of mixing the desserts in with the main dishes. I mean like wrapping pigeons in pie crust and putting prunes and apricots in the stew. Get serious. No sir, there's nothing like good, American, government-inspected beef and grease. Would the U.S. Army eat it if it wasn't healthy?"

Ted laughed, but was puzzled by the peculiar relationship these people allowed themselves with the military. Although not one of them, he'd bet, would have considered serving in the armed forces, they didn't object to—in fact, they relished—wearing odds and ends of army surplus, feasting off PX food, and masquerading as a ludicrous commando unit. He had also watched with astonishment their sidelong glances of respect when Phil had introduced him and told a bit about his combat experience.

Maybe they simply believed he was the right man at the right moment; any other time they wouldn't have touched him. But he wouldn't have liked being in their position, helpless, completely dependent on a person they didn't know and couldn't control. Or were they one step ahead of him, aware of what they were doing and confident they could use military tactics for a specific purpose, yet not be trapped by them? They might have decided to ditch him once the job was done. He'd have to keep his eyes on this bunch.

As Puff ladled out the beef stew, Ted's stomach rumbled. She passed him a steaming plateful and, while waiting for the rest of them to be served, he steeled his nerves against what was coming. He'd been caught off guard the first night and angry afterward for not speaking his mind. Now, although he hadn't gotten used to it—he didn't believe he ever would—he was resigned, as he had become to so many of their idiosyncrasies.

When everyone had a plate, they stood, clasped hands, and chanted a chorus of Oms. On the ground at their feet the servings of stew smoked like votive offerings. Bert was between Ants and Ted, and as he put his hand in her moist palm, she tenderly crooned as though he'd touched a vital spot at her core. His right hand was in Phil's bony fingers. Fortunately no vibrations passed between them.

Led by Puff, the chanting rose to a crescendo and died in a volley of echoes which must have reached the village on the far side of the valley. Then they sat down to dinner, Ted prickly with embarrassment. If pushed, he'd have conceded that he believed in God, but he no longer saw this as the answer to anything. It struck him as just another question. Normally he would have objected to grace before meals and been infuriated by this pimply pantheism, or whatever they called it. Yet he stayed silent. There was no sense wasting his breath.

When he looked up, he could read nothing on their faces. They certainly didn't seem self-conscious. But he still was and glanced beyond them to the Volkswagen bus, which was painted in luminous psychedelic swirls of Day-Glo. On the side panel, spilling from a silver cornucopia, a jumble of red letters spelled THE GRAVY TRAIN!

"I been here long enough now to be let in on the secret," Ted broke the silence. "What the hell's The Gravy Train?"

"That's us, man," said Ants.

"That *was* us," Puff corrected him.

"We'll get it together again."

"I don't know whether I want to. Too much has happened. Too many of the best people have split. Remember when we started? Remember how many of us there were?"

"Yeah, fifteen."

"No, at the very beginning, when we left San Francisco, there were more like twenty." She chuckled. "Of course Jenks and Bibby split as soon as we hit the state line. They couldn't conceive of living anywhere except California." Puff put down her fork. Her face alone was visible, framed by the hood of the djellabah. Below it, draped in thick wool, her massive body looked preposterously ill-formed. "It was such a great scene then, being together with no hassles, no hang-ups, no hard times. No matter how many straights we met during a day, it meant nothing because we had our own thing."

"If you're talking about the Haight, that didn't last long." Pulling the soft center from a piece of bread, Bert poked it into the stew. "The narks and tourists and psychos saw to that."

"Christ, yes," said Ants. "For every cat doing a Ken Kesey and the Merry Pranksters number, there were two on a Charles Manson trip. We were lucky to cut out when we did."

"I haven't forgotten. But it was a mistake to leave. We were like those people who panic when a black moves onto the block. We should have outlasted the weirdos or talked them down from their bad trips. We could have created a real community. What was the sense in heading for India?"

"It sounded like grins," said Ants. "Didn't get far, did we?"

"We got too far. I wish we'd stayed in the States," said Puff. "We had something going there. For the first time my head was really right. I mean I was up every hour of every day, and not on dope either. It was the idea of belonging, of knowing there were people like us. For once everybody didn't have to look like Joe College or a bouncy little cheerleader. If you don't believe things have changed, just think of the early sixties." She chuckled again, but didn't seem to think it was funny. "Sick times, man. Mind-bending. I remember being a freshman at the University of Indiana and going through sorority rush. Me! Imagine it! Picture this six-foot-tall freak in size-twenty Villager clothes and size-twelve Papagallos gallumphing through those tea parties. Man, they threw me out on my ear. They thought I was making fun of them, trying to put them down, when I only wanted to look like them."

"Come on, Puff," said Ants, laughing. "They didn't kick you out."

"Well, not really. But they sure as hell didn't let me in."

"You should of started your own sorority," said Ted.

"We had something better when we were together. But one thing I learned was you can't take it on the road. You have to stay with people who understand. Like over here they don't have a clue what we're into, and we've been hassled and ripped off left and right."

"Face it," Phil interrupted with uncharacteristic gruffness. "Sooner or later reality would have intruded regardless of where you were. You can fly in that artificial atmosphere only so long before you crash. Gypsy told me it didn't take much time for this trip to go bad, even with kilos of hash to keep you hiked up. It sounded like one big bummer."

"It wasn't that bad," she muttered, slumping as if she'd been struck a low blow.

"That's not what I heard. Gypsy described it in Technicolor—the mono, the hepatitis, the pregnancies, the abortions, the busts, the people bailing out to fly home sick or screwed up or spaced out." Phil spoke in a preachy, fastidious voice, and when he used slang, he grimaced, as though it brought a bad taste to his mouth. A teacher to the marrow of his bones, he didn't let anything undercut the case he was building against them

Finally Ants said, "Hey, we don't need a lecture."

"You need something."

"We need to get Gypsy out of jail, that's all. Right?"

"Then what?" Phil demanded, his thin face red. "If this experience doesn't change how you act and how you see yourselves, it's been a waste. You'll bumble along, letting somebody else—your parents, the police, me, Ted, anybody—clean up the mess after you."

The three of them looked too miserable and lost to argue. But then Puff picked up her fork and, slowly chewing a bite of stew, said, "I'll tell you, it's changed me. Gypsy and I are going back to the States and look for a place to settle. We'd like to have a baby."

"That's great," Ants assured her, although Phil didn't appear to think so.

"Yes, it'll be nice, won't it?" A wan smile shone from under the shadow of her hood.

"What about Polo?" asked Ted. "Was he part of the original group?"

"No. He came later," said Ants. "We met him in Marrakech when there were the four of us left. We were low, man, very low, and he had all his equipment and bread and muscles and contacts up at Kénitra. It was like Santa Claus had sent him."

"Some present," Puff said bitterly.

"Don't dump on Polo now that he's not here to defend

himself. He bugs me, too, but he did give us a lift."

"That's about all he gave us. The rest we paid for—either by putting up with his political bullshit or running guns for him."

"How's that?" asked Ted.

"The whole time he was doing that heavy dealing at Kénitra, we were his cover," said Puff. "Each time we went there for supplies, he'd buy a gun and hide it in the bus for Gypsy to bring south. Only he didn't tell us. So the one day that I stayed behind in Agadir, the cops stopped Bert and Gypsy at a checkpoint near Tazenzit, found a pistol under the back seat, and busted them."

"Why did he want them anyway?" asked Phil.

"Who knows? Who cares?" said Puff. "That's probably how he gets it off."

"Okay, cool it," said Ants. "Everyone has his way. No doubt about it, he should have told us what he was doing. But I don't recall anyone refusing his help, and after the bust we believed what he said, even though we weren't into violence like him."

"What did he say?" asked Ted.

"You know, that a revolution was coming, and we had to be ready."

"And you believed that?"

"Well, it sort of made sense."

"You can't be serious," said Phil. "You've as much as admitted it. Without his food and money you wouldn't have listened to that nonsense for a minute."

"That's not true. I'm not claiming he changed me into a radical or anything. But what he said added up after what we'd been through. I mean, we'd been trying to get it together and live on our own peacefully, not bothering anybody. We didn't ask much, but it didn't work."

"Whose fault is that?"

"Polo said it was the system. He said we'd never make it until the system was responsive to our needs and we had control of the sources of power."

"Old buddy, you had a long wait ahead of you if you meant to put those ideas into practice here."

"We weren't at that stage," Ants said sheepishly. "We were just talking."

"And while you were talking, Polo was stockpiling weapons," said Phil.

"I don't believe he'd actually have used them."

"I wouldn't bet on that," said Puff. "But I promise one thing. I'd never have gone along with one of his silly-ass schemes."

"You are now," said Phil. "He's the one who said we should free Gypsy."

"That's different." She blushed angrily.

"Sure. It's always different when it's someone close to you."

"What the hell, he's your brother. Are you telling me..."

"I'm not telling you anything. We've been through this. I'm here and I'll help, but that's not saying it's right."

After a moment's silence, Ted turned to Bert, anxious to have the facts straight. "You were arrested too?"

She nodded, pushing a crust of bread through the last of her stew.

"You weren't convicted?"

When he'd waited half a minute for an answer, Ants said, "She didn't come to trial. Gypsy took the rap."

"Look, why the hell are we talking about this? It's a goddamn drag." Bert sailed her plate like a Frisbee into the darkness. "We're going to get him out, aren't we?"

Her eyes, swimming widely with tears, were on Ted, who

was sorry he had spoken. He was tempted to take her hand and tell her, Yes. You can count on it. We'll spring him. But he was afraid to get in over his head. When he said nothing, she blinked once and returned to staring at her feet.

3

TED carried his bedding far from the cars onto a large, flat rock which felt as if it was growing cooler as he touched it. He should have cushioned it by building a platform of pine branches or palm fronds, but it was too late, the terrain too stony, for him to stumble around in the dark searching for a tree. So, lacking a sleeping bag or a canvas drop-cloth, he doubled an army blanket underneath him, pried off his shoes, which he wrapped inside his ski parka for a pillow, then rolled himself in a quilt and stretched out on his back, waiting for body heat to accumulate and warm him. A tiny trumpet of frost formed on his breath.

Christ, he thought again, I'm too old for this camping in the boondocks. He was lonely, depressed, and worried, and wished he had a drink. A little bourbon to sip until he fell asleep. Out of habit, he ran his hands over his arms and chest to rub away the goosebumps, and, also, to test his muscle tone, as someone might pat his pockets to be sure he had his car keys, credit cards, and checkbook. His body was his bankroll, and since it ached terribly, he feared it had begun to fail him. That was all he needed. He'd watched his father die, a big, strong man doubled up with arthritis, so twisted by pain that they had to break his bones before they put him in the pine box. Ted knew if he didn't escape this life soon, he'd end up like him, like all the decrepit, wormy dirt farmers in Appalachia.

Well, he consoled himself, the others had to be just as

uncomfortable. Bert and Puff slept on the floor of the VW
bus, and Phil and Ants had squeezed onto the back and
front seats of the Renault. During its ten months in
Morocco, The Gravy Train hadn't done much to make itself
at home. Living wretchedly, like refugees, these kids
seemed to have forgotten their own country and learned
nothing from the locals. As Phil had said, they'd blown
their best opportunity, preferring to buy canned goods and
sweets from the Navy PX, rather than tents, lanterns, sleeping bags, and air mattresses.

Almost as amazing to Ted, they'd had scant contact with
the Moroccans, since their Arabic was nonexistent and
their French a string of mispronounced infinitives. Even
Phil and Polo, who as graduate students must have studied
foreign languages, understood little and could express less.
So Ted, who'd taken three years of French in high school
and had had two tours of Vietnamese bars and brothels to
sharpen his grasp of the idiom, acted as their interpreter as
well as—what could he call it?—"tactical advisor." There
was a nice bullshit title for you.

Hell, he was tired of trying to understand this bunch.
Sometimes, in spite of their youth, they seemed as old and
melancholy as he felt. Ted hadn't counted on this—the
familiarity of their emotions, their vulnerability, their
humanity—and it troubled him. At first, put off by their
appearance, their behavior, and slang, he'd made the mistake of believing they weren't real, didn't feel—not as he
felt at any rate—and couldn't reason. But he should have
known better, since he had led hundreds of soldiers their
age. People were much the same.

Yet this didn't afford him any comfort. In fact it threw
another unknown into the equation. The job was already
difficult. Once he thought of them as people, it might be

impossible. Being careful and considerate of them, he'd
screw himself up. You gotta keep them at arm's length, he
thought. Don't let them use you.

"Are you awake?"

Stunned, Ted struggled to sit up, but the quilt had him
strait-jacketed, pinning his arms to his sides. Lunging to the
left, he unraveled the cloth and had crawled to his knees
when he realized it was Bert.

Barelegged and barefoot, she stood there in her denim
shirt, holding down the tail with both hands. His heart
thudded sickly; he was angry and embarrassed that she had
managed to move two feet from his shoulder without his
hearing her. In battle, he'd have been dead. He'd grown
rustier and sloppier than he'd ever suspected.

"I didn't mean to scare you."

"You didn't." Was there a hint of mockery in her voice?
Though her legs—nice ones, he noticed—were within
reach of his hand, he couldn't see her face clearly. "What
is it?"

"I have to talk to you."

"What about? Who sent you?"

"No one. Can I come onto the blanket? My feet are
cold."

"You should of worn shoes," he said gruffly. "There are
scorpions here." As he made room for her, she sat beside
him, shivering and hugging her knees to her chest. "Bundle
up in this." He handed her his parka. "I were you, I
wouldn't go sneaking up on anyone like that. It's a good
way to get hurt."

Covering her legs with his parka, she whispered in a
quavering voice, "You have to help us."

"I said I'd think about it. That's what I was doing."

"I'll bet. To you this is just another job, isn't it? But I've been in jail and know what it's like for Gypsy."

"Where was this?"

"The women's jail in Agadir." She had lowered her head and even in the dark wouldn't look at him.

"I thought you weren't charged."

"I wasn't, but the Moroccans held me for two months while they made up their minds."

"I'm sorry. I didn't know."

"Don't b-b-bother." Bert's teeth were chattering.

"I *am* sorry. No one mentioned that."

"They don't like to remind me, but I haven't forgotten."

"I don't guess you could forget it." Drawing nearer, he briskly rubbed her thin, shaking shoulders. Bert stiffened at his touch, but didn't pull back. Then slowly she relaxed, and her long hair felt fleecy under Ted's hands. He thought he'd better stop.

"You can't imagine what it's like," she murmured.

"I think I can."

"First they strip you. The room's cold, and they're all there watching."

"You don't have to tell me."

"I know I don't have to," she said, "but I'm going to. They clean you with cold water and alcohol. For medical reasons, they say. Then they examined me inside and out. They claimed they were looking for dope. They even had one of those metal things gynecologists use. The cops were laughing, and I was so scared and tense from trying not to cry that it felt like a knife going in me. I started screaming and couldn't stop. But at least then I didn't have to watch what they were doing with their fingers and that goddamn metal tube."

"Look, don't talk about it." He put his hand on her again to calm her.

"Why? Are you bored? You acted bored today. Don't you care about anything except your money?" She was crying, and her voice broke.

Ashamed that he hadn't hidden his feelings any better, Ted slipped an arm around Bert and tenderly rocked her. As she sobbed, her silky hair caressed the underside of his chin. "Of course I care."

"Then you have to believe me. I'd rather be dead than back in jail. Gypsy'll be dead if we don't help him."

"I believe you." He spoke softly to soothe her, but she didn't stop trembling. He knew she'd have to tell everything before she'd be silent. So he held her head to his chest and waited, listening, feeling the warm movement of her lips through his shirt.

"After they searched me, a guard took me to a cell that had three fat women in it. They weren't Moroccans. French or something. He said they were prostitutes and very tough, and it'd be better for me to have a cell of my own where he could protect me. I knew what that meant, so I said no, and he shoved me in with the women. He must have known what they'd do. Maybe he'd planned it with them, because after he left, they jumped me and tore off this cotton smock they gave me to wear. They threw me on a cot, and while one sat on my shoulders and another pinned my legs, the third woman came at me with this ... this long stick, like the end of a broom handle. I'm little and not strong, and all I could do was scream and hope someone would hear me.

"The same guard came back, and I thought he'd stop them. But he let them go ahead for a few seconds so I'd know what it was like. Then he unlocked the cell, shoved them aside, and asked again whether I wanted my own place. I said yes, Christ, yes. I was wild by then and anything seemed better than those women and that stick."

She sat up gasping for breath, her shoulders still shaking, her teeth chattering. "I was there two months. He never really hurt me. But that didn't make it easier, and when they let me go, I learned I'd never been charged. What I did was for nothing."

"I wouldn't say that. You did what you thought you had to."

"No, don't make it sound better. I know what I did. I know."

"You said yourself you didn't have a choice."

"That's wrong. There's always a choice. I just didn't make the right one. I didn't think it mattered, but it did."

"What could you have done?"

"That's not important," she said, recovering some of her composure. "The point is you have to realize what freeing Gypsy means to me. It's not a political game, like Polo thinks. And it's not just a job, no matter what you think. Wait till you see the inside of that jail. Then you'll believe me."

Ted felt himself being drawn in, and his throat ached as though a noose had tightened around it.

"One more thing," she said. "I watched how you handled Polo. He deserved it. Someone had to put him down. But don't overdo it. Don't gang up with Phil and lecture us and treat us like kids. We're in this together."

"I had to take care of Polo."

"I understand. Do you?"

"I do now."

"Then you'll help?"

"Yeah, I'll help." The noose couldn't yank tighter than that.

"Good. We need you."

"Well, I'm here." Trying not to sound resigned or sorry that he was, he patted her shoulder and kissed the crown of her head in a paternal fashion. But misunderstanding the gesture, Bert lifted her lips to his. At first the urge to comfort her and reassure himself aroused Ted more than desire. And though this was a sadly limited means of expressing his concern and sympathy, he couldn't, at the moment, imagine another. So he was determined to put all his emotion into that one kiss and be done with it—the pity, imperfect comprehension, an apology for appearing not to take the situation seriously, a sense of his own loneliness, and, only in the end, passion.

When he ran a hand down her spine and cupped her bare, cool behind, it flexed with youthful force, flooding him with memories and piecemeal images. But while his body began to follow the familiar course, his mind remained in a much different groove. He'd done this too many times before and didn't wish to now, for he had developed a deep dislike for senseless repetition, for bedding down with strangers in the dark. He'd rather be alone.

But he wasn't, and couldn't be. Already his thoughts were cluttered and the rock they reclined on seemed to contain many more than their two straining bodies. Her curves evoked the tangle of nameless women he had waded through; his hands carved them from her cool sides. They surrounded him like stacks of cordwood, and it struck him as cruel to drag Bert into that crowd of corpses. She was too young and had had too much trouble. This is a mistake, he thought, after what she's been through.

Ted attempted to draw back, but there was nowhere to retreat, and what could he tell her? The truth was wounding. He was worried about himself as much as her. You're nuts, he thought. Don't do it. Don't tie yourself down like this. Yet there was nothing to do except press straight ahead, through Bert to whatever lay beyond. Certain the whole time that he couldn't carry her with him, he hugged tight and hurried, telling himself he couldn't afford to care. But she quickly caught up, her small hard body arching under him, her deep breathing echoing in his ear. Then they were together whether he wanted it or not.

4

Polo pulled off the road, stomped the accelerator, and pushed the Land-Rover across a rocky field, flinging pebbles and dirt clods against the gravel pan, outracing the low beams which waved feebly like broken insect antennae. The massive bumper sheared off the tops of two cactus plants; the thorny stumps raked the differential. Thick, cleated tires pounded the bumps flat and took the deepest potholes in thunderous leaps. Slamming into one, he flew off the seat, hitting his head on the roof. His spine compressed, pile-driven into the springs, but he didn't slow down. He felt he was fighting the car, fighting the whole damn, obdurate countryside. This, and the punishment he accepted and dished out, acted as a release for Polo as a scream might have for someone else.

Entering an almond orchard, he snapped off a sapling in a shower of pink blossoms, then wrenched the wheel to avoid a larger tree and rocketed between rows of gnarled trunks. As low branches buggy-whipped the roof and side panels, a limb reached in the open window to slap his face. Swearing, he stood on the brake. The engine coughed, lurched, died. Too late he stepped on the clutch.

He punched off the headlights and saw white dots before the night closed in quickly to blink them out one by one.

His left cheek was warm and wet where the branch had slapped him. He touched the scratch, then put his fingers to his tongue and tasted blood. With his shirt-sleeve he wiped it clean.

When his hoarse breathing quieted, he heard the engine block ticking as it cooled. His heartbeat was almost audible and Polo shivered as a breeze cooled him, too. But his anger continued to crackle hotly.

He had warned Phil they couldn't afford, and didn't need, help. An outsider meant trouble. They should have engineered the escape themselves. But Phil's years as a graduate student had sapped his self-assurance, and he wouldn't take any step until he'd done his homework and consulted an expert. Christ, Polo knew the type—an admirer of Henry James doing a dissertation on William Dean Howells, carefully constructing a façade of manners and morals between him and the fact that he feared boldness and the grittier side of reality.

So he should have expected Phil's last-minute objections in the name of moderation. If there was a dull way to do something daring, Phil would back it. Well, he has his expert, thought Polo, and the son-of-a-bitch is taking over. He'd warned Phil about this, too. Scratch a redneck and you found a fascist. Even if he didn't betray them, Kuyler was bound to simplify and subvert their objective. In it for the money, his first concern would be his own safety and only secondarily Gypsy's rescue. As for any greater goal— liberating the other prisoners, succeeding with style, proving something to themselves, and to the Moroccans—they could forget that.

And there was another point, by no means the least important. They couldn't pay Kuyler. They didn't have four thousand dollars. He and Phil knew it; the rest of them didn't. They could scrape together the two thousand advance, but there was no chance of raising the balance. Though Phil was fearful and conscience-stricken, Polo had told him not to worry. What could Kuyler do after they crossed the border?

Now Polo wasn't sure it would be that simple. There was no saying what Ted might do, and it would be hard to handle a man like him who, for all his limitations, wasn't a fool and had a mad dog's immunity to fear. Remembering the incident on the rock, he was glad Kuyler hadn't called his bluff. Not that he was afraid to fight. No, he was far more afraid that he might have used the rifle and killed him rather than lose face in front of the others.

He's their problem now, thought Polo, and they're welcome to it. Let them explain why he isn't getting paid. Let Phil deal with Kuyler after the double-cross. He'd be lucky if Ted didn't cripple his other leg.

But Polo couldn't kid himself and couldn't give up the plan that quickly. He'd waited and worked too long, and he'd done it not just for Gypsy or because he felt responsible, but for himself. After so many cop-outs, defeats, and compromises, the jailbreak had become the focus for his yearning, the cure for his frustration.

In the past he'd come close, but had always stopped short of cutting the strings that tied him to the familiar, the comfortable, the secure. And when he stopped, wherever he stopped, his family was there waiting for him with bemused expressions of sympathy. Whether paying off his bad debts, appealing for favors to influential friends, or bailing him out of jail, they *understood* what he'd done—and, of course, discounted it. No matter how violently he resisted, he seemed to prove them right, and when their smooth faces smiled, it was as if he saw his future. Sooner or later, they assumed, he'd end up like them. Did he have to go mad to make them admit he was different, and they were ridiculous?

Though he had a sense that he was marked for something special—that the times required it—Polo had started to question whether he was equal to it. Boredom, a niggling feeling of smallness, fed his anger. Boredom, he believed, was the acutest agony, the cancer of the age, but despite its virulence, it brought on desolation, not the saving grace of death.

As he'd gathered more often with friends to express his fury at public indignities—racism, poverty, corruption, the war—he began to suspect this masked a deeper personal rage that they couldn't upset the utter predictability of their lives, much less the course of governments and countries, unless they were ready to push themselves harder, farther. They had struck a shabby bargain with life. They'd ask little of it as long as it demanded less of them and guaranteed that their troubles would be small and manageable. Feeding on self-deceit, retreating in fact, if not in theory, from any commitment that threatened their security, they'd hedged themselves in with cars, houses, families, careers. By nature Polo wasn't docile, but like a bull in a ring, he'd chosen a smaller arena, his *querencia*, graduate school, to lie down and quietly die in. What if, he had wondered, I broke the bargain, tore up a contract I never signed with full consent, and took what came?

For months afterward nothing came, and his mind circled crazily, searching for an answer, any answer, until it turned on itself like an animal willing to gnaw off its leg to get out of a trap. Fed up with introspection, he had decided to win his freedom by confronting what he feared, by running any risk to escape the thousand diminishments which left a man half-dead before his days were done.

And now that he'd started, Polo couldn't bear to fail again. He'd gone too far and might not have another chance. No matter how much Kuyler and the others rubbed his nose in it, he had to go back. He couldn't let that hill-ape control things.

He appreciated the appeal of Ted's plan. It sounded safe and reasonable, especially as he explained it with his laconic, low-rent amiability. But Polo thought it was an obscene evasion not to accept an element of risk. If danger wasn't there, they had to create it. Otherwise this caper was no better than a college prank, and they would waste an opportunity to free themselves from their old assumptions at the same time as they freed Gypsy.

Yes, he'd return, but not until morning. Reaching around, he arranged a bunk on the back seat—a Moroccan blanket for warmth, a small leather hassock for his head. But as he slipped off his boots, he wondered why he was huddling behind locked doors. What was he afraid of? Nothing, and yet his first thought was to stay in the car. Because of the warmth? Comfort? That was reason enough to drag his blanket through the dew-wet grass beyond the almond branches and bed down in a clearing. Kuyler slept out. He would too, here in an unprotected spot.

Polo didn't care about the cold, for he believed he had found in discomfort the power to change and grow. When he'd left the University and the States—how inextricably they were linked in his mind!—he'd sworn to savor every new sensation. Why exclude pain, terror, and what timid people called evil? To extend his range of responses, he'd hurled himself into filth of all sorts, eating whatever was set in front of him, sleeping wherever fatigue fell upon him, and enduring the caprices of a country which ignored straight lines, schedules, and timetables.

At first he'd also fucked as many whores as he could afford—tough, stringy *pieds noirs* who'd stayed on after the French had gone; Berber girls, barely pubescent, with blue tattoos on their faces and henna on their hands; devout Arabs, their vulvas shaved; fat black Haratin women, still warm from the desert, with pink slits between their thighs.

Well aware of the theoretical implications of sexual experiments, he realized they could be revolutionary, mocking marriage, parenthood, the family, and bourgeois morality. But he'd learned that for him the bed wasn't a battleground for metaphysical rebellion. Not that he regretted doing something wrong, rather that he'd failed to do anything sufficiently immoral to violate the entire concept. Having attempted to do the unthinkable, he had discovered that sexually nothing was. In the end it had bored him, depleting his body, wallet, and imagination. There was nothing worse, he thought, than the laws, not of unjust authority, but of absolute nullity. After exhausting human orifices, only an inhuman void remained. He preferred to struggle against real limits, drawing the line between himself and an enemy, between his strength and theirs, his ideas and theirs, instead of masturbating in a vacuum.

As night insects attacked, Polo concentrated on what might happen tomorrow. One thing he knew, he wouldn't explain or apologize. Words seldom worked. They watered down what he felt, or when they weren't useless, they were insidious, blurring distinctions, substituting subtleties of deceit for truth.

You couldn't convince anyone of your good intentions. They all lived in a world without trust, and nobody had time to impress the rightness of his ideas on everyone. Polo simply had to act, alienating as few as possible and hoping people would eventually appreciate what he was doing—enriching life for them in the long run. If they'd just cooperate in the meantime. But they rarely did. They'd been forced to go against their own interests for so long, you couldn't count on their common sense or gratitude. Even as you rescued them, you had to be ready for hostility. And when you couldn't persuade them, you had to be willing to push.

Phil and he had often argued this point. Predictably, for Phil it was enough to have the right intentions. Counting on quiet commitment and gradual reform, he said he'd never force anyone against his will. Which was all very well in the abstract, but, as Polo maintained, ineffective in reality. For the present system didn't permit sympathy and charity to have any impact. Morocco should have proved that to Phil. It had to Polo.

Once he had driven from Marrakech over the mountains to the desolate, sandy plateau around Ouarzazate, where the brightness burned cavities in his eyes and the empty expanses induced agoraphobia. While the sun was scorching hot, the wind was cold and stinging with grit. Sweating and shivering at the same time, Polo didn't understand how anyone survived on this high desert.

Yet there were barefoot women staggering through the countryside, carrying scraps of wood and twisted, thorny branches on their backs. The loads were so large some of the women had wooden staffs to prop themselves up, and they trudged along like weird, three-legged creatures.

Polo's instinct was to help. Yet it seemed ridiculous to offer them a ride. Where were they headed anyhow? And who'd help them tomorrow? Still, he thought, there had to be something he could do.

When he noticed eight of them next to the road, waiting for him to pass so they could cross, he slowed down. The women shielded their faces from him and from the dust dug up by the tires. He stopped and brought out a big bag of oranges. Several of them ran, or rather tried to run. The heavy bundles harnessed to their shoulders kept them from going very far, and the others, who had spotted the oranges, called them back.

With the fruit in his hand, he approached cautiously, not wanting to scare them. As the women waited, their eyes on the oranges, they leaned away from Polo, ready to run again. At first, from their crooked spines, he'd thought they were old, yet though their seamed faces were braised like slabs of meat and their teeth were chipped, discolored, and mossy with tartar, they were young, a few no more than children. The blue, cryptic tattoos on their foreheads and chins were still bright. Wriggling their fingers, they chattered in Berber, begging for the fruit, but kept backtracking, too frightened to take it.

Polo tossed an orange to the closest girl, who caught it, giggled, and showed it to her friends. A bigger girl promptly snatched it from her. Polo threw her another, but the same girl stole this one too. So he lobbed an orange at the bully, who dropped the two she had to catch the third. She missed, and all three rolled in the sand as the girls shouted, pushed, and scratched for them.

When Polo stepped in to separate them, they trotted off a few yards, then paused. Picking up the oranges, he held them in one hand and the whole bag in the other, motioning to the girls. There were enough for everyone. But they crept toward him warily, shoving and snarling at each other, tottering beneath the gnarled limbs strapped to their backs. Just beyond his reach, they resumed their begging and pointed to their mouths. They were hungry.

He was tempted to dump the bag and leave. But he knew they'd fight and was afraid the smaller girls would be hurt and get nothing. He considered taking it with him, but couldn't do it. That would be too cruel. So, in despair and absolute disgust at his helplessness, he started pitching out the oranges. First he overwhelmed the bully until she couldn't carry any more, then made sure everyone else had a share. But the big girl continued to claw and fight, and the others defended what they had. Screeching, they sounded like scavengers as they scurried around, kicking the oranges when they couldn't bend over to grab them. With the sharp sticks as weapons, they flung themselves at one another in a kind of feeding frenzy, and Polo had a vision of himself hurling raw meat into an alligator pit, then watching the blood flow.

One small girl, reeling from a hard blow, fell flat on her back, pinned on a bed of barbed branches. Her cries of pain shocked the rest into silence. As she pleaded with them, the girl's arms and legs squirmed, and she looked like a turtle that had been turned on its shell. Slowly they drew near, mumbling sympathy, but didn't put down their oranges to help.

When Polo moved in, they ran off and this time didn't stop. He leaned over and saw her eyes were whirlpools of pain, but she was more terrified of having this strange man touch her than she was of the thorns in her skin. Scissoring her legs wildly, she walloped him in the jaw. Polo protected his eyes and waded again into the pinwheel of her arms and legs to work at the shoulder straps. His hands fumbled, slick with blood—hers and his own, for his fingers had been forced onto the thorns.

She was shrieking and spitting at him, and her bony fists

beat his head when, after loosening the harness, he grabbed her upper arms and lifted the girl. The bundle clung for a moment. He shook her once, it fell from her flesh, and she sank her teeth into his chest and didn't let go until he set her on her feet. Howling, she limped into the desert, her wounds leaving a trail of blood through the oranges that littered the roadside.

That, he had told Phil, was humanity in its current state —a man causing pain as he tried to help, a little girl pinned on a bed of thorns hysterically resisting every effort to relieve her suffering. These conditions made it futile and maybe worse to offer aid to anyone incapable of accepting it. And it was equally useless to expect to reason with people while they kicked and screamed in pain. Till the entire context changed, you had to harden yourself against the agony of individuals and fight to eliminate the greater misery that had whole civilizations pinned and wriggling on their backs.

But talking to Phil—to anybody—changed nothing. Tomorrow he had to start acting, and what he might ultimately accomplish, even Polo couldn't imagine. Lying awake in the almond orchard, staring up at the stars, he felt like a man far off at sea. He had no precise idea of the course he would pursue, yet he didn't mind as long as he was under way.

II

TED WOKE once when a rooster crowed in the earliest hours of false dawn, then again at the harsh, asthmatic heehawing of a donkey in a distant village, and finally and thoroughly as the sun shone full in his face and he realized for the third morning in a row that he should have slept in a shady spot. Aching and uncomfortable, he waved futilely at the flies. His joints had stiffened, his arms itched from mosquito bites, and his shoulder was sore where a sharp stone had dug into it.

Beside him, Bert was cocooned in the quilt, one hand shielding her eyes. Her face, its delicate features flushed from heat, seemed troubled by bad dreams. Her eyes fluttered under the thin lids, her mouth twitched at the edges as though she couldn't quite open it to speak. In the pitiless light she looked very young and frail, and Ted had an instinct to protect her, though he couldn't have said from what. A dangerous emotion, he didn't have to be told. One he'd seldom experienced. Yet he liked this girl, who was clearly stronger and gutsier than she appeared.

Picking up his parka, he went to slide it under her head, but Bert woke with a start, squinting into the sun and groaning, "Oh god, what is it?"

"Nothing. Go to sleep."

"Who is it?" she asked, frightened.

"Me. Ted." He leaned forward to block the light. "You okay?"

"Now I am. I had a nightmare. What time is it?"

"Early. Want to move into the shade?"

"No, I'll stay awake." She dragged a hand through her hair, arranging long, dark locks on either side of her face. "It's getting so I hate to shut my eyes."

"Like some coffee?"

"Not now. We'd wake the others."

"It must of been that PX food that gave you nightmares," he said.

She looked at him, smiling. "Yeah, and this wasn't the softest bed I've slept on. Another night on it and I'd be ready for one with nails."

Ted grinned and grasped the downy nape of her neck. "What the hell, you had the whole cover."

"Sorry about that. Were you cold?"

"Not really."

She leaned back, rolling her head against his hand. "That feels good."

"Glad to oblige. What's your name anyhow?"

"You know."

"No, your real one."

She grimaced. "Mary Bertrand Riley."

"Who started calling you Bert?"

"I did. Mary's so . . . so dull and ordinary."

"No, it's not. And originality isn't everything. Mary's a pretty name."

"Pretty things are boring. Ugly ones have more character."

"I guarantee you I've known some ugly characters who were pretty boring. You just like to be different."

"Doesn't everyone?"

"Seems that way. Maybe I'll be different and call you Mary."

"Not in front of the others. They'd make fun."

"Let them. We're going to need some laughs."

"Not at my expense. You call me Mary, and I'll call you Captain Kuyler."

"Okay. You win. I'd hate anyone to think I was a damned officer."

As his hand caressed her neck, Bert asked, "Are you married or anything?"

"No, I'm not married. Or anything," he added. "Would it matter?"

"It might. It'd depend on you. Why aren't you married?"

"No time. I never stayed in one spot."

"It doesn't take much time. Have you ever come close?"

"Sure. I came close last night."

"Okay, wise guy, how many times have you come that close?"

"More than I remember."

"Big deal." She seemed slightly hurt. "What's the record anyhow?"

"I wouldn't know. I don't keep count."

"Look, if you'd like to forget last night . . ."

"That's not what I meant."

"If you change your mind, tell me. I'm no good at playing games."

"Neither am I."

Ted was bringing her close for a kiss when, just before his eyes shut, he saw a huge, hawk-shaped shadow sweep over the rock. Roughly he shoved Bert behind him, whirled toward the sun, and was momentarily blinded. As he blinked, a man with a rifle stepped clear of the orange glow. Ted groped about the blanket for a weapon of any kind, but there was nothing.

"A very pretty scene," said Polo. "Pardon me for breaking into your bedroom."

"What the hell are you doing?" he jumped to his feet.

"Didn't you post guards?" Polo had cradled the M-16 to his chest.

"What for? You're the only one I'd expect to find sneaking around here."

"I didn't sneak. I didn't have to. You should have heard me."

Ted couldn't very well deny this. Twice in twelve hours he'd been caught napping and had nobody to blame but himself. You don't watch it, he thought, this guy, for all his greenness, is going to march those big black boots right over your chest. But Polo didn't look angry or threatening as he smiled.

"Go to the bus," Ted told Bert.

She stood up, the quilt wrapped around her bare legs. "Are you coming?"

"In a minute."

"I'll call Ants."

"Let him sleep."

When she had clambered awkwardly off the rock, Polo coughed up a chuckle. "You don't waste time, do you? She any good in the sack?"

"Watch your mouth, buddy."

"She's so little I imagine it's . . ."

"I said cut it out."

"Ah, I see. An officer and a gentleman."

"Neither one. Don't push me."

"So who's pushing?" Polo squatted down, propping the M-16 between his spread knees, and rubbed the polished barrel against the bristles of his two-day beard.

"You get such a big kick out of that rifle, I'd like to see your face when they catch you with it."

"The Moroccans? Nah, never happen."

"The Americans, dick-head. You think they're not going to bother looking for it?"

"How'll they know who has it?"

"They'll start by knowing who doesn't have it. The serial number on the rifle is registered to the trooper it's assigned to. Probably a marine at the navy base. When it turns up missing, the MP's will question the guy and keep on him until they learn how he lost it. Then they'll look for you and won't quit. They're never happy to lose a piece of hardware like that, specially in a country where they're not supposed to be in the first place. You positive you all aren't being followed?"

Polo shook his head no. "We've been on the move ever since Gypsy was convicted. I haven't noticed any Americans after us."

"How about Moroccans? I'd of thought they'd be watching. You're lucky they didn't arrest the whole bunch of you."

"They questioned us. And they kept an eye on us before and after the trial, but no more. They see us every week at the jail. Maybe that's enough for them."

"Yeah, maybe. Meantime, I were you, I'd keep the M-16 hidden."

"Nice to know you worry about me."

"I don't give a damn about you, buddy. I just don't like the thought of being linked to that rifle. Why'd you come back?"

"I missed my friends."

"I don't buy that bullshit."

"It's the truth. I thought it over last night, and I want in. And face it, you need me. You've got the brains to know that. I mean Ants is a good guy and so's Phil. But one's a kid and the other can't do much lugging that crutch."

"And you're such a great human being you had to help us. What's in it for you?"

"A hell of a lot less than you're getting. Look, I know it's partly my fault Gypsy's in jail. I'd like to set that straight. I also know you're liable to try and break him without me. Somebody might get hurt because you're shorthanded. I don't want that to happen."

Ted thought about this a moment. Everything Polo said made sense, which is exactly why Ted was suspicious. He didn't believe anyone could change his attitude that quickly and completely. Yet he did need help. "All right, I admit we could use you, but not unless you agree . . ."

"You're the boss."

"That's not how I'd put it."

"But that's what you mean, and it's okay by me. We'll have it all your way—except one thing. I'll leave the M-16 as long as we take a pistol. I just don't feature being un-armed."

Though anxious to play it safe and use no more force than necessary, Ted knew you could never be certain how much that was. With chilling clarity, he relived that instant when the dark shadow sliced over Bert and him and he had fumbled for a weapon that wasn't there. When things started to break, you had to have something extra to call on, and a man like Polo backing you up. You might not be able to trust him until the last moment, but he looked like the type who'd hang tough in a tight spot.

"Okay," said Ted. "I'll carry the pistol."

Polo smoothed his moustache. "There's a .38 and a .357 magnum. We could each have one."

"No dice. I carry the gun. Take it or leave it."

"Sure, man, I'll take it. Just thought I might make it easier on you." Polo rose. "Let's see what Puff's got for breakfast."

Bert crept into camp quietly. No one was up, and the embers of last night's fire had stopped smoking. She tried to climb into the bus without disturbing Puff, but the big blond girl was awake, chewing the fleshy pad of her thumb, her complexion unusually pale except where blue smudges bagged beneath her eyes. "How'd it go?"

"Not bad."

Dropping the quilt, Bert pulled on her Levis, then lay on the sheepskins which covered the floor in back where the seats were folded down. The skins had been dried, not tanned, and they had a gamy smell as Bert rested her cheek on the warm fleece. When Puff crawled close to her, they cracked like parchment.

"You act down. Won't he help?"

"No, he'll help."

"Great! Thank god." She gripped Bert's shoulder. "Thank *you*. That's beautiful. How'd you do it?"

"Look, he said he'd help. Isn't that enough?"

The hand hopped off Bert's shoulder. "Sorry."

"No, I'm sorry." She patted Puff's broad knee. "I'm in a bitchy mood."

"Why? He didn't get rough, did he?"

"No, nothing like that. He's not what you think. A hard-hat or something. He wouldn't hurt anybody."

Puff suddenly seemed uneasy and averted her eyes. Each

girl found it difficult to face her friend. "Should I fix coffee?"

"Yeah. That'd be nice."

Before leaving, Puff whispered, "Thanks again, Bert. I won't forget."

Bert didn't answer. She wished she could forget. Nothing had gone as she'd expected—what ever did?—and when she recalled what she'd done, she was wracked by shame, guilt, and anger at herself.

Last night, shortly after they'd bedded down, Puff began crying. She attempted to hide the tears and muffle her sobs, but her soft, trembling body had betrayed her. At first Bert remained silent, reluctant to embarrass her and make the situation worse. Puff wasn't shy. She'd talk when she was ready to. But as the sobbing continued, the sound growing hoarse and frantic, Bert couldn't stand it. "What's wrong?" she asked.

"I'm scared."

"Don't be," said Bert, although she was too and had been for months. For both of them, it seemed, the bottom had dropped out of life. Puff had lost Gypsy, and at times Bert felt she'd lost even more.

"But I am. I can't hack it any longer. The waiting, the hassles, this rapping about tactics has me half out of my head. Now Polo's gone, which is right on with me, but if this new dude doesn't help, we're dead. We'll never free Gypsy."

"It'll work out," Bert muttered.

"Christ, don't say that. You know it won't. Phil's liable to leave next. Then what? Who's going to foot the bills?"

While Puff went on, fretting and wailing and shredding the flesh on her thumb, Bert didn't waste her breath saying, I wish there was something I could do. I had that chance, she thought, and I blew it. While Gypsy was taking the rap, she'd shacked up in the cell with the guard. Although the two weren't—could not have been—connected, she sometimes felt she'd personally sentenced Gypsy to five years.

But during the months in jail, nothing had mattered except her safety and the knowledge that she had a small corner on one man's selfish concern. She'd expected to be there for years, free only to choose her brand of rape. For the first time in her life she'd felt defenseless, of no consequence to anyone except herself, and had begged not to be thrown in with the others.

In return she had let the guard do what he liked, telling herself this was nothing, that he'd never really touch her. She'd slept around a little in the last few years. What difference did one more make when so much was at stake and there was no alternative?

Not until afterward did Bert realize the price she'd paid. She could have refused and fought. Made it miserable for him. Threatened to kill herself. Or just owned up to what she was doing—paying with her body and, more important, her self-respect, for what she wanted. Anything except pretending that since it was mechanical, it didn't matter.

"But if this new guy helps," Puff ran on, "I'm positive we'll pull through. Did you see how he put Polo down? The man's tough as a tire iron and not dumb." After a pause, she said, "He seems to like you. You could convince him."

"What? How?"

"Talk to him. He'll listen to you."

Bert sat up, not sure she understood. "What are you saying?"

"Talk to the man. That's all."

"You've already talked to him. Phil and Polo talked to him."

"But you haven't."

Then she was certain Puff meant sleep with him, screw him, do whatever it takes to change his mind. And Bert's best gauge of what she'd lost was that this didn't upset, insult, or anger her. Without a word, she'd stepped off the bus and stumbled over the sharp stones. This time she didn't delude herself. She'd learned that there was very little that didn't matter. Actions had a life of their own. You released them like pigeons and ultimately they all returned to the roost, but that was not to say they followed the course you plotted for them.

She was eager to help Puff and help herself by doing something for Gypsy. That'll be the difference, she thought. I'm doing it for someone else as well as myself. But as she walked barefoot through the darkness, numb from the cold air and a kind of inner freezing, she knew how much this was going to cost her. There were many ways to commit suicide. For Bert, indiscriminate sex had become one of them, a piecemeal method, not because in the intensity of the moment you forgot yourself, but because afterward there seemed less of you left.

Now nestling on the fleecy sheepskins, she was confused. She'd gotten much more than she'd planned to give. She'd come away with more than she'd brought. She wasn't even an honest whore. She tricked him, and it did no good to tell herself she hadn't intended to.

Nobody knew the whole truth about her time in jail. She hadn't laid that heavy load on anyone. Yet she'd cried and told Ted at once. Why? That wasn't part of the contract. It was supposed to be a straight business deal. Using her body, she'd keep herself out of it. But talking to him, unconsciously playing on his sympathy, she had exacted his promise of help, then slept with him, though it was obvious he hadn't really wanted to. And afterward she'd spent the night beside him because she felt safer there.

She'd had the best of the bargain, and it amazed her how little it took to transform the same act from a meaningless twitch of the nerves into something warm and human. Yet when she thought it over, there was no mystery about it. At its best, sex never rolled back reality for Bert. It brought it closer. What had happened, then, was quite simple. She'd talked, and he'd listened. She'd confided, and he'd been considerate and consoling. When they touched, it was as though more than their bodies met. She'd felt she could trust him. She didn't have to sleep with him—he'd already agreed to help—but by then she'd wanted to.

Bert didn't regret that, but she was sorry about the deception. If she confessed now, he'd never have faith in her and might not free Gypsy. Though she considered not making love again until she could be honest with him, that too was impossible. Then he'd know he'd been used. She had to hold up her end of the bargain and hope they pulled through safely and that Ted never learned the truth. For if he did, she was afraid she'd lose the first person who had mattered to her in a long time. Maybe, she thought, hoping again, it meant something to him too.

2

BY THE time they finished breakfast, the group had welcomed Polo back with a good-natured indifference which proved to Ted they didn't have an inkling how difficult it would have been without him and how much their plan depended on a few men spread too thin. But since it would have upset them and inflated Polo's fat head, he didn't bother to jolt their complacency.

They broke camp quickly, packing up their belongings and abandoning a pile of refuse. In the rear-view mirror Ted noticed stew cans, cellophane wrappers, plastic bottles, and the heaped wet ashes of their fire. Though he didn't like leaving this mess, they had to get to Tazenzit, talk to Gypsy, and put the touch on one of the guards. A raven was circling the garbage.

In front, Puff rode with Polo in the formidable grey Land-Rover, while Ants and Phil followed in the VW bus, and Ted and Bert brought up the rear in the Renault. Thumping over the unpaved washboard trail through the Ammeln Valley, they kept a careful space between cars so they wouldn't be blinded by the red dust or have their windshields shattered by gravel. They met no traffic moving toward them save for an ancient Berber slung sidesaddle on a mule. He goaded the animal to the edge of the road, waved to The Gravy Train, then plodded on toward Sidi-Abd-ej-Jebar which, at his present rate, he'd reach by noon.

When they arrived at the asphalt road, the sun was lighting the last of the massive boulders around Tafraoute, which to Polo had always resembled the ruins of an ancient city rather than unhewn rocks. Lining the hills, strewn across fields, and stacked atop one another like pinnacles about to tumble, the stones actually served a more practical purpose as props, foundations, and walls for the town's pink and orange pisé houses. Constructed of mud and gravel, clinging to the crevasses from which they'd been quarried, these buildings embodied a paradox peculiar to Morocco, the revenge which reality exacted of art. Regardless of their beauty and grandeur, the casbahs were water soluble and, after a few hard rains, would wash away.

Polo kept this in mind as a caution against their seductive charm and a protection from his own sense of failure. He had explored all the villages in the area, but had made contact with none of them. Seen from the road, they presented uncanny geometrical patterns, misleading perspectives, and brilliant *trompe-l'oeil.* Yet the instant he set foot on the first street, an essential aspect of the overall design disappeared. You couldn't enter a work of art and expect satisfaction.

Once, while walking toward a mosque whose ornate minaret hovered over the town, he had roved through narrower and narrower streets till he wound up in a garbage dump where dogs, cats, rats, birds, and insects fought for what the people had discarded as absolutely inedible. Here he was, it had suddenly occurred to him, searching for beauty, swimming in a sentimental bath of abstractions, while behind the pastel walls, inside the perfect cubistic forms, human beings were suffering. He'd sworn then to avoid the ambiguities of these cool, cumin-scented alleys until he'd discovered a way of breaking through to the people and to deeper parts of himself.

As he drove by, he wondered whether he was any closer to that breakthrough. A little, he thought. At least I've started. He refused to look again at the tall, flaming stones, the palm grove they passed through, or the almond orchard where the wind whipped up a blizzard of fallen blossoms.

When the road left the valley, winding into a range of low rolling hills, Bert asked, "Do we need Polo?"

"He'll help," said Ted.

"Why? Will it be dangerous?"

"Could be. Not scared, are you?"

"No. Neither are the rest of them. It's sort of unreal to think of us breaking somebody from jail."

"It'll get realer as we go along. Sure you're not having second thoughts?"

"No. We have to do it. That's what's so weird. I don't remember the last time I *had* to do anything."

"You'll do fine." He placed a hand on her knee. "I'm fixing it so nothing can go wrong."

"Good." Bert leaned over and yanked his hair. "Why don't you let it grow?"

"I don't like lugging a comb. When I'm walking the weight of it throws me off-balance."

"Buy one for each pocket."

"Tell you what. You wear dresses, I'll wear my hair long."

"Oh, wow! You and my mother ought to meet."

"She likes dresses, too?"

"The longer and lacier the better. Every time I'm home I have to dress like a Kewpie doll."

"Is that what you'll do after this? Go home?"

"I suppose so. It's as good a place as any to decide what to do next."

"How much does your family know?"

"Nothing. They'd wig out. I told them I'm traveling with Puff, and that's it. Once in a while they write and send money, and I answer with breezy post-cards full of beautiful lies. It'll be hard to be around them again. What'll we talk about?"

"What do you usually talk about?"

"As little as possible. Don't get me wrong. I'm not dumping on my parents. They're good people, and I love them and don't like to hurt them. But they're in another world. At our house the clocks stopped in 1954 "

"A fine year."

"Be serious. They're probably as uncomfortable around

me as I am around them. So we smile and talk about when I was a little girl and discuss *things*. Stuff they relate to. The lawn, the car, clothes, the dog, my mother's club, my father's job. Whenever I mention an idea that matters to me, they squirm. You can hear their hearts thumping and read their minds. 'Suppose she tells us she's on drugs? Or she's got a black boyfriend? What'll we do?' "

"I take it you won't stay long."

"I couldn't or they'd notice I've changed, and that'd blow the whole scene. No, I'll play it cool, take a lot of baths, eat everything on my plate, let my mother buy me a few dresses, then split. Isn't it a hell of a thing when all home means is warm water, clean sheets, good food, and new clothes?"

"Sounds nice to me. For some people it's a lot less."

"Hey! Whose side are you on?"

"Nobody's. My own."

"I'm beginning to believe it."

Ted wasn't smiling when he said, "You've been in Morocco ten months. You see how they live here. Like to trade your home for one of theirs?"

"Okay, you've got a point, but it's not the answer, or you'd be in the States yourself, living in Levittown. Maybe nothing beats America. That's another argument altogether. But there has to be something different, someplace for people who don't fit in the same bag. That's what I'm looking for. My parents love each other. It works for them, and that's great. But I couldn't stand a life like theirs."

"Then you won't have one."

"You better believe I won't. I'm not going to wake up one morning and walk into my mother's world."

"All right. I know what you don't want," Ted drawled.

"Why don't you tell me what you do want?"

"The truth is, a lot of women don't know what they want. They have such an ass-backward upbringing, it's a wonder they even know who they are. They're given names they'll have to change, educations they're not expected to use, and lives they're not allowed to control."

"I'm still listening. What is it *you* want?"

"Well," Bert was working her hands through her hair, braiding and unbraiding a single lock. "I used to say I didn't want anything. Not the normal things. I didn't care about money or a career or success or marriage. I just wanted to be happy and free. I said that like it was nothing, like anybody could be happy and free. But I don't fool myself any more. They're the hardest things to get, especially if you're not materialistic. I mean, apart from objects, what is happiness for most people? Define it. How can you be sure when you have it and when you don't?"

"Everybody knows what makes him happy," said Ted. "What does it for you?"

"Being on my own. Having the freedom to be myself."

"That covers a mighty big piece of ground."

"I need a lot of ground. Take a person like Puff. She's searching for somewhere to settle. All her life she's looked odd and for once she'd like to feel at home. Well, much as I might look like other people, I'm not like them. Deep down, I'm different and if I'm always going to be out of it no matter where I am, I'd rather be moving."

Ted glanced at Bert, whose hands shuffled more rapidly through her hair, and since she seemed agitated, he spoke calmly. "How does that help?"

She shrugged and said without much conviction, "I don't like to be tied down. I've always had a feeling if you hope to do anything special, you have to be free of strings."

"I used to think that. It didn't work for me."

"Why not?"

"I don't know." Now he shrugged. "Just being alive ties you down. There's nowhere to run. I've been on the move almost twenty years and never really got anywhere or did anything special. I don't know anybody who hit the jackpot that way. Seems to me, if you sit tight, good things are about as likely to happen as when you're hustling around."

"Where does that leave you?"

"It leaves me agreeing with Puff. I'm tired of traveling. I'm ready to settle awhile."

Bert was scratching at the frayed patches on her Levis. Her hair curtained her face from Ted, yet he could hear a change in her voice. "Maybe you're right. I'm turned on by good times and new places, but in the end it comes down to people. If you're not with people you like, nothing's worth it." Brushing back the hair, she forced a faint smile. "And you, where are you going to live? I'd like to hear about this magic spot."

"No magic to it. It's an island in the British Virgins. When I was stationed on Puerto Rico, I used to go down there every chance I got. By boat it takes only four hours, but you'd think you were in a different century. No tourists, no roads, no electricity. Just terrific scenery, friendly folks, and water that's blue and clear and full of fish. I figured it'd be a good place to start a little charter business when I retired from the service."

"What are you waiting for?"

"Well, for one thing, I didn't retire."

"I don't get it."

"I left the army after fifteen years. I wasn't eligible for retirement and I didn't have a cent saved to buy a boat. I was hoping to work until I put some money aside, but, with one thing and another, I never got that far ahead of the game."

"Is that why you're helping us? For the money?" She flattened the friendliness from her voice.

"There's lots of reasons, but I reckon that's what they add up to."

"It's true, then, what Polo and Phil say?"

"What's that?"

"That you're a soldier of fortune."

Ted broke into laughter.

"What's so funny?"

"You people, the whole bunch of you, are too much. You couldn't be farther off base. Soldier of fortune! Shit, I'm just the opposite. How do you say it?" He was still laughing. "A soldier of misfortune, of fate."

"Meaning?"

"Meaning you or anyone else thinks a man gets rich in the army or doing what I do, you're nuts."

"Then why do it? Why did you join the army in the first place?"

"I was about to be drafted. So I enlisted."

"A lot of guys don't go."

"It was a little different back in 1952. You wouldn't remember that. You must of been a baby then, and I wasn't much more when they sent me to Korea. I fought because they told me to. It's as simple as that. When you're eighteen and some second looey is shouting at you from behind and someone's shooting at you from in front, you don't stop and ask, Is this right? You fight to survive."

"But you stayed in fifteen years. You had a choice."

"Yeah, and I admit I didn't muster out when I should of. I waited till after my second hitch in Vietnam. But I could of sat tight, you know, and retired in five years. The way they were promoting people, I might of been an officer by now. If I had, you can bet I wouldn't be here. I'd be toasting my bones on that island." He smiled and smacked her thigh. "Better be glad of that. Don't go reforming me too fast. Not till after your friend's free."

She returned to picking at the patches on her Levis. "Why did you quit the army?"

Ted wondered whether it was worth explaining. She seemed eager to find fault with him, and he didn't enjoy discussing the subject. He'd been over it in his own mind too many times. Yet he liked Bert and was anxious for her to understand.

"Well, I won't pretend I'm a pacifist or any better than the next guy, but Vietnam's a tough war to take. It's so confusing, no matter what you say about it one minute, you'll look like a fool the next. Some of it's very quick, clean fighting and for long stretches the life's not that bad even in the combat zones. They're using television and electronic gear and tons of air support, and when you're in from a patrol, the food's good, you pop a beer, flick on your radio, or take an R & R, and if you catch some shit or your time's up, a helicopter flies you out. And you think to yourself, nobody's going to beat us.

"But it's funny. The equipment's fantastically effective, but the men who work it, a lot of them, are the same kind who used to throw spears or shoot arrows. Sometimes they can't control themselves, and when they don't, who's controlling those machines? I'll tell you, no one is. They keep rolling on their own. They're scarier than the Cong.

"Then the other fighting, what the infantry, the grunts, do in the field, that hasn't changed in years. It's close and mean as hell, more like a barroom brawl than a battle. We couldn't win and Charlie couldn't win, but neither of us could bear to lose. So we kept going at it. Ever watched two evenly matched men street fight? Pretty soon, when they know neither of them can win, they forget about that and try to scar the other guy, make a mark on him. Half the time that's what we were doing—punishing hell out of people. They'd fire a mortar; we'd mess up a village. They'd booby-trap a body; we'd cut off a few ears. They'd march American prisoners through Hanoi; we wouldn't take any prisoners. I reckon the war'll end sooner or later, but I decided it'll have to be without me."

There was a puzzled arch to Bert's eyebrows. "Then why do this?"

"Trying to talk me out of it again?"

"I'm serious. After what you've said, how could you fight in Nigeria?"

"Crazy, isn't it? Me, a white cracker down there with all those spades. Now it doesn't make much sense to me either, but at the time I was in bad shape. No money and no prospects. There are just so many jobs you qualify for with an automatic rifle, or a grenade launcher, or a flame thrower. So when this friend put me in touch with an Ibo relief agency in Switzerland and they laid an offer on me to fight, it sounded pretty damn good. Fifteen hundred a month and expenses. I thought by the time it was over I'd have a nice nest egg. And I gotta be honest, it was more than the money. I was out to prove something to myself. That was my first mistake. Whenever you're set on proving anything, you end up in trouble. But I aimed to show I didn't quit the army because I was scared, and I wanted to fight for the good guys, the underdog, for a change. Everybody was rooting for the Ibos, so I said to myself, why not give them a hand and pick up a little loot at the same time? Of course it didn't turn out like that."

"How come? I was never clear about the issues in that war."

"Oh, the issues are the easy part. They always are. The Ibos said they were being oppressed and broke off from the rest of the country. Both armies had outside help. The Nigerians a lot from the British, the Ibos a little from the French. But in battle that stuff doesn't matter. You couldn't care less what the issues are or who supports you, as long as they're sending ammunition. The point is to stay alive and kill a few of the enemy while you're at it.

"It was the same story. Neither side could win, but nobody was about to surrender. The Nigerians dug in and waited for the Ibos to starve. Everybody except the army was going hungry. You've seen pictures of it. Thousands and thousands of kids and women and old men with their bellies swollen and their hair turning orange. After a while, no one had the strength to bury the dead. The whole country smelled like a slaughterhouse.

"It made Vietnam look almost sane. I mean here I had next to no ammo or equipment, but I'd plan these missions and lead a bunch of boys through the boondocks. We'd lay down a line of fire into the bushes, but we might as well of been spraying a garden hose. That jungle just sucked up bullets. Every once in a while you'd find a dead body or hear a scream, or more than likely take a casualty yourself, then you'd retreat into your own territory and watch the people starve and wait for someone or something to stop it.

"For me it ended in a little mud and straw hootch. I was separated from my men and humping my way back to home base when I got to this abandoned village. It was late afternoon, and I had no idea where the hell I was at. First I skirted the clearing, thinking it was a trap. Then when I figured it wasn't, I started through.

"I heard them before I saw them. It sounded like an army crashing in around me. They didn't expect to find anyone there and they didn't bother being quiet. I ducked into one of the hootches, hoping they wouldn't search the place. They didn't, but they stopped and set up camp—about a dozen Nigerian soldiers, and a few women and kids tagging after them, begging for food. I couldn't do a damn thing but stay put.

"While I was waiting, one of the kids, a boy about nine, wandered toward my hootch. Just curious, I guess, like most kids. Or maybe he was sick and looking for a place to lie down. He didn't seem to belong to anybody. At least nobody noticed when he left the fire.

"He was so skinny, you could see his skeleton and his heart beating like a little bird behind his rickety ribs. He had that orange hair and those eyes that looked like they were standing out on stalks. I was wedged in the corner, praying he'd go away, but he walked right in and saw me. Before he could shout, I grabbed and dragged him clawing and kicking into the corner. I've never seen anyone his size fight like that. My hand was over his mouth, and he bit into it till it bled. I didn't mean to hurt him, but I was afraid they might hear him thrashing around, so I hit him with my fist. That stopped him, but not for long. He about dug his teeth into my bone. So I popped him harder and put him out.

"He laid there in my lap, half-naked, skinny, and sweating, with blood from my hand all over his face. I asked myself, what the hell's with you that you're beating up on little boys? But before I had an answer, he was awake and wiggling, and this time when I punched him, I busted his nose. Now he had my blood and his on his face, and before he went out, he had the strangest look in his eyes. Maybe he was wondering, like I was, How the hell long is this going to keep up? Am I going to go on punching him in the head all night?

"Well, that's what I did. There was nothing else to do except surrender, and I might as well of committed suicide, because when they captured mercenaries, they took those people apart. You see, it was too late to ask whether it was worth it—the money and helping the Ibos and proving I wasn't chicken. Nothing counted except keeping that kid unconscious and myself alive. I've never done anything more mechanical in my life. I pounded him like a drum."

"Did you kill him?" Her voice was very even.

"I don't know. It was dark. I swung whenever he moved. Then he didn't move any more. He might of been dead. I didn't check. I didn't want to know. When the soldiers were asleep and the fire died, I dropped him and ducked into the underbrush. I never fought again. The war kind of collapsed after that. The Nigerians broke through, and the mercenaries—the volunteers—we were airlifted from the country. I never got my last pay-check. I looked for that relief agency in Geneva, but it'd folded."

When he was silent, Bert said nothing and avoided his eyes. Now you've done it, he thought. Loused up everything. It shouldn't have mattered what she thought, and yet it did.

"I went home for a while," he fumbled on. "When that didn't work, I came here, looking for a job. There was this company in South Africa . . ." He tried to wind up the story in a way that wouldn't leave them silent and estranged, but couldn't say anything that sounded right.

Finally Bert saved him the trouble. "I'm sorry."

"Why? You got nothing to be sorry about."

"Yes, I do. I'm sorry I asked you to help us. Sorry I've been talking to you like this."

"Don't be. You just hadn't heard the whole story."

"You're the one who doesn't know the whole story. I wouldn't want you to do anything like that for us. I . . ." She started to say more, then shut her mouth.

"Look, this'll be a piece of cake. When it's over your friend'll be free and I'll head for that island. It's the last time out for me. You can count on that," said Ted.

3

At Tiznit they turned north where the land leveled and widened and the wind, with nothing to slow it, sluiced loudly through the gum trees which lined the road. Shoals of slender green leaves eddied over the cars, swimming off in their wake. It was market day in town, and trucks, donkey carts, pushcarts, and men on motorscooters, bicycles, and on foot crowded the narrow ribbon of asphalt. Even a cripple rolled past in a wheelchair, churning along the graveled apron.

In the scrubland beside the road, mules plodded beneath mountainous loads of lumber, charcoal, and grain, and caravans of camels, though maintaining a steady pace, appeared to pause before each step, as though they were uncertain whether they could or would go on. Among them, much slower and infinitely more miserable, shuffled women bent under bundles of cork oak, firewood, baskets of fruit, and bread boards on which mounds of unbaked dough had been stacked.

Still in the lead, the heavy Land-Rover held a straight course into the wind, but every gust buffeted the VW bus and sent it skidding toward the opposite lane. As it fell farther behind, it began to belch black smoke. Ted passed it and Ants waved, pulling onto the shoulder, sounding his horn. Ted sped up to signal Polo, and together they circled around to ask what was wrong.

Ants said he thought the VW had blown a gasket. The Gravy Train had traveled over a hundred thousand miles and the bus was about shot. Since they were two hours from Tazenzit, it was decided that Ted should go ahead with Polo, while Bert and Phil waited with the VW, and Ants and Puff drove the Renault into Aït-Melloul to hire a mechanic. They'd meet that night at a campground on the beach in Agadir.

"Suppose they can't fix it?" asked Ants.

"Junk it," said Polo.

"Hey, we can't do that. It belongs to Gypsy."

"Have it towed," said Ted. "We'll need it." Then, after saying good-bye to Bert, he guided Phil to one side. "About that two thousand advance, I'd like to have it soon as possible."

"You've made up your mind?"

"Yeah. Lemme have about half in small bills. Dirhams and dollars."

Looking down, Phil leaned on his crutch. "You're sure you won't reconsider once you see the inside of the jail?" It sounded almost like he wished Ted would.

"Is there something you're not telling me?"

Phil shook his head. "I just don't care to cash the traveler's checks unless you're positive you're going to do it."

"You get the money. I change my mind, I'll pay you back with interest." He clapped the crippled boy's bony shoulder, but couldn't coax a smile from him.

In the Renault, Puff rearranged her flowered tent dress

so that it cloaked the bulky contours of her body. Once she was motionless, her awkwardness disappeared, and her size and weight gave her an air of gravity few women her age could claim.

"It might not have been a red-hot idea to leave those two alone," she said to Ants as they sped toward Aït-Melloul.

"Who, Bert and Phil? Let's trust them together. Phil's a very low-key cat."

"Not them, you simple tool. Polo and Ted."

"They're old enough to look after themselves."

"Just so long as they don't look after each other. That was a bad scene yesterday."

"Ted had it under control," said Ants. "Believe me, there's one guy who has his shit together."

"Last night you were defending Polo."

"Okay, I was showing both sides. But I'm tired of Polo coming on so strong."

"You really dig this new dude, don't you?"

"He's a good head. I have a hunch Bert thinks so too. I saw her sneaking back from his sack this morning."

"Oh?" She managed to make this one word express surprise and disappointment, as though she'd known nothing about it. She told herself she had to protect Bert. But from what? They were out front about these things. Puff knew it wasn't Bert she was protecting. "Well, she needed somebody," She mumbled to herself as much as to Ants. "But I'm not sure she picked the right person."

"Hey, wait a minute. I hope you're not saying that because you don't like her consorting with the hired hand."

"I'm not joking, Ants. He isn't one of us. It's hard to make it with a man like Kuyler. On top of that, he must be twenty years older than her."

"So you're an Age Segregationist as well as an Elitist

Pig-Dog. Puff, I never suspected this. Say Ted was black and I talked about him like you're doing. You'd accuse me of being a racist."

"Won't you ever be serious?" She poked him playfully in the arm.

"I am, I am."

"I thought she'd wind up with Polo."

"I bet he did too."

"Or with you, if you weren't such a silly shit."

"Oh, no, I'm saving myself for you, Puff. Soon as you lose ten pounds, we'll fit together snug as a jigsaw puzzle."

"You bastard!" She blushed, but couldn't stop laughing. "I've told you, I'm never going to reduce. Dieting is a world-wide conspiracy of puny finks like you. Besides, what's the difference between being a tall, goofy-looking fat chick and a tall, goofy-looking skinny one?"

"Then I'll put on weight. Say I do a body-building number and get up to one-fifty, do you think I could hold my own?"

She stroked his soft, bearded cheek. "Son, you've been holding your own so long, it's a wonder you haven't grown warts on your hot little hands."

Now they were both laughing.

"Watch the road before we wind up in the ditch," she warned him. "And keep those hands on the wheel where I can see them."

When Polo had run through the gears and they'd reached open road, he said, "We should get rid of that damn bus. It's been nothing but trouble. This could happen later. Then what?"

"It'll come in handy," said Ted.

"How? I got news for you. It'll never last in the desert."

"Not like this tank." Ted smacked the dashboard. There was a solid *thunk!* No rattles.

The Land-Rover did resemble a military vehicle. Big, drab, and boxy, it cornered stiffly and could call on great power in the low gears. The deep tread of its tires hummed monotonously on the asphalt, reminding Ted of every ride he'd taken in army transportation. With four-wheel drive and heavy-duty brakes, it could easily handle the steepest, unpaved trails, its grey, sheet-metal sides suggested armor plating, and the spare tire mounted on the hood might have been a machine-gun turret. Though comfortable, the interior looked stripped down and mercilessly efficient.

Proudly Polo showed Ted his Westinghouse 4-band, portable shortwave set and the panel he'd built behind the dashboard for the M-16. The pistols were hidden under the floor in the back. Only a thorough search could have uncovered the weapons, yet they were close at hand in case of trouble. As Polo wrestled the wheel and muscled the gears, which would have meshed with no effort, he wore a satisfied smile. Here, in the Land-Rover, he was in command.

"Nice machine. How much it cost?" asked Ted.

"I don't remember."

"Must of been a bundle. Funny how a revolutionary like you could afford it."

"I saved my allowance and sold magazines door to door."

"Look, I don't care what it cost, but someone said you're wanted in the States."

"So what?"

"So I'd like to know how you paid for this car. If it was with a check, it might of been forged. I don't want the job falling through because you were dumb enough to string paper around here."

"You sound like a cop."

"I'm trying to think like one."

"Relax. I bought it in London and I paid cash."

"How'd you get out of the States?"

"I might have hijacked a plane."

"Cut the crap. Do you have a passport?"

"Yeah."

"In your own name?"

"No, I'm carrying Canadian papers."

"How'd you get them?"

"Simple. I used another man's birth certificate. That's what James Earl Ray did. Amazing what you learn by reading the newspaper. Of course they're not looking for me as hard as they were for him. I haven't had any problems."

"Not yet. Then you are wanted? No bullshit?"

"Yeah, I went underground with the Weathermen after the Days of Rage in Chicago."

"When were you in Algiers?"

"I wasn't," he admitted after an instant's hesitation. When Ted smiled, he said, "I never claimed I was. I let people believe what they like. I'm on the lam, man. I don't have to tell everyone my life's story."

"Then why spread it around that you're wanted?"

"Well . . . I trust Phil and the others and I thought you . . ."

"Friend, you got more shit in you than a Christmas turkey. You were trying to impress those people. Oh, come on now," said Ted, as Polo's face darkened, "don't get pissed off. I don't care how you pull your chain. Just don't try to pull mine. Did you do anything stupid in the States I should know about? Anything that might foul us up here?"

"I didn't do half what I should have. For a couple weeks I hung around Chicago expecting a general rising or something. When that fell through, I left. I was looking for some real action for a change."

"Find any?"

"I arrived in Morocco right after the attempted coup."

"Too bad. I bet you could of turned it around," Ted applied the needle again, prodding and pressing Polo, hoping he'd tip his hand if his sudden change of heart was a trick. But Polo wouldn't take the bait.

"I'll get my chance. This country's ripe for a revolution."

"You sound like you're on a soapbox, old buddy. I know a lot of things Morocco needs more than a revolution."

"No, I've analyzed it, and that's the only way. It doesn't take a genius to imagine a better life than this."

"Maybe you have too much imagination."

"And you not enough. Christ, man, how can you look . . ." With a sweep of his hand, he included everyone streaming along the road. ". . . and not feel for them?"

"I didn't say I don't feel for them. I just don't have the answer."

"Have you asked the right question? Somebody has to find an answer. They deserve help. They're beautiful people."

"I like them, but I don't know how it'll help to shove something down their throats. If what you said was true, you wouldn't have to force them."

"Look, people are always being pushed one way or the other. They pay taxes, obey a lot of fucked-up laws, and play it straight because they have to, not because they like it. But our side is never supposed to use power. We're supposed to persuade people with logic and good will. That's horseshit. It doesn't get you anywhere. Not when some bastard's standing over you with a club or a gun. Everybody talks about violence. You were moaning about

it yesterday. But when the crunch comes, who does it?
Who's really into violence? The cops, the army, the government, that's who. So don't talk to me about force. That's
what we need."

"And that's what you aim to offer?"

"Yeah, when the time's right."

"My friend, your daydreaming doesn't mean diddly-shit
to me as long as the time's not right in the next week."

As Polo gripped the steering wheel tighter, his calloused
knuckles yellowed, and it looked like he'd been punching
a cinder block as part of his training. "Don't sweat it. I
won't screw up your tight-ass little plan. I want Gypsy out
and I'm willing to play ball with you. But don't push me,
Kuyler, and get one thing straight. You may be patting
yourself on the back for helping us, but in the long run it
adds up to zilch. You're in for a penny. When the ante rises,
you'll back off."

"We'll see who backs off."

"No, I guess you'll stick this out. Why not? You're getting paid."

Ted stayed very still. After seven years as a top sergeant,
he found it tough to take static and was aching to belt this
big-mouth. But he didn't have the U.S. Army behind him
and, although he allowed himself better than an even
chance of beating Polo, he realized whether he won or lost
the fight, he'd lose the battle—and the four thousand
bucks. So he smiled, as he often did when he was angriest,
and dropped into his hill-country drawl. "You sure know a
lot about politics and revolution, don't you? Where'd you
learn all that? At the university? But did you ever kill a man?
Or are you like one of those boys who's never had a piece,
but does nothing except talk about pussy?"

Though Polo had been struck at his weakest point, he

didn't buckle. "Okay, you've had experience. But there're a lot of ways to learn. I saw things clearly after the Cambodian invasion and the killings at Kent State and Jackson. Everyone was hiked up higher than a kite, claiming it was the most crucial moment in American history. At the rap sessions and committee meetings they'd ask, Are you part of the solution or part of the problem? But it never dawned on them that if the problem is real, the solution has to be real too. One minute they were saying the country was in a crisis, the next they were on their knees begging kids not to walk on the grass or occupy the ROTC office. You don't change government policy like that. You do it by closing the campuses, Congress, the army, big corporations, and to do that you need muscle. Admit it, violence works. That's the Establishment's dirty secret. Now everyone's in on it."

"All right, it works. So do other things."

"Name one that's as effective. Impossible! Only power stops power. There's no denying it, violence is the heaviest trip."

"Sometimes it takes you where you don't expect to go."

"So what? At least you're not standing still with your thumb up your ass. Look, for years in the civil rights movement, then with the antiwar movement, it was always the same. You'd listen to a few speeches, then march into the streets and meet the pigs. They'd say unless you broke it up, they'd bust you. So you'd sit down, scared shitless, and start singing Southern spirituals and staring up the street to where the pigs were getting it together.

"They'd look like the Green Bay Packers—big beefy mothers, whacking those wooden sticks against their thighs, chewing wads of gum so huge their jaw muscles flexed like biceps, laughing at us, really gearing up. And I'd think to myself, No, it's not going to happen this time.

"But there'd be a signal and they'd storm down on us, crack our skulls, and cart us off to jail. It went like that every fucking time. I knew they didn't agree with us and were doing their jobs and following orders, but I didn't understand why they'd bust somebody's ass for that.

"Then in Chicago it was different. We had the clubs and helmets, and we were dishing it out. I can't explain how it felt. You must know from being in battle. Having the power changes everything. It's a high. There's no other word for it. We marched up Michigan Avenue and savaged everything in sight. Bap! Bap! Bap!" He slapped his palm on the dashboard. "Cars, store windows, cops, pedestrians. It wasn't revenge. I didn't think about all the times I'd had my head handed to me. There was just this great sense of release. Nothing but a bullet could've stopped me. Any cop feels half as high as I did, there's no hope of talking reason to him. He's not listening to speeches and spirituals. He's grooving on something heavier. I learned then, if you mean to stop them, you have to crush them before they do it to you."

"And you really think that'll work?" asked Ted, not testing or taunting Polo, just anxious to know why anyone with a choice would commit himself to such a course of action. Although he recognized the unswerving determination, he'd seen it before only in hardened soldiers and half-crazy tribal politicians who mistook military strength for moral superiority and wouldn't settle for anything less than absolute victory. Polo might be genuinely concerned about his ideas and about the Moroccans, but in Ted's experience, the cause rarely justified the body count.

"Don't look so shocked, man. You're a soldier. It's gotten to be a cliché, but power does grow from a gun barrel."

"That's the truth, old buddy. But the fact is, there are a

mess of guns and even more people willing to fire them. You're going up against professionals. I were you, I'd find another place where power grows."

"More speeches and spirituals? To hell with that."

"Then you'd better learn to shoot straight."

"We will. In due time."

Ted was about to ask Polo if he'd seen the kind of holes bullets left, or smelled the stench of corpses, or felt the sickness when that battlefield high wore off. And what if this solution he favored was part of the problem? Some solutions caused new problems. Violence fed on itself, and there was always somebody willing to push it a mile farther, somebody who didn't care whether he died or who he killed.

But it was useless. No one could change Polo's mind, and Ted preferred to have these knuckle-headed notions in the open. It's when he stops acting and talking like King Kong that he'll be ready to clobber you. Maybe he's right about one thing, though, Ted thought. It'll take a bullet to stop him. But not me. I'm out of this. Let someone else do it after I've used him for the job.

Atop a gradual knoll rose the red walls of Tazenzit, concealing everything in town except the tallest minarets and palm trees. Some of the ramparts had fallen into disrepair, their rubble dissolving into the wind-swept plain. But surrounding the center of the city, the battlements bristled with parapets and crude, hand-cut crenellations as if in imitation of the awesome High Atlas range, whose frozen peaks formed a bulwark thirty miles behind the town.

A laterite road funneled traffic toward the medina gate. As Polo honked the horn, a shepherd and his flock casually claimed the right of way and slowed the Land-Rover to a crawl. Passing under the high arch and through the wall, they lost sight of the sun. Squat and hive-like, the houses created an impression of warmth, but the tunneling streets, tinged by the scent of urine, were shockingly cold. Swirls of wind chased dust devils through the alleys, billowing the blue robes worn by women who pulled their veils tighter as the Land-Rover approached. Each of them had only one deep-set eye and an indigo-tinted hand exposed.

Polo sounded the horn steadily now, nudging into the crowd, but there was no room. Young boys trotted beside them, smacking the metal panels and screaming, *"Fluss! Fluss!"* Though Ted had no loose change to throw them, he could have patted their heads or touched the matted straw which helped hold the mud bricks together. The road was that narrow. Ahead of them, a man had a live goat slung over his shoulders and, walking with him, a friend bore a goatskin water bag. Plugged shut at its feet, mouth, eyes, ears, and anus, it reminded Ted of the carcasses he had seen on the roadside, their bellies blown big from gas.

At last a shaft of light, laden with smoke and dust, appeared in front of the Land-Rover and, leaving the medina, they entered an immense, sunbaked square. PLACE DES CHA-MEAUX read a sign, and in parentheses under it, an indication of change, CHAMEAUX INTERDITS DANS LA PLACE. Bordered by arcades and rows of keyhole arches, the square could have contained the entire population of Tazenzit, but it was almost empty, for the crowd combed through the arches into the market.

A mist of flies rose, then resettled as they rumbled around a dead dog. Polo drove to the west end of the *place* and parked next to the jail. When Ted climbed out, the smell of the dog was on the wind.

The Sûreté Nationale looked new and sturdy, built of

concrete instead of crumbly pisé. The windows were barred by iron grates, and a massive wooden door, reinforced by brass rivets and hinges, loomed twice as tall as a man. For day-to-day business a small hatch had been sawed through the planks.

After buying bread, cheese, fruit, candy, and cigarettes at an *épicerie* in the European quarter, they returned to this hatch, which Polo shoved open. With a bag of groceries on his hip, Ted crouched and stepped into a corridor as dank as a cave. Huge and high-ceilinged, it was feebly lit and foul from unwashed bodies. A fierce, penetrating chill stole from the cement into his bones, and he couldn't stop shivering.

In a corner six guards sat around a charcoal brazier which gave off more smoke than warmth. Opposite them, bundled like an Eskimo, a clerk slumped in a cage of heavy-gauge wire. Polo was speaking to him in laborious French, asking to see James Powell. Ted should have interpreted, but he was shivering so badly he was afraid his voice might crack. So he let Polo seize the initiative and told himself he wasn't scared, just stunned—by the cold, increasingly by the stench, and by the conditions which must have been almost as unbearable for the guards as for the prisoners.

Although the frigid air should have killed them off, flies were an added affliction. Hundreds hovered near the guards at the brazier and, as they cruised closer to the heat, one fell with a moist hiss onto the coals. Others beaded like sooty tears at the edges of their eyes. No one bothered to bat them away.

Polo slapped Ted's arm. The clerk had emerged from his cage and gone to a door at the end of the corridor. As they passed the guards at the brazier, not one looked up. In their grey uniforms, the men seemed frozen solid as ice statues.

They had unbuckled their cartridge belts and put their holstered pistols on the floor. Three Matka 47 submachine guns stood in the corner.

Glancing into the grocery bags, the clerk took two tangerines and a pack of cigarettes.

"Is this the one?" Ted asked.

Polo shook his head no.

Drawing his hands, the tangerines, and cigarettes into his djellabah, the clerk pressed his shoulders to the door and kicked his heel against it as a mule might have. Ted couldn't tell what the man's blank eyes registered and was relieved that they didn't have to deal with him.

When the door swung in, a sickening smell washed over them, a staggering compound of odors among which urine and vomit were the least offensive. Walking from one windowless room to the next, it was as if they'd moved closer to a cavern where garbage was decomposing. Suspended from the ceiling by a black cord, a single bulb in a wire basket bled miasmal light.

Yet a surprisingly dapper little guard met them. Locking the door, he pocketed a weighty ring of keys and appeared to get great pleasure from patting them down, checking for concealed weapons along the inseams of their trousers. Polo signaled that this was their man.

As the guard stood up, Polo said, "This is Driss."

"Welcome. You are my friends." After shaking Ted's hand, the guard kissed his pink fingers, touched them to his heart, then repeated the ritual with Polo. "You are well, I hope." This seemed to exhaust his English and he lapsed into French. *"Avez-vous des cadeaux pour votre ami?"*

Guiding them to a table, he emptied the bags, clucking delightedly like a housewife over each item. Driss had a hat on, and the polished visor and insignia gleamed in the dim light. His uniform was clean and tailored to his plump figure. Unlike the other guards, he had kept his cartridge belt and holster on, and it creaked as he bustled about. When he'd divided the food and cigarettes into two piles —one for Gypsy, one for himself—he smiled, showing a glint of gold teeth. "You are very generous," Driss said in French. "I am sorry your friend won't be with us much longer."

"He tells us you've been kind," Ted answered.

"Oouff." Shrugging, Driss puffed his sleek, hairless cheeks, imitating an expression he'd seen in French movies. But he looked more Oriental than Gallic. His left eye was marred by a milky cast over the pupil. Driss had trachoma and without medical attention would probably be blind in a few years. "I am a poor man, but I do what I can. I like the Americans."

"And I the Moroccans."

He studied Ted an instant before saying, "I shall bring your friend."

Unlocking yet another door, Driss marched down a row of cells, his leather heels loudly clicking. Though the odor had assumed new and nauseating dimensions, Ted ignored it as he sized up this room, the corridor of cells, and their relationship to the outer hall. The doors bothered him. He was more convinced than ever that they needed inside help.

Keys jangled, a cell door clanked, and a slender boy came to Driss. As the two of them approached Ted and Polo, the prisoner's feet were silent, for he wore rubber-soled sandals. Shivering and stoop-shouldered, he hugged his chest for warmth, but had big goosebumps on his neck and hands. Dressed in tattered dungarees and a denim shirt, Gypsy Powell bore a striking resemblance to his brother, Phil—the same red hair and freckles—except that he was a little taller, wore wire-rim glasses, and was much thinner.

As they shook hands, Ted could have counted every bone in the boy's fingers. It was beginning to eat at him. He'd intended to stay neutral, detached, but he was growing angry as well as worried. The group hadn't exaggerated. Gypsy would never survive five years of this.

After six months he had a sickly prison pallor, accentuated on his fingers by nicotine stains, and one of his front teeth had gone bad, having been knocked loose by a punch or deadened by the poor diet. His eyes revealed no curiosity, no emotion at all, when Polo introduced Ted as a friend who had joined The Gravy Train. Gypsy had learned already to count on nothing and give nothing away.

"How do you feel?" asked Ted.

"Fine. Mind if I sit down?" He fell onto a straight back chair at the table and hurriedly peeled a tangerine, eating the pulp, then the skin.

While Ted and Polo sat opposite him, Driss stood at the head of the table, a smiling master of ceremonies.

"Will he leave?" Ted whispered to Polo.

"No."

"You bring anything for the roaches, rats, bedbugs, and other prisoners?" asked Gypsy, who'd finished the tangerine and was gnawing a slab of cheese.

"Yeah, and a few crumbs for our friend here."

"Oh, him, he's the lord of the flies," Gypsy mumbled through a full mouth.

As Driss inclined his head, the milky eye became opaque. Though it was impossible to judge his grasp of English, Ted thought they didn't have to play it safe. "Are you strong enough to travel?" he asked Gypsy.

"Yeah. They should transfer me to Casablanca pretty soon. I'm looking forward to the change."

"I was thinking," said Ted, careful not to blink or bring his gaze around to Driss, "there might be someplace you'd like more."

"There are a lot of places I'd like more." Gypsy munched a piece of candy along with the cheese. Although he appeared to be intent upon nothing except the next bite, the veins in his skinny neck had drawn taut.

"We might fix it so you don't go to Casablanca." Polo put his boot on Ted's foot and pressed down hard, but Ted asked, "That appeal to you?"

"I'm up for anything." He tossed some candy to Driss who, quick as a cat, wasn't caught off balance. "Eat it. You'll like it."

"*Merci.*" He placed it on his pile of food.

"Like a cigarette?" Ted asked the guard. Polo had lifted his foot, but looked frantic.

"Not now, thank you. Perhaps later."

"We're discussing a trip through the country. Do you have any suggestions?"

"I know Morocco very well," said Driss. "We could have tea one evening and . . ."

"How's Puff?" Gypsy interrupted, and Driss's eyes, alert to new possibilities, glazed over in confusion.

"Terrific!" Polo blurted, as if to blast from the guard's head everything he'd heard. "She misses you."

"And Bert?"

"Better all the time. Ted's seeing to that." In Polo's lap, his fists clenched and unclenched. "Ants and Phil were coming today, but the bus broke down. They're in Aït-Melloul having it worked on."

"We're lucky it's lasted this long. How about the weather? Is it warm?"

"Some days it is."

"In here it's hard to tell."

"Aren't you cold?" Ted asked Driss.

"I manage to stay warm." His ambiguous grin displayed its gold.

"Tell me how you do it," said Gypsy in passable French.

"Someday I shall. But now you must return to your cell."

"Great. I'm dying to get back." Lifting his glasses, he rubbed the pinch marks on the bridge of his nose and attempted to hide his disappointment.

"You won't be here much longer," said Ted.

Gypsy nodded. "That's nice to know."

When Gypsy slipped a hunk of cheese into his pocket, Driss said, *"Non, non. C'est défendu,"* and told him to leave it on the table.

As they shook hands, Ted said to Gypsy, "Be a good scout and remember the motto."

"Don't worry about me, man. I'm prepared."

"Be seeing you," muttered Polo, his face drained of blood.

"I'll be in the same place. Drop by anytime."

Then the skinny boy folded his arms against the chill and reentered the cellblock, his head hanging low.

While they waited for Driss, Polo whispered, "Are you completely crazy? We may not get out of here. You see how he cut the visit short. Why'd you mouth off like that? I say he pulls any shit, we swipe his gun and make our break now."

"Forget it."

"The two of us could take him. I swear he knows why we're here."

Grabbing Polo's pumped-up arm, Ted dug in his nails. "Get a hold of yourself. Everything's okay."

But his own heart was pounding heavily and, despite the

freezing air, he felt moisture under his arms. Maybe he'd made a mistake and misjudged Driss. Polo was right. Getting a jump on him, they could overpower the neat, little guard. But there were too many more in the hall, and Ted doubted it would help to take Driss hostage, since they'd most likely just as soon shoot him too. Remembering the Matka 47's, he had trouble swallowing.

When Driss returned and locked the cellblock door, he didn't seem to suspect anything, yet somehow his holster flap had unsnapped, exposing the deep crosshatchings on the handle of his revolver. From the table he picked up the piece of cheese Gypsy had tried to pocket. "Yes, I like the Americans. They are so . . . so . . ."

As he gestured elaborately, struggling for the word in English, Ted thought, He's going to go for that gun. And to distract him, he said, "So rich."

"Ah, yes. That too." Smiling, he bit into the cheese, resting his free hand near the pistol.

"Would you take a glass of tea with us this evening?" Ted asked. "We'd like to talk to you about our vacation."

"I would be delighted, if we could meet at a quiet place."

"It's your town. Wherever you say."

"I find the Café de la Paix in the souq very *sympathique*. We could rendezvous there in an hour, if it would be no inconvenience to you."

"Not at all. We'll be waiting." Ted shook the man's hand, then watched him kiss his fingers and touch his heart.

When they passed into the corridor, both the stench and the chill dissipated. The clerk had crawled back into his cage; once again nobody looked up from the fly-spattered brazier. Driss slammed the door behind them. Polo straightened, but didn't turn. Then they ducked through the hatch. Blinded as they stepped into the bright square,

Ted and Polo paused while their eyes readjusted to the sunlight. The air tasted pure and burned when they breathed.

"What do you think?" asked Polo.

Ted brushed a hand through his hair, which felt cold and stiff as copper wire. "I don't like those damn doors."

"To hell with the doors. How about Driss? Should we trust him?"

Ted's eyes narrowed as he scanned the square. "Tell you in an hour or so."

"Suppose he comes after us with those cops?"

"He won't. Why would he let us go, then do that?"

"Jesus, are you joking? You as much as told him to his fat face we're springing Gypsy."

"You don't know how much he understood. I just hope it was enough. We had to tell him sometime."

"I'd feel safer with a gun. Lemme get one from the car."

"No guns. Wise up. Our friend does double-cross us, I don't fancy being arrested with an unregistered weapon."

"And I don't *fancy* being busted at all."

"We won't be. He's got nothing on us. I have a hunch we can do business with this fella."

"And if we don't, we're screwed. One chance is all we have."

"Okay, I'd rather take that chance over a cup of tea than in there up against those mothers and their Matka 47's. Come on, we'll look around the souq for the best route to follow."

4

CROSSING the Place des Chameaux, Ted counted his steps, measuring the distance from the jailhouse door to the arched entrance to the market. But halfway, the dead dog blocked their path and, as they detoured to avoid the smell of rotten flesh, he lost count. The animal had been there for days; little was left except a sack of matted fur and a mass of flies and maggots.

When they reached the arcade at the opposite end, Ted reckoned they had walked the length of a football field. How fast could he do a hundred-yard dash? It didn't matter. No one was faster than a bullet, and if a single guard with a Matka 47 stayed in the square, he could cut them down as they squeezed through the hatch, blinded by the sun. They had to have a way not just of drawing the guards out of the jail, but far from the *place*.

"Someone who knew how to shoot," said Polo, musing along the same lines as Ted, "could move onto a rooftop with the M-16 and cover us in case the cops came back."

"I've got a better idea."

"Yeah? What?"

"Tell you later."

It irritated Polo to have Ted always a step ahead of him. But as he tried to anticipate Ted's strategy, they entered the souq, and that was the wrong time and place to think. His eyes darted about, dazed by the vain search for a neutral space, and despite his determination to stay calm, his pulse quickened.

Though he'd wandered through dozens of them, Polo was mesmerized by Moroccan souqs where selling assumed the aspect of religious ritual and aesthetic experience. Yet he couldn't have said whether his fascination outweighed his uneasiness, for he was assailed by smells that sickened, sounds that split the ear, tactile sensations that turned his spine to gooseflesh.

Slants of light slashed through the awning of reeds over the street, zebra-striping the crowd. Amid the raucous cry of vendors and the pungent scent of spices, incense, and burning cedar, they passed a profusion of merchandise at rows of stalls. But few of the browsers bought anything, and it was a mystery how so many shopkeepers supported themselves.

"Watch out!" Ted shouted, shoving him aside as a donkey, loaded with firewood, stumbled into the crowd. Behind it the owner, holding the animal's tail in one hand and a stick in the other, bawled loudly, *"Balek! Balek!* Make way! Make way!"* With the sharp stick, he drove the donkey faster, gouging a raw welt on its flank.

Struggling to locate landmarks, Ted and Polo staggered through the street shoulder-to-shoulder, their goal, for once, mutual. Polo knew he'd have to remember this route, but had difficulty concentrating and instead retained an impression of an army of Arabs, acres of rotting fruit and flesh, and miles of fetid alleys. The air had a terrible taste, and had he been able to, he would have rejected it just as he would any scrap of food from the smoky stalls. He felt squeamish even about the soles of his shoes touching the pavement into which so much dung, urine, and garbage had been squashed.

Yet, at the same time, he was transfixed by the faces he saw and ogled them like animals in a zoo. Unlike in the States where pedestrians resembled a parade of fat thumbs skinned of their prints, every person in Tazenzit seemed to be distinctive, to have one bad eye, a mutilated ear, a missing patch of hair, or a hideously mashed nose. It was as though they wore on the outside their deepest secrets and most shameful weaknesses, failures, and manias.

"Imagine driving through here," said Ted.

"Yeah, you were right," said Polo. "It'll be hard enough on foot."

"But harder for anyone to follow us. If there's a gate at the end of this street, we've got it made."

"Good luck. I'm lost. For all I know we're walking in circles."

"No. We're headed east. See, the sun's way behind us. We'll run the rest of them through this tomorrow. To be on the safe side, they should be able to do it blindfolded."

"I wish I were blindfolded now."

They were in a meat market where blood streamed through the street. Hundreds of cow and goat carcasses swung on chains from overhead beams as butchers in gory aprons chopped them into slabs with giant cleavers. Though the animals had been recently slaughtered, the flesh was dark, the bones blue-tinted, the fat a rancid yellow. Tossed onto metal trays, the internal organs oozed and bubbled in their own fluids like submarine creatures.

At a couple of stalls camel heads hung from rusty hooks. Skinned down to the purpling meat and muscle, they still had their eyes and appeared perfectly serene, as though they weren't aware that their bodies had been severed. Below them, like dusty, rundown shoes outside a mosque, their feet stood in neat lines—calloused pads, bracelets of hair, and, extending to the shattered knees, slick pink joints of bone.

As they passed the courtyard where *peau fraîche* was cured, Polo held his breath. On the ground, sheepskins steamed and stank as they dried. Then the smells grew sweet at a pastry shop where the soft candy and fruit tarts in the window were alive with insects. Bees, drunk on sugar, blew back and forth, benign as yellow feathers.

Farther on, olives bobbed in buckets of brine, and dates

and figs were stacked in waist-high walls that trapped flies and dust. A spice seller, wearing a necklace of braided garlic bulbs, seemed sunk in profound somnolence, asphyxiated by the odor. Opposite a fish stand, a used-shoe shop offered sandals and *babouches* which smelled of low tide, but looked more edible than the merchandise its neighbor sold. Deep in the last stall a woman wallowed in old underwear and shreds of linen, sorting the rags for sale, or perhaps simply pulling each piece through her hands to assert her ownership.

Finally the wall was in front of them and, cutting to the left, they discovered a gate, actually no more than a narrow passageway, that led to an empty lot. A road ran across the lot, then swung to the east toward the mountains, Ouarzazate, and the desert. As wind sprayed sand around their legs and piled it against the wall, Polo leaned over, hands on his knees, like a man who had sprinted a long distance.

"We'll leave the cars here," said Ted. "We do the job late in the afternoon, the sun'll be behind us and we'll drive into the dark. Look, it's already night in the mountains."

Polo didn't answer.

"You all right?"

"Yeah." Hocking deep in his throat, he spat into the dust. "It's my stomach. Feels like rats eating at my guts."

"Can you walk?"

"Sure."

Ted touched his shoulder. "Come on. We'll find that café and have something to drink."

They wandered around the souq and had to stop twice to ask directions before they saw a jarring sight—several Arabs in caftans and turbans playing pinball machines at the Café de la Paix. Now that it was dark, every appliance in the place had been switched on and would remain on until the generator died at midnight. Drawn like moths from the medina, people in fluttering robes milled about shouting and clapping, celebrating the brief hours of artificial light as if the day's sun hadn't been sufficient.

Those who didn't go in—the children, dogs, and women —bathed in the golden pools which flowed through the front windows. From that vantage point, the café appeared bright, warm, and lively, but inside, the noise of the radio was deafening, the air reeked of hastily splashed disinfectant and sawdust, and the blue walls and ceiling bathed the room in underwater distortion. Every face glowed an eerie aquamarine. With his heavy beard and meaty cheeks, Polo looked bloated and sick.

"You sure you're all right?" Ted asked.

"I will be once I've had a beer."

Standing at the bar, they ordered two Storks, a Moroccan brew which Ted contended was called that because it was fermented from beaks, feathers, and claws. It had a flat, metallic taste, but it quenched thirst better than hot tea, and was safer to drink than the gritty tap-water, which left sediment in the glass and a grumbling disquiet in the stomach.

As they sipped the beer, Ted watched the crowd in the warped mirror behind the bar, but didn't spot Driss. The bartender broke his concentration, pointing proudly to a shelf next to the radio where a huge stuffed rat was displayed. Its hairless tail had stiffened into a curlicue, its thin lips lifted above needle-sharp teeth. Nearly the size of a fox, it was supposedly the largest rat ever trapped in Tazenzit. Yet the bartender said he'd seen bigger ones in the grain *fondouq.*

"Quite a drawing card," muttered Polo, as the lines at his

eyes and mouth dissolved. "Jesus, I bet I'm working on an ulcer."

"Not worried, are you?"

"Shit, yes. You and this goddamn plan of yours have my guts churning overtime." But his growling sounded good-natured. Leaning against the bar, he'd lost his military bearing and was making an honest admission, not bitching. "I've always had a nervous stomach. But ever since I got to Morocco—even before you came along to mess me up—I've been losing weight."

"No kidding. You look pretty damn healthy to me. What'd you used to weigh?"

"About two-twenty."

"God awmighty, you're making a mistake. You should be in the States playing football."

"I did for a while."

"Where's that?"

"In high school, then a few years at Stanford."

"Big as you are, you should of gone on to the pros."

"No, at that level, everybody's big. You've gotta have something extra going for you, and you've gotta want to do it. I didn't any more. Even in college it was more like a business than a game. What the hell, I started playing just to piss my parents off. After I'd made my point, there was no sense beating my brains out."

"What did they think, that you'd get hurt?"

"No, they didn't like me mixing with the other kids. You see, I went to public school in San Francisco. That's another thing I did to piss them off. They said I should go to private school. Almost everyone in class was Chicano or Oriental, and we must have had the smallest and worst football team in America. Like our two tackles weighed a hundred and ten apiece. The only reason they survived is they ran faster backwards than most guys could forward. Because I was big, they put me at fullback. I carried the ball just about every play, but I don't remember winning more than two or three games the whole time I was there."

"That doesn't sound like fun."

"But it was. No pressure and lots of laughs. And those great little guys so desperate to be like real Americans. Stanford's where the game got to be a drag. Long practices, pressure, and hundreds of rules about how to look and act. The campus was turning on, but we were supposed to be Dink Stover at Yale. Hell, I had better things to do. Besides, by then my stomach was bothering me."

"Maybe you should drink some milk to settle it."

"You can't be serious. That's what they use in Morocco instead of arsenic. Even mother's milk must be curdled. You ever smelled anything worse than that souq?"

"Yeah. In the jail."

"Don't remind me." The tense lines returned to his face. "Jesus, Gypsy looks terrible, doesn't he? Just guess how he got like that." Polo was tearing the label from the green beer bottle. "Ah, screw it. I don't want to guess. In a few minutes we'll be dealing with Driss and if I'm thinking about Gypsy, I'm liable to lose my temper and punch his teeth in. I'm no good at this. Negotiating, compromising. Never have been. I wish it'd boil down to something direct, a simple one on one."

"It seldom does. But you don't have to hit people head-on to have an effect. We get Gypsy out and we've won. What's the difference whether Driss has his teeth and a few extra dollars?"

"There's a big difference to me. It's not just winning that matters. I'd like to teach the bastards a lesson, break their asses and have them realize what it's like to be at someone's mercy. One time it's bound to come down to that kind of head-on collision, and when it does, I'll be ready."

Ted gripped Polo's thick wrist and felt the thudding pulse. It seemed he'd been repeating himself all day, but this guy hadn't gotten the point. "You know, most head-on crashes are a deadlock. So why waste the sweat? Believe me, you let these feelings of yours run free, you won't get what you're after, I won't get what I'm after, and Gypsy'll stay in jail. Or worse."

"Yeah, you're right." Polo signaled to the bartender for another beer. "I'll put Gypsy out of my mind and play it cool."

"That's the secret," said Ted. "Never let the other fella see where you're weak. We're going to pull this job so smooth it'll be like slitting somebody's throat with a razor blade. They won't know what hit them till their heads fall off."

Polo grinned. "I'm looking forward to it."

"Good man. Keep an eye peeled for Driss. I'll be in the can."

Strolling through the café, Ted studied the customers, but didn't recognize anyone from the jail. As he went through a dim alcove where a solitary Arab sat shrouded in his djellabah, he could already smell the latrine. Leaving the door open, he stood far from a foul hole in the corner. His arch of urine barely made the mark; others had fallen short. Soon, unless someone stopped them, the less devout Moslems, who didn't squat when urinating, might test their aim from the alcove.

There was no toilet paper, and the walls were streaked with arabesques of excrement, an extreme form of graffiti, the strident poetry of the poor who demanded in these dismal, smelly dungeons the satisfaction they couldn't obtain outside. So what if it disappeared as soon as they pulled the chain? Every man's a king in the water closet, thought Ted. Although he didn't read Arabic, the pictures were universal. They asked for everything, at once, and for nothing. He wasn't that greedy. He'd be happy to get through this alive with four thousand dollars.

As he came back to the alcove, the Arab spoke quietly in French, "Would you care to take a glass of tea with me?" Gold gleamed under the hood of Driss's djellabah.

"How long have you been here?" Ted recovered quickly.

"Since before you arrived. I was waiting to see whether you'd notice me. Disguises amuse me. But, of course, with its walls and veils, Morocco is a very easy country in which to hide. Don't you agree?"

"I'm beginning to. Let me get my friend."

Driss's plump, copper arm snaked from the djellabah, his hand encircling Ted's arm. "Couldn't we talk alone? His French is poor, and I don't find him *sympathique.*"

"No. We're together."

"Comme vous voulez." The arm coiled into its hole.

"Would you like a beer?"

"No. Please bring me a glass of mint tea."

Polo tensed when Ted tapped him on the shoulder, then gave another start when he was told Driss had been watching them. "How the hell did he sneak behind us?"

"He was here first."

"Is he alone?"

"I think so. At least he's sitting by himself. Relax and let me do the talking."

"Okay, but be careful."

"Don't worry. He's dressed for business."

Driss had to know they were here to ask a favor, Ted thought. Otherwise why had he worn the djellabah and remained anonymous until the last moment? But though he'd entertain an offer of petty bribery, he might balk at something this big, and that could be the end of the ball game.

Ted glanced around, searching again for familiar faces, but spotted none. In case of trouble, should they run? No. The door looked distant. And the car? Christ, they were miles from it.

"Anything goes wrong," he said to Polo, "don't panic. Remember, they've got nothing on us."

They ordered two bottles of beer and tea for Driss. The glass, stuffed with mint leaves and stems, warmed Ted's palm. In the alcove a grimy globe contained the overhead light and from it loomed the enlarged shadows of insects that had crept in and beat against the hot bulb. A skeletal outline of their wings was reflected on the blue walls.

Setting the tea on a spindly table, Ted took a chair opposite Driss. Polo sat next to him and folded his arms. The stench from the toilet was overwhelming, and seemed a test of their nerve. If Driss could stand it, so could they. And from the little that showed of his face, Driss, who was smoking a cigarette from one of the packs they'd brought Gypsy, wasn't bothered by the odor.

A copper arm came out for the tea. Raising the glass under his hood, Driss smacked his lips. "Very good," he said in English, then went on in French. "You mentioned a trip through Morocco?"

Ted knew no reason to be oblique. That wouldn't persuade Driss, and he'd rather save his energy and patience for the bargaining. "Our friend, Monsieur Powell, is very sick. We hope you'll be kind and help him."

"Unfortunately, after this week, that will be out of my power."

"You could do what's necessary before then."

"But how? And what might that be?"

Ted bent forward. "Set him free."

There was a sudden agitation inside the folds of cloth. Polo also reacted, swiveling around to see whether anyone had overheard.

"Impossible."

"No. It's possible. You could let us free him."

"Vous êtes fou."

He hesitated a long moment, allowing Driss time to get up and go. Or call for the cops. When he did neither, Ted continued more confidently. "I mistook you for a man of imagination and courage, a man who would like to earn a great deal of money in a short time. The reward would be large, the favor I ask, so small."

"No. The favor is enormous, and extremely dangerous."

"But very profitable for you."

"If we failed, you would be put into prison. I might be executed."

"If we're careful, we won't be caught."

Driss crossed his legs, right over left. He was wearing pointed-toe yellow *babouches,* leather slippers with the backs bent down, and he wriggled his right foot, slapping the *babouche* against his sole. "What precisely do you propose?"

Now that Driss appeared interested, it was Ted's turn to take his time. He sat back, sipping the beer. It occurred to him Polo and he were staring dumbly at a bundle of brown wool in which a revolver could have been hidden. The thought gave him an extra moment's pause before he said, "We plan to divert the attention of the guards and, while they are away from the jail, free our friend. With your help, of course. We'd pretend to threaten you and force you to unlock the cell. That way you wouldn't be blamed."

"Oh, make no mistake, I would be blamed and punished." The hand that fumbled for the glass trembled slightly. "How would you divert the guards?"

"By an explosion or a fire in the medina. Would that work?"

"Yes, they would have to go if I ordered them. Everyone, that is, except the clerk."

"We'll see he doesn't cause trouble," said Polo, who had been following the conversation intently and was eager to prove it.

When Ted translated, Driss said, "No, I would. He is neither intelligent nor rich. A little money will increase his natural tendency to forget things."

"What do you think of our chances?" Polo asked in halting French, impatient at being left out. Ted's facility with the language irritated him. He sounded so formal and stilted, not at all like the redneck he really was.

Driss gave a monumental shrug. "To free your friend with my help is no trouble. After that it will be more difficult. You couldn't stay in the country. Yet how could you get out?"

"That's our problem," said Ted. "Once we leave the jail, your part is finished. There would be very little danger for you."

"But there would have to be great danger. How else could I convince people that I had no choice? You have guns, I hope."

"Yes, many."

"Good. No Moroccan could be expected to resist armed American bandits." Driss grinned at his own cleverness. "But one question troubles me. How could I be certain that when . . . I should say *if* . . . you are captured, you won't implicate me?"

"You can't. Just like we have no guarantee that you won't

turn us in. But you can be sure we have a good way to escape the country. And to take care of you, if you double-cross us.''

"Yes, then we must trust one another. It's always a plea-sure to help friends and, at the same time, earn money." Driss was fishing a sprig of mint from the glass. "You real-ize it would be foolish of me to do this cheaply?"

"Of course. What is your price?"

"One thousand, I think."

"Dirhams?"

Driss let out a moist, perfunctory laugh. "Very amusing. Dollars."

"The figure we had in mind was five hundred dirhams or a hundred dollars."

"You insult my intelligence and belittle my ability. Or perhaps you do not appreciate what you're asking me to do." Driss spoke in an amicable voice, devoid of anger or genuine emotion. But the yellow *babouche* flapped more rapidly on his foot. As he rejected the first figure, he cal-culated his next demand.

Ted was reminded of the men he had bargained with for hours in various markets. Although eager to end the discus-sion and escape this rank café, he knew no Moroccan would quote at once the amount he expected or accept the first offer. The price would be arrived at only after a lengthy ritual. So settling himself on the hard wooden chair, he fielded the outrageous figures which Driss flung at him and bounced lower ones back. Gypsy's freedom, and maybe much more, hung in the balance, but they kept haggling as if over the cost of a carpet or a brass tray.

As the gap between them gradually closed, Driss seemed completely caught up in the exchange, conducting himself according to unwritten rules. Though he didn't show it, this puzzled Ted, who realized they had no room for maneuvering. Driss could have asked a steep price and stuck to it, forcing them to pay or forget about Gypsy. Didn't he understand this? Or was he luring them into a trap?

Then finally Driss was firm. "Out of friendship I would like to help, but I cannot go lower than six hundred dollars."

That was a lot of money for Driss. Half a year's pay, probably. But Ted would have felt better if he'd been even greedier. Probing for a weak spot, he purposely overplayed his hand. "Three hundred and fifty is honestly all you are worth, but I'll raise it to four. That's my last offer."

"I refuse! You take me for a fool. You act like a fool yourself. Your friend is sick. Isn't his life worth more than four hundred dollars? I should ask for two, three, four thousand. What would you do then?"

"Nothing. We don't have that much."

"Obviously, or you would have gone to a higher authority. You are not rich. I know that by your clothes." Driss pulled the hood of the djellabah away from his face. "Neither am I. Do you see my eye? It happens to many people here. I know what it means. I'll go blind unless I have money for a doctor. We both have our reasons for striking a bargain. Let's admit that, and set a price that is fair."

Ted felt relieved, almost elated, and, at the same time, rotten as hell. At last they had a bit of leverage. He didn't like to play on this man's misery, but he'd been working for an angle and had to take advantage of what he'd won. Cursing his own callousness, he said, "We can give you five hundred, no more."

Driss nodded. "I understand, and even though that's less than I deserve, I'll agree. Do you have the money?"

"Of course not," said Ted, trying to make his oversight

sound like wisdom. He wanted to close the deal, but never expecting things to move this fast, he hadn't brought that much cash. They'd have to meet again, taking the chance of being caught and giving Driss time to change his mind. "I'll have it tomorrow."

"Yes, you must, because the day after, on Thursday, there is the weekly market in the Place des Chameaux. That's the best time for your plan. The town will be crowded, and the confusion should be to our advantage."

"All right, we'll arrange it for Thursday. Where do I meet you tomorrow?"

"Near the butcher stalls at noon. Don't be late. I won't wait long. And don't look for me. I'll find you. Have the money ready and pass it to me immediately. There will be no opportunity to talk."

"*Entendu.*"

"Which currency?" asked Polo.

"We were talking about dollars."

"No. It's got to be dirhams." Polo spoke English to Ted. "It's illegal to trade in foreign currency. They could nail us for that, and if they decided to pin a bigger charge on us, they'd use the dollars as evidence."

"Your friend doesn't trust me," Driss said in French.

"It's not that," answered Ted, grateful for Polo's presence of mind. He'd forgotten the currency problem. "But we have to pay you dirhams, and maybe there should be two installments. Half tomorrow, half once our friend is free."

As he leaned forward, both of Driss's pink hands poked from the djellabah. His wrists looked frail enough to snap like twigs. "There may be no 'later' for you or for me. Whatever happens, I will be punished. I may be beaten, or lose my job, or be put into prison. It depends on how well we play our charade. So I insist on having the money in advance."

"You'll get it tomorrow," Ted assured him.

"If you change your mind, I won't pay you back."

"We won't change our minds. Expect us late Thursday afternoon."

"Good. Then there's nothing more to discuss." He shook Ted's hand, kissed his fingers, and pressed them to his heart. "You go first. I haven't finished my tea. Until tomorrow, *inshallah.*"

As the two of them started for the door, Ted was tempted to glance back. But what would he have seen? A bolt of brown material adding substance to the shadows from which a seamless voice had issued, smoothly discussing matters of life and death. They had struck a bargain in this semi-darkness. Now they'd have to carry it through in broad daylight.

Monstrous insect wings webbed the blue walls. The stuffed rat sat sleekly behind the bar, while the radio whined with breathless nasality, nightmare music from Marrakech. As they walked through the pools of light in front of the café, Polo asked, "Can we trust him?"

The question deserved no answer, and he didn't repeat it.

A wooden wagon, whispering by on bald tires, led them into the souq. The horse was half asleep in its traces, the driver deeply asleep with the reins wrapped around his wrist. Behind him, on the flat bed, hulked what appeared to be burlap sacks of grain. But one sack stirred, a hand emerged, and scratched. Buried in their burnooses four passengers fitfully slept.

Several stalls were still open and people sat in the lantern light, holding skillets over charcoal fires. Slivers of cumin-coated meat sizzled in grease. After a day's begging the cripples were being collected. A young boy piled them onto a pushcart and departed with his wretched cargo.

But Polo noticed that the most mutilated scrap of humanity had no one to help him. The man looked as if he'd been sawed in half at the waist, and too poor to buy a wheelchair or pay the boy, he wore leather sandals on his palms, hobbling crab-like along the street. He never spoke and couldn't lift a hand to beg. Struggling from stall to stall, he waited mutely until someone took mercy on him and dropped a piece of food in his mouth. Then he dragged himself away.

How does it happen, Polo wondered? And why? Two people lie down and by their pleasure produce an artifact of the unknown. Afterward, perhaps they're haunted by a fear that something horrible has always been inside them. Now it's out. From darkness to darkness.

It seemed to him they lived in a world of total chance. Some had everything. Others nothing. And in the end everyone's number came due. That gave you just so long to even things up. So don't think of this one, Polo told himself. He's hopeless. Think of the others, the ones you can help.

The wagon wheeled down a side street, a lantern on its rear axle swinging in time to the measured clopping of the horse's shod hooves. Ted and Polo walked on through the smoke and incense and shadows and silence to the square. Polo would have stepped on the dead dog if Ted hadn't grabbed his arm and guided him around it.

5

"CAN WE trust him?" Bert repeated the question which Polo had asked three hours earlier, echoing verbatim the question Puff had asked half an hour ago as the six of them sat in the VW bus discussing the deal Ted had made with Driss.

Bert and Ted were in the Renault, she lying on the front seat, he on the back. He hadn't invited her; she hadn't asked. It was simply assumed. She'd slept with him last night and would again tonight. Though this, too, troubled Ted, he didn't care to be left alone with his thoughts. For while the rest of them argued whether they could trust Driss, he was bothered more by memories of the man's milky eye, of Gypsy in that icy, stinking jail, of the entire town of Tazenzit with its covered streets, cripples, and crumbling mud houses.

The feeling—no, it was a fear—had been building in him that he'd gotten in too deep. This was supposed to have been a simple job. Something he could do with his left hand, then be finished for good. But every day he discovered new problems. Now he had his shameful disregard of Driss to regret. The guard hadn't lied. He'd be punished. In helping Gypsy, how badly would they hurt Driss? What if he were put into prison, in a sense as a replacement for Gypsy? How could they justify that?

And what about Bert, Ted wondered? What did she expect of him?

Rain rang on the roof. The campground bordered the sea, and he had parked a few feet from a spot where waves rushed over the bulkhead. Above the sound of the storm, he heard the rattling wash of debris against the rocks. When should he break with Bert? Tonight and face the loneliness? Or tomorrow morning and feel like hell for having strung her along?

She was young and different from the women he'd been with lately, and he couldn't imagine why she was interested in him or how she'd act when she learned he had been alone too long to change. Though he liked her, and was getting to like her more, he'd been through this often enough to realize it couldn't last.

"Well, can we trust him?" she insisted on an answer.

He gave her the same one he'd given the group. "We have to. We can't take the place without an inside contact. There are eight guards and three doors to go through."

"How's Gypsy?" This time she quoted Phil. Was she double-checking his honesty? Or simply breaking the silence?

"Skinny and sick. But he said he was strong enough to travel."

"You're so quiet. Are you worried?"

"Not a bit. We're in good shape. Don't you worry either."

"Have you worked things out? I mean, how will we . . .?"

"I'd rather not talk about it tonight."

"Not even to me?"

"Specially not to you. Get a good night's sleep. We'll discuss it tomorrow."

"You're acting pretty damned paternal. We're not kids, you know."

She was right. They were a bigger headache and less predictable than a pack of kids. It would do no good to tell them the truth, explaining his doubts and pointing to dangers that hadn't dawned on them. That might rattle them, but they wouldn't give up on Gypsy and, despite his misgivings, Ted wouldn't either, now that he'd met the boy. It wasn't just the money. It was the pitiful slope of Gypsy's shoulders, his pasty coloring, the eyes from which all emotion had vanished.

But damn Polo for mentioning the other prisoners. Don't think about them, Ted told himself. Or about Driss. You already have too many problems. Don't go taking on every-body else's. They didn't hire you to save the whole god-damn world.

Thrashing around noisily, Bert knelt on the front seat and gazed at him. Clouds formed in the cool air by their breathing had curtained the windows with silvery conden-sation, but Ted could see clearly inside the car, and as she stared at him, the hollows of her face held fine triangular shadows which offered an insight into the depth of charac-ter she'd gain with age. Haunting and lovely, rather than haggard and worn, her expression would show its troubles, yet triumph over them.

But you won't be around to see that, Ted thought. It's going to be tough leaving her. Reaching up, he touched her lower lip and this appeared to release her powers of speech.

"Tell me more about that island of yours."

"Not much to tell. It's beautiful and quiet."

"At night do you hear the sea?"

"Not like this. The Caribbean's calmer. But sometimes when the tide turns, you'll wake from a sound sleep and hear these slow breakers rolling toward the beach. It's like they're not in a hurry. They're just taking it easy. It's such a peaceful sound you could fall asleep before they get where they're going."

"What did you do there?"

"Nothing much."

"You must have done something."

"Mostly I fished. I had a little shack on an inlet, and every evening I'd heave a couple of lines from the front porch. For its size, that inlet was the deepest harbor I've ever seen. The natives swore the *Queen Elizabeth* could put in there and never touch bottom. They said the water was bone-deep. I like that. Bone-deep. Well, in the evening, I'd toss out these two lines—one a twenty-pound test, the other a nylon rope that I'd tie to a post on the porch. It had a hook on it big as your hand and I'd bait it with a bloody hunk of meat. I was after something huge.''

"What'd you catch?"

"'A lot of nosy damn sea turtles and a few blowfish with big mouths and bigger ideas.''

Bert laughed. She had a strong, deep laugh for such a small girl, and Ted laughed with her.

"What I wanted was a shark or a whale," he said. "But I reckon one of them would of dragged me and the house out to sea.''

"Ugh! Are there sharks there?"

"A few, like everywhere else. They don't bother you unless you do something stupid." Reaching up again, he stroked her hair.

"Hmm, if I saw one in the water with me, it might be hard not to do something stupid. You know any people on the island?"

"Not many."

"Won't you be lonely?"

"I'm used to being by myself."

"Would you like company?"

Lowering his hand to cover her eyes, he said, "I don't think you'd care for it.''

Bert shook off his hand. "Are you kidding? It sounds like paradise.''

"Well, it's not. Last time I was there they didn't even have electricity or indoor plumbing.''

Nodding, she bit at the inside of her cheeks and sank down on the seat. When Ted sat up to look at her, she rolled onto her side, away from him. "Don't bother. I get the picture.''

"No, you don't. Sure, it's a nice spot. But it's no place for a woman."

"Oh, bullshit," she said wearily. "What is? A kitchen?"

"You'd be sick of it in a week."

"Why? I've been surviving here without electricity and indoor plumbing. Look, I said it. You don't have to explain. I get the picture."

"No, listen, if I took you with me, we'd be . . ."

"Wait a minute." She was shaking angrily. "I didn't ask you to *take* me. I said I'd *come with* you. There's a difference, you know. Say one of the guys wanted to go to your island, would you . . ."

"It's not *my* island."

"But say they asked to go with you, would you act like this, like somebody had popped your balloon?"

"No, I suppose not."

"Then why me? Why the hell get uptight when I say— when I merely suggest—I *might* like to come with you?"

"You're the one that's upset. And be honest. It's not the same. I wouldn't be sleeping with some guy."

"We could change that. We don't have to sleep together."

He shook his head in frustration. "I'm trying to level with you and save us both a lot of trouble. That island's nothing like San Francisco or living with The Gravy Train. There aren't more than twelve white families, none of them the kind you're used to."

"Maybe I dig black guys. Is that what's bugging you?" At once she was sorry she'd said this. "Oh, what the hell are we arguing about? I'm not going to beg. You can do what you damn well please and be alone."

Ted leaned back. He hadn't expected her to fight and force him to admit what he was doing. It wasn't Bert he was worried about. He was afraid of himself. For years, in every-thing he agreed to, he'd included an escape clause. If the island didn't pan out, he could always junk the idea and move on, just as he could abandon The Gravy Train if things got too tangled. But with Bert along, it would be much harder. Hell, she might like it there and make him keep his word and stay in one place long enough to know it. That scared him.

To pull through this job in one piece he'd thought he had to harden himself and look at Driss and Gypsy, all of them, even Bert, as objects in his path, as hurdles he had to leap and leave behind. But now Ted knew the price was inhu-manly high if, as he withdrew to the island, he cut himself off from everyone else.

Sitting up, he extended a hand toward Bert, who rolled over with tears in her eyes. "I'm sorry," she said before he had a chance. "I've fallen into this habit of asking you for favors."

"No, I'm the one who's sorry. It wasn't a favor you asked. Just a question."

"Okay, but I don't have the right. You don't owe me anything. I've already asked you for too much."

"No, you haven't. And I should of come clean and an-swered."

"I wish you had. I don't see why people can't say what they think and feel. I like you. I'm not afraid to say it. But if you don't want me around, tell me. You don't have to make excuses."

"No. I like it when you're with me."

"You'd better think it over. You might change your mind."

"So might you. People do all the time. The point is, I like you and hope we'll keep on this way. But it won't be easy. I've gotten damn selfish."

"No, you haven't."

"You don't know me."

"But you think you know me?"

"I'm beginning to. Why don't you come here and we'll both get better acquainted?"

Bert climbed over the back of the seat and they stretched out together. "I know more about you than you think. You're no mystery man. You're patient, and you care about people. I saw it in your face tonight when you were telling us about the jail and Gypsy."

"Okay." Ted chuckled self-consciously. "You've convinced me. I'm a great guy." Slipping onto his side, he gave her more room and ran a hand along her spine. "Now you, you're not so easy to understand. Who ever heard of a pretty little girl dressing like a sharecropper?"

"I'm not 'a pretty little girl.' " She frowned. "Being small is such a drag."

"No, you're not little." He pinched her bottom. "That's a handful."

"Just soft from no exercise."

"And your face"—with his fingertips he explored the hollows that held shadows—"sometimes it looks so damn sad."

"I'm not sad. Not really. My grandfather used to say I'm black Irish, which means grumpy, I guess. I lose my temper one minute and feel better the next. I'm fine now."

"So am I."

When they kissed, Bert rolled onto his chest. Though she was nearly weightless as far as Ted was concerned, the pressure of her body felt firm and insistent. She unbottoned his shirt and warmed her palms by rubbing his chest. He eased inside her blouse and watched her wince until his hands were warm, too.

As they worked free of their clothes, Bert stayed astride

Ted, kneading her fingers into the front of him, massaging the muscles of his stomach and chest in a slow circular rhythm which rocked both their bodies. Her eyes were shut, her head shoved far back, and he could see the pale underside of her jaw. It was not her darting, tense dexterity that pleased him most, but the total expressiveness of her face, the mobility of her features, the flicker of light and dark in the hollows beneath her cheekbones. As she'd said, she wasn't afraid to show what she felt, and what she felt, Ted saw at once and seemed to feel too, enjoying his own, as well as her, pleasure.

He held her hips as the rocking grew more rapid. Her hands slowed, her spine was rigid, her head fell forward. Suddenly she raised herself till she was almost clear of him and crumbled against his chest, her breathing warm on his neck. Then Ted heard and saw nothing as he lost himself inside her.

III

NEXT morning when the clouds lifted after a night of hard rain, the houses, streets, and tall hotels of Agadir had a laundered look. After the earthquake of 1962, which killed ten thousand people, the city had been rebuilt around the wide bay, and its raw slabs of poured concrete seemed precarious on their foundations. The slender, tossing palms and banana plants along the boulevards also appeared to have a weak grip on the dry soil which a wind off the Atlantic raked from under their roots.

Ted and The Gravy Train sat in the lee of the VW bus eating breakfast, the group strangely reserved and silent. As Phil handed him his two thousand dollars, they acted as though they'd witnessed a secret ceremony, but Ted was having none of their solemnity.

"All right, halfway home. This'll keep me in couscous a couple of days. Now, there's this five hundred bucks for Driss . . ."

At that their faces dropped farther. Everybody except

Polo, who hadn't expressed an opinion lately, agreed it was best to bribe the guard, but no one had mentioned the money. Now he thought he knew why.

"Hey, what the hell, are you all broke?"

"Not exactly," Phil mumbled. "But this could be a problem."

"You don't pay him, it'll be a bigger problem." And if you don't pay me, he thought. I'm not going to be jerked around by this bunch for two thousand bucks. Did they have the dough or didn't they? And if they had his, how about travel money for themselves? It was a hell of a hike from Algeria to the States.

"Our budget's close to the bone," said Polo. "We had to stretch it to pay you. We didn't count on this bribe."

"You see," said Phil, concentrating on his crutch, "my father won't send any more checks. After the trial and the appeal and the payoffs fell through, he said it was hopeless and told me to fly home and let Gypsy serve his sentence. So . . ."

"So he's using his own bread," said Polo.

"Is that right?"

Phil nodded.

They stared at the eggs on their paper plates. Though Ted didn't like to look cheap in front of Bert, he was flustered. Somehow they'd scrape together the dough for Driss, but what about his? They better have it or . . . Or what? He was afraid to ask. If he refunded the first two thousand, he wouldn't have enough cash to keep his car in gas. And these dummies were liable to go ahead and pull the job alone.

"Listen, seeing how you bent yourselves out of shape to raise four thousand for me . . ." When Ted paused, no one denied this. "I . . . I think . . ."

"Everybody should chip in," said Ants.

"I'll buy that," said Puff.

"You too." Polo cuffed Ted's shoulder in a friendly fashion. "You're the one who suggested we bribe that bastard so your job would be safe. You should foot the whole bill."

"Wait a damn minute. I don't have all my money yet."

"Ants is right," said Puff. "Each of us'll kick in a share. Anyone who disagrees, I'll pay back once we're in the States."

"No, I will," said Phil.

"Why don't you two fight for the honor later? I'll give a hundred and fifty, and I don't want it back." Polo turned to Ted. "How about you? I'm sure it's tax deductible."

It seemed pointless to carry them financially. But Bert was watching, and when he remembered Driss's bad eye, he didn't mind so much matching Polo's one-fifty. The thought that the guard would get medical attention glossed over some of his guilt.

Ants, Phil, Puff, and Bert put up fifty apiece, and he quickly collected it, along with Polo's money, glad to be done with that.

"What's the story on the bus?" he asked Ants.

"The mechanic fixed it, but kind of hinted it wouldn't last long."

"What exactly did he say?" Polo asked.

"Man, I couldn't *exactly* quote him." Ants pushed back his blond bangs which had curled in the damp air. "He spoke English, but you know Moroccans. They have opinions like they have children. I mean they come on with a dozen, hoping one'll be a winner. And you should have seen this outta-sight garage. Two gasoline drums with hand pumps, a corrugated steel shack, and a parking lot full of rusty parts. It looked like there'd been a twenty-car collision. The mechanic was a big funky dude, the king of the pit crew. He was wearing a workie tee shirt and had axle grease up to his elbows. He must have combed his hair with transmission teeth. You could have plunked him down in New Jersey and he'd have been right at home.

"He told me the bus had a blown gasket, sticky pistons, a leaky radiator, a clogged carburetor, a slipped clutch, a degenerate generator, a busted flywheel, a frayed fanbelt, bad brakes, bad breath, a headache, hemorrhoids, and a hard-on. Then he charged a grand total of eight dollars to repair it and said name your price and I'll buy it. Now you sort out that jive."

Polo, who didn't laugh with them, said, "It won't be so damn funny when it breaks down in the desert."

"No problem," said Ted.

"How's that?"

"We'll talk about it tonight. First, my friends, we have to take a group tour of the lovely town of Tazenzit."

Ants and Phil rode in the VW bus, Ants at the wheel, Phil beside him. As they listened to the tinny, Morse code messages tapped by the failing motor, the exhaust pipe sent distress signals to the cars behind them.

"Maybe that mechanic was right," said Phil.

"Nah, carbon monoxide never hurt anybody."

When they were out of Agadir, driving east, Phil pushed back on the taut, leatherette seat and steadied himself against the bus's badly sagging suspension system. "Let me ask you something, Ants. Suppose Gypsy was in prison in the States. Would you help him escape?"

"For sure. Why not?"

"Wait a minute. Say he was at the Marin County Courthouse about to be sent to San Quentin."

"Okay, I read the papers. What are you trying to do, gimme nightmares? Like I really don't believe this is the best time to remind anyone of that Jonathan Jackson horror show."

"I can't imagine a better time."

"How about never? No one'll mind."

"Then you wouldn't do it?"

"I feel like a shit for saying it, but I probably wouldn't."

"Because of the danger?"

"That's a good enough reason."

"Is it the only one?"

"What is this? Twenty Questions?"

"Just curious. Are there any other reasons?"

"Hundreds. It's not the same scene." Ants darted a quizzical glance at Phil, who gripped his crutch like a crozier. "You know what I mean?"

"No. Why don't you tell me?"

"Hey, this stinks of school talk. No teacher-student games."

"It's not a game."

"All right, if Gypsy had been busted in the States, he'd be out on bail. Your father would have hired a hot-shot lawyer. You see? And say he was convicted, he'd have umpteen appeals, a chance for early parole, and even at San Quentin he'd be better off than at Casablanca."

"What you're saying, then, is you respect the American system and wouldn't take things into your own hands. Here, in Morocco, you think you have a right to."

"Do you have to put it like that? You sound like my father."

"But that's the reason, isn't it? Respect."

"I guarantee you I respect their marksmanship. American cops get more target practice."

Phil, laboring methodically toward a conclusion, didn't laugh. "You know what it adds up to? Our plan, our whole attitude? Racism. A very subtle, condescending form of racism."

"What are you talking about, man? I dig these people."

"Maybe, but because they do things differently, because they don't have the money to imitate us, you think we can do whatever we want here. For you—for all of us—this country is a kind of funny farm, a playground we enjoy because we don't have to live in it. Or at least not live like the Moroccans. Soon as something goes wrong, we split. If that isn't racism or worse, what is it?"

"So what's the answer? Suppose it's true—and I'm not saying it is—what do we do? Gypsy's in jail. You rather forget him?"

"No, I'll go through with this, but I like to admit what I'm doing."

"How's that help?"

"It keeps me honest. Or at least lets me know when I'm fooling myself."

Phil had gone over it incessantly and confessed he had betrayed his better judgment, but he wasn't fooling himself. Though Polo believed he'd talked him into backing the prison break, Phil hadn't needed convincing. Gypsy was his brother. It was as basic as that. Family sentiment had overcome intellect, and much as Phil regretted this, he saw no alternative.

Yet, although he was in it deeper every day, he still had faith in his intellect. He just hadn't located the key to this problem. I'm a student, he thought, not a genius, not a saint. I know what's right and I'm doing what's wrong. There's nothing extraordinary about that. But as he searched for an answer, he felt the wrenching pain of separating what he believed from what he did.

"Do me a favor," he said to Ants. "Don't repeat this to anybody. I was thinking out loud."

"Next time switch on the radio so I don't have to hear. Jesus, the Marin County Courthouse! Don't remind me." But Ants was smiling.

2

BEYOND Aït-Melloul the fields were green and wet beneath the lattice-work of gum and palm trees, and last night's storm clouds, combing inland, cast shadows over them as they scattered toward the mountains. Where citrus groves crowded the road, windfallen fruit had rolled under the tires of passing cars, turning the pavement slick and sweet-smelling.

The itinerant merchants, who had stopped yesterday in Taroudannt, were setting off for Tazenzit to prepare for tomorrow. Some owned sixth-hand automobiles and trucks to which they tied their merchandise, but most of them went on foot, whipping their donkeys, cows, and goats before them. One woman carried a raffia basket containing two tiny white-faced lambs. A man on a motorcycle had stacked four wicker baskets full of chickens on his rear fender, and feathers and fresh droppings flew out in his wake. Far off the highway, etched against a gold leaf sky, a train of one-humped camels clumped along the horizon exactly as it might have hundreds of years ago, bringing north the spoils of black Africa—ivory, ebony, incense, and ostrich feathers.

Then suddenly the crowd converged at a single spot in the center of the road. Signaling frantically to Polo behind him, Ted stood on the brake and brought the Renault to a skidding halt at the edge of the circle. But few people bothered to swing around and see where the screeching came from.

"What is it?" asked Bert.

"Don't know. There's a cop."

Elbowing a path through the crowd, a policeman motioned for the automobiles to advance one by one. As Ted ground the Renault into low gear, he feared it was a roadblock and hoped Polo had hidden the guns well. To gain time and study the situation, he proceeded slowly, stalled the car, then restarted it. Had Polo noticed the cops? There were three of them. Driss might have tipped them off. Would they all be arrested? Or only Polo and him? He thought of gunning the Renault and running for it, but that was crazy. They'd hit half a dozen people.

"Don't get shook," he said to Bert. "Sit back."

"What's wrong?"

"They may stop us and ask questions."

Then they saw the black Mercedes with the cracked windshield. On the asphalt, fifty feet in front of it, lay a little boy in a pool of blood, a rusty bicycle wrapped around his body. His arms and legs were looped awkwardly over his chest like strands of rope hastily tied to hold him together. Where his face should have been only a raw purple sore remained.

"Don't look," he said too late.

"Oh god," she groaned. "Shouldn't we stop? Can't we do something?"

"It's no use. He has to be dead."

Bert sucked in her breath as though, despite the mangled body, she couldn't believe him.

The policeman whistled and waved Ted on. As he accelerated, he glanced at the rearview mirror. Polo, then Ants, paused uncertainly at the accident. Like Bert, they no doubt had difficulty believing this ugly smudge on the highway was death, and had a harder time yet admitting there was nothing they could do. Though Ted had been through this many times, he too experienced a sick sense of inadequacy.

"He was there so suddenly," said Bert, her voice choked, "you didn't have a chance to . . . to . . . Why didn't they cover him?"

Ted didn't know and couldn't say anything that sounded sensible. Picking up speed, he put miles between the accident and them. The sight might unhinge this group. He, himself, was shaken. Jesus, you are getting old. But maybe it was an instinct he'd regained, not an advantage he'd lost. He'd never found anything admirable about some soldiers' indifference to death.

He circled the red walls of Tazenzit and parked on the pebbled lot. Wind was soughing through the emptiness when the others arrived. No one mentioned what they'd seen, and Ted moved them out before they had more time to ponder it. Gathered in a gloomy knot, they followed him through the souq, pacing off the distance between the landmarks he pointed to, paying strict attention to his instructions. For once no one interrupted with questions.

Then, from the shade of the keyhole arches, they stared across the dusty expanse of the Place des Chameaux to the Sûreté Nationale.

"It's about a hundred yards," said Ted. "The hatch in the door is smaller than it looks. Careful to step up over the sill. One of us trips, the rest of us'll fall flat on our faces. I've clocked it and we should get from the jail to the cars in fifteen minutes. That's at a reasonable walk, no running."

"There'll be a crowd tomorrow," said Polo.

"I took that into account. One of us'll stay here under the arches with the djellabahs. We'll put them on afterward and blend with the people."

"What if the cops come back, spot us, and start shooting?" Polo sounded upset, and was scaring the others, who had already been spooked by the dead boy.

"They won't," said Ted and returned with them to the souq. "While I pay Driss, you all buy supplies. Get canned food, a lot of it. Enough for a week. We need gasoline too so we don't have to stop before we get to Algeria. Find a few ten-gallon drums and have them filled. Do we have anything to carry water in?"

"A couple of canteens," said Ants.

"Better buy three or four water bags. But before you pay, be sure the plugs are tight. Meet you at the cars when I'm finished."

When they left, he started for the butcher stalls. To avoid suspicion and, also, to hold all the cards in his hand, Driss had said he'd do the searching. But Ted didn't want to be caught from the blind side and kept an eye open for the prim, little guard and his buddies from the jail.

Strolling over the bloody cobblestones, he had a fleeting, queasy vision of that boy smashed against the asphalt. As Bert had said, it happened too quickly, before you recognized what was wrong. Then it was gone, yet the memory remained. You got trapped off base once in life and that was it. He wouldn't have minded half as much if you knew when to expect it. But you didn't, and though it was far from a perfect defense, you could only be careful, and when caution wasn't the answer, be courageous, and when courage was futile, be quiet.

Five hundred dollars worth of dirhams were wadded in his pocket. He hadn't known how else to carry the money. He'd considered sealing it in an envelope, but feared anything that might link him to the bribe. This way if Driss turned him in after the payoff, they couldn't prove the dirhams were his. And if they nabbed him carrying the roll, he'd claim he was shopping for carpets.

As he drew near a counter where the shopkeeper was spooning brains from the cracked skull of a cow, a weak-voiced beggar weasled up beside him, whispering, *"Donnez-moi l'argent."*

Ted would have ignored this whine, which was like a ceaseless litany in parts of the country, had an insistent hand not grabbed his arm and spun him around. The beggar, badly bent inside his djellabah, appeared to have a hunched back, but, also, youthful skin and a gold tooth.

"L'argent pour un pauvre, s'il vous plaît," Driss pleaded, dragging him from the meat stall.

When Ted was slow in producing the dirhams, the hand tightened until he pulled out the sheaf of bills. Driss received it deftly, sliding his arm up the loose sleeve.

"Merci, monsieur. Merci, merci," he mumbled, hobbling away over the cobblestones.

Ted expected stronger hands to seize him then. But he stood perfectly still, counting to ten before walking to the next shop, where a butcher had paused with his dripping cleaver poised over a camel's hump. When Ted looked down the street, Driss had disappeared.

There was something Ted had forgotten to have them buy. So he stopped in the European quarter at a hardware store and got two gallons of grey metal primer and four brushes which he lugged through the souq, shouting, *"Balek! Balek!"* like a donkey drover. Several boys trailed after him, offering help, but he outdistanced them and soon reached the passageway in the wall where Ants relieved him of the bucket. The rest of them were in the Land-Rover— Polo and Puff up front, Phil and Bert in back—staring at the high wall, as if at a drive-in movie screen.

"What's this?"

"They're jumpy," said Ants. "No one'll talk about anything except how we could screw up."

"Polo?"

"Not just him."

"You?"

"No way." As he grinned, the pale whiskers on his chin might have been streaks of milk he had neglected to wipe with a napkin. "I'm looking forward to tomorrow."

Ted slapped his shoulder. "I admire your spirit, old buddy. It's your sanity that bothers me."

"You don't have to worry about me."

"I won't. You're my main man. I have something special for you to do."

"How'd it go?" Polo called as they crossed the vacant lot.

Ted didn't answer until he was next to the Land-Rover, which had gasoline drums lashed to the roof. "Quick and quiet."

"What'd he say?"

"Thanks."

"That's a well-raised Moroccan for you," said Ants. "Polite and personable."

Polo flexed his fingers on the steering wheel. "Seems to me we're depending too damn much on Driss."

"What choice do we have?"

"None now."

"What's in the bucket?" asked Phil before Ted could respond.

"Something to keep us busy this afternoon. Let's roll before you people begin peeing your pants."

He went to the Renault and sped north on a dirt track toward the mountains. Ants, in the VW bus, followed at once, while Polo brought up the rear. The scene in his side mirror reassured Ted a bit. He'd managed to squeeze through a tight spot. But if he wanted to keep this crew from collapsing in anger or panic, he had to be careful of what he said and did from now on. Yet there were things he couldn't control. An accident, another death on the road, any reverse might ruin them.

North of Tazenzit the countryside became barren and sere, then broke into jagged gullies and ridges. Incessant wind and seasonal rains had skimmed the topsoil from a bed of sharp stones, and the spiny vegetation, shimmering in mirages of mid-afternoon heat, reminded Ted of antlers of ocean coral. Yet there was no water here, not even in the wide riverbeds which had carved runnels through solid rock. These dry washes—the *oueds*—held big, smooth boulders, tons of silt and salt crystals, and cedar stumps that had floated down from the High Atlas during flash floods. Peeled of bark and polished silver-grey, the cedar had been sculpted into vaguely human shapes, so that it looked like broken arms and legs of beautifully grained marble lying amid the rubble.

The road, really no more than a path for goats, donkeys, and shepherds, would be slippery and dangerous after a storm. But the sky was cloudless now and the three cars bore on over the rutted trail, rising with the land onto a grassy plateau where sheep and cattle grazed.

In the foothills, a mud village had been built on stone terraces, forming a small amphitheatre at the edge of the arable land. Below it, fenced from the wind by cypress and gum trees, fields of tall grain swayed slowly as women wielding hoes and sickles walked through them. While cultivating the crops these Berbers wore colorful clothing of gold and silver thread and bright polka-dot bandannas.

Next to an irrigation ditch, almond trees had bloomed, the palms bore waxy orange clusters of dates, and an olive grove provided shade. Ted parked and motioned for Ants and Polo to stop. After the engines died and the last door had slammed, total silence settled over them. In the fields the unveiled women glanced up, shading their eyes with hennaed hands, then went back to work. Gradually they heard the chocolate water sucking at the banks of the irrigation ditch, and a breeze harped through the highest branches.

"Wow, what a beautiful place," whispered Puff, snapping off a spray of almond blossoms. She tried to wear it in her hair, but it was too fine to hold the flowers. She thrust the pink petals into Bert's thick, black mane.

"We'll camp here," said Ted.

"Yeah." Hands on hips, Polo surveyed the spot. "This is as good a time as any to talk things over."

"Not now. First we have to camouflage the bus. There's a bucket of primer and a few brushes in my car."

"What for? It won't last. I told you that. So did the mechanic."

"What are you saying, we should junk it?" Puff asked indignantly.

"I'm afraid we'll have to," said Ted. "Polo's right. It's too big a risk to drive the bus across the desert."

"What do you think?" she asked Phil.

"Gypsy'll have to understand. I go along with Ted," he said, but was far from enthusiastic in his support.

"Okay, gimme a goddamn brush."

"Just a second." Polo's burly arm blocked her path. "Since we're ditching the VW anyway, why paint it?"

"We're not ditching it. We're going to use it. But not like it is. We might as well be riding around in a kaleidoscope," Ted said.

No one smiled, and there wasn't a single face unclouded by questions or accusations. Even Bert, who along with Ants was always on his side, had a puzzled expression. Perhaps, expecting the kind of obedience a sergeant could command, he had asked too much and not told them enough to gain their confidence. But he wouldn't back down for Polo, who insisted, "How are you going to use it?"

"Tell you when the time comes. While you all are painting, Phil and I'll scout around the town."

"For what?"

"For the hell of it."

A rocky path angled across the wheat fields, bordered on one side by the irrigation ditch and on the other by a quagmire of mud. Although Phil was agile with the aluminum crutch and could walk easily on level ground, the slightest change in terrain, the shallowest pothole, the smallest stone sent him stumbling. Yet, as always, his greatest struggle was not so much against pain or his physical limitations as against resentment, which was futile, and self-pity, which was worse. Even anger was a luxury he didn't allow himself. He depended on brains and the standards of integrity he'd set for himself. Only when he abandoned them did he feel maimed and inferior. And he felt that way now with Ted, whom he liked but was cheating. Phil dreaded being revealed as a liar more than anything Ted might do to him.

At the entrance to the village, they encountered a staircase of hewn stone. Ted let Phil go first, and he attacked each step in three stages, planting his crutch, putting down his good foot, then pulling the bad one up behind him. His fleshless jaw was clenched in a false smile; his stringy muscles and veins stretched tight. Dark blood, pumping through his freckled face, seemed about to spurt from his red hair. Yet he had the strength to mutter, "Strange town. Ever seen anything like it?"

The section they climbed through had decayed and crumbled. A few houses had caved in altogether, the walls warped and water-stained like cardboard boxes left too long in the rain. Tall stalagmites of stone—interior columns in the old buildings—rose above the weeds. But, farther up the hill, the houses were new, the pisé hard-packed and glowing a warm orange. The handprints over the doorways as protection against the evil eye looked like tracks left by a mysterious creature capable of climbing sheer walls.

Rather than repair its old homes or rebuild on the same foundations, the population had moved higher and begun again. Though the process must have been repeated every generation, the people never deserted the past, which awaited them at the bottom of the hill. Phil thought of the entire village as an elaborate piece of surrealistic sculpture in which youth and old age overlapped on the same face.

When they gained level ground, Phil and Ted sat on a low retaining wall and looked back at the campsite. A canopy of palm and olive branches concealed the cars, Ted was pleased to see. Below them a man was stacking mud bricks to dry in rows, like loaves of bread. In a cramped courtyard, a blindfolded donkey blundered round and round a dusty track, rotating a massive stone which ground ripe grain into flour. The miller, his skin and clothes powdered pure white, the index finger of his free hand stuck in his nose up to the knuckle, sang absent-mindedly as he flicked a leather thong at the animal's haunches.

Phil clung to the crutch as he caught his breath. "Too bad you can't live in a spot like this."

"A lot of folks do."

"They don't know any better."

"I wouldn't say that. It's a hard life, but those two fellows look right happy."

"I couldn't be, and not just because of the conditions. You know, the discomfort and disease. These places are unreal."

"Oh, they're real all right."

"No, I mean they'd be unreal for an outsider. Gypsy and his friends used to yammer about returning to the land, living an elemental existence close to the earth, but I've never bought the bucolic myth."

"The what?"

"The pastoral tradition. The joys of being in the country, growing your own food, living organically."

"You're talking about farming, I grant you it has its drawbacks. I watched a lot of men around home bust their humps on bad land. But it's got its good points too."

"Almost everything has its good points. But in a country like Morocco, going native and living organically means catching worms, hepatitis, or dysentery and dying of old age at thirty-five. Hell, even hiding has advantages, but it's no answer, and it irritates me when people talk about it like a great triumph instead of a retreat."

"Hey, hold on. I'm thirty-nine. According to your time table, I'm four years overdue. I better haul my ass out of this town."

Though he chuckled politely, Phil was too earnest to

regard his ideas as jokes. "I was telling Ants this morning, we won't suffer any more than we have to by living here. When it stops being fun, we'll shove off. But these people" —he motioned to the miller and the brick maker—"they have to stay. And beautiful as it is, you can't convince me they wouldn't leave if they could."

"Maybe, like you said, they just don't know any better. What'll you do after this?"

"Finish my dissertation, then next fall teach at a black college in the South or in a ghetto school."

"They'll be lucky to have you."

"I'll be the lucky one to have an opportunity to do something worthwhile. In grad school you lose yourself in the grind, the hustle for grades. But I don't want to be the type who demands more of books than he does of himself and forgets why learning's important, what really matters."

"What's that?"

"People. Books, education, degrees, they have to be directed toward people. Being in Morocco has proved to me that bad as things are in the States, there's still a chance to change them. We have fantastic advantages over this country."

"Could be. But advantages have a way of balancing off. It depends what you're after."

Phil felt self-conscious. Maybe, he thought, I sound too much like a do-gooder, a missionary. That was always a problem when he was talking. Or am I trying to show what a great guy I am, even though I'm rooking him? "What are you after?" he asked.

"Nothing much. Peace and quiet mainly. There's this island I know where I'll do a little fishing and drinking. I don't mean to discourage you, but I've had my fill of crusades. This is my last one."

"Some crusade!" He doodled in the dust with his crutch.

"It's not a bad one, as these things go."

"You don't have to talk me into it."

Ted drew a hand across his cheek where a stubbly red beard was beginning to itch. "Good. I'll be counting on you tomorrow. You stay calm and the others will."

"I'll do my best."

"Everyone else does the same, we'll be safe." Ted scratched his chin again. "Look, what I've decided is you should take one of the pistols and guard the cars."

Now the crutch tapped the toe of his orthopedic shoe. "What you're saying is, *wait* at the cars, out of your hair."

"No. It's an important job."

"Have somebody else do it. Not me."

"You're the right man for it."

"Why? Because I'm crippled?" When he didn't answer, Phil said, "Of course that's it. Well, I won't do it, Ted."

"Listen, I understand how you feel, but . . ."

"No, you don't. Goddammit, you couldn't. It's not your fault, but you don't understand. Gypsy and I aren't close. I'm four years older, and after I had polio, there were more differences between us. I tried not to, but I resented him. He probably resented me too. Our parents were always warning him to be nice to me, to help and be patient. Whenever he forgot, I reminded him. It got to the point where he was scared to do anything that might make me feel . . . I don't know . . . inferior or different. But it was impossible. I mean, I *am* crippled. He couldn't change that. I guess the pressure got to him. When he was nineteen, he left home instead of going to college. I'm responsible for that and what he got into. Now I'd like to make it up to him."

"I see, but it's not that easy."

"Do you really expect it to be dangerous?"

"Could be."

"That doesn't bother me. I'll take my chances with the rest of you."

Ted was reluctant to hurt his feelings or to frighten Phil, but there was no sense lying. "I appreciate you want to do your part, but having you along won't help. You saw that square. Tomorrow it'll be swarming with people. Suppose you can't keep up? Say you fell?"

"Leave me. Don't bother stopping."

"I don't doubt you've got the guts to bring this off, but nobody's going to leave you. We'd stop and carry you, and it'd slow us up. Are you ready to risk everybody else's neck as well as your own?"

"Dammit, that's not fair. You've loaded the question against me. Everything's a risk. Having me along is just one more. I accept that. If you don't, *you* should wait at the cars."

"I was thinking of you and . . ."

"Don't! I'll take care of myself."

"It's up to you," said Ted, wishing it weren't. "You change your mind, tell me."

At the campsite under the tent of trees, evening had descended and a dusky green light filtered through the palm fronds. Ants, Polo, Bert, and Puff had finished painting the bus and were floundering knee-deep in the irrigation ditch, laughing, joking, and scrubbing flecks of primer from their hands and arms. Dipping into the murky stream, Ants splashed Ted and Phil.

"Dive in," cried Puff. "It's warm as bathwater."

"It's not Saturday night," said Ted. "And that trough looks like it'd leave a ring around me."

"You're liable to catch schistosomiasis in there," said Phil.

"It'll have to catch me first," said Ants.

"It might. I'm serious."

"You always are."

"What is it?" asked Puff.

"A disease that attacks about half the population in some parts of Africa. People defecate in these irrigation ditches, and that infects a snail that infects the people."

"Christ, now he tells us." Puff, whose dress had been dovetailed between her legs, scrambled from the ditch. After slapping beads of moisture from her ponderous thighs, she tugged down the hem of the dress and covered them.

"I don't see how I can catch a damn disease I can't pronounce." But Ants, too, hopped out of the water and reached back to help Bert.

Unrolling the cuffs of her Levis, she moved close to Ted, slipping an arm around his waist. "Like it?" She nodded to the bus, which was drab grey.

"Not bad. I was betting you'd do the windows too."

"I think it's sad," said Puff.

"Looks like a hearse," Polo called from the ditch.

"Nice sense of humor," said Ants. "Like at least your mother and black cats must love you."

"I'm going to miss it," said Puff.

"Gypsy'll buy a new one," Phil consoled her.

"There's a man with confidence." Leaping onto dry land, Polo crossed to the Land-Rover, put on his socks, stepped into his boots, and leaned against the front fender. "Care to discuss a few details about tomorrow?" Though he acted casual and unconcerned, his words had a cutting edge.

"Sure. Go ahead and discuss," said Ted.

"What's on tap? Maybe you ought to refresh our memories."

Disentangling himself from Bert, Ted, too, tried to appear affable and unconcerned.

"I figure we'll have Puff wait outside the wall with the cars. Bert'll hide under the arches with the djellabahs. Then the four of us'll drop by the jail and spring Gypsy. After that, it's a question of beating them to the border."

"Will Phil be with us?"

"Yes," Phil spoke for himself.

"You said something about a diversion."

"Yeah, that's where the bus comes in. Ants'll drive into the medina and set off an explosion in it. The noise and fire and smoke should draw those guards."

"Where'd you buy dynamite?" asked Polo.

"I didn't. I got a gas can in my trunk. We'll make a glorified Molotov cocktail by using a long, oily rag as a wick and having a cigarette burn down to light it. That'll give Ants plenty of time to scram before the bus blows."

"I suppose you know what you're doing."

"I reckon I do."

"Will that be loud enough?" asked Ants. "It'd have to be a hell of a blast for them to hear it in the jail."

"Even if they don't hear it, somebody's bound to report the fire. Then Driss'll kick those guards out."

"I think it's a mistake to have Phil with us," said Polo.

"We talked that over, and it's a chance I'm willing to take, if he is."

"What if he falls behind?"

"Let me worry about that. I'll . . ."

"No one'll fall behind," Ted cut Phil short. "Do what I tell you and there'll be no trouble."

"Okay, fine," said Puff. "Nobody'll fall behind and we're

willing to do what you tell us, but there are some questions you haven't answered. Suppose the plan doesn't go like you say?"

"That's what I've been asking," said Polo. "We should consider all the angles and have a contingency plan in case Driss diddles us."

Ted had to guess what kind of game they were playing. Had Polo put them up to this? And was it fear or anger or plain orneriness that kept them chipping away at his self-control? "All right, what's our option? The way I see it, they catch us, they catch us. We could try to buy them off. Beyond that you'd just be kidding yourselves. Better count on Driss."

"We don't have to surrender," said Polo. "We could fight. Claw our way out if we have to."

"That's what you're after, isn't it? A chance to crack heads."

"I didn't say that. It just doesn't make sense to me to break our asses springing Gypsy if we're not willing to fight to stay free ourselves."

"How about you all?" Ted appealed to the others.

Bert shook her head apologetically. "I'm with Polo. I'd do anything to stay out of jail."

"This is silly," Phil pleaded. "For one thing, it won't happen, for another, how will we fight them?"

"Silly or not, I won't surrender," Puff swore.

"I'll fight," said Ants, as if it were a simple favor he'd been asked.

Polo clapped his meaty palms. "Motion carried four to two."

Though irked, Ted didn't answer. Like Phil, he thought the discussion was stupid. If Driss did trick them, how the hell were they going to fight?

3

THEY didn't build a fire that night for fear someone—anyone other than the villagers—might notice it and creep up for a closer look. It was unlikely that soldiers or cops patrolled the area, but Ted preferred not to take a chance. So they sat in the dark, surrounded by the cars, eating peas, cassoulet, and ravioli from cans. As the cold food fell heavily to their stomachs, no one spoke.

Then Polo went to the Land-Rover for his shortwave radio. A tiny bulb illuminated the rows of numbers and the thin, silver aerial that quivered as it was extended. He tuned the set to the Armed Forces Network, which broadcast the news, an interview with Spiro Agnew, then the latest albums. Though the noise and music were as dangerous as a fire, Ted didn't object. He should have gone over the plan until each person understood his role, but he knew if he was tired of talking about it, they had to be sick of hearing it.

So he held Bert's hand against his thigh and listened to the music, which carried no memories or meaning for him, yet curiously had an effect. Drifting into a pensive mood, he added up all the years that had passed since the last time he'd danced. A decade at least. Now he rarely heard new records, and his songs, not the tunes his parents used to hum, were the old ones. That was strange to realize and tougher to swallow. Christ, he was ancient.

Bert, as if mulling over the same subject, said, "Know what I miss most about America?"

"McDonald's hamburgers," said Ants.

Everybody laughed.

"That, too. But I was thinking of music. Dancing."

"So dance," said Ants. "This isn't the Fillmore, but the footing's good."

"Not now. Tomorrow night."

"Hope it doesn't slow you down to have sand in your shoes," said Ted. "We'll be in the desert."

"We'll all dance tomorrow night," said Puff. "Gypsy's the biggest fumble-foot in the world, but we're going to wail until dawn."

"I know how you'll be wailing," said Ants.

"You better believe it, son. Now there's what I miss."

"Join the crowd." Polo's deep voice was surprisingly soft in the obscurity.

"Yeah, who doesn't miss that?" asked Ants.

"You don't, you twink. You can't miss what you've never had," Puff teased him.

Phil said, "I miss my books."

"Oh, bullshit," said Polo. "Nobody's giving you a grade for this. Loosen up. What do you really miss?"

"I like books."

"Okay, what else?"

"Friends."

"So we're not good enough for you?" Ants protested.

"No, no, I can't imagine anything better than spending my whole life with you guys, sitting next to this scurvy stream, picking bugs out of my food."

"What do you miss?" Bert asked Ted.

"Nothing. I've forgotten what there is to miss."

"Come on, it's the moment of truth. There must be something."

"Well . . . there's liquor. I'm talking about bourbon."

"Boo! Bourgeois," Ants razzed him. "All poison and no insight."

"Old buddy, you don't have a clue what a real trip is till

you've tossed down about six straight shots of Tennessee sipping whiskey. That stuff'll perk you up, then lay you low. You'll be knee-walking drunk, having visions that'd knock your socks off."

"Hey, sounds terrific," said Ants. "What do you do, smoke it or sniff it?"

Ted laughed along with them.

"I miss Sunday," said Polo.

"They have it here too," said Ants. "Strangely enough they sandwich it in between Saturday and Monday."

"Okay, smart-ass, but can you find the paper on your front porch? Can you have orange juice, bacon, and eggs for breakfast? It's the whole Sunday feeling I miss. Resting up and getting ready for Monday. Then, in the afternoon, you flick on the tube and watch the professional football games."

"What the hell, you heard every one of them on the radio. Remember the night in Safi when we sat on the sea wall listening to the Super Bowl?"

"I'll survive without football," said Puff. "What I miss is pizza, chocolate sundaes, banana splits, baked potatoes and sour cream."

"Wow, we have to stop," said Bert. "It's bringing back too many things. Suddenly even bad ones sound good. Hair dryers, telephones, movies, mirrors . . ."

"Cellophane, supermarkets, Crunchy Granola," Puff picked up the chorus.

"Crunchy *what?*" asked Ted.

"Crunchy Granola. A health cereal," said Ants. "Man, you *have* been away too long."

"I reckon I have. It's like you're talking about a foreign country. Will anyone besides me miss Morocco?"

"Yeah, about as much as I'll miss dysentery," said Polo.

Well, I will, thought Ted. And what else? It was a hell of a fix not knowing any more what was worth missing. Resigned, if not indifferent, to the isolation and loneliness of the last few years, he had been only half alive, he realized. Was there anything in America he missed? His family, since the death of his parents, was a fading memory and the town of Clifton Forge the merest shadow of one.

He certainly didn't miss the army, although there were parts of the life he had liked. The routine, the system of promotions and rewards, the security, occasionally the camaraderie. Bert said the clocks at her house had stopped in 1954. In the military, during the deep, soothing sleep of the Eisenhower years, it had been a lot like that. Every American base, no matter where it was located, had bathed in the complacency of a small, rural town, the type you were raised in as a boy, or wished you had been.

But Vietnam had destroyed that illusion. The bases, with their movies, bars, launderettes, cafeterias, swimming pools, palatial PX's, and football fields, hadn't changed, but when built in that burnt-over countryside and barricaded by barbed wire, they had seemed shameful. And even the archest patriot had to suspect that the side which was willing to sacrifice most—the side that could survive without massage parlors or smack shooting galleries—would win.

Though like most people he missed being young and had enjoyed his share of good times, there weren't many days he'd have asked to relive. If Ted felt nostalgia for anything, it was for the future, not the past. Nostalgia probably wasn't the word for it, but what he missed most was the island and now, after last night, the idea of Bert there with him.

Although she nestled next to him, her hand on his leg, he longed to be closer to her. It pleased him, then, when Phil pulled himself to his feet and said he was sleepy. Fumbling in the dark, they unpacked their bedrolls, choosing spots in the dusty compound formed by the three cars and the irrigation ditch. But Ted was unwilling to spend the night in this improvised stockade. Clasping a blanket under one arm and encircling Bert's waist with the other, he crossed the ditch and waded through the fields.

Each footstep steeped them in the scent of crushed grass and moist earth, reminding him of boyhood summers. As they ambled on, frogs and crickets sounded the alarm, then fell silent while the breeze, blowing in mild freshets, made a waving green ocean of the grain. Above them to the left, a few fires flickered in the village, filling the air with cedar smoke, and Ted was astonished by all he remembered and missed. The very first time he'd breathed the sweet, thick aroma of burning cedar it had seemed to him he'd already smelled it somewhere and missed it. Maybe his blood had been born with memories.

Holding hands at arm's length, Ted and Bert wheeled as if in a slow dance, while the field whirled away from them, spinning beyond the patch of grass—an island in the ocean of grain—which they trampled down for a bed. When Ted shook the blanket, it stayed aloft on the wind, then sank with a *whoosh* to the ground. Removing their shoes, they felt the rough wool on the soles of their feet. Bert seized his shoulders, raising herself by her own slender strength till their lips were together.

As they separated to undress, Ted lost sight of her in the dark, but knew where she was by the sound of her clothes falling to the blanket. Only after she had shed everything could he distinguish her shape from the deep night that hid them from the village, the campsite, and the awesome mountain wall. Bert's body appeared pale and fresh enough to smear, so that he hesitated to touch her. Ted was two-toned—tanned on the face and arms, white everywhere else. Compared to her, he thought his skin looked blistered and aging. But she hurried to meet him in the middle of the blanket, straining against him, her feet once more off the ground, her hair unfurled over his arms.

"Tonight it's your turn," he whispered and set her on the ground on her stomach. Sliding his hands along her flanks, he found them tight and cool. He massaged Bert, warming her back, thighs, and calves as well as his own hands, until she rolled over, protesting, "Don't. You'll spoil me."

"I mean to."

"No. We should share." She spread her arms in a wide gesture of welcome. "Come here."

He braced his weight above her on his elbows and knees, but she wouldn't allow it. Pulling him closer, she pinned them both to the blanket, which had grown damp and fragrant from the field. He heard the wind humming in the grain, bending the stalks, brushing her hair gauzily against his face.

Afterward Ted lay on his back with Bert on his chest and tucked the blanket around her, hugging her for warmth. Here was one thing he'd remember and miss whenever they weren't like this.

But when she murmured, "I love you," his impulse was to answer, No, don't say it. Words would add a burden to what was best left unspoken. Yet he said nothing and she didn't seem hurt. She was telling the truth, not baiting a trap.

"I wish I were going with you tomorrow," she said.

"You are."

"I mean into the jail."

"No. Your job's important. Can I count on you?"

"What if you're captured? I won't stand there holding those damn djellabahs. I'll come help."

"No. Promise not to do that." Easing Bert onto her side, he cupped her chin in his hands so he could watch her eyes. "Gimme your word, anything goes wrong, you'll run to Puff, drive the Renault to Casablanca, and catch the first plane out of the country."

"What are you talking about? I won't do it. You'll need me."

"I'll be okay if I'm sure you're safe. But if I'm worrying about you, I'm liable to hold back from what I have to do."

"What's that?"

"You know the plan."

"You're not hiding anything from me?"

"What's to hide? It should be a cinch."

Shivering, she huddled in the blanket. "I don't believe you."

"You gotta trust me." He took her trembling hands. "Don't make it harder. I'm being very selfish about this, I admit, but do me a favor. At the first sign of trouble, get the hell away and stay away."

"Suppose you get to the lot and I've gone."

"The Land-Rover'll be there."

"You don't understand. How will I know you're safe? How will you know where I am? We have to have a place to meet if we're separated."

Recalling the tiny hatch in the jail's tall, wooden door, Ted didn't care for his chances in case of a double-cross. But if it pleased Bert to arrange a rendezvous, he wouldn't deny her.

"Why not meet in Spain?" he said.

"Where? We've got to have a specific place. Do you know the Costa del Sol? We could meet in Marbella. There are planes from Morocco to Málaga. And boats from Ceuta and Tangier."

"Fine. That's it, then."

"I'll be at the Hotel La Fonda. Will you remember that?"

"Of course. The Hotel La Fonda in Marbella. Feel better?"

"I guess."

"Good. Now you've gotta swear to catch the first flight from the country."

"I promise," she whispered disconsolately. When she was dressed, Bert curled on her side, drawing her arms and legs into a knot. "You just don't know what it'll do to me if something happens to you."

"Nothing'll happen to me. Day after tomorrow we'll leave for the island." Pulling the blanket up to her neck, he tried by vigorous rubbing to stop her from shivering, but that didn't help and he said, "I'll bring another blanket from the car."

"Ted."

"Yes."

"I love you."

It took so little effort to answer, he couldn't hold back this time. "I love you too." And once he'd said it, it sounded true.

The instant he stepped beyond the circle of crushed grass, Ted became a stalking animal, urged on by a strong flow of adrenalin he'd often experienced on night patrols. In springy strides, he'd covered ten yards before realizing he was still naked. Blades of grain slashed his ankles and calves, and his toes stubbed dirt clods and stones. He should have turned back, but suddenly exhilarated, he started to run instead, his feet barely grazing the spiky undergrowth. The wind rushed in waves over his chest and down his spine. There came, along with the speed, an improvement in his vision and balance, as if the darkness had allowed him to relearn his body's secrets.

When he stopped, the wind slackened. Only the beat of his heart and lungs was audible. Then other sounds resumed as the field seemed to shrug off its sleep. Oblivious to him, insects chirred. Several landed on his arms and legs, and he let them be. At the irrigation ditch, he crouched by the muddy water which purled through its narrow canal, floating a few olive leaves which he mistook for minnows. Ted shivered and his skin was feathered by gooseflesh.

Across from him slept Ants, Puff, Phil, and Polo. One of them rolled over, snoring, while Ted luxuriated a moment longer in the advantage he enjoyed of being awake and invisible, watching them. *I haven't lost it, after all,* he thought. Like his father, who had taught him how to hunt, he could glide silently over dry leaves and steal through the deepest thicket.

Ted leaped the ditch and crept to the car. The door opened easily. Bending over, he fumbled under the front seat, found the blanket, and had begun to back up when he bumped into something cold and solid. He didn't need to look. He knew it was a pistol, and his body stiffened as he waited for white heat to explode from the icy barrel and sever his spine.

"What do we have here?" asked Polo, chuckling quietly.

"Take that thing off me."

"What are you doing?" Polo insisted, pressing the pistol into him.

"Getting a blanket. I'm cold," he shouted to wake the others.

"I wonder why."

"I'm not going to tell you again. Get that goddamn gun off my back. Is this your idea of a joke?"

"Yeah, that's it. A joke. A game called catching Natty Bumpo in the nude. I thought it'd be good practice for tomorrow." Polo pulled back, but didn't lower the revolver. "Thanks to you, we'll be going in that jail naked."

"But we'll be coming out alive."

He swung around slowly to Polo. The dark, unshaven face on its thick neck was thrust forward at him, and Ted thought, If I had a gun, I'd kill him. Not just in revenge for this ruthless humiliation, but because of all the bad blood that had built up between them and was bound to be spilled.

But Polo had the pistol pointed at Ted's bare stomach. He couldn't see whether the safety was on or off. Though tempted to grab the gun and smack Polo's head against the car, he knew no matter what happened or who won, he might as well forget about tomorrow. After a fight, much less a shooting, this bunch would fall apart and there'd be no time to patch them up.

"You shouldn't have come snooping like this," said Polo, no longer smiling.

"I was getting a goddamn blanket."

"How would we know? This is the wrong night to screw around."

"Who's that?" Ants groggily called.

"Me. Ted. Go back to sleep." Slinging the blanket around his shoulders, he pushed by Polo and strode toward the ditch, conscious of a dull stinging in the soles of his feet. But he didn't show it. It was bad enough to be retreating. He wasn't about to limp.

His shoulder blades, which had drawn together when he

presented his back to the pistol, didn't relax until he'd reentered the island of trampled-down grain. Swaddled in the blanket, Bert slept soundly. Kneeling next to her, he whispered to himself, What's that son-of-a-bitch after? How many times had he stuck out his hairy kisser and dared anyone to swing at it? No amount of money was worth much more of this.

And yet he realized Polo was right. It was stupid to have stumbled into camp without waking them first. When he was calmer, he put on his clothes, wrapped up in the cover, and lay awake listening for footsteps.

IV

TED HAD grown used to the raucous crowing of roosters, and they could no longer rouse him. But that morning he woke to the call of wild birds. Scraps of shiny black clattered close by, then across the sky trailing their harsh hunting cries and the crisp snapping of their wings. Twisting around to follow them, he found a straggling member of the flock stalking the field beside him, its feathers wet with dew and sleek as patent leather.

When he sat up, the raven didn't row off on its wings. It cocked its head, parted its curved beak, and peered at him through one implacable eye. Half-expecting it to strike at his bare arms, Ted went rigid. But the bird pecked at the sod and snatched up a tiny green snake. With the triangular head clenched in its bill and a murderous claw over the tail, it stretched the snake till its spine snapped.

When Ted clapped his hands, shouting, the raven clapped back with its lacquered wings, shrieking as it ascended, the dead snake dangling from its talons.

"What's that?" asked Bert, not actually awake.

"Nothing. Roll over and go to sleep."

She did so at once, and he kissed her cheek. Overwhelmed by tenderness for her, Ted felt, as he had before, the need to protect Bert and keep her near him. But today it was better for them both if she stayed away.

Lying back, he didn't shut his eyes. Though tired, he was still suffering the after-effects of last night and resisted the false consolation of sleep. Behind him the sun soared from a curtain of haze, shrugging off clouds and carving the mountains into sharper relief. At first the peaks were obscured by shrouds of mist, but as the sky brightened, they assumed their true mass and the contrast of colors between snowcaps above and dark crags below. Even here the wind bore an icy intimation of the High Atlas, and he shivered.

Once they left that freezing crypt of a jail, he'd feel much better, for he had less fear of the maze of streets in Tazenzit and the drive over the mountains and through the desert. Driss had said it. Morocco was an easy place to hide. If nothing else, it had hundreds of barren miles, and in this landscape of lost souls, people disappeared all the time and any medina offered anonymity.

But the jail, with all its doors, was a different matter. The moment they stepped into that concrete box, they'd be prisoners, and Driss alone had the key out. Their lives hung on the honesty of the guard, who'd given no indication he understood what the word meant. Yet Ted had more faith in him than in the crew he commanded. Driss could help them or refuse, and they were likely to learn at once what he'd do, whereas Polo, Phil, and Ants possessed a constant and incalculable potential for causing problems. Once again he was glad he'd agreed to take the pistol. It gave him the edge he needed, now that he was as worried about Bert as he was about himself.

*   *   *

When Bert was awake, they walked to the campsite,
where the group was up, babbling like the ravens that had
clattered past, hungrily seeking something to seize upon.
Though they had plenty to eat, The Gravy Train was fam-
ished for security and believed they'd found it in loud ban-
tering. Even Polo joked about the awful coffee and the
baggy bib overalls which Puff wore instead of her tent
dress. He was wearing a clean suit of army surplus fatigues,
while Ants had on a patchwork shirt and dungarees embell-
ished with bright appliqués of birds, insects, and flowers.
But what caused most comment was the leather cut-out of
a woman's head sewn to the crotch of his pants. He explained this was his plainclothes outfit.

No one mentioned last night or what they had to do
today. It was more important to make noise, to keep the
sound waves moving, linking themselves with light-hearted
chatter. Ted didn't object, but neither did he join in. He
was in no mood to gab.

Then, after breakfast, when he went to the trunk of the
Renault to get the gas can, neither were they. A strained
silence fell over the group as they gathered their bedrolls
and cleaned the campsite.

"Ants, come here," he called. "The rest of you empty the
bus and split up the food, water bags, and suitcases between my car and Polo's."

As they did what he told them, he was glad to see they'd
bought a dozen round loaves of Berber bread, along with
boxes of canned goods. At least they wouldn't starve.

"You called, captain?" Ants executed a left-handed salute.

"Jeezus." Ted had to smile. "I bet you stole that outfit
from a circus clown."

"It's my camouflage, man."

"Stand back. You're blinding me." Hoisting the gas can from the trunk, he unscrewed the cap and stuck a finger in the spout. Then he spilled a long draught into the dust.

"What are you doing?"

"There's gotta be an airspace at the top." He stood the can between his feet and plugged the spout with a rag which he'd used to wipe the dip-stick. Hanging over the side, the rag ran for a few inches along the ground. "See that? That's how you should fix it on the back floor of the bus. Then light a cigarette, get it going good, lay the unlit end against the fuse, and shut and lock the doors. Better haul ass after that."

"Sounds simple."

"It is. Just don't go spilling any gasoline before you light the cigarette. Now screw the cap on tight and stow the can in the bus."

The others were at the rear of the Land-Rover, loading supplies, when Ted said, "Before you finish there, lemme have the pistol."

Polo lifted a floor panel and handed him a Smith & Wesson .357 magnum with a four-inch barrel. Ted nudged open the chamber, spun it, and emptied the shells. They were hard ball cartridges, the kind packed by Military Police, the tips of the bullets painted black. Armor-piercing, they could crack the block of a truck.

"Where's the other one?"

Polo pointed to the floor panel.

"Lemme see it." Prying up the panel again, he showed Ted the .38. "Be sure you leave it there. I'll take a box of ammo, too. You ever shoot this?"

"A few times."

"What's it like?"

"Loud."

"Look, does it pull right or left or what?"

"I didn't notice," Polo answered, irritated by Ted's aura of expertise.

He wondered whether Polo had cleaned it, but didn't want to rile him by asking. Before reloading, he glanced down the bore. It didn't look dirty. Though he'd have liked some target practice, he was reluctant to fire the pistol. Bert, Puff, and Phil were bothered by the sight of it, and the noise might bring someone nosing around.

Sticking it under his belt, he tucked his shirt over it. The revolver left a sizeable bulge, much heavier than he'd expected, and its barrel felt unpleasantly familiar against the bare skin of his belly.

Patting it, Puff did a passable imitation of Mae West. "Is that a gun in your pocket, big boy, or are you just happy to see me?"

"Both, baby, both," said Ted. "We might as well shove off."

They rode behind the Land-Rover with the windows rolled tight, yet a fine powder stole in through the cracks and crevices. The sun seemed to inflate with the heat, burning off the shade. Wavering blue mirages welled up in the low spots, then streamed away as the cars drew near. Ted's eyes ached, his teeth were gritty, and sweat plastered his back to the vinyl seat. When his hands left wet prints on the steering wheel, he told himself it was the heat, not his nerves, and lowered the window an inch. By the time they reached the paved road, his shirt was damp and the shadows had shrunk to nothing. As he cranked the window down, a cool breeze caused him to shiver.

Bert cleared her throat twice before asking, "Did you hear a noise this morning? A loud screech?"

"A few birds flew over."

"Funny. I'd have sworn you shouted something. It scared me."

"I told you to go back to sleep. You must of been dreaming. Listen, I left a lot of money locked in the glove compartment in case you have to catch a flight from Casablanca."

Bert folded her arms. "I won't need it."

"Don't make me go through it again," he said. "You promised."

"Okay, but I told you how hard it'll be if anything happens to you."

"Quit talking about it. Nothing will."

She didn't act reassured. "So far it's been one way between us—you giving, me receiving. There hasn't been time for me to do a damn thing for you."

"Who's keeping score anyhow?"

"I am. I'd like to do something for you."

"You've done a hell of a lot for me."

"I want to do more," she said. "I want to help take care of you. Not in any big way. You're pretty self-sufficient. But I'd like to buy a bottle of that bourbon you talk about and fix you a drink every evening." She shook her head. "Crazy. Must be a Mother Hubbard instinct."

"You'll get your chance," said Ted. "And it won't be long before you're tired of it."

She scratched self-consciously at her arms. "Next thing you know, I'll be bitching about having a baby." Bert sounded almost ashamed of herself.

"What's wrong with that?"

"Some people say they wouldn't bring children into a world like this."

"Isn't that generous of them? Hell, the world's a big

place. What they're really saying is they wouldn't raise kids in the small part they've made for themselves."

"Or messed up for themselves."

"Maybe. I've messed up more than my share of places, but I wouldn't mind having kids. Mostly it's a matter of meeting the right person to have them with. I don't buy this business about the world being rotten. It's people. If there are too many bad ones, then we gotta have more good ones, and there's just one way of doing that. In Vietnam and Nigeria the folks went on like they knew things would get better, like they believed kids'd make them better. Life's hard, but it beats the hell out of whatever's in second place."

"That's ignorance. Once they're educated they'll learn..."

"What? Life's not so hot?"

"They'll learn to use the pill."

"Hey, that'll help. I don't fancy having a family as big as a football team."

Bert laughed and let him take her hand.

Traffic streamed sluggishly toward Tazenzit, and for miles they made grueling progress behind an old man who pedaled a bicycle which had a sheaf of long reeds strapped to the rear fender. From that angle he resembled a monstrous insect with feeble wings. But when they passed him, he looked wretched, weary, and all too human, like someone who had struggled and failed to discover the secret of self-propelled flight.

As they entered an argan forest where squat, gnarled trees clung to the otherwise bare ground, Bert showed Ted the goats that had climbed high among the branches to nibble the tenderest shoots. But then the eerie improbability of the scene forced her to reflect in silence upon the even less probable scheme they had embarked upon. If it had been up to her, they would have turned back. The heat, the sun, the bizarre countryside conspired against reality, and she didn't believe that anything starting under these circumstances—especially not her relationship with Ted—could proceed rationally. But they had to get Gypsy out. She'd wait until afterward to worry about herself.

Parking on the lot beside the town wall, Ted had them pull the cars around, pointing east, ready to depart.

"Should I stay here?" asked Puff, hitching the straps of her overalls. From the neck down, she might have been a stout farm worker, but her face was fair and, in its way, handsome.

"No, we'll look around first."

"You know where the pistol is," Polo said to her. "If there's trouble later on, use it. Without the cars we're dead."

The word did terrible damage to everyone's expression. Their eyes glazed over, and nobody looked at anyone else.

"Follow me," said Ted. "Stick together."

Once they'd gone through the gate, the crowd swept them up in its current, but it flowed toward the square, and they didn't fight it. Bobbing in an ocean of Arabs and Berbers, they seemed to coast at the crest of a breaking wave. For once even the women wearing veils and long robes couldn't deny their corporeality. Squeezed against several hefty black Haratin, Ted experienced a slow sensual sinking and heard them giggle.

The swell collapsed in the square, and the six of them stopped to collect themselves.

"God, get a load of this mob," said Ants.

"Let's look around," said Ted, and led them toward the

jail, holding Bert's hand, searching for the best path . . . It was going to be difficult to dash through here, dodging all the obstacles. But at least there wasn't a single clear line of fire.

Every Thursday the tribes from the countryside traveled to Tazenzit with the itinerant merchants to display their wares in the Place des Chameaux. Much of what they had to sell was identical to the merchandise in the souq—fresh fruits and vegetables, mounds of fly-ridden meat, bright hand-loomed carpets, and lavishly tooled leather goods. A few had built temporary stands of reeds and bamboo poles, shaded by broad banners of canvas, and in front of them, boisterous hawkers worked the crowd, physically collaring customers.

But other vendors knelt on the ground next to scraps of cardboard on which their meagre goods were strewn. These seemed to sell nothing and must have returned each week out of habit, or a longing for excitement and human contact. Dressed no better than a beggar, one man sat crosslegged with a dozen rusty nails, three hinges, and a few hard-boiled eggs in his lap. A toothless Berber had shriveled lemons and garlic bulbs. A woman roosted behind stacks of English, American, German, and Italian magazines. It was hard to imagine where she had unearthed them or who she expected to buy them, but though they were dog-eared and years out of date, they were too valuable for her to discard. Cleaning their covers with a fluffy ostrich feather, she preserved the slick periodicals like priceless icons.

Only the owner of a table littered with false teeth did a brisk business. He had whole sets for sale, as well as individual molars and incisors which might have popped from his own purple gums. Customers pressed the pieces of cheap plastic into their mouths, trading off with each other until they found ones that fit.

The same man also sold an astounding variety of amulets and charms—rabbits' feet, snake skins, flattened lizards, dead scorpions, porcupine quills, rodent fangs, crab claws, and an entire stork which was much marveled at although it was little more than a rank ball of feathers and buzzing flies with two stalk-like legs.

Ted tripped over corroded batteries, lengths of copper tubing, crushed tin cans, old license plates, burnt-out light bulbs, and broken tools. It seemed a tidal wave had dumped half the world's trash in the square, and these people had to support themselves by selling it. He quit searching for a safe route through the rubble. Since more buyers and sellers arrived every moment, eddying and swerving from one stand to another, he decided that when they came out of the jail with Gypsy, they'd have to pick the path that looked best at the moment.

Pausing beside a barber who whipped up lather in a porcelain bowl, applied it to a young man's head, and shaved him bald, Ted said, "I've seen enough. Why don't you all wait in the souq while Ants and I poke around in the medina for a place to leave the bus?"

"We should watch the square," said Polo.

"And have everybody watch you?"

Polo motioned to a rooftop restaurant overlooking the market. "No one'll notice us up there."

"Okay. Meet you in a few minutes."

The medina was quiet and uncongested except on the main street, where a gang of boys played an improvised brand of soccer with a ball of rags. For blocks the wall of houses was unbroken. Doors were shut, the small windows shuttered.

At the first intersecting alley, Ted said, "Not this one. Farther from the square. We want a spot where you won't be bothered while you're working and nobody'll get hurt when the bus blows."

"The way it's leaking oil, there should be plenty of smoke. But will it explode or just burn?"

"You tell me. You're the demolition expert."

"Good luck, man." Ants arched his eyebrows, yet didn't act very concerned. "Maybe you better lay another lesson on me. I haven't had much practice in this line since they banned Fourth of July fireworks."

"Just unscrew the cap and stuff that rag in the spout for a fuse. Stretch it out to give yourself time to get clear. Then light a cigarette and set it so it'll burn down to the rag. An important thing to keep in mind, old buddy, is once you uncap the can, don't dilly-dally inside that bus while the fumes build up, or we'll be tweezing tin and glass from your fanny for the next few months."

"I dig. Thanks for the warning."

Six blocks into the medina, when they could scarcely see a slice of the square behind them, Ted and Ants ducked down a blind alley where the scent of urine was sharp and stinging. The mud walls, matted with straw, appeared to be no more than an arm's span apart, but Ted measured and it was wide enough for the VW.

"Drive to the end of the alley," he said. "Careful not to block any doorways. Then loosen the license plates and bring them to me. We might as well make things as hard for those cops as we can. Soon as you're sure the cigarette's burning, lock the doors and light out of here. You don't have to run, but hurry the hell back to us."

Sniffing, Ants sourly twisted his face. "This isn't a spot I'd like to linger in."

But for a moment, both of them did.

"Do me a favor," said Ted. "Stay cool and concentrate. The rest of the plan depends on your doing this right. If something goes wrong, use your head. Say the cops nab you. Play dumb. Pretend you don't know what they're talking about. You're just some jerk smoking in the back seat of his bus with a gas can beside him. Whatever you do, don't drag them to us. I've got this gun and that could be bad. When things calm down, I'll bail you out. They'll have no call to hold you. Brass it through. Understand?"

"For sure."

"One other thing. Say you can't reach the square, or we're arrested or separated from you for some reason. Forget us, walk around the walls, and hustle to the cars. The girls'll be there. I'm trusting you to take care of them. There's money in my glove compartment. Drive to Casablanca if you have to and catch a plane out of the country."

"But what about the three of you?" For the first time Ants seemed troubled.

"Don't bother about us. We'll meet you later. Bert knows where."

With obvious misgivings, Ants nodded.

"I'm banking on you, buddy. When you leave, be sure Bert's with you."

2

JOINING the group at the rooftop restaurant, Ted ordered mint tea and almond pastry for everybody, and they sat eating and drinking along the balustrade, gazing at the action on the Place des Chameaux. Panning left to right they had an unobstructed view of the keyhole arches at one end, the main street of the medina opposite them, and the Sûreté Nationale at the far end. Polo had picked an excellent observation point, and Ted told him so.

As the afternoon lengthened toward evening, the crowd grew larger and louder, and palm readers, dancers and drummers, acrobats, snake charmers, and storytellers entertained it. Beside Ted, Bert rested her hand on his bare arm. The pistol barrel jabbed into his belly, and he leaned back in the chair to ease the pressure. All around them rose the racket of voices, the beat of drums, the clinking of finger cymbals, and filigrees of reedy flute music.

"Isn't this square out of sight?" shouted Puff. "Reminds me of the one in Marrakech. Pajama el-what's-its-face."

"The Jemaa el Fna," Phil corrected her. "It translates as Meeting Place of the Dead. It . . ."

"Yeah, that's it. Last time Gypsy and I were there we practically lived in that square during the day. At night we'd go to a good restaurant or bar. For once we weren't doing the rat tour. No camping and eating roots and berries. It was right after his birthday and he decided to blow all the bread his old man had sent.

"We stayed at the Mamounia, and it was like a museum, only with real dead bodies, not wax ones. The joint was crawling with these English dudes in short pants, safari jackets, and pith helmets. Like they expected to meet a lion on the parking lot.

"We crashed into that scene like a couple of creatures from outer space. They let us have a room, but took one look at our freak threads and said Monsieur et Madame can't eat in the dining room. We didn't give a damn. We ate out or called room service. They've got terrific cheeseburgers.

"Some evenings we'd hire a carriage and go trucking through town. There was this one groovy driver with a big whip and a badge cut out of cardboard and tinfoil. He handed us a card saying 'Englihs Spoke,' but the fact was, he didn't speak much of anything. He was tongue-tied and mostly pointed and grunted.

"One night he drove us into the countryside. I don't know what for. It was nothing but an empty plain, even worse than Indiana. It looked like it had been plowed and sown with rocks. But he drove on and on and Gypsy said, 'Ah, I get it. He's showing us what the UMA has accomplished.' 'The what?' I asked. 'The UMA!' he explained, like everyone had heard of it. 'The United Moroccan Appeal. It has a famous program for planting stones. Over the years they've managed to transform fertile land into desert.' Well, I laughed like I . . ."

Puff was winding tighter rather than running down, and while she went on talking, Ted didn't have to check his watch. The town wall served as a sundial of sorts, changing colors according to the hour from rose pink to orange to carmine to terra cotta. The crowd swarmed in wide rings, wheeling from one show to the next, the long lines of their shadows like bars of wrought iron forged by the day's heat into one intricate arabesque. Then the sun passed behind a bank of clouds and the pattern disappeared as the market plunged into gloom. The temperature dropped ten degrees in ten minutes.

"Excuse me, Puff," said Ted. "It's time."

She stopped in mid-sentence. The meandering story may have occupied her mind, but she hadn't lost touch. Standing up, she was ready to start.

"Ants, go with the girls. Easy in the medina. There's no rush. Phil, Polo, and I'll sit tight till you're finished with the bus. Then we'll wait under the arches until the cops come out. Any questions?"

When there were none, he was nonchalant. No pep talk,

no warnings, not even a warmly whispered, Good luck. It was better for them to assume it would be a snap.

But Bert had to blink the tears from her eyes when she said, "Good-bye."

"No need for that. I'm not going anywhere. Here, you keep the car keys. Be with you in a few minutes."

After Ants, Puff, and Bert left, the three men were separated by silence and empty chairs. Straining forward to watch their faltering progress across the square, through the arcade, and into the souq, Ted was glad Bert didn't glance back or wave. Don't worry, he told himself. She's safe. And so are you. You're not going to catch it today. You're going to be careful and get through this. He stared at the main street of the medina, his lean body relaxed, his grey eyes revealing nothing.

Polo couldn't sit still. Fidgeting and chewing at his moustache, he slouched low in the chair, lifting his face toward the spot where the sun should have been. "It's going to rain. The clouds are blowing in from the sea and that . . ."

At an exasperated glare from Ted, he trailed off. He wasn't scared. Just itching to get on with it. His big body had hardened; his mind had coiled tight to crush its questions and nagging doubts. He experienced a keen tension and excitement, like he had before football games, and later as a graduate student before important exams, and recently during poker games when, regardless of the cost, he'd stay in for the last card to see what he'd draw.

But then, in an annoying reversal, he remembered what an erratic card player he was and made himself review the plan. The details were tedious, infuriating. The emphasis on safety and strategy had subverted his original purpose.

How was the project important, if he could compare it to a football game, poker, or graduate school exams?

Suddenly it all sounded trivial, and to regain his grip on the critical issues, Polo considered the possibility of something going wrong. What if one of them were killed? What if he were killed? This seemed more absurd than sobering. People died, but not him, not here.

It was more likely that he'd be captured, and in a mechanical fashion he mulled over what that would mean. A long prison term, torture, boredom, broken health, and perhaps the impossibility of returning to the States and reconstructing his old life.

The last point appealed to him, but he couldn't bring himself to believe it would happen. For despite the example he had of Gypsy, he could imagine his capture, trial, and conviction as another in a series of international *causes célèbres*. A few years in jail would certify his credentials as one who had done something extravagant in the name of freedom. Queasy with recognition, Polo admitted how difficult it was to exclude base motives from what should be selfless ideals. While convincing himself he meant to crack the mold and escape the entire asinine charade, did he want to take a fashionable detour and, after a few deceptive gestures of independence, wind up at the head of the class?

Polo cursed this temptation to cheapen his commitment. Indignantly he drove the questions from his mind. He wasn't going to carry them or any other shoddy baggage into the jail with him. Your reasons are right. There's no need to cross-examine them. Better not to think than do that. Better to push yourself to the edge, then over it, beyond the point where anyone can accuse you of being cautious and self-seeking.

Phil was going through it again, asking questions which

were painful or impossible to answer. It's one thing, he thought, to betray your most deeply held beliefs, and a different, more serious matter to betray a person. But that's what he was doing, and it didn't make things any better to tell himself he had no choice, that Gypsy's freedom was worth forsaking his values. For in the last few days, he'd realized Ted might have helped them anyhow, if they told him the truth.

But whether they told him or not, Phil would have felt guilty. Had anybody bothered to wonder, much less ask, if they'd convinced Kuyler to act against his beliefs? Or wasn't he supposed to have any?

Yes, it was a classic case. Polo, with his half-digested Marxism and outspoken sympathy for the poor, ought to have recognized that. Ted was lower class, as close to the *Lumpenproletariat* as they'd ever come. Polo should have loved him. Instead they were at each other's throats. Why didn't Polo see the irony?

Face it, thought Phil. You hired a Hessian to do the dirty work. And though no one admired a mercenary, how about the people who paid him? Or who didn't pay him, but depended on him? It frightened him that he had no control over what they were doing. Neither did Polo. They were dangerously beyond their depth and foolish to go through with this.

In his palms, moistened by perspiration, the metal crutch felt oily and unfamiliar. "Look, I think . . ."

"There's Ants," said Ted, and he and Polo stood up.

The blond boy with the Prince Valiant bangs and wispy goatee came across the square carrying the license plates.

"I don't think we should . . ."

"Let's shake a leg," said Ted. "Who knows how long that fuse'll last?"

As they started for the stairwell, Phil was tempted to call

them back. But then he clamped the crutch to his elbow and limped after them. He'd have to think this through later.

They stole along the edge of the market, expecting to hear an explosion, studying the sky over the medina for smoke. Braziers had been lit for dinner and against the evening chill, and the scent of hashish and incense blended with the charcoal haze. But there weren't yet the black, muscular billows that Ted had bargained on.

Thoroughly disguised by a djellabah and with five more over her arm, Bert was in the depths of the arcade. Seeing Ted, she stepped forward, but he waved her away.

Ants held his thumbs up in triumph.

"Any trouble?" asked Ted, as they huddled behind a broad pink pillar.

"None. It'll blow any second."

"Good." Ted glanced at his watch. It was five of five.

"Maybe Phil should get a head start," said Polo. "He could go halfway across and pretend to be shopping."

Phil's face was dead white as he nodded. "I'll signal you if I see anything."

He walked smoothly at first, swinging his bad leg and the crutch, but as he entered the mob, he had to fend off people with his free hand and scuffle for space. His red head bobbed awkwardly as he moved to the middle of the market.

"Christ, couldn't we have talked him out of this?" asked Polo. "It's not just that he'll slow us down. He could get hurt."

"He wouldn't listen to me," said Ted.

Half-moons of sweat had spread under the arms of Polo's fatigue shirt. "What the hell, if he can't keep up, I'll carry him."

"He's a gutty guy," said Ted. "He may end up carrying us."

"What time is it?" asked Ants, who wasn't smiling for once.

"A little after five."

"Any minute now," he muttered, looking at the medina. There was still no more smoke than usual. Ted prayed for a powerful, earpopping explosion, and that it would happen soon. Polo's boots were pawing the ground. Ants whistled absent-mindedly through his teeth. Maybe we should go and meet Phil, Ted thought. Anything to move.

"What's the hold-up?" Polo smacked his hand against the pillar, sending out a cloud of powder.

"Easy. There's no hurry."

"You sure you lit that fuse?" Polo snapped at Ants.

"Sure I'm sure. But we didn't know whether it would explode. It might be burning quietly."

"With no smoke?" said Polo, seizing him by the collar. "You little asshole, I oughta cold-cock you."

"Knock it off." Ted squeezed between them and grabbed Polo's arms.

"I swear it was lit."

"How the hell would you know? You were probably too busy shooting off your mouth."

"I said that's enough."

"The cigarette was burning," said Ants, "but it could've gone out."

"Yeah, maybe." But Ted thought it was also possible someone had seen the smoke, broken into the bus, and yanked the fuse. Or called the cops. What could Driss be counted on to do?

"Send him back to light it," said Polo.

"No, I'll go."

"Let me, man," pleaded Ants. "Honest, I did what you told me."

"I believe it, but someone might have spotted you. You snoop around again, they'll get suspicious. They won't notice me."

"What if they do? Suppose somebody's there?" asked Polo.

"I'll go out the gate and circle around the wall to the cars. Wait here half an hour, no longer. I'm not back by then, meet me there."

"And what if you're not there?"

"We'll come help," said Ants.

"No. Leave my car and drive the Land-Rover to Agadir. I'll see you at the campground."

"What if you don't make it?" Polo pressed him.

"Then Gypsy'll have company in that icebox."

"I won't let you do this," said Ants.

"Quiet! Lemme talk. Say they hold me, you'd better leave the country fast. Be sure Bert's with you. Drag her if you have to."

"Christ, man, I didn't . . ."

"I'll be right back."

Ted went to the end of the arcade. For a moment the beat of his heart muffled the noise of the square. He wished he could wave to Bert or, better yet, kiss her good-bye. But he didn't trust her or, at this point, himself. If he turned around now, it would be for good. Ted plunged into the Place des Chameaux, hurrying toward the medina.

The main street was hushed, dim, and deserted. Blowing from the town gate to the square, wind lashed at the loose sand, but made little sound. As the temperature tumbled, Ted had to quicken his pace to stop shivering. The boys were no longer playing soccer. Their ball, he saw, had fallen into the tangle of rags it really was. This was a bad sign. They might have gone to the smoldering bus. Or to the police.

Inching along the last mud houses, he pressed his hands flat against them to dry his palms. Despite the cold, he was sweating and his shirt had dampened to a clammy plaster on his back. The gun barrel jabbed into his belly as he craned his neck around the corner and peered up the blind alley.

Ants had driven the bus deep into the dead-end. But a thin Arab boy perched like a sparrow on the rear bumper, gazing at Ted, not at the back window, which was opaque with an oily patch of smoke. Ted halted twenty feet from the VW and called, *"Viens! Vite!"* If the fuse was burning, the bus might blow any moment, and the boy would be killed.

"Viens ici!"

The little boy looked up, leaped from the bumper, and loped to Ted, his bare feet slapping the unpaved alley. Filthy and raggedly dressed, he shivered uncontrollably. He pointed to his eye, then to the VW. *"J'suis gardien."*

"Oui. Bon. Merci beaucoup." Rapidly backtracking, bringing the boy with him, Ted dropped a dirham into his hand and hustled him toward the square. *"C'est tout. Va-t'en. Merci encore."*

He braced himself, then reentered the alley. He'd taken several wary strides when he realized that stalling wouldn't help. Dashing to the door on the driver's side, he knew if it blew now he'd be burnt to a crisp, studded with shrapnel and slivers of glass. The bus was dense with smoke, but on the rear floor he noticed no flicker, no flame.

Relieved, he pushed the button on the door handle, and immediately his relief vanished. Racing around to the passenger's side, he found that door locked, too. Battling his panic, Ted tested the back door and the rear window, but Ants had obeyed orders. Senselessly he slapped his pants pockets, although he knew he didn't have the keys.

Then closing his eyes, he leaned his forehead on the cool window and whispered, Think. Keep calm and think. If he had a coat hanger, a piece of wire, a fork . . . But he didn't, and couldn't go to get the keys from Ants. They'd lost too much time already and someone was sure to see him scurrying back and forth.

Dropping to his hands and knees, he crawled around the evil-smelling alley, scrabbling for a rock, for anything heavy and hard enough to crack a window. His fingers slithered through muck, and the odor of urine, and worse, was sickening. When he stood up to escape the stench, there was someone beside him. The little boy had come back.

Ted chased him from the alley, but because he had no reason to believe he would stay away, he ran to the bus, pulling the pistol from his belt, and swung the butt at a window. The sound astonished him. He thought the gun had gone off. But the window had shattered into a spiderweb, and he had to hit it again to punch a hole in its center. Reaching his arm gingerly past the spikes of glass, he unlocked the door.

On the floor in back the cigarette had rolled off the rag fuse and burned down to a nub. Ted tossed the butt into the alley. There was no time for that. The VW smelled of gasoline, but he retwisted the rag, tightened it in the spout, then fumbled a book of matches from his pocket. Striking one, he extended it toward the fuse, which struck like a snake, snatching the flame from his hand. A forked tongue of blue fire flicked at him as it ate up the oily cloth.

The fuse was burning faster than he'd expected. Slamming the door, Ted sprinted for the corner, where the boy was watching him, bewildered. He'd seen everything, but there was nothing to be done about that. Grabbing him to his chest, Ted didn't break stride as he raced up the street, his face streaming icy sweat.

In the square, he unloaded the boy at a crowd listening to a storyteller. At that instant, there was a loud crumping noise and the ground shook slightly. Though puzzled, the storyteller gave the impression he had created this special effect. But the people turned from him to look at the medina.

By the time Ted got behind the pillar, a thick stem of smoke was climbing toward the clouds. Touching the low grey ceiling, it blossomed like a black orchid. Everyone in the market—even Phil, his red hair far away in that sea of dark, uplifted faces—had swiveled around to stare at it. But Ted watched the jailhouse and was the first to notice the hatch swing in on its hinges and the six guards saunter out, strapping on their shoulder harnesses and holsters. Three of them had Matka 47's, and they acted irritable at being disturbed until they saw the flames that had licked over the rooftops. As they rushed to the fire, most of the crowd— some frightened, others merely curious—surged forward, following them into the medina.

Ants smiled as they stepped from under the arcade, through the almost empty square, toward the Sûreté Nationale. But Phil, who fell in with them, wasn't smiling, and neither were Ted and Polo. Ted took the VW license plates from Ants and tossed them on a stand where there were hundreds of old plates. Near the last stall, on the far side of the market, he spotted the sawed-off cripple they had seen two nights ago in the souq. He had slipped the sandals from his hands and was sifting through a garbage heap.

Shoving the hatch with all his strength, Polo stumbled when it opened effortlessly. He was the first one in, Ants and Phil were next, and Ted went last, shutting the hatch behind them. There was a metal bolt which he slid home with a loud clank, locking the guards out and them in.

Polo had hauled the clerk from his cage and forced him against the wall.

"No need for that," said Ted. "He knows why we're here."

But Ted wasn't sure. Bundled in his djellabah, the man said nothing and didn't show any reaction. When Polo let go of him, he shuffled down the corridor, leaned his back to the door, and dealt it a kick.

"Tell him to take out his hands," barked Polo. "He could be armed."

Ted repeated the order in French, in a softer voice, and the clerk brought forth his fists which were blue and chil-blained. The brazier in the corner radiated less warmth than usual, and the flies seemed thick enough to smother the coals.

Polo was kicking the door, too. "Where the shit's the gun? Jesus, get ready."

When Ted drew the .357 magnum, Phil and Ants drifted to the left, Polo to the right, dragging the clerk with him. On the other side of the door, a key ring jangled, the lock untumbled, and Driss appeared, smiling benignly.

"Welcome, my . . . ."

Polo clapped a hand to his mouth, wrenching his arm into a hammerlock, and Driss's visored cap clattered to the floor. "All right, fuck face, unlock the door."

"Are you crazy?" Ted stepped in to separate them, but had to be careful of the pistol. Ants helped him, yanking Polo by the belt.

"Il est bête! Il est absolument fou," Driss spat out indignantly.

"Another trick like that," said Ted as he twisted the front of Polo's sweaty shirt, "and you're finished. Hear me?"

"I don't trust him."

"Shut up and keep your hands off him."

"Please," said Phil, "we're wasting time."

"Since your friend insists on being theatrical," said Driss, recovering his dignity along with his battered cap, "let him save it for the prisoners."

Ted motioned to the cellblock. *"Ouvrez la porte."*

The neatly groomed guard flung the door wide, crying in French, "You'll never get away with this. We'll capture you and kill you." He held trembling hands over his head and cowered into the corridor, speaking now in Arabic to be certain everyone understood. "You're mad. You'll be punished."

Polo ripped the key ring from his belt and raced to Gypsy's cell. Though the boy wore a wide grin, he appeared not to believe what he saw. Phil limped after Polo. A little color had brightened his cheeks, but he still wasn't smiling. When the bars slid back, the brothers embraced.

Ted stood near the entrance to the cellblock, covering Driss, who crouched in front of him, gibbering in well-rehearsed panic, while the clerk seemed to cling listlessly to Ants, not so much held as supported. The prisoners had pitched to their feet, shaking the bars and shouting in Arabic. They looked skinny and sick and every bit as miserable as Gypsy, but Ted tried to ignore them by concentrating on the other end of the corridor, where the three of them took their time, far too much time. Polo was whispering to Gypsy, who nodded and spoke to his cellmates. Suddenly Phil wedged himself in the doorway in an attempt to block the Moroccans, but they pushed past him.

Ted couldn't say who screamed first. He cried, "Stop!" as Polo started to unlock the other cells, and at the same instant Driss shot to his feet, shrieking, *"Non! Non!"* Whirling on Ted, he yelled, "This was not part of the bargain. Only your friend! Only your friend!"

But a dozen prisoners had charged into the corridor, and the rest of them raised a clamor of entreaties and threats. Polo didn't need encouragement. Speeding through the cellblock, he had freed everyone when Driss jumped back from Ted, babbling in French and Arabic, tore loose his holster flap, and fired into the crowd.

The shot deafened Ted; smoke singed his nostrils. For a second he was blind. Then as his eyes cleared, the prisoners were squeezing to either side, away from Phil, who was caught up in a crazy dance with his crutch. He staggered back and forth, looking for a place to lie down, but the aluminum crutch propped him upright. "Help. Help me, Gypsy," he whimpered. But when Gypsy, trapped in the crowd, couldn't get to him, he appealed to Ted, one hand outstretched.

A purple sore had swollen his right cheek, and from a bullet hole in its center poured a stream of blood. His legs crumbled, the crutch flew from under him, and Phil crashed to the floor, bleeding bubbles from his mouth.

The sound of his fall confused Ted, for it was followed by an insanely outsized echo. Driss had fired a second shot. A prisoner toppled to his knees.

"Kill him!" Polo hollered, and like everything Ted saw and heard, the words seemed to reach him from another planet. "Kill that bastard!"

Only as he aimed at Driss's temple did a familiar dread force things into focus. This was what he had feared, what he had hoped to protect himself against, and so, rather than shoot, he said, "Drop it."

Driss squeezed off a third round, and a prisoner fell. Ted grasped the guard's arm, still thinking there had to be another way to stop him. But Driss spun abruptly, knocking Ted back. *"Toi ... toi ..."* he stammered, leveling the gun at his chest.

Ted lifted his hand, as if to deflect the bullet with his bare palm, and started to retreat, but he was already against the bars. "Wait a minute." His French failed him, not that it mattered. As he saw from Driss's eyes—the one milky and mild, the other narrowed in anger as he aimed—there was nothing he could say to save himself and a single thing he could do.

From the hip he shot first and, hit by the hard ball cartridge, half of Driss's plump face flew apart. The flesh, ear, eye, and bone blasted up under his cap, splattering the polished visor and ripping it off his head. Then everything washed away. Ted felt the splashing wave on his fingers and wrist as Driss smacked against the bars, bouncing to the concrete, dead before he hit the floor.

The inmates flooded forward, hurdling the bodies of the two prisoners, then Phil and Driss. Breaking loose from Ants, the jail clerk backed into an empty cell and shut the grate. He was safe, since none of the Moroccans wanted to waste the time to find the keys and kill him. They streamed into the other room, ran down the hall, and through the double doors to the square.

"They should've stuck together. Where are they going?" Polo mumbled to Gypsy who was bent, dumbfounded, over his brother. Phil was on his face, a jagged hole at the base of his skull.

Ted grabbed Polo by his coarse, black hair and banged his head against the bars. "You son-of-a-bitch, are you satisfied? Are you?" He jabbed the gun barrel into the soft, whiskery underside of his jaw. "See what you did? See what you made me do? We gave that man our word."

"I didn't know . . . I didn't think . . ."

"Shut up! I warned you. I told you not to pull anything. You dumb fuck, look what you did."

"Why didn't you stop him?" asked Polo, his eyes wide and wild.

"I said shut up." Ted banged his skull against the bars again. "I'm watching you. Do you hear me? One more screw-up and I swear I'll kill you."

Then he turned to Gypsy, who was tugging at his trouser leg.

"Help me. We gotta do something." He had tears on his glasses; the lenses looked like two silver disks.

Gypsy had rolled Phil over, so Ted couldn't see where the shell had burst through his brain. But blood oozed from the hole in his cheek and from his mouth, and now from his nose and ears. His eyes were open, and they had filled with blood too. Ted put a hand to Phil's scrawny chest, then a finger to his pulse, and felt nothing. Though still twitching, he was dead.

He stood up, sick to his stomach, and pried Gypsy's hand off his pants. There was no sense checking on Driss. He went to the two prisoners, who were alive, but just barely and wouldn't be for long. One had gotten it in the chest above the heart, the other in the throat. Ted had seldom seen so much blood.

"We gotta get him to a doctor," moaned Gypsy, still kneeling next to his brother.

"It's too late," said Ted.

"No. Look, he's alive. He's moving."

"I'm telling you it's too late. Let's go."

"No. I won't." He clung to Phil's arm like a life line.

"Gimme a hand," Ted said to Ants, who was also in tears. "Drag him if you have to."

"Phil?"

"No, Gypsy."

"What about Phil?"

"He's dead."

"We can't just leave him."

"We have to. The guards may be back any minute."

He hauled Gypsy to his feet, but the boy wouldn't stand on his own. So Ted shoved him on Ants while he rifled Phil's pockets. There was a little loose change and a few keys on a chain, which he left. But he took Phil's wallet with its identity papers, thinking this might slow down the Moroccans, and that they, themselves, might need the ID's.

Then squatting there among the dead and bleeding bodies, he tried to control his hoarse breathing and think what else he could do. Because of the wound, Phil's face was almost unrecognizable. He was an anonymous, skinny redhead dressed in drab khakis. Ted had a ghoulish idea, but thought it was worth trying.

Twisting the crutch from Phil's elbow, he set it aside, and stripped off his orthopedic shoes and blue lisle socks.

"Gimme your glasses and sandals," he said to Gypsy, who shook his head, whimpering.

"What are you doing?" asked Ants.

"Hurry! Hand 'em to me. We don't have much time." But Ted had to do it himself. He yanked the rubber thongs from Gypsy's feet and slipped them onto Phil's. Then he threw Gypsy's rimless glasses to the floor. One lens cracked.

"Have you flipped? What are you doing?" Ants asked again, although he must have known. It looked like Gypsy lying there dead. And that's what Ted meant for the authorities to think. Now there was nothing to involve them except the word of the other prisoners, and no one would believe their story.

After forcing Gypsy's feet into Phil's shoes, Ted stuffed the socks into his own pocket, picked up the crutch, and said, "Let's get out of here." He held Gypsy by one arm, Ants had the other, and they towed him toward the door.

Polo darted in front of them. "How about this one?" He pointed to the stony-faced clerk who sat in a new cage.

"Get out of my way."

"He could identify us."

"I said move."

When Ted gestured with the gun, Polo gave ground, saying, "Wait. I'm telling you, we've gotta kill him. He's the only witness."

"You asshole, there was a jail full of witnesses. You set them loose. I shoot anyone, it'll be you."

But Ted knew though no one would believe the prisoners, they might take this man's word. Still he couldn't bring himself to kill the clerk. Pausing at the cell, he said in French, "Don't tell anyone about us. If you do, they'll punish you too. Blame it on the prisoners."

There was no sign that the clerk understood.

"See," said Polo, "we can't leave him alive."

Ted and Ants went by him, into the other room, and down the hall with Gypsy. Polo overtook them in the shadow of the tall, double doors flung open by the fleeing prisoners. The square, with its stalls and braziers unattended, was unnaturally quiet. The sawed-off cripple didn't make much noise pawing through the trash.

"I don't like this," said Polo, his face pallid behind the stubbly beard.

"Then stay here."

At that, Polo hurried into the marketplace. Ants, Ted, and Gypsy moved out deliberately. Above the medina, the column of black smoke was snowing white ashes. When they heard gun shots, Polo stopped.

"Keep going," said Ted.

As they reached the middle of the market, the racket grew louder, and on the main street of the medina Ted saw people coming toward them. The prisoners had run into the crowd at the fire. Now the police, in pursuit, were shooting at everybody.

"Steady," said Ted. "There's plenty of time."

But Polo broke into a sprint, his boots kicking up dirt. Though they urged Gypsy on a little faster, he and Ants didn't panic. By the time they'd gone under the arcade, people were crushing into the square, shoppers and prisoners alike scattering for cover.

Given enough targets already, the guards didn't notice the group go up the street through the souq. Behind them, there was the metallic stutter of an automatic rifle. Someone had cut loose with a Matka 47. Angry and appalled that he couldn't stop the slaughter he'd helped start, Ted hurled Phil's crutch onto the roof of a grain warehouse.

"Ted, Ted," cried Bert, doubling back to them. "I was going. Honest, I was. But I thought you'd need these." She held up the djellabahs.

"There's no time."

"Why? Where's Phil? You've got blood all over. What happened?"

"Phil's hurt. We have to help him." Gypsy dug in his heels, but didn't have the strength to struggle for long.

"Please, somebody tell me," said Bert.

"Phil's dead," said Ted. "So are three other men."

"Oh god, no." She tried to turn, but Ted wouldn't let her.

"There's nothing you can do," he said, steering her up the street, steeling himself against that desolating knowledge. Over the years he'd left many people and places behind, and now the mess on the cellblock floor added immeasurably to the list. It was all he could do to keep moving.

The souq was almost deserted. While everyone else had gone to the fire, the oldest women and youngest children minded the shops. Among them, a few beggars who couldn't budge on their own waited for the pushcart to collect them. In the grisly street of butcher stalls, the carcasses rotated on hooks—massive, macabre mobiles.

Far in front, Polo waved and shouted for them to hurry. From the clammy tunnel in the town wall, they came onto the vacant lot where Puff clambered from the Land-Rover to greet Gypsy with a great whoop of joy. But when he was in her arms, he whispered to her and she went wooden. "No. It can't be," she cried.

"Into the cars," called Polo, striving to command.

Puff led Gypsy to the Land-Rover, Ants took Bert toward the Renault. Ted wavered between the two cars, tempted to tell them to go on without him, that he wanted nothing more to do with them or their goddamn money.

"What the hell are you doing?" asked Polo, revving the engine.

Ted reacted slowly and hazily, lowering his head instead of answering. His gory fingers still gripped the nickel-plated pistol. Blood splotched the right sleeve of his shirt up to the elbow. But, of course, it was Driss's or Phil's or those Moroccans'. It was always someone else's on his hands. He could wash it off and get away clean, yet he couldn't forget what he'd done, no more than he'd forget these people. Without him they didn't have a prayer. They'd soon spill more blood, most likely their own. Their one chance was to go on together. Thrusting the .357 under his belt, feeling hollow and half-dead, Ted slumped into the driver's seat of the Renault.

V

AS THEY sped toward the High Atlas Mountains, the peaks were lost in clouds which had sunk lower until they'd massed solidly at the snow line. Devoid of sun and shadow, the land disclosed its true starkness. The mountains became a forbidding, monotonous barrier. The rich colors of the countryside changed to dull sepia. Any suggestion of warmth or softness had vanished.

Howling across the plains, the wind twisted the gum trees, tearing loose leaves and limbs and shearing one trunk flush with the ground. It had crashed across both lanes of the road, ripping down the telephone and telegraph lines. Ted, then Polo, detoured onto the bumpy shoulder, around the tangle of green branches and black wires. That's a break, thought Ted. The snapped lines would give them more time, and every minute counted.

At a fork in the road, they veered east toward Ouarzazate, and the Anti-Atlas range hunched before them, its barren foothills curving just under the clouds. The wind wailed at their backs now, goading them on with violent gusts that got into the cars through the cracks and needled grains of sand at their necks. As the asphalt snaked through steep terrain, the air cooled considerably. A few shepherds, heavily shawled and with rags wrapped around their faces, tended herds of sheep that seemed to graze on stones. They saw no one else, and met no cars moving toward them.

When something hissed at the windshield, Ted thought it was sand and didn't switch on the wipers. Even a moment later, when he realized it was rain, he waited, not willing to concede that anything more could go wrong. They had to drive all night and didn't dare slow down. Hitting the button for the wipers, he pushed harder at the gas, hoping to outdistance the rain before the road turned slick.

In the back seat Bert stared blankly through the window, her arms folded tight, her hands tucked under them for warmth. Though she refused to meet Ted's eyes in the rearview mirror, he didn't have to be a mind reader to imagine her thoughts. Her small-boned face bore more sadness than seemed possible. Her tears had dried, but their red tracks remained as she grappled with an experience for which nothing—not even her months in jail—could have prepared her.

Ted wasn't doing any better. This was one area where they were all amateurs. Although he'd watched a lot of men die, he'd learned nothing from it except how to hide his feelings and to keep functioning. That was a well-practiced skill—sheer self-protection—that involved no understanding. When he was honest with himself, the thought of death reduced him to mute incomprehension. People talked about dying well, but nobody did it much different or better, and nothing he'd heard of made it easy. When your time was up, you went out like everyone else, alone and like a rookie.

The storm, which had started as a stinging mist, began to beat in big drops at the roof. Rain pocked the mud at the roadside and orange rivulets flowed into streams. The land couldn't absorb much water, so it drained off onto the asphalt, transforming it into a spillway, awash with silt, stones, and twigs. Plowing uphill, the Renault spread great fans of spray which must have blinded Polo, who drove dangerously close behind.

Ted steered clear of the shoulder which was losing ground to the flood, and struggled not to grow angry or bitter at the way they'd botched the job. He had to concentrate. One skid off the pavement and they'd spend hours hauling the car out.

Yet Polo sounded his horn, forcing him near the edge of the road. As the Land-Rover lumbered by, unfurling sheets of water, no one in either car exchanged a glance. Gypsy and Puff sat at opposite ends of the back seat, wearing identical expressions of bewilderment.

Polo, as usual, looked angry—at the weather, at his car for not going faster, and perhaps at himself.

Ted was furious too, and couldn't believe he'd ever trusted that bastard. I should of shot him instead of Driss. But by then it was too late. That one lapse had cost four lives. Maybe more by now. And for what? He must have had something in mind. A revolution with the prisoners as his personal, ragtag army? The imbecility of the notion enraged Ted. In the heat of the moment, why had he hesitated? Now there was no way to get rid of Polo, except killing him in cold blood.

The road was little more than one lane and as the cars climbed, the clouds coasted down to meet them. Swallowed

by fog, Ted could distinguish Polo's taillights, a jagged
ledge of rock on the right, and absolute emptiness to the
left, where nothing marked the end of the asphalt and the
rim of a canyon. Though he hugged the rock wall to the
right, that, too, had its hazards. Fallen slag clattered under
the tires, and oozing mud made it impossible to steer a
straight line or negotiate the curves at anything more than
a nervewracking crawl.

When Ants said, "It's snowing," Ted thought the boy
should have known better than to joke. But then Bert said,
"No, it's hail," and after a closer look, Ted knew that it was
neither. It was sleet, and since they were in the clouds, the
icy pellets seemed not to fall. They appeared with a metallic
ping! on the windshield and hood.

The wipers quickly acquired a crust, rattling uselessly in
front of his face. The road became a sheet of beveled glass
and at a corner the tires lost their grip. There was a terrifying instant of total drift as Ted, drawing on reserves of
self-control, turned into the skid, toward the cliff. That
straightened the Renault, and at the next curve he did the
same thing, advancing in a series of tense power glides.
Low gears ground, tires whined on ice. There was no other
sound.

Despite its four-wheel drive, the Land-Rover fishtailed,
too, and the brake lights blinked and swayed in Ted's eyes,
so that he feared he'd follow them over the edge, thunder-
ing down to the thorny canyon floor. Even had they wanted
to stop, there was no safe place to pull off the road. They
had to push on until the weather let up or they got to level
ground.

Eventually the weather and terrain both changed, but
there was no let-up. While the road crossed a broad valley
swept by winds that lashed the cars, the sleet turned to

snow. Hard-driven lines of it buried the macadam beneath dry powder. Through this treeless waste, telephone poles were the only landmarks, and they didn't always march parallel to the road. Several times as he set his course by them, Polo was thrown back by gullies, ruts, and boulders.

When the telephone and electricity wires cut to the south, the two-car caravan continued east into the darkness. For miles they drove blind, blundering off and bumping back onto the pavement. The Land-Rover easily withstood the pounding, but Ted was afraid the Renault would fall apart. Finally Ants had to get out and lead the cars, searching for the road with his feet. They moved safely then, but with agonizing slowness.

Once they came to a clearing where the wind had wiped the asphalt clean, Ants climbed in, and they drove at a normal speed. A few miles ahead, however, the scooped-up snow waited for them in what resembled a broad sand dune. Polo never slowed down, and the Land-Rover piledrove through the drift. But Ted didn't have the power, and the Renault snagged at its crest.

Floundering hip-deep, he and Ants rocked and heaved at the rear bumper while Bert gunned the accelerator. Polo staggered around to lend a hand. By the time they'd worked the car free, new snow had filled their footprints, and the drift looked like no one could break through it.

"Do we go on?" Polo was panting.

"Have to."

"No one's after us in this."

"We got through. So could someone else. Let's roll."

Though the telephone poles reappeared, driving was no easier. Now it was dark and the distance between poles had lengthened. Through these empty spaces they glided silently, while the lines, sheathed in ice, drooped lower and the wind threatened to sweep the cars into this electric web.

When they saw a wire that had snapped of its own ice-encrusted weight, Polo parked and struggled back to Ted. "We're nuts to go any farther."

"We'd be crazier to stop. We have to cross the border before those people in Tazenzit put things together."

"We won't make it tonight," said Polo. "Not in this weather. And how the hell will it help to get lost or have a wreck? We could have taken a dozen wrong turns already. Why not camp here?"

Ted glanced around. There was no cover, no break in the wind. "We'll freeze."

"No, we'll keep the cars together and build a fire between them."

"Someone'll see it."

"Who? We haven't passed anyone."

He studied Polo's face instead of the storm. Against the white background, he looked darker, more intense than ever. Why, after his earlier panic, was he so damn eager to stop?

"Come on, man. Another drift like that last one and you'll drop your transmission." He stamped his feet, blowing on his bare hands.

"Okay. But don't go far from the road."

They parked the cars side by side, protecting the space between them from the wind and blowing snow. While Polo attacked one of the telephone poles with an axe, the rest of them dug away the icy crust with shivering hands. The ground was frozen solid. Tufts of grass bristled like wire brushes. No one spoke. No one looked at anyone else for fear he'd have to speak. They listened for a car, a truck, footsteps, any sound of a pursuer. But they heard only the wind and the *chuck-chuck-chuck* of Polo's axe, measured, deliberate, muffled. As he leaned his weight into each stroke, Puff and Bert winced as if he were hacking at them. Then they stood bolt upright as the pole splintered and fell.

Polo brought back an armful of kindling and several sizeable logs. After gathering scraps of trash from the Land-Rover and the Renault, he lit a small blaze and fed it slivers of wood. When the flame grew tall and steady, he tossed on a fat section of the telephone pole, sending up an explosion of sparks that sizzled as they sank in the snow. Now that Polo had recovered his confidence, Ted knew he should have stepped in to reassert command, but bothered by bigger problems and sick of the constant seesawing battle between them, he said nothing.

The bonfire gave off a great deal of smoke, a pungent, tarry smell, and surprising warmth. They squatted on their heels around it, leaning against the cars. While Bert opened a few cans for dinner, Ted stared at the embers, weary and depressed. In the army, he'd known troopers who returned from every mission elated, convinced no one could kill them. The bloodier it had been, the fewer that had survived, the more they thought it proved their point. They were invincible. But each time Ted returned, it had been with a profounder sadness for those who hadn't made it and a sense of guilt that he had.

He was experiencing the familiar emotions now—guilt and sorrow. They all felt horrible about Phil and showed it by their concern for Gypsy. But didn't anyone, Ted wondered, care about Driss and the other two? And the prisoners who'd be captured and punished, didn't they count?

He thought again of Driss. He'd never shot anyone that close, or anyone who wasn't an enemy. To learn about killing, you had to do it at that range. No amount of plinking at stick figures from two hundred yards, seeing them drop like bugs, was the same. The only thing he could compare it to was pounding the little boy senseless that night in Nigeria. Was Gypsy's freedom worth it?

No, the question was unfair. Or at any rate futile.

Gypsy shivered and sweated. The fire highlighted his prison pallor, and his head drooped low on the slender stem of his neck. Though Puff had wrapped him in a blanket, then in her large arms, he trembled and his weak eyes watered with sadness and smoke. He won't last many nights like this, thought Ted. They had to get him to a doctor as soon as they were in Algeria.

Rooting in the Land-Rover, Polo returned with the shortwave radio and his guns. He stuck the pistol under his belt, stood the M-16 against the car, sat down, and flicked on the set. Scratchy and faint from static, the Moroccan stations played uninterrupted music—yowling, nasal chants accompanied by high-pitched string instruments and tinny cymbals that set one's teeth on edge. There were no announcements.

"That's bad," said Polo, but he looked delighted as he tuned in the American Armed Forces Network and heard the news that for the third time in two years there had been an attempted coup in Morocco. Though the king was believed to be out of danger, Rabat was under strict curfew and army troops patrolled the streets. Most of the fighting was taking place in provincial towns in the south, where resistance to the government was surprisingly stiff. There was sporadic gunfire in the larger cities, but more serious violence was thought to have been averted by an early show of force and the mass arrest of student and leftist leaders. In a brief statement to the press, the king blamed communists and agitators from Libya for the disturbance. Casualty figures weren't released, but at least one American was reported to have been killed.

When the commentator turned, then, with no change in tone or tempo to the sports, Polo switched off the radio, and Ted felt much worse. As always their advantages seemed the result of other people's suffering, yet his mind raced to sort through the news. Would the borders be closely guarded? Or, if the situation were as serious as it sounded, would they be able to slip like minnows through a net cast for larger fish? Clearly, in case of a coup, the army and the police would have more important things to do than look for them. And if the clerk kept his mouth closed, if they believed Phil's body was Gypsy's, no one would bother about them at all.

"Soon as the storm lifts, I think we should go back," said Polo.

"You heard the man. Phil's dead," said Puff, who had tears on her lashes.

"Maybe he didn't mean Phil," Gypsy muttered.

"I'm sorry," Ted said. "But he couldn't of lived with a wound like that. He was gone before I got to him."

While everyone, except Ted, had his head down, Polo darted a glance at them, then said, "We should still go back. After all, we started this and we should finish it. Those people need us."

"What the hell are you talking about?" asked Ted.

"It's simple, really. There's a revolution on, and we started it. We didn't intend to, but now we have an obligation to the people. I say we head for one of the towns where they're fighting and offer our help. With a little luck and organization, we might . . ."

"Are you out of your goddamn mind?" said Ted. "We started anything, it was a slaughter, not a revolution. You wouldn't last a week. Those folks you *liberated* aren't likely to last that long."

"Okay, the odds are against us, but Castro had twelve men in the Sierra Maestra. It can be done. It depends how much you're willing to sacrifice. Anyone with me?"

What Polo suggested was so stupid, Ted didn't have to object. They'd had horrifying problems breaking Gypsy from a cracker-box jail. How could they lead a revolution that probably didn't exist? He wasn't convinced that Polo himself was serious. He seemed to have proposed the scheme—and not with his normal belligerence—out of some dim inkling of what he ought to do.

Though angry, Ted was afraid to humiliate Polo. Badgering him into a face-saving escapade would only jeopardize their chances. From that day's ride, he realized they couldn't bank on the Renault. Snow had slowed it; the desert might stop it dead. They needed the Land-Rover. If Polo decided to leave, Ted had to stop him and he was willing to do almost anything rather than use the gun.

"Look, friend, there's one thing you're forgetting. That was an Armed Forces broadcast. How much of their news do you usually believe? Nothing, I bet. For all we know, there might not be a revolution. There might not even of been any shooting except in Tazenzit. The king could of taken that as an excuse to settle a few political scores, then covered his tracks with a lot of bullshit about a communist coup."

"He's right," said Ants. "You always told us not to trust the news."

Polo's shoulders were bobbing like a boxer's before a fight. "Still, I'd like to have a look."

"Suppose someone's chasing us? You'd smack right into them. After what we did, they won't slap us behind bars a couple of years. They bother having a trial, we'd be up for murder."

"Shit, didn't I tell you we should have shot the clerk? We'd be in the clear. Now if there's been an uprising, how the hell are we going to get past the army?"

"Same plan," Ted said calmly. "Tomorrow, we'll hole up somewhere till dark. Traveling at night we should reach Algeria in ten, twelve hours."

"That's no answer. There must be troops in Ouarzazate, Agdz, and Zagora, and they'll set up roadblocks."

"They don't know which direction we're headed," said Gypsy.

"They won't have to. They'll broadcast an all-points bulletin."

"By that time, we'll be far from here," Ted assured him. "As for roadblocks, we'll circle around the ones we can. Those we can't, we'll bluff our way through. Nobody spotted the cars, and Gypsy'll have Phil's papers."

"I spent six months with those people at the jail," said Gypsy, shivering, "and I bet nobody'll give an accurate description of what happened. The prisoners will lie to protect themselves, and no one's likely to believe the clerk."

"You're right," said Ted. "He'll be rooting for us to escape. They capture us, we might finger him, and the first thing he'll have to explain is why he's alive and Driss isn't."

"I'll write a letter and tell them why," Polo grumbled, glancing into the pot which Bert held over the fire. "That ready?"

"Whenever you are."

After she'd passed the paper plates of pork and beans, Puff asked them to stand, and they formed a circle around the fire. Ted contained within himself too many conflicting emotions to be bothered by embarrassment. Extending a hand to Bert on his left and Ants on his right, he squeezed tight and chanted the chorus of Oms as fervently as anybody. Though he didn't know to whom the prayer was directed, they were obviously begging for deliverance.

As they ate, Polo started to seethe again and, ripping chunks from the loaf of Berber bread, he reflected upon the new concession he'd agreed to. Of course, he could have gone back alone. At last there was a revolution. Wasn't that what he'd waited for? But he knew he wasn't going, and wondered how much more of himself he could surrender before he had nothing left.

Beneath the heat of his anger, he was agitated by a cold terror that had needled into his heart and couldn't be pried loose. Ashamed, he recalled what a coward he'd been. His mind and mouth had functioned in something like slow motion, and he couldn't have killed the clerk. He'd barely been able to hold himself together. Then in the square, hearing shots, he'd scurried for cover while everyone watched him blow his cool.

He glanced at Ted, and his anger and fear struck a fitful balance. A bastard like Kuyler, born without a brain in his head, could convince people to follow him, and in a face-off, he never flinched. Polo hated him for this, yet wished he could combine one half of the hick's strength with his own commitments. That's the kind of man you had to be if you hoped to accomplish anything. A nerveless redneck, not bothered by blood. But how did you acquire a soul like shoe leather? Suppressing a shudder, he remembered the moment when Ted had pulled the trigger and Driss's temple exploded. As the guard's hat and face flew away, Ted hadn't so much as blinked.

*   *   *

Then the Arab stumbled in from the dark. Puff shrieked, and Polo dropped his plate and drew the pistol. The six of them swung to the right where a wraithlike figure was confused by the scream, temporarily blinded by the firelight. Since his djellabah was bleached by snow and hoarfrost, he could have vanished just as suddenly as he'd appeared by withdrawing two steps into the storm. Instead he came into the camp, wailing and waving his hands.

"Stop!" said Polo, and if Ted hadn't wrenched his arm, he might have shot.

When Ants bounced up to block the man, Ted said, "Leave him alone."

"What the shit, he could be a cop." Polo cocked the pistol.

"Take another look. He's no cop."

The Arab wore sandals, and his broken-nailed toes were blue from the cold. The fire melted the snow on his djellabah, exposing makeshift patches and spots of fraying dry-rot. Shivering and sobbing, he thumped his chest, knocking the hood back from his face. Sun and wind and sand had pinched his eyes into perpetual squints and scorched his cheeks the color of overcooked meat. A black beard, unevenly trimmed, traced the line of his jaw to the point where his sideburns would have begun. A filthy turban covered his shaved head.

"What's he saying?"

"Shut up and lemme listen."

As the man moaned in Arabic, Ted recognized a few French words—among them, *berger* and *moutons*—and gathered he was a shepherd who had lost his flock. Since the animals apparently weren't his, he had good reason to be sorry, for the owner would punish him. With hands as knotted and dark as cypress knees, he pointed beyond the cars, cursing the snow and begging them and Allah to save him. He didn't seem surprised, though, that no one answered his prayers.

When his sobbing subsided, Ted led him to a place next to the fire, and Puff fixed him some beans and bread. Sitting in the mud, he moved the plate an inch under his chin, squeezed the beans into compact balls, and shoveled them into his mouth with his right hand. If he thought there was anything extraordinary about finding these foreigners, a fire, and food during a blizzard in this barren mountain pass, he didn't show it. On the surface, at least, he accepted the encounter as natural. Or as natural as anything in a life dominated by the inconsistencies of richer men, the seasons, and superstition. When he finished eating, he unwound his turban, mopped his face, blew his nose on a corner of the cloth, then rewound it.

Polo checked the action on the M-16. It clicked sharply as it closed. "I'm going to have a look around."

"For what?" asked Gypsy.

"While we're diddling ourselves, this guy could have friends near here. I don't care to be caught with my pants down again."

"Not even by a shepherd?" asked Ants.

"Not by anybody."

"Shit, man, save yourself the trouble. Say you spot someone, what'll you do?"

"That depends." He tapped the butt of the .38 to be sure it was secure under his belt.

"You're liable to get lost," said Bert.

"Don't build my hopes up," muttered Ants, throwing a paper plate into the fire.

After a last look at them, almost as if he wished they'd stop him, Polo left.

"You don't think he's dangerous, do you?" Bert asked Ted, nodding to the Arab.

"No."

Yet the man could create problems. If an army search party found him tomorrow, he could tell what he'd seen and which direction they'd taken. Maybe, thought Ted, we should drag him with us for sixty miles or so, then dump him. But that might be more trouble than it was worth. What if he refused and fought?

The Arab had flung himself full-length on the ground in front of the fire. Warmth and company were two of the very few consolations in his life and, on this night when he'd lost so much, he had no intention of leaving them. His djellabah steamed as it dried, loamy-smelling like a forest after rain. Folding his arms under his head, he shut his eyes and slept.

"Nothing like having a live yule log in the house," cracked Ants.

"What must he think of us?" asked Puff.

"Not much," said Gypsy. "There were guys like him in jail. Berbers from way back in the mountains. Some of them hadn't met more than a dozen people from outside their villages. You'd think they'd be scared or curious, but they weren't. They acted like we were unreal or part of the furniture."

"Let's hope this fella thinks we're unreal," said Ted, "and that he has a short memory."

Polo was sorry as soon as he left camp, but was too stubborn to turn back. The snow was deep and difficult to slog through. The wind had piled up drifts as high as his hips, hiding gullies and ravines. He tripped into one and had to dig himself out with the rifle. This is dangerous, he thought, and stupid. I could break a leg and freeze to death, for all anyone would care. Yet he pushed on as a kind of penance for his panic that afternoon.

Behind him a hazy dome of light arched over the cars. You really want to prove something, keep walking till that's out of sight. Get off on your own, in over your head, and see what happens. But he knew he wouldn't, and it nagged at him like another defeat as he circled within striking distance of the fire. Though he was desperate to snip the threads that bound him, this valley was too broad and dark, the night too deep, to break loose now.

As ice beaded on his eyelashes and moustache, he whistled through the frozen whiskers of his nose. His toes and bare fingers tingled, and he wondered whether he'd have the strength or agility to aim and shoot the M-16. And would he have the guts?

This has got to end, thought Polo. I'm just torturing myself. I'll make my move and take a stand when the time is right. Then an idea, cutting and cold as the wind, occurred to him. Hugging the rifle to his chest, he trudged through the snow toward the light.

No one reacted when he entered the area between the cars. He'd meant to surprise them, to prove how ill-prepared they were, but they continued talking about the Moroccan. Polo's moustache and hair had been powdered white, as though the hike had aged him forty years. Tossing his head, he stepped to the fire and slapped the snow from his field jacket.

"Can't see a damn thing out there. They could be camped right next to us."

"Who?" asked Ants with exaggerated innocence.

"The cops, you asshole. A whole fucking army."

"A few hours ago you swore no one was following us," said Ted. "Why are you so rattled?"

"I'm not rattled. I'm being reasonable. He found us, didn't he?" Polo thrust the rifle at the shepherd, who slept on through the noise.

"You don't still think he's a cop?"

"No. But he wandered in here before we saw or heard him. So could somebody else. We have to be ready, post guards, and . . ."

"Why? You just said you couldn't see a thing."

Polo bit at his wet moustache. "It's better than doing nothing."

"I don't know about that, old buddy. Seems to me like you're aching to have us as shook up as you are."

"I'll tell you this . . ." He glanced around as if searching for an enemy, then prodded the Arab with his rifle. ". . . he's gotta go."

"Why? He's not bothering anybody," Puff protested.

"He doesn't even have shoes," said Gypsy. "He wouldn't last the night."

"That's the point. Either we send him off to die or we kill him ourselves. So make up your minds. Which one'll it be?"

"You're sick," said Ants. "He hasn't done a damn thing."

Polo grimaced at their slackness. "Not yet. But he could do a lot later on. He's seen us and the cars. If that clerk ever tells who we are and what we look like, this one could say where we went."

"We'll be long gone by then," said Ted.

"Maybe. Maybe not. You said something about laying low tomorrow. What if he tails us? What if he shows the army where we are? Stop bullshitting yourselves. It's down to survival. Him or us."

"I'm not killing anyone else."

"We're the ones who're going to be killed unless you face facts."

"For chrissake, man, he won't remember us in the morning."

"That's your story." Polo spoke louder, goading himself on. "I'm not risking my ass for it. You called the shots at the jail. You told us to trust that little prick. This time we're doing what I say." He drew a bead on the Moroccan.

"Don't!" shouted Bert, and the man drowsily raised his head, more puzzled than frightened.

"You shoot him," said Ted, pulling his .357, "and I'll kill you." He braced his elbows on his knees, steadying the revolver with both hands, aiming at Polo's heart.

"You wouldn't."

"Try me."

Polo's shoulders were bobbing and twitching again. While he wouldn't look at the pistol, the Moroccan squinted quizzically into the muzzle of the M-16. "You mean you'd kill me, but you wouldn't shoot him?"

"You're fucking-A right. His life isn't worth any less to me than yours. Four men have died today because of you. I'm not sitting here and watching you go for number five."

"Jesus, man, you don't make sense. You'll shoot me and that'll be six." He flexed his hand, bringing it near his belt.

"Stay away from that pistol."

"Listen, we have to do it to save ourselves. What you don't . . ."

"I'm tired of talking. Put down the gun." He slid to the left, farther from Bert.

"You people are incredible. Haven't you got the guts to admit what we're up against? We leave him and none of us'll make it alive."

"Then I'd rather not make it," said Ants. "A minute ago you were begging us to fight for men like this. Now you say we should kill him on the chance he might—just might—rat on us. You have real head problems, Polo."

"I don't like to do it any more than you."

"Then don't. Look at him," said Gypsy. "He doesn't know where he's at."

"I'm so damn sick of guns," said Puff, standing up, "I don't . . ."

Ted shoved her from his line of fire. "Time's up, Polo. Drop the goddamn gun."

His shoulders quit bobbing and the rifle slapped against his leg. "I believe you'd do it."

"You'd better."

"And the rest of you'd sit and watch. You're going to be sorry about this," he said to Ted.

"I'm already sorry about a lot of things. Ants, take the rifle and pistol." While the boy stripped Polo of his weapons, Ted got up, wondering where to go from here. He couldn't cover him all night.

"I should have expected this," muttered Polo.

"What you oughta do is shut your mouth."

"You cocksucker, I . . ."

Polo stepped into a straight left from Ted and staggered back against the Land-Rover. Tossing aside the pistol, Ted followed up his first punch with a right cross to the jaw. Polo never had a chance to protect himself. Pinned to the side panel, he bellowed while Ted's fists cut his face like scalpels, fattening his lips, bloodying his nose, and slicing an eyelid.

Ted felt the big body sag and thought he should stop, but instead he pumped Polo's thick, jacketed midsection. It was like punching the heavy bag. There was a loud popping of canvas, and Ted soon grew arm-weary. He gave a flurry of punches with both hands as Polo slumped to his knees, then he switched to his feet, kicking twice before Polo curled into a fetal position.

No one moved. They stared, mouths agape, like children

who had come for cartoons, but had wandered in on a heavy-weight match by mistake. Polo was moaning hoarsely. Ted stuck his hands under his arms and waited for a second wind. The Moroccan murmured deep in his throat.

Flopping next to the Renault, Ted buried his fists in the snow. Bert kept her distance. After digging the .357 magnum from the mud, Ants left it, the rifle, and the .38 near Ted, as though he wanted nothing to do with them. Puff had pulled herself together and was tending to Polo. Pressing snow to his forehead and cheeks, she revived him and washed his cuts. His left eye had closed to a slit, and he wouldn't look at Ted.

When Ted's hands were numb, he pulled them from the snow. The skin on his knuckles had split and his left fist was so swollen he could barely close it. Painfully juggling the guns, he crawled into the car.

2

BY THE time they bedded down, the storm had passed and a few faint stars shone through the scattered clouds. Mothering two men now, Puff led Polo and Gypsy to the Land-Rover. But Ants insisted on sleeping next to the fire.

When Bert slipped into the front seat of the Renault, Ted was busy with his arsenal in the back. After drying the M-16 and the pistol with his shirttail, he broke down the .357 and cleaned the chambers and barrel. Like Puff, he was sick of guns, but thought he'd better have them handy tonight.

"Aren't you going to sleep?" asked Bert.

"Maybe later."

"Would you like me to come back?"

"I'd love it," said Ted. "But it'll be safer if you stay where you are."

Sitting up, she looked where he was gazing now through the window. Since the clouds had broken, the night, even without a moon, was bright because of the snow, and as wind flattened the drifts, the field didn't contain a single shadow big enough to hide a man. They would have spotted anyone approaching from that direction and, silhouetted against the snow, he'd have been an easy target.

When Ted swung around to the Land-Rover, she said, "Do you expect more trouble from Polo?"

"Who knows what he'll do?"

"Would you have shot him?"

"Yes."

"You're serious?"

"I sure was then."

"You shot someone in the jail?"

"Yes." He felt he should say something more, that she deserved an explanation. "The guard named Driss. The one helping us."

"It must have been horrible."

"It was." He told her what Polo had done, then what he had had to do to Driss. "He wasn't standing a foot from me. His head . . ."

"Ted, you don't have to go on. I know you didn't have any choice."

"Hell, yes, I had a choice. Shoot him or get shot. So I shot him. But the real choice was way before then. When I took this job, I told myself it'd be safe. I should of known I couldn't predict that, not with somebody like Polo to foul us up. I had my doubts about him, about this whole deal, but once we were in the cellblock and the shit started to fly, it was too late."

"Don't blame yourself."

"Why not? I did it. I conned myself into believing I could pull the job by using my brains. I should of remembered

I'm better with a gun than I am at thinking."

"Who'd have guessed this would happen?"

"That's what I was paid to do. Now we're in it up to our asses. I'm going to bust my hump to get us out, but who can say what it'll cost? Look at tonight. Polo had shot that guy, I'd of killed him. Christ, what kind of choice is that?"

She leaned over the seat to touch him, then asked with amazing composure, "Do we have a chance?"

At once, Ted was ashamed of himself. He held her hand in his. "Of course we do."

Though Bert let him have her hand, he couldn't hold her eyes. Again she was gazing at the empty field to the east. "I kept my promise, you know. When I heard shots, I started up the street. Not fast, but I was moving."

"Good. I may be asking you for a lot more promises before we're through."

"Why don't we take them one at a time? It was damned hard doing that today." She combed her hair forward so he could see less of her face. "I have a favor to ask you."

"Yes. Just name it."

"If we're about to be captured, will you give me your gun?"

"What?"

"Promise to let me use your gun," she said evenly.

"What the hell for?"

"I told you, I'd rather do anything than be back in jail."

He squeezed her face in his hands, tilting it to study her eyes. She looked as serious as she sounded.

"Will you?" she asked.

"Nobody's going to catch us."

"But if they do . . ."

"Don't say that. They won't."

"Then you won't promise?"

"Hell, no."

"I kept my word."

"It's not the same." He suspected he was clenching her jaw too tightly, but dreaded loosening his grip. "Look, why are we talking about this? I tell you, it won't happen."

"It's important to me, Ted."

"You want a promise, I'll make one. The best." He gave her head a firm shake. "I promise no one'll get you. And here's another. Right after this, we'll fly to the island."

"How can you promise that? You just said you don't know what it'll take to get to Algeria."

"Whatever it is, I'll do it. Don't you trust me?"

"I trust you."

"Okay, you know I'd never let you down. Stop talking about this. Don't even think about it." He kissed her forehead, then closed her eyes by kissing them too. Her face looked pale, waxy, and perfect as a death mask. "Lie down," he told her, so he wouldn't have to see it. "Get some sleep."

3

TED WOKE with a jolt, his cheek against the foggy window, a pistol in his lap. Bert, he judged by her steady breathing, was still asleep up front. Buffing the glass with his shirtsleeve, he saw the sun was high and had been for hours. He checked his watch—eight o'clock—and was shocked he'd slept so late.

The air was warm, and all around him he heard the gurgle of melted snow. A crust of ice coasted on its own quick melting over the rear window down the sloping trunk to flop in the slush. The treeless field already had a few bare spots, steaming as the sun struck them. By noon there would be nothing left of last night's storm. The army, if it's after us, won't miss this campsite, he thought. They had to shove off soon.

But as he looked at Bert, who had her head cradled in her arms, he hated to wake her. Who could say when she'd sleep this soundly again? Ted wished she could have dozed through all of it—what had happened and what might be ahead. But he could do only so much—spare her a little worry, protect her, create an illusion of security. He'd be damned if he'd give her his gun. Where had she gotten that idea? He knew so little about her, he didn't doubt she'd do it. He didn't doubt anything she said.

Leaning back, he thought if it hadn't been for her, this is when he'd have left. He had half his money, and there was nothing to link him to the shoot-out in Tazenzit. He could have driven to Casablanca and bought a ticket to Spain. But he was staying. That surprised him. Maybe he didn't know much about himself any more either.

What if, he wondered, Bert and I bugged out together? No, she'd never do it. Imagining her anger and disappointment in him, he felt uncomfortable for considering it. These people would be helpless without him. He might as well have shot them himself and saved the Moroccans the bother.

Yet he was also aware that the six of them traveling together meant trouble. It would be hard to hide and harder still to keep track of them all. You never knew when one of them would try some bone-headed trick.

Watching Bert sleep, Ted thought again, I have to take care of her. She was something to fight for. Their future was something to believe in. He was anxious to be alone with her, far from this bunch and their problems. In a bed, a big double bed, not like two kids in the back seat of a car.

In a house with a shower where, after a quick splash, they'd stretch out on fresh, smooth sheets with a whole afternoon in front of them and an entire night ahead, knowing they'd be together tomorrow and the day after.

Shrugging a blanket from his shoulders, he draped it from the steering wheel to the back of the seat, building a tent of shade for Bert. Sleep, he thought. Sleep a few minutes longer. That's all I have to offer now, but later . . .

The door of the Land-Rover squeaked. Polo had climbed out and was closing it. Ted's hand fell to the pistol in his lap as Polo studied the dead fire, his face puffy, bruised, and lopsided. He had to swivel his whole body, like a man with a broken neck, when he looked toward the road. Then noticing Ted, he spread his arms in dejection and let them fall to his sides. Ted put on his ski parka, tucked the revolver under his belt, and slid silently from the car.

The morning was balmy and bright, more like spring than the middle of February. The snow muffled every sound except that of its own melting. Ants was asleep, snug in his blanket in a spot of shade beside the Renault.

"What is it?"

"He's gone," Polo whispered, as though their last chance were lost. More than his face looked beaten. His big body appeared to have turned to baby fat.

"Who?"

"The shepherd."

"So what? Did you want to invite him to breakfast?"

Polo sighed, too tired to argue. "You're the boss. I'd just like to know where he went."

"That way." The tracks crossed the snow to the road, then disappeared down a gully.

"There might be a village."

"There's no smoke."

"Fine. Forget it."

But a few hundred yards beyond the gully, a rabble of dark birds circled and dived. Something was dead or dying. The shepherd? Ted thought he'd better have a look. "You wait here. I'll be right back."

"I'd rather come."

And on second thought, Ted realized he'd rather have Polo where he could watch him. He nudged Ants with his foot until the boy's blue eyes opened. "Wake up, old buddy. Polo and I are going to look around. You stand guard. Get a gun from the car and signal with two shots in case of trouble. I mean real trouble. Don't go shooting at your shadow."

"How about me?" asked Polo. "Shouldn't I have a gun?"

"Take the .38. But watch it. I haven't forgotten last night."

"Want me to wake the others?" asked Ants.

"No. Let 'em sleep."

They walked single file, with Polo well in front, tracing the Arab's tracks, which had melted at the bottom to bare ground. Wet snow clung to their cuffs and soaked their shoes. At each step Polo's boots squelched. A mild breeze blew from the west, the air pure and heady, and in the red ski parka Ted started to sweat. Dressed like this, he made a great target. Another mistake, he thought. Should of taken it off. Perspiration purled along his flanks.

He had the pistol in his hand as he scanned left to right. The glare was bad in the east and while he squinted, he might have missed someone. The land sloped from the road, broken by ravines where a man could have hidden.

When they reached the rim of a deep gully, the tracks descended in a zigzag path, then collapsed near the canyon floor into a straight skid mark. The man had rolled the remaining distance, and from where he'd landed, the foot-prints led east. Polo was floundering down the slope when Ted hissed and shook his head no.

Crouching low, they skirted the gully to where the birds wheeled and swooped and shrilly cried. Their flapping wings beat against the blue bowl of sky as if to poke holes in it. The sun magnified their shadows on the snow so they looked the size of eagles.

Ted stood up, holding the heavy pistol loose against his leg, blinking each time a bird darted past his face. Polo straightened too, his forehead and moustache moist. In the canyon, about twenty feet below, dozens of dead sheep and goats, half-buried in snow, appeared to be bobbing to the surface like corpses from a river. They'd stumbled off the cliff. The fall had killed them, then the storm had frozen their carcasses into grotesque shapes, so that even in death they seemed to be struggling against this new torment.

As vultures, ravens, and kites swept over the animals, sampling exposed parts and waiting for the sun to finish its work, the shepherd raced at them, wielding a stick and swearing, lunatic with anger or despair, vainly defending his flock. But the birds weren't bothered much. The kites and ravens skittered away, and the shabby vultures shot their wings wide, sailing beyond his range. Behind him others landed. Almost all of them had gone to the ground now and were stabbing their beaks at the hard bodies. Lunging with his stick, the man did little more than dig up the snow and thump the bellies of the sheep and goats.

Ted didn't notice Polo snap off the safety on his pistol, but he saw him lift it and thought he meant to kill the Moroccan. Before he could do anything, Polo had his hand high above his head and fired four times in the air. Ted's ears popped, deafening him to the echoes that rattled through the gulches and ravines. He could only watch and feel the wind from their wings as the birds exploded like sheets of slate blown from a roof. The morning erupted with feathers and snow and scraps of flesh that fell from their bills as they accelerated in a whirlpool pattern.

The shepherd looked up, his face speckled with dirt. Spotting Ted and Polo, he didn't act surprised, no more than he had when he'd wandered from the blizzard into their camp. To him they must have been like mysterious elements of his fate. Shaking the stick, he spoke. Ted's hearing had returned, but if there was any gratitude or relief in the man's keening wail, it escaped him. With no enemy to strike at now, he began to beat the bodies of his sheep and goats.

Rapidly, Polo and Ted retraced the tracks through the snow.

"You shouldn't of done it," said Ted.

"What else was there to do for the poor bastard?"

"Anybody in the valley had to of heard that."

"I'm sorry."

Ted didn't push it. He was sorry, too, and more dumbfounded than angry. He'd never met a more dangerous man than this brooding crazy who'd nearly killed the shepherd last night, then had risked their necks this morning for a gesture of sympathy.

Everyone was out of the cars, huddled together, Puff looming over them like a mother hen. But they're sitting ducks, thought Ted. Dead ducks. They don't even know enough to take cover.

Ants gingerly shouldered the rifle.

"For chrissake, don't shoot," hollered Ted. "It's us."

The Moroccan's footprints had expanded to gigantic proportions, and he and Polo loped from clear patch to clear patch across the road and the snowy field. When Bert hurried to meet him, Ted gave her a brief hug and said, "We have to get out of here."

"What was it?"

"Nothing. We shot at some birds."

She plainly didn't believe him, but there was no time to convince her.

"Everything okay?" asked Ants.

"Yeah. Point that the other way, friend."

"I was about to come help, but I thought you'd rather have me here."

"You did the right thing. Into the cars. Gypsy, Puff, let's move. Don't bother about that," he said to Polo, who was shoveling snow over the ashes of their fire. "It's melting anyhow, and they'll see the chopped-up pole. Let them figure it out."

4

WITH Ted in the lead, they sped south-southeast, spraying high waves of slush and unspooling black threads of asphalt under their tires. Then for a few moments he stopped on the crown of a hill and studied the rearview mirror. The road was bare for miles behind them, shrugging off its crust like a snake losing its skin. When he was sure no one was following them, he started again.

The valley buckled at its borders into spiny ridges and sheer, icy mountains. There were no villages and very little vegetation. Ted branched off the paved road onto a track that corkscrewed toward the mountains. During dry weather the *piste* would have been a faint scrawl in the dust. Now, because it held more snow than the macadam, its trail was distinct and they made perfect prints, but these dissolved a few minutes after they'd passed.

Not far into the foothills, the track narrowed to a path used by shepherds leading their flocks to higher pastures for summer grazing. It was too steep for cars. Ted rolled a few yards in reverse and parked behind a big boulder and several scrub bushes. Polo squeezed in beside him.

Though their backs were to an immense stone wall, they overlooked the land sloping toward the road and commanded much of the valley. Anyone tailing them would have to take the same route, exposed to their view and to their gunfire, if it came to that. Unless the Moroccans brought up mortars or called in air strikes, Ted knew they could hold on for days.

But that was thinking in military terms. A rescue mission wouldn't arrive no matter how long they lasted. We're not here to make a stand, just lay low, he thought. And it's not a bad place for that. No one was likely to spot them unless he was looking through field glasses and got very lucky. Only the glare of sunlight on the windshields might give them away.

"Find something to cover the windows," he said as they climbed from the cars.

"Can I cook?" asked Puff.

"No fires."

"Where do you reckon that goes?" Ants pointed to the footpath.

"The mountains."

"Should we explore?"

"Don't bother."

"What if we have to leave that way?"

"Not me, buddy. I'm going the way I came. You wouldn't have a chance up there this time of year. Gimme the rifle. I'll stand first guard."

After Ants handed him the M-16 and they'd all gone to

eat a cold breakfast, Ted popped the trunk of the Renault. Phil's grey Samsonite suitcase had been locked, but the key was tied to the plastic handle. When he had difficulty unknotting it, Ted gave a good yank, snapping the string. He set the suitcase on the spare tire, inserted the key, and punched a button to flip up the metal clasps.

Phil's belongings were so neatly packed, Ted hesitated to touch them with his raw-knuckled hands. Pairs of khaki pants were creased and folded, shirts were sealed in plastic bags, socks were rolled, and even his underwear was meticulously arranged. As he grubbed through the clothes, Ted's fingers left smudges and flecks of dried blood.

Phil had slid his passport between two books—*Christianity Without God* and Albert Camus's *The Rebel.* Ted took it, then fanned the pages of the paperbacks, but found no money. During a swift, second search he discovered a slender diary in a side pocket. Tucked between January tenth and eleventh were three fifty-dollar traveler's checks.

He pocketed them and read an entry, as though that was what he'd been looking for.

> By a typical modern inversion of values Polo strives to attain a romantic transcendence, a kind of negative religious experience. Predictably he believes he can succeed only by indulging in what used to be considered base and immoral—i.e., sexual experiments, gratuitous crime and violence, a random violation of laws. Hasn't it ever occurred to him that decency and kindness and rational action might allow him to reach the same goal by . . .

Ted flung the diary into the trunk and rifled the suitcase one last time, tossing the books aside, rearranging the clothing, unraveling the socks. His swollen fist throbbed so badly he had to hold his breath. Then exhaling, he threw everything back in, snapped the clasps, and locked them.

Where the fuck were his two thousand bucks? Angry and confused, he flopped onto a flat rock behind the boulder, the M-16 across his knees. He had to think, but the sun was hot and achingly bright. His face burned in the thin air. His scalp itched, and he smelled his dirty, baking hair. The elastic wrist bands of his ski parka were wet with perspiration. Peeling it off, he stuffed the red nylon jacket under him.

Cool down, he told himself, and though he said it silently, his lips mouthed the words. Polo or Puff has the dough. Or maybe Phil put it away for safe-keeping. No one's going to screw you. They wouldn't dare. You've got Gypsy and somebody'll pay for him. Or he'd take it out of their asses.

No, don't start that. It was the wrong time to be racked off. He already had more than enough to worry about. And he couldn't bring up the matter of money before Phil's body was cold. What the hell, there's always the Land-Rover, he thought. He'd claim that as collateral. So don't let it bother you.

Stripping off his shirt, he scooped up two handfuls of snow from the shade of the boulder and scrubbed them like bars of soap over his face, chest, and underarms, sucking in his breath sharply at the frosty shock. That cleared his head and gave him the illusion he was clean. After a shave and a few hours of sleep, he'd be a new man.

Bert brought him a slab of Berber bread, a cup of water, and a can of corned beef. "Aren't you freezing?" she asked.

"No. It's nice."

"Hungry?"

"You bet." He smacked the rock for her to sit beside him. Though aware of a false heartiness in his own voice, he was

still uneasy and didn't know how else to contend with the
hollowness of hers.

"It is warm in the sun, isn't it?" Spreading corned beef
on the bread, she passed it to him.

"Yeah. Thanks, babe. Bring some for yourself?"

"I had a bite. I'm not very hungry."

"You oughta eat. You're . . ." Bothered again by the
phony, paternal tone, he didn't finish.

She picked up his blue shirt and scratched at the sleeve
that had been splattered by Driss's blood. Part of it might
have been Phil's and the Moroccan prisoners', but it had all
dried the same shade of rusty brown. "This won't wash.
Why don't you throw it away?"

"Right. I'll leave it here."

She turned, then, as if to look him straight in the eye, but
wound up staring over his shoulder into the valley. "Do you
mind if I ask something?"

"Of course not."

"You promise to tell the truth?"

"Sure," he said, though he feared she'd bring up the
business about borrowing his gun.

"Did you kill that Arab?"

"What Arab?"

"The shepherd. Did you shoot him?"

"Hell, no. I told you, there were some birds. Why do you
ask?"

"I had to be sure," she said as though she still weren't.

"I don't get it. What are you driving at?"

"I thought you . . . well, maybe you didn't want Polo to
do it last night in front of us, but this morning you decided
you had to."

"Christ awmighty, you make me sound like a hired gun
or maniac."

"I'm sorry. It's just . . ."

"Just what?" he asked angrily.

"I guess it's getting to me—what happened to Phil and the fight with Polo and now this talk about guns and shooting people. It's totally unreal, you know?"

"I didn't plan it that way, but there's nothing unreal about it. You all hired me to help, but you haven't done a hell of a lot to help yourselves. I should of known better than to mess with a bunch of amateurs."

"I'm sorry," she repeated. "Don't be mad."

"Okay. I didn't mean to yell. It's not you I'm mad at."

Ted shut his mouth for a moment, thinking, Don't take it out on her. She's afraid, that's all. Sliding his hand up her arm and shoulder, he kneaded the downy nape of her neck. "Tomorrow this'll be over and we'll forget about it."

"I won't forget Phil."

"Neither will I. Or Driss and the other two." He clasped her to his chest, tucking her head under his chin. Her hair was smooth, warm, and fragrant. "Honest, I don't like hurting people, and I'd never let anyone hurt you."

"I'm being silly. I'd better go help Puff."

"You believe me, don't you?"

He held her until she answered, "Yes."

"Gimme a kiss."

Touching a hand to his warm chest, she brushed her lips past his, then, without looking back, went between the cars and sat with the others against the Land-Rover. At least he didn't kill the shepherd, she thought, relieved for him and also for herself. That was one thing she couldn't be blamed for.

But he had shot Driss, and though it wasn't his fault, that set him apart. Everyone except Ants, she noticed, had begun to look at him like an uncaged animal. Ted was capable of killing. He'd done it before and was ready to do it again if he had to. Although he was trying to protect them, they were baffled and frightened by him.

Bert was afraid *for* him, and ashamed of herself for persuading him to help. She loved him and desperately didn't want him to kill anyone, especially not on her account. But they'd gone too far, she thought, and things had gotten too tangled for her to tell him the truth now.

"Anybody want this piece of bread?" asked Ants.

No one spoke. No one acknowledged the question. It was so quiet he could hear them spooning up the uncooked food and swallowing. When Polo got to his feet and clumped away from the cars, Ants dropped the crust of bread and went down to the boulder where Ted stood guard.

He'd own up to what scared him, and wished they'd talk about it. Until yesterday he'd never seen anyone die and hadn't once thought of dying himself. Now he couldn't think about anything else. Death, wasn't it life's best-kept secret? He'd somehow assumed it had died with his grandparents when he was too young to attend the funeral. Or if it still happened, wasn't it only to the very old? Wasn't it always a mistake which should have been prevented? That's why bodies were smuggled out at night and swiftly buried.

But no, he'd seen it now, and felt as dazed and cold as Phil had looked lying on the concrete, bleeding from the nose, ears, and mouth. Luckily Ted had been there. If he had to go through it alone, Ants didn't know what he'd do. Scream, cry, panic like Polo, do something insane? I'll watch Ted, he told himself. I won't go wrong imitating him.

"Finished eating?" asked Ted.

"Yeah, half a can of greasy cold meat. The kind with jelly

all over it." He rubbed his stomach. "One minute it starts to come up. The next it seems to be settling in for the season."

"You oughta try C-rations that have been mouldering in some damn warehouse since World War II. Once at Fort Benning they fed us . . ."

Gypsy couldn't shut off their voices, which were scratchy and indistinct, then suddenly deafening, as if they'd shouted into his ear. He'd had this experience on mescaline, like someone was tuning a radio in a distant room, then turned it full blast and shoved the speaker against his head. And something similar had happened one time in jail, when through the light shaft high on the wall he'd heard Americans talking and believed his voice was among them. As he answered, holding up his end of the conversation, the words echoed in the corridor and the guards thought he'd cracked. He'd talked himself down from that bummer, but when the voices faded, he thought part of him had gone too.

Now it seemed a bigger part of him was missing. Without his glasses his vision swam blearily. Yet the instant he'd stepped from the cell, even before Ted had taken his glasses, everything had been large and out of focus, and he felt very small and of no consequence. When Polo whispered he was going to set the prisoners loose, it had sounded reasonable. Or as reasonable as anything at that moment. Then the shooting had started, the noise pounding through his skull, and Phil was on the floor bleeding.

At last he was free, but Phil was dead. A straight exchange at an absurdly high price. His frail body bent beneath an impossible obligation. He'd have to tell the family, explain, and make it up to them. But how? And what if more people died because of him?

No matter what, he knew he couldn't help. Wearing Phil's orthopedic shoes, he wasn't much better than a cripple himself, and almost worse than his weakness and his wavering vision, he couldn't concentrate. Starved of fresh air and sunlight for six months, he found open spaces unsettling, his spine bore a permanent rash of goosebumps, food had no taste, and his skin stung wherever it was touched.

He slumped against the Land-Rover, letting Puff hold his hand, and thought of Phil. He'd always felt guilty about his brother's bad leg. It wasn't his fault, he'd continually told himself, yet the fact remained. While Phil wore a brace and had to hobble along, Gypsy's legs were perfectly formed. From the same family, the same room, the same bed, polio had picked Phil.

As a boy, every time he played sports or danced, he was reminded of Phil. Finally he'd decided it would be best not to move at all, at least not where Phil would see him, and best not to show he was ever enjoying himself. When Phil became interested in books, Gypsy didn't compete, didn't indicate he cared, although he liked to read too. He'd let his brother have his books and "the life of the mind," as he called it.

But now what? Now that Phil had been killed springing him, what adjustment could he make? Didn't Puff understand he had to answer that before he considered the future? He spoke to her in monosyllables because there was nothing more to say. If he told her he was grateful and loved her, that would only add to his obligation, and he already owed too many debts.

Puff said, "I know how you must feel about Phil," yet the truth was, she didn't. She believed she could help Gypsy, if he'd let her, if he'd look at her, if he'd speak. Had one of her sisters died, she'd have needed him all the more. But he withdrew into himself, baffling her by his indifference. After six months the waiting should have been over, but this was as bad as having him in jail. Worse in a way, for though she could talk to him and touch him, she got no response. He'd locked himself in and her out, closing a cold door between them. Had Phil's death killed off everything?

She was chattering and worrying too much to listen for answers. Falling into a role that disgusted her, she found herself acting like her mother. Fretful, bustling, ridiculous, she petted and caressed Gypsy, asking, Do you feel better? Can I bring you anything? Did you have enough to eat?

In her mother, Puff knew, it wasn't love but a sense of inadequacy which led her to offer obsessively what would be rejected. Now she was doing it. But what choice did she have? She was afraid to keep quiet and let Gypsy think things through. What if he decided he didn't love her? No, Puff had to make an extra effort, since she was sure no one would meet her halfway.

Hearing her high-pitched, nattering voice, Polo was about to holler, Shut up! For Christ's sake, shut your goddamn mouth. But silence would have been worse.

He crouched on a rock in the sun, his head held gingerly in his hands so that his bruises wouldn't ache. It seemed his life had smashed against an unyielding limit, and he lacked the strength to fit the pieces together. Yet he told himself it was that fat, silly bitch who prevented him from thinking.

He might have moved farther away, but he already felt isolated, and didn't need more reminders of how alone he was, how little they cared, how utterly he'd failed. Action was supposed to bring people together, build solidarity. That's what he'd read. But his thumping defeat had driven them apart, and the plans that had propped him up for weeks had been cut from under him in less than twenty-four hours.

It was fear that did it—a fear more enormous and enduring than he'd ever imagined. Last night before his eyes had glazed over and he'd gone down for good, he'd caught a glimpse of the others petrified with fright. Kuyler could have killed him, and they'd have done nothing.

Then there was a physical revulsion augmenting the fear. The tiniest details still triggered his terror. The memory of Driss's face flying off, scattering bits of flesh and hair. Kuyler wiping the slime from his fingers. The bullethole in Phil's head, big enough to stick your fist into. This morning he'd discovered a scrap of dried skin stuck to the toe of his boot, and it had turned his stomach, like finding a maggot in his food.

Only Kuyler could survive under these conditions. But why bitch when that's what you had to be like if you wanted to win? And when you played this game, you had to win. There was no prize for the runner-up.

Polo stretched out on the rock, unbuttoning his shirt to bare the matted hair on his chest. From football he suspected he'd been beaten even before Ted punched him silly. The best players didn't have to destroy you. They countered your strength with their quickness, blunted your anger with their savvy. They tricked you, trapped you, blindsided you. Dreamlike, the runner danced beyond your reach; the blocker snarled your feet. You might think you were handling your man easily until you glanced at the scoreboard and saw how badly you were being humiliated. Then the harder you fought, the more infuriating it became, as you learned your opponent wasn't just clever. He was faster, smarter, stronger, better.

He had to admit he was learning a lot from Kuyler, but

always too late, so that at every step he fell farther behind. How could he settle the score when he couldn't stay even? It was unnerving. Each time he thought he'd caught Kuyler off guard, he outsmarted himself. Yet Polo wouldn't give up. Failure made him more defiant, for he feared that the closer they got to the border, the fewer chances he'd have . . . for what? To prove he could contend with Ted and back up his beliefs?

He'd done that, hadn't he? Heedless of the consequences, he'd acted on impulse. No one could accuse him of caution or of being self-seeking. It would have been inhuman to leave the other prisoners locked up. It was as simple as that.

But something had gone drastically wrong—something in addition to Phil's death, which was gruesome enough. One gratuitous act had committed them—the whole country, it seemed—to a course of events which they couldn't escape. His first step had led them onto a narrow ledge, and much as he wanted to stop until he'd figured things out, there was no turning back. Unless they hurled themselves over the edge, they had to pursue this path to the end.

5

THE CAR came shortly before noon. From Ted's vantage point, the road appeared to split the valley halfway between the horizon and him, and the car took ten minutes to traverse it, heading west toward Tazenzit. It never slowed, never swerved, and made no noise. Though at this distance it looked like an industrious bug, it was a big, black sedan with the sun glinting dully on its broad hood. Ted couldn't tell whether it was a military vehicle. He had to sweat through another hour, while two more dark sedans drove by, before he spotted several cars that clearly belonged to civilians—a red sport model, a yellow convertible, a green VW camper—and was certain the road hadn't been closed.

"Good deal," said Ants. "Why not start?"

"That doesn't mean there aren't checkpoints and road-blocks. I'd rather do them after dark."

That'll be the hardest part, thought Ted, bluffing our way through the roadblocks. The army was sure to set them up at bridges, towns, and gorges which you couldn't loop around. Whether there was a general alarm or a specific search for Gypsy, they'd have to hope for sad-sack soldiers, peeved by night duty, indifferent to this crisis and its causes.

Many Moroccans couldn't read the Western alphabet. He'd often seen officials examine documents upside down, from right to left. What the hell, he thought, his hope rowing, he couldn't read a word of their language. Why should they do any better with his?

But even an illiterate would recognize the bluish-grey cover of an American passport, and that might call for a thorough check and questioning. The coppery hairs on his arms stiffened. Well, the group had voted to fight.

Ted wondered, though, whether they had any fight left. They looked whipped, past the point of listening to advice or orders. Everyone, except Ants, winced at the sight of a gun or the sound of anything louder than a fart, and like Bert, they acted more afraid of him than of the Moroccans. He wouldn't have minded if it meant they'd obey. But he didn't believe they would.

Again, except for Ants. The boy, who still wore his bright, patchwork shirt andgappliquéd pants, looked more like a clown than ever. But maybe you can count on him, thought Ted. He'll do what you tell him, and he could take care of small stuff, while I handle the heavy action.

He'd known this boy's type. How old was he? Eighteen? No younger than a private. A nice, eager kid. A kind you met in the army. Puppies, he'd always called them, because they were affable and liked to follow. If they survived the first few battles, they became good soldiers. But you had to watch how friendly you were with them, because they drew flak like magnets and usually didn't last.

No, I won't do it, no matter how tight things are. He liked this puppy too much. A very unprofessional attitude. But what the shit, why take advantage of Ants's good nature? So Ted was back to hoping for poor soldiers on the other side and a long string of luck on theirs.

After the snow melted and the pools of moisture evaporated, the low spots in the valley filled with heat mirages. For relief Ted fixed his eyes on them, reminded of freshwater lakes in the Blue Ridge Mountains, and he savored memories in his mind like a sweet soothing drink on his tongue. Cooling in the shallows, the fish he'd caught would be strung through the gills. On another line he'd have a six-pack of beer. In the evening he'd build a fire and fry the fish in batter, so the meat would snap crisply from the delicate ladder of bones, and he'd wash it down with foamy mouthfuls of beer.

The road also looked liquid, like a glistening stream, and as a few fat cars bobbed by, Ted's stinging eyelids drooped. Tired and thirsty, he told Ants, "You take over. Keep track of what passes, specially army or official-type vehicles. Anything stops, call me."

Groggy from heat and fatigue, he fumbled into the bloody shirt which Bert had begged him to throw away, and staggered toward the cars.

Polo didn't raise his lumpy, discolored face. Bert, who had her chin on her knee, didn't look at him either. Gypsy's head was on Puff's padded lap, his unblinking eyes staring through Ted like he wasn't there.

"I'm going to lie down. Lemme have the shortwave set. Maybe there's some news."

When no one answered, he told himself, Don't get pissed off. You've only got another day or two to put up with them.

Fetching the radio from the Land-Rover, he quietly closed the door, as though this were a hospital recovery ward. In the Renault the vinyl upholstery burned through his clothes, and even with the windows covered, there wasn't a cool spot in the car. So he climbed out and lay in a shady patch near the front bumper.

He couldn't locate the Armed Forces Network, and the Moroccan stations still played constant, chanting music. But a BBC broadcast said the country was tense and, though the king was in control, some fighting continued in smaller towns. Did that mean the situation wasn't any worse? Or simply that the government wasn't talking? Maybe both.

Although he couldn't be sure there was a connection between their trouble in Tazenzit and the attempted coup, it seemed things were tough not just for The Gravy Train. It was going to be harder on a lot of people in Morocco for a long, long time. He knew there had always been a chance they might be captured, but that was nothing compared to what had happened. It was like they'd thrown a boomerang and had it fly back at their throats as a big razor blade dripping with other people's blood.

Ted shut his eyes, leaving the radio on, as he'd sometimes done as a young boy after he'd gone to bed. Back then, listening to the news or dance music from Detroit and Chicago had brought on a wistful, melancholy mood. The world had seemed very large, and he'd wanted to see it all. Now he'd settle for a lot less. But for the first time he wondered what he'd do if he lost Bert.

His eyes snapped wide. What kind of chicken-shit question was that? Everything goes right, she won't realize half the problems you've had. If it goes wrong, she won't know what hit her.

That was no way to keep his promise, yet for years he'd depended on it himself. He always believed he'd pull through—it was the other guy who bought the farm—and if his turn came, Ted told himself, it would be over in a second. But when he applied this to Bert, he felt sick inside.

If I had one person to count on, to take over if anything happens to me . . . But Ted didn't, and considered staying where they were. Rationing the food and water, they might last a week. Maybe the Moroccans would abandon the search and lower the roadblocks. Or, with time to organize, would they bring in spotter planes, helicopters? And the waiting would be hard. After a few days on this fly-blown heap of rocks, they'd be basket cases. No, they had to leave tonight. Speed and darkness were their only advantages.

So don't go over it again. You know what you have to do. Though he didn't delude himself that it would be easy, Ted relaxed a little and snatched a few hours of sleep.

As he dozed, the sun descended and the sky darkened. He didn't see the clouds spread from the mountaintops to canopy the valley, but he felt the air grow cool and rolled over, letting a breeze dry his back.

VI

POLO WOKE him when it started to rain. Actually it was no more than a brisk sprinkle, but thick clouds threatened much worse and obscured any trace of evening light.

"Where's Ants?" asked Ted.

"There on the rock."

"Why didn't anyone relieve him? He's been on guard for hours."

As Ted side-stepped down the trail, he tested it with his shoes. The *piste* felt solid under the slippery surface, and unless the rain got heavier, they could coast safely down-hill, around the hairpin curves, to the road.

But Polo said, "It's bad, isn't it?" and in spite of his somberness, he seemed satisfied, as though everything was going against him and this proved it. Sweat and rain had beaded on his bruised, unshaven cheeks. He didn't bother to wipe them dry. Polo was beginning to feed on his gloom like a fat, cellar-swelling fungus, and men in this mood, Ted knew, generally did one of two things. They gave up, turn-

ing your gut with their groveling and ass-kissing. Or, convinced they didn't have a chance anyhow, they lashed out
in one last attempt to even the score. Either way, they didn't
make good company.

"Yeah, it's real bad," said Ted, leaving him to stare at the
mud.

"How you getting along?" he asked Ants.

"Swimmingly." The boy did a breast stroke in the drizzle.

"Anything go by?"

"Twenty-three cars, four buses, and seven trucks. Nothing that looked like the army or the cops. The road's been
empty for an hour. You think there's a curfew after sun-
down?"

"Could be." Though he spoke calmly, Ted thought,
Christ, that's all we need. "You keep watching. We won't
leave unless there's some traffic. I'll spell you after I eat."

"Why not have Polo take a turn?"

"I don't trust his eyesight." He slung an arm around the
boy. "You won't fall asleep, will you?"

"No way. Too damn many bugs."

"And I thought they were all on me. Come on up soon
as you see anything."

As Ted ascended the slick path, he heard angry, arguing
voices. Or was it rainwater babbling through the rocks? No,
Puff was speaking, then Bert answered, her words low, intense, and bitter. But he couldn't tell what they were talking
about, and by the time he reached the cars, the group was
silent and uneasy, as if they'd just stopped discussing him.

"Don't lemme interrupt."

When Ted sounded them with his eyes, Polo studied the
back of his hands. "We'll eat before we go," said Ted.

"Anyone hungry?" Puff sprang to her feet, struggling to
pump some enthusiasm into her voice.

No one answered.

"Well, I am. And sore. My built-in upholstery must be wearing thin." She slapped her fleshy rump.

"Better eat," said Ted. "Could be a long time till the next meal."

Polo mumbled a few words, which Ted didn't understand and knew better than to ask him to repeat. There was no sense starting anything or, since whatever had gone wrong was well under way, no use aggravating it. Peeling off his blood-spattered shirt, he squatted beside Bert. His upper body broke into goosebumps, but more than the cool rain had caused his skin to prickle and quilt. What was the matter with them?

"How are you, babe?"

"Not bad." She refused to look at him. When Puff passed a can of cassoulet, she swallowed two spoonfuls, then seemed to gag, and wouldn't touch any more.

Polo wasn't eating either, and Puff had to feed Gypsy as one would a child, wheedling and coaxing him to accept another bite. Finally he snapped, "For chrissake, that's enough."

She shoveled the beans into her own mouth and stuffed down a wad of bread as if to staunch an internal wound.

"Hey, look, you people, what the hell's happening to . . ."

But Ants cut Ted short. "Four or five cars went by."

"Which direction?"

"Both. There's no curfew."

"Not yet."

"What's with this group?" asked Ants, sitting in the mud. "Don't you have the brains to get in out of the rain?"

"We didn't want to ruin our record for consistency," said Polo.

Puff lifted her face to the bleak sky. Her cheeks were wet with tears and raindrops.

"What's this?" Ants asked.

"Nothing," she murmured.

"Listen up," said Ted, anxious to hit the road before they were all bawling. "Here's how it'll be. Puff and Gypsy in the Land-Rover with Polo, Bert and Ants with me. The guy in front has to watch his rearview mirror. We gotta stick together." He paused, expecting Polo to ask, Suppose we're separated? But he said nothing and didn't appear to be paying attention. "Probably there'll be roadblocks, but don't let that rattle you. Our story should be short and sweet. You all are students, I'm your teacher. We'll tell them we've been out of touch the last few days, up in the mountains studying village life. We don't know anything about Tazenzit, never even been near it. But the main point is, while they're questioning us, I want you to stay in the cars with the motors running."

"How's that?" asked Ants, and Ted was grateful someone was listening.

"I mean, sit tight, buckled in your seats, and wait. That way we'll have cover and mobility. Let me do most of the talking. You people in the Land-Rover only need to remember two words—*étudiant* and *professeur*. Don't run off at the mouth."

"Suppose they don't buy it?" At last Polo spoke.

"They will."

"Don't hand me this 'they will' business. Say they don't? What do we do?"

"I notice anything really wrong and figure we oughta bug out, I'll signal by flashing my high beams. We'll drive down one of these tracks and lose them in the dark. Is that clear?"

"Say someone else sees trouble first." Polo was warming up.

"Be sure you're right. Then flash your lights. But don't do a damn thing till I blink back. No free-lancing. I want Puff, Gypsy, and Bert to hit the floor. Duck down and stay down. There could be some shooting."

"How about us? Do we shoot back?" asked Polo, his voice edged with the old abrasiveness. But his face looked like raw hamburger, and Ted found it difficult to read through the sullen, self-pitying mask.

"Yeah, we'll fire till they take cover. That'll give us the jump we need to get away." He heard the rainwater rippling faster through the rocks. "One last point. They ask about Polo's face, why it's puffed and bruised, better say he ran into a door or something."

Shivering in great spasms, Gypsy rubbed his nicotine-stained fingers on his pants legs. "Isn't there any way to do this so no one gets hurt?"

"Nobody's going to get hurt," said Ted. "Not if you do what I told you."

"Yes, but look, I . . . It seems to me, you know, I could give myself up and you could . . ."

"Forget it." While the rest of them turned to Gypsy, Ted swung around to Polo. Was he behind this?

"What kind of trash are you talking?" Puff wailed.

"L-lemme explain." Gypsy stuttered as he spilled his words in a rush. "I c-could t-t-turn myself in and you'd get away."

"They'd kill you," said Puff.

"No, there'd b-be a trial. It'd take a long time."

"I wouldn't bet on that," said Ted. "Anyway, like I told you before, we don't know whether they're after us. If they're not, it'd be twice as stupid to surrender."

"B-but meanwhile you'd escape."

"No, don't you see? Once they nabbed you, they'd real-

ize you didn't break jail on your own and they'd come looking for us."

"I-I wouldn't t-t-talk."

"You wouldn't have to. They won't stop hunting us no matter what you do," said Ted. "Too many people have been killed. You can't change that."

"Listen to him," Puff begged Gypsy.

"I p-promise I'd do it to help."

"It won't," Ted assured him. "We're wasting time."

He stood up, and they dropped their tin cans and bread crusts and started for the cars. The rain was falling harder and the mountainside streams rushed louder through the gullies. Ted was shivering as much as Gypsy as he rooted around in the trunk of the Renault for a clean shirt.

Polo had followed him, waiting for a chance to speak.

"How about me carrying the M-16?" asked Polo, as Ted pulled on a starchy work shirt.

"You've got a pistol."

"I'd rather have the rifle. I've shot it before. Ants hasn't."

"I'll use it," said Ted.

"Suit yourself. But there's the panel in the Land-Rover. They shake you down, you'll be sorry you have it."

A chill crawled his spine as he imagined the damage Polo could do with an M-16. And, almost as bad, when they needed him most he might do nothing but stand there like a shabby bear. He'd frozen yesterday. He might again tonight. At least Ants could be trusted to point at the enemy and pull the trigger.

Yet Polo was right about one thing. The boy would have problems with the automatic, and the panel in the Land-Rover was the logical place to put it.

"Okay, switch with Ants. But believe me, buddy, you start any shit and I won't waste my breath asking questions. I'll kill you."

"Thanks. That's great for the morale."

"What's that word to you?"

"Nothing you'd understand. Look, I'd like to ask one question. Don't get pissed off. I have to be sure about something. Would you keep Gypsy with us if he didn't owe you two thousand bucks?"

"What the hell are you saying?" Ted grabbed his shirt front. "You tell me not to get pissed, then say something like that."

"I have to know." In the dim light Polo's dark eyes might have been two more bruises on his face.

"I keep you around, don't I? And you're not worth a dime to me." He shoved Polo. "Get away from me. Get in your car."

Polo lingered like he had more on his mind, but wasn't sure whether to say it. Ted tried to calm himself. He couldn't afford another fight. Ripping Phil's passport from his pocket, he thrust it at Polo. "Take this to Gypsy." Then he slid behind the wheel of the Renault before Polo could speak.

Ants sat in front, Bert in back, her legs folded underneath her. This was the safest arrangement, but he doubted that's why she'd done it. She wanted him at arm's length, Ted thought. Yes, he understood everything now. Polo probably claimed he was in it for the money and convinced Gypsy to test him. If Ted told Gypsy not to turn himself in, it was because of the bread. But if he encouraged him to do it, he'd come across as a heartless bastard anyhow. Heads I win, tails you lose. He wouldn't argue with them. They'd think what they liked. But how could Bert believe Polo?

The tires whined as the Renault skidded onto the trail, plunging downhill before Ted touched the gas. Polo was close behind him. One broadside swerve and the Land-Rover would plow into the Renault, so Ted maintained a strong head of speed until they gained the macadam.

Once again, as yesterday, the asphalt was a water course, awash with red silt and pebbles that raised a hollow din in the wheel wells. The rain wasn't that hard; the flood had deepened with the drain-off of melted snow from the mountains.

"Jesus, it's going to be a long night," muttered Ted.

"Couldn't be half as long as this day," said Ants, who had stuffed the .38 under his belt and tucked his shirt over it, imitating Ted.

"Yeah, it dragged on, didn't it?"

"How many hours to the border?"

"Depends. If we don't drown here or die of thirst in the desert, we should be there before daybreak."

"Wow, that's some 'if.' "

"Only joking. You all right?" he asked Bert, who had lain down.

"Yes. Just a little tired."

"I'll wake you when we're in Algeria." That was the answer. Put everybody to sleep and wake them when it was over. They were no help to him anyhow. They might as well be asleep. Oh Christ, poor you, with so damn many problems. Don't do it. Don't add self-pity to the list.

"Ever shot a pistol?" he asked Ants.

"Yeah, one of those pellet guns at a shooting gallery."

"This's a little different, old buddy. Don't fiddle with it till I tell you how. First thing to remember . . ."

As he instructed Ants in the handling of the .38, Bert wished she *were* asleep and would wake, not in Algeria, but days ago when she'd first met Ted, before she'd told any lies and things had gotten snarled and hopeless. What good would it do to be in Algeria? That wouldn't blot out what she'd done and seen and heard.

Now it was all out front. At least for everyone except Ants and Ted. At the last moment Polo had explained that they didn't have the two thousand to pay Ted. Crumpled against the car, dumpy and black as a sack of coal, he'd said, as if he took delight in bringing bad news, "I thought you should know. Hope it doesn't ruin your ride tonight."

"Jesus Christ," said Puff, "what'll he do when he finds out?"

Polo shrugged. "Kick our asses. Kill us. The question is, what should *we* do?"

"Pay him. That is, promise to pay him."

"Oh, yeah, we'll promise. But we did that number once. Who knows whether he'll buy it again?"

"Why the hell did you offer more than you had?" Gypsy roused himself.

"Hey, man, your brother and I were bargaining for your life. We weren't going to let two thousand bucks hold us back. Of course, if you don't think you're worth it . . ."

The strength bled visibly from Gypsy's spine. "I know this. I can't call my father and tell him Phil's dead, then in the next breath ask for two thousand dollars. It'll take time."

"Which is exactly what we don't have. Unless I miss my guess, Kuyler'll demand his money the minute we cross the border."

"So what are you suggesting?" asked Puff.

"I've run out of ideas. I've run out of everything except the feeling that we're fucked. What do you think?" he asked Bert.

"I think you're a prick. We all are. Whatever he does, I don't blame him."

Polo's face split into a lopsided smile. Then they heard Ted's feet on the muddy path. "Do we tell him now or later?"

No one answered. And no one had told him.

She believed Ted was liable to shoot someone, Polo most likely. She'd have told him the truth herself, if she hadn't feared that. Yet he'd learn sooner or later, and what would he think of her? That she'd lied all along? That she'd never loved him?

When they got to Algeria, if he'd listen, if he'd let her, she'd explain there had been a mistake and promise to pay him his money. But Bert wasn't sure that would work.

"It's heavy. Hold it in both hands, if you have to," Ted said to Ants. "Don't yank the trigger. Squeeze nice and smooth."

Bert felt feverish and depressed. Her back ached and her stomach had knotted with cramps, but she suffered more from a stricken conscience, a strange sickness, a deep disappointment with herself and the others. After months of aimless drifting, her mind had come into clear focus and she recognized them and herself for what they were.

This morning Ted had called them amateurs, yet he couldn't conceive of the extent of their callowness, and it wasn't a temporary condition. They were permanent amateurs at everything—pampered, privileged, lifelong children. While they liked to think they'd preserved their innocence and enthusiasm, they had only ignored the consequences of their actions. Now there was nowhere to hide.

Until her arrest and Gypsy's conviction, it had all been an elaborate game. First they'd played at being travelers of the open road, on their way to India to live the unstructured life. Then they'd been dope dealers, laughing at the law and those sailors who shopped for them at the PX. And finally, after the bust, under Polo's influence, they'd dabbled at the role of revolutionaries.

But the guns they'd bought in Kénitra didn't become dangerous until Ted touched them. Before that, she'd never believed they'd shoot them, never believed for a second they'd crash into that jail and free Gypsy. The talk, the plans, the boring rap sessions and political wrangling had, she thought, simply been to soothe Phil, who was so upset, or satisfy Polo's baroque fantasy life, or to waste time until someone or something—the solution remained vague, yet inevitable—arrived to set things straight.

Instead, Ted had shown up and, because of the money, but also because of her, he'd made the mistake of taking them seriously. Then with Phil's death, they'd learned the guns fired real bullets and that amateurs, regardless of their intentions—or perhaps because they had no specific intentions—often did great damage.

"You don't want to shoot wild. Aim at the chest and catch a piece of him. Lead your man as he . . ."

The talk terrified her as it never had before. She'd heard it at political rallies, then constantly from Polo—tiresome harangues about offing pigs and power growing from gun barrels and violence being a valid political alternative. But Ted meant it. He'd done it, and would again to bring them safely across the border.

Though Bert realized she was being unfair, she'd have liked to blame him for what had happened, for not seeing through their silliness. They were fakes, not into the heavy stuff. They'd never been serious, not like this—riding through the rain with revolvers in their belts.

"Pack your pockets with shells and duck behind the dashboard when you're reloading. Synchronize with me so we don't go empty at the same time."

Yes, she was tempted to hate Ted for taking the money and, worse, for taking her and the rest of them at their word. For Phil's death. For all that had gone wrong. Because she'd been a bitch. Yet he said he loved her and felt she was worth worrying about. Because she was afraid these four days were all they'd have, and that there'd be no time to straighten out her false start.

"Don't get rattled. Pick a target and pull the trigger. Squeeze. Just squeeze." He crooked his finger as if beckoning to a friend.

But she couldn't hate him. She didn't even hate Polo for pushing the jailbreak to the point of catastrophe. Or Puff for persuading her to ask Ted to help. They had all used each other, and it was impossible to say where one person's blame ended and another's began. But she did hate herself for what she'd done.

Bert had always agreed that anything was permissible as long as it hurt no one else. That had seemed a wise, yet harmless enough notion. But what could you do that didn't affect the people close to you? And how could you predict the wider influence of your actions? Sometimes the laws of logic and physics were refuted. You had to expect an opposite and immensely magnified reaction. You dropped a single pebble into a still pond and the rings of water didn't diminish. Instead they spread out and drowned everyone.

Now as Bert's actions backlashed on her, it appeared to be the end not only of her own delusions, but of something larger, of the deception and self-indulgence of so many people she knew. Limits existed, she thought, whether you recognized them or not. She'd collided with one and had no idea how to recover. She just had to stay out of the way and try to make it easier on Ted. Though she didn't believe she deserved anything herself, she hoped he'd pull through unhurt and without hurting anyone else.

*   *   *

The rain had slackened, but water was still deep on the road and their hubcaps clanged with debris carried along on the stream. Then as they snaked down from the mountains, pumping their wet brakes and cautiously rounding sharp curves, the flood outraced them, bubbling in torrents over the embankments and trenches.

"How fast are you going?" asked Puff from the back seat of the Land-Rover, where Gypsy slept with his head in her lap.

"Fast as I can," said Polo.

"Christ, we're crawling. Why not speed up?"

"Look for yourself. You're lucky to see ten feet in front of you."

"How far have we come?"

"About forty miles."

That relieved her a little. "Then I feel forty times safer and the feeling gets stronger every mile."

Actually every mile brought them closer to the threat of a roadblock at Ouarzazate, but for Puff, movement lightened the load on her mind. At last they'd escaped that sun-scorched hillside and abandoned the broad valley whose bleakness alone had been enough to unhinge her. Somehow she'd survived the numbing moment when Polo had told them they didn't have the money to pay Kuyler. Then five minutes later, she'd eased past the even more terrifying instant when Gypsy had volunteered to turn himself in. Nothing that lay ahead, she thought, could be worse than the last twenty-four hours.

As a child Puff had enjoyed going for rides at night with her parents, for as darkness fell over the plains, concealing the sterile stretches of green and giving the countryside a texture it didn't have, she could pretend they were anywhere on the way to someplace better. Now she didn't have to pretend. She was happier than she'd been for months. Tomorrow in Algeria she'd get a doctor for Gypsy, and once he'd recovered, they'd call his parents and hers and ask for money. Enough to fly home. And to pay Kuyler, if they could swing it. Of course, there was Phil. They'd have to tell Gypsy's family and . . .

Suddenly it sounded like a shell had been cupped to her ear, full of the fury of a stormy sea. "What's that?"

"Damned if I know," said Polo, lifting his foot from the gas pedal.

As they chugged downhill in low gear, Ted's engine quit and he, too, heard the noise, like an enormous, churning motor.

Bert sat up. "I hear something."

"Could it be a helicopter?" asked Ants.

Popping the clutch, Ted had gunned the Renault to life when the road dipped abruptly and disappeared, and the headlights lost themselves in a yellow glare. His stomach fell, and he thought of the brakes, but his reflexes weren't as fast as his mind. Before he realized what was wrong, he'd plunged into a *oued* that had swollen with rain and melting snow into a swift-running river. His high beams barely reached the far bank, but there was solid pavement beneath him and the tires had traction. Ahead, in the deepest part of the stream, a bridge appeared to be standing. At least the tops of its white railings broke the smooth sweep of the current.

"God," said Ants. "Stop!"

"Ted, don't," Bert shouted.

But it was too late. As the tide fought to wrench the wheel from his hands, Ted could gauge its strength by the strain in his forearms and knew if he stopped or the car stalled, they'd be washed away. Coaxing the gas and the clutch, he steered for the white brackets of the bridge railings and, between them, felt safe for a second. Then something bashed his right front fender, and he nearly lost control.

A dark shape grabbed at them with dozens of wet tentacles. It was a monstrous cedar stump that had shot down from the mountains, tossed along miles of wild water. Too big to flow through the culvert, too heavy to float over top, it banged against the bridge, clutching at them a second time, its roots whipping the roof and cracking the rear window.

Then they were past it, speeding through shallow water. When Ted got on high ground, he paused to pump his brakes dry, and behind him heard the Land-Rover smashing through the net of roots. It emerged scratched and mud-streaked, but undented. As soon as Polo was ready, they set out again.

"God," Ants repeated in a much different voice.

"How did we do it?" asked Bert.

"I don't know. Damn good thing I didn't see that coming or we'd still be on the other side."

"You mean back there with my heart and half my dinner," said Ants.

"Yeah, and about ten years of my growth. You hanging on?" he asked Bert.

"With both hands." She was sitting up, leaning forward to be near them. "For a second I thought we were floating."

"That stump nearly stove us in."

Ants combed his blond curls from his face. "I was wondering what the hell an octopus was doing here in the desert."

"There's an inch of water on the floor," said Bert.

"It'll drain off. Don't get your feet wet."

"Feet wet!" said Ants. "My pants are wet."

"Hold your water, buddy. Don't go peeing your britches. Your momma isn't here to change you every time we slip by a little tight spot like that."

As they joked and laughed loudly, even Bert joined in, Ted was glad to see. That was a bad one. He could always tell how tense it had been by the need he felt to talk afterward, and this time he could have chattered until dawn.

2

ONCE OUT of the mountains, they drove south on a wider road across a plateau through the spitting drizzle. Mixed in with the rain, grains of sand buzzed at the cars, and a gusty wind buffeted them from side to side. They skated over the wet asphalt, as if on ice.

A few fire-lit villages huddled next to the road, and as the Renault and Land-Rover approached, people rushed from mud huts waving glittering chunks of amethyst. Some stood in the center of the macadam, trying to stop the cars and sell them rocks. But at the last second they jumped aside in a great swirl of robes, then sprinted after them as the tires spun gravel in their faces. The starless night seemed necklaced with jewels.

The jewels became brighter in Ouarzazate, where arc lights lined the main street, each bulb a swarmy beehive of blowing sand. Along with the lampposts, a parade of gum trees marched into town, the wind clipping off leaves in a flurry of green. They encountered no cars coming toward them, but there were a few people on foot, battling to keep their djellabahs from ballooning. As protection against the sand, the men had pulled strips of their turbans across their faces, so that they, like the women, appeared to be in *purdah*.

Ouarzazate had no walls, but a pink arch over the road forced traffic into two narrow lanes. Beyond this was a guard house, and in front of it a dozen soldiers surrounded a fifty-gallon oil drum, holding their hands above a bonfire. When they swung around toward the cars with rags wrapped over their faces, they resembled mummies squinting through slits in the cloth. The material at their mouths puffed as they exhaled frosty clouds of condensation.

Ted slowed, tapped his horn twice, waved, then went on. A Moroccan officer started to move, thought better of it, stayed near the fire, and waved back. Polo couldn't bring himself to blow the horn. That was pressing your luck too far. But he snapped his arm up in something like a salute and sped off.

"Can you believe it?" asked Puff. "They waved."

Though he believed it, Polo didn't like it. He'd been prepared for anything except this. He checked the rearview mirror to be sure no one was following, then searched the darkness ahead, still edgy and alert. Had the soldiers mistaken them for members of their own army? Ridiculous as that seemed, the Renault did have Moroccan plates and the Land-Rover could have passed for a military vehicle.

Farther on, there were more soldiers staring from behind telephone poles, trees, walls, and buildings. Yet no one ordered the cars to halt. Maybe they assumed the soldiers at the arch had questioned them. Or were they being drawn into a trap?

On a stony abutment overlooking the town, the fortress-like Grand Hôtel du Sud was bathed by floodlights. Surely, thought Polo, it would have been shut down and darkened if they expected trouble. Speeding up on a straightaway, he kept near Ted, then cut left as the road curved through the perfect place for an ambush.

To the right a crumbling casbah of the Glaoui family

brooded over its battlements, the slabs of pisé looking like tombstones, their intricate designs like illegibly scribbled epitaphs. Opposite it the Club Méditerranée, constructed of sterner stuff, duplicated the lines of the casbah, but its flawless cubes of concrete had the appearance of papier-mâché. In a striped tent beside the hotel, stroked by flattering lights, tourists had congregated for an evening of Moroccan folklore.

At the far end of town, Ted waved to more soldiers. Polo didn't bother. When they were a few miles beyond the city, he punched his high beams on and off, signaling Ted to the side of the road.

"What do you think?"

"I think you oughta climb into your car," said Ted. "We have a long ride ahead of us."

"Look, man, there's no alert," he said, as if irritated that there wasn't. "That's obvious."

"Like hell it's obvious. It could be different at Agdz or Zagora. The more time we waste here, the better their chances of getting word about us."

"Yeah, maybe." He was chewing at his moustache.

"But it looks good so far," Ted added, wondering whether that was what Polo wanted to hear.

Polo didn't answer or act encouraged as he returned to the Land-Rover. By the time Ted hurried the Renault through the gears, he had moved into the slipstream and dimmed his lights.

"What'd he expect?" asked Ants. "A victory dance right there in the road?"

"Hard to say. He sure didn't look happy, did he?"

"The hell with him. I am." Bert had one hand on Ted's shoulder, the other on Ants's.

"I knew there wouldn't be any hassles," said Ants.

"What'd you do, read that on your ouija board?" asked Ted.

"Nothing like that. No magic jive for me. I paid off the cops."

"All of them?"

"Yep. Every mother's son between here and the border. The entire army's on the take. You saw it. The secret is to wave as you go by."

As she laughed again, Bert's face lost the last trace of whatever had been bothering her. So, although he was puzzled by Polo's behavior, Ted laughed too.

The terrain began to buckle and roll and as the road plunged through steep gullies, it gave them the sensation of riding a roller coaster. The car seemed to soar, the tires out of touch with the asphalt, and their bellies floated free, giddy with relief, then fell in a resounding jolt. Ted didn't slow down until they came to an unbanked curve.

They had ridden into another mountain range. Though clouds cloaked the moon and stars, he could distinguish broad ledges of rock that continued for miles like lines on a giant graph, but it wasn't until he noticed lights in a canyon far below that he realized how high they'd climbed. At Tizi-n-Tinififft the sign said 1600 meters.

The asphalt coiled tighter and tighter as they squealed down through a series of switchbacks toward the lights of Agdz. Ants and Bert fell silent, and they were all aware of the wind once more, goading them on. Near the outskirts of town, they flashed past a few fires and lanterns—tongues of orange and pinpricks of red. Then there were electric bulbs, but the night deepened around them, much darker than it had been in the mountains. A couple of passenger cars advanced in their direction, driving toward Ouarzazate. At least they're letting some people through, thought Ted, as they entered Agdz.

Soldiers milled through the main street. Some lounged along the sidewalk, others clustered around fires. A platoon of armed men, in no particular formation, shuffled toward The Gravy Train, and at a command which Ted couldn't hear, they closed ranks to block the road. A man with a lantern motioned for the cars to stop. As Ted hit the brake, he realized the Land-Rover should have been in front where he could watch Polo. It was too late to switch.

From what he'd seen before the line of soldiers slammed like a gate in his face, the street was straight for a few blocks, then angled around the town square. Agdz was too big to break through, and this platoon was just the first of his problems. In a burst of speed he might smash through it, but with more soldiers farther on firing from the sidewalk, they wouldn't have a chance.

"Get your hand off that," he told Ants, who was fingering the pistol in his belt. "Bert, how much room did Polo leave me?"

She craned her neck, peering through the cracked window. "Six or seven feet."

"All right, sit back and relax. Everything's okay," he murmured, although the situation didn't suit him a bit. Glancing at the rearview mirror, he couldn't see much of anything in the Land-Rover. That's where it'll start, he thought. Even if they aren't after Gypsy, Polo could cause trouble, and I won't know till it's too late.

Ted tried the side mirror. That was better. He could make out Polo's huge shoulders hunching over the wheel. Look around, you damn fool, and figure the odds. They're against us, and the M-16 won't make any difference.

The soldiers had broken formation to encircle the Renault, more curious than hostile or suspicious, it seemed to Ted. Hanging back a short distance, their rifles still strapped to their shoulders, they jostled and joked with one another as they looked in at Bert, Ants, and him. If anything went wrong, Ted believed the men on the right could be counted on to shoot half their buddies on the left and vice-versa, but in the crossfire the Renault would be riddled.

An officer swaggered forward, balancing a clipboard, a nickel-plated flashlight, and a ballpoint pen in his hands. The troops braced for a moment, but almost immediately crept in for a closer look as he copied the license number of the Renault, scribbling from right to left.

When he came to the driver's side, Ted lowered the window six inches.

"Your passports," he said in French.

"Of course." Ted handed him the three booklets and rolled up the window.

The officer rapped his knuckles on the glass. "Leave it open." He used the familiar.

"Il fait froid."

"All the way down," he demanded and, leaning in his head, scrutinized each of them in the direct glare of the flashlight. The man, who smelled strongly of woodsmoke and spices, had a heavy, smoothshaven jaw and thick lips discolored by the cold and the light. Below the polished visor of his cap his eyes were invisible.

When he'd studied them to his satisfaction, he stood up and shone the light on the passports, leafing from back to front, examining each page, even the empty ones, as though they contained a secret code. For the first time, as he sought to unscramble the enigmatic alphabet, he was unsure of himself.

Ted shot a second glance at the side mirror. No one was checking Polo's papers. Apparently this officer would handle that too. Ted tried to count the soldiers, but there were too many. The six in front squinted into the headlights, which he'd left on along with the engine. These he could blind with his high beams and nail the officer first. Another pointblank shot. Backing up and turning north, he'd be gone before the others unshouldered their rifles. But the Land-Rover would bear the brunt of it.

Lowering his long jaw again, the officer stared at Bert, then flicked his hidden eyes several times from the passport photo to her face.

"It must be my hair," she said. "It was shorter then."

"Mademoiselle has changed her hair style." Ted spoke at the man's jaw as if into a microphone.

"Yes, her hair is different, and his is too long." He indicated that Ants looked very little like the picture which had been snapped several years ago.

"But they are the same people. See where it says about their size and weight, the color of their hair and . . ."

He didn't bother. He was having too much fun flashing the light in their eyes.

"Would you care to see other identification?" asked Ted.

The officer shook his head irritably at the idea of wrestling with more unintelligible print. "Where are you going?"

"South," said Ted.

"Obviously, but where?"

"Zagora."

"Why?"

"I'm a professor. These are my students," said Ted. "We're studying Moroccan village life. It's been very . . . "

He jabbed the flashlight nearer Ted's face. "You don't look like a professor."

"I don't follow you." He fought not to blink.

"I said you don't look like a professor. You don't dress like one."

"In America this is how we dress when we do field research. We've been hiking and camping in the mountains."

"Did you notice anything unusual?"

"No."

"There were no soldiers in Ouarzazate?"

"Yes, there were soldiers."

"And isn't that unusual?"

"I wouldn't know. What the army does is no business of mine."

"Did they question you?"

Ted couldn't guess which was the wiser answer, but took a chance and told the truth. "No."

"That's interesting." The officer scrawled something on the clipboard, and Ted had a sinking feeling that he'd said the wrong thing. "And you saw nothing unusual today?"

"No. I told you we were in the mountains."

"Yes, by the looks of you, you've been there too long. Where have you come from tonight?"

"Not far from Ouarzazate."

"Where exactly?" Ted caught the full force of his spicy breath.

"Tiffoultoute," he mumbled a name he'd noticed on a sign.

"Tiffoultoute isn't in the mountains."

"I didn't say it was. We ate there after we drove down from the High Atlas."

"How could you? It has no restaurants."

Realizing the light would exaggerate any reaction, Ted

had frozen his features into one expression. But at this he was afraid he had flinched. "Would you move that? I can't see."

"There's no need to see. Just answer."

"We don't eat in restaurants. We cook our own food."

Though he lowered the light, the officer's broad jaw hung near the window ledge. Red dots popped in Ted's eyes. The engine of the Renault sounded as racing and erratic as his pulse. His foot trembled on the gas pedal, but he didn't remove it for fear the motor would die. Ted wondered whether the man was suspicious only because of the coup. Probably they were cross-examining everyone who had a foreign passport. Yet this questioning could upset Polo, who might spill too much with his broken French. Or in a fit of panic or pique, fall back on the M-16.

At last he lifted his long jaw and, cradling the clipboard in the crook of his arm, copied the information from their passports. Ted could do nothing except take small comfort that the man was once again scribbling from right to left. Raising himself in the seat, he saw that the officer hadn't translated the words into Arabic. Instead, he attempted to duplicate the Western alphabet, whittling laboriously at each letter like a wood carver.

When he'd finished, he flung the passports onto Ted's lap. "There's a curfew. You must be off the road by midnight."

"Why?"

"There's been trouble in Rabat and in several towns west of here."

"What's wrong?"

"Nothing you need to know about. But you would be smart to stay in Agdz."

"Thanks for the warning." Ted looked at his watch. It was nine-thirty.

"Are you staying here?"

"No. We're going on to Zagora."

"To the Grand Hôtel du Sud?"

"Yes," he said, glad to give him a false lead.

"If you don't arrive by midnight, you'll be arrested. But do as you like." He brought his hand up in a brusque salute of dismissal.

"The people in the next car are also my students. I'll wait for them."

"No. You'll go now."

"They don't speak French. They won't understand you."

"But you said they were students," the officer taunted him.

"They are, but not of languages. They lack your excellent knowledge of French." He took a stab at flattery.

"Then I'll offer them a lesson."

Abandoning his own orders and all caution, Ted started to get out. "I'll be your interpreter."

"I said go." As he slammed the door, Ted yanked in his leg just in time.

At that he went immediately, speeding through the street, which was thronged with troops. His headlights gleamed on scraps of polished metal—buckles, badges, bandoliers of bullets, and rifle barrels.

"What'll we do?" wailed Bert.

"Wait on the other side of town."

"Suppose they're busted?" said Ants.

"See anything back there?" he asked Bert, who was looking through the shattered window.

"No. It's too dark. Ted, we have to help them."

"You heard the man. He said go and he meant it."

And again Ted wondered why. Was that big-jawed bastard just another officer who got his rocks off by pushing people around? If he suspected anything, he wouldn't have hesitated to hold them, unless he had a surprise waiting ahead. He might have telephoned the next guard post by now. Maybe he split us up to make the arrest easier, thought Ted, and was tempted to turn onto a side street and leave town by a different route. But he didn't know where the alleys might lead, and if Polo did pull through, he'd never find them.

For a second, despite himself, this possibility appealed to a shameful part of him. Polo and Gypsy were the weak links. With them gone, the odds would improve. Yes, Ted liked his chances of escaping without them.

But then why had he bothered to free the boy in the first place? Only for the bread, as Polo claimed? No, his clock didn't start and stop for four thousand bucks. Pressing on through Agdz, he promised to give them more than their money's worth so no one could accuse him of being a mercenary. But he knew when a thing was useless. He wouldn't go back and get himself killed. If the three in the Land-Rover were lost, his job was to look after Ants and Bert.

"There's a roadblock," said Ants.

"Be ready to duck," he said to Bert. Shooting a glance at the side mirror, he saw nothing. A chrome-framed circle of black.

An officer blocked the street, swinging a lantern whose flame described a faint red semicircle. Ted's headlights silhouetted other soldiers at either side of the road. Far too many to take on. A sedan had halted in the northbound lane, and the passengers slid out to show their papers. Damned if he'd do that. Agdz ended twenty yards up the road and at his first inkling of trouble, he'd run for it.

"Heads up, Ants. Leave the pistol where it is, but click

off the safety. Don't fire unless I do." He shifted into low gear, surging forward with a loud, revving sound, ready to accelerate.

"Should I roll down the window?"

"Don't bother."

The officer studied their license plate as they rumbled closer.

"I think they . . ."

"Quiet." Ted had one hand on the wheel, the other on the knurled butt of the .357.

Then the officer waved them on. Ted smoothly picked up speed, while Ants swiveled around in the seat.

"No sign of the Land-Rover."

"We can't just leave them," said Bert.

"They'll be along in a minute."

As they cruised around a lazy curve, and the town and its lights vanished, Ted was trying to figure whether, and how long, they should wait. Polo knew the plan. Under other circumstances, he'd have driven on and let him catch up, but you couldn't say what that guy would do.

"Shouldn't we stop?" asked Bert.

"I'm looking for a safe place."

"It's all the same," said Ants, staring at a vast moraine of rubble and slag. To hide the car they'd have to roll far off the road, where Polo would miss it too.

Ted bumped from the pavement onto a patch of gritty pebbles, cut the engine, then the lights. Polo would see them here. So could anyone else. "We'll give them fifteen minutes."

"And if they don't show?" asked Bert.

"They'll catch up later."

"No, I won't do it."

"Yes, we have to. There's no sense circling back. Those

soldiers bust Polo, they'll be after us too. Now, let's get out of the car."

He hustled them across a field of jagged, ankle-twisting rocks, and about thirty yards from the Renault they bellied down in a shallow dry wash where they could watch the car and the road. Ted had drawn his pistol, and so had Ants, but if troops came, he knew it would be silly to shoot. At this distance, in the dark, they'd be lucky to hit a house and they'd just draw fire in return. It'd be smarter to slip away silently.

Ted was about to dash back to the Renault and collect as many of their supplies as he could carry, when a car came around the curve, its high beams raking the field of rocks. He ducked, pulling Bert down with him. Then when the lights moved around on the straightaway, he lifted his head to see the car slow as it neared the Renault. It wasn't the Land-Rover, but he couldn't tell much more. A Fiat maybe. Ted stood to lose a lot more than the map, food, and water. His money was still locked in the glove compartment. Did he dare defend it?

But the car sped south, and Bert said, "How much time do we have?"

"About ten minutes."

"You two go. I'm not."

"I'm not leaving you."

"Then why leave them?"

"I'm not going anywhere yet. But how'll it help for us to get caught too?"

"I don't know." As she shook her head, her hair whisked the sand.

"No way," said Ants, his voice thin and breaking.

Then they heard a second car and fell flat as the head-lights probed the darkness around them like twin tines of a giant fork. Ted's free hand dug into the sand, which was warm just below the surface. His other arm was around Bert, and as she held her breath, her heart beat furiously at the cage of her ribs.

"It's stopping," hissed Ants.

The car was on the far side of the Renault. Ted couldn't identify the model. Leaving the headlights on, a heavyset man, hands on his hips, got out to look around. He wore a uniform of sorts, but he was no soldier.

"Hey, Polo," Ted shouted.

The stocky figure froze. "Yeah?"

"It's us. Is anyone with you?"

"Just Puff and Gypsy."

"Switch off the goddamn lights."

Leaping up, they loped across the gravel. Ted had the pistol in his hand, just in case.

"Christ, what kept you?" cried Bert, but she went to Puff and Gypsy before Polo said, "He asked a lot of questions."

Polo was wet, blown, and panting like a plowhorse, his fatigue shirt plastered to his underarms.

"You sure they're not tailing you?" asked Ted, eying the curve.

"Pretty sure."

"What'd he ask?"

"Everything. Where we'd been. Where we're going. A lot of it I didn't understand, and I pretended I followed less than I did. That's what took so damn long. He kept repeating himself and so did I."

"He ask about us?"

"You bet your ass. I told him we were students, like you said to. I figured he let you through, he'd let us."

"Any problem about Gypsy?"

"No. He compared his face to the picture on Phil's passport a couple times, but that's all."

"What about your face?"

"I told him I fell."

"Did he take your names?"

"Yeah, and the license number." Like Ted, Polo was watching the bend.

"He worked that ballpoint like a soldering iron," said Ants. "Maybe he didn't copy them down right."

"Yeah, maybe," Ted murmured.

Polo hocked, but there was no moisture in his mouth. "I don't get it. He acted suspicious. Why didn't he bust us?"

"Be damn glad he didn't," said Ants. "That was one mean-looking mother."

"Shit," said Polo, trying to spit again.

"I don't think they're after us, or they'd have recognized Gypsy's last name. And they're not rounding up every foreigner who rides by." Ted spoke slowly as he pieced things together. "He didn't even ask about Tazenzit. This has to be a general alert because of the coup."

"So what do we do?"

"Shove off before we have company."

"Same direction?"

"I don't feature turning back."

"Neither do I. But now they know we're heading south. Later on if word comes through about us, they'll have our names and the license numbers. They link up a few facts and we're fucked. They can always phone Zagora or Mhamid."

"I thought of that, but I'm not about to sit here or set out over these." Ted kicked a stone. "You start first. Stay in front."

"Lemme ask a stupid question. Say we hadn't gotten through. What would you have done?"

"You're right. It's a stupid question."

"I'd like an answer."

"I'd of left."

"That's what I thought."

"And that's what I'd want you to do, if I was late."

"So that's the way it is."

"Don't be an asshole, man. It's the only way. Come on, Bert."

They drove in the Dra Valley, the river on their left crackling over its rocky bed, the banks lined by small villages and fields of grain and fruit. The wind had quieted to a whisper, the dust was still. They soon outdistanced the clouds and when a quarter moon and a profusion of stars appeared, the difference seemed as dramatic as between night and day. But this was a day of submarine shades and illusions. The land looked pale, blue, and liquid. The palms waved their fronds slowly, like sea fans in underwater currents and the casbahs and *agadirs* resembled miniature Atlantises, elaborate sandcastles that had somehow lasted.

To the west hovered the Anti-Atlas range, a deeper blue than the sky or the lowland. Tall and stark, the outline of its peaks might have been scratched with a nail on a sheet of polished tin. Though the mountains looked near enough to touch, the distance was drastically foreshortened by the darkness, and they were at least forty miles away.

In the east, across the river, rose the Jbel Kissane, spiny and sawtoothed, like the high comb of a rooster. Donkey paths zigzagged up its steep slope into boulder-strewn wastes, but the cars couldn't crawl over it, and there was nothing on the other side except more mountains and desert.

So they were trapped in this deep ravine, with a deceptive amount of space in which to maneuver, yet only one way to escape—south to Zagora, then on to Mhamid and the border. But somehow Ted felt he was driving in the wrong direction down a one-way alley toward a dead end. Bert and Ants seemed to feel the same, for they didn't joke or talk about this close call. And, of course, Polo, always attuned to the worst, had gotten a glimmer of the truth. Since that officer had their names and license numbers, it would be easy to trace them if he or anyone else ever added up the information.

3

POLO WAS exhausted. For two days his body and mind had been a battlefield for conflicting emotions, and he was afraid he was about to falter. In the lead, he drove the Land-Rover erratically, flooring the gas pedal one moment, hitting the brake the next. With a nightmarish sense that someone was gaining on him, he couldn't flee fast enough. Yet he had no desire to be separated from the others or to cross the border until he'd done—at least learned or decided—something definite.

At the roadblock in Agdz, he had come close. As that son-of-a-bitch badgered him, Polo had computed precisely how simple it would have been to lean forward, as if fumbling for more identity papers, unlatch the panel behind the dashboard, and pop up with the M-16. Jesus, it would have given him a kick to blast the guy, and if it had to happen, he hoped his first shot iced someone like that.

But with each tiny town they tore through—Timiderte, Tansikht, Tamezmoute, Taakilt, Timesla, Tilmesla, Tinezouline, Tissergate—he thought he had lost another opportunity. There were no soldiers or roadblocks in any of them, and he began to suspect it was going to end like this, anticlimax after anticlimax, with a tedious drive through the desert, his ideas and energy drying up like the perspiration on his back.

By eleven o'clock the Dra Valley had widened and the river, siphoned off to irrigate fields, was silt-filled and sluggish. The village of Zagora seemed to be asleep. Though the local and last Grand Hôtel du Sud was illuminated, few other lights shone in the oasis. Then as the main street forked, the right branch leading to Tagounite and Mhamid, they saw several soldiers squatting around a charcoal brazier. One of them stood up and, with a weary wave of the hand, signaled for them to stop.

Polo liked these odds. There were six of them, and they looked sleepy and bored. Rolling down the window, he smelled simmering food. Reluctantly, they got up and, in groups of three, checked both cars at once, glancing cursorily at the passports, indolently asking where they had come from. Where could they have come from except Agdz, and where could they be going except south? The soldiers scarcely listened to the answers. Letting The Gravy Train go on without mentioning the midnight curfew, the Moroccans returned to their meal.

"God, we did it! We did it!" cried Puff as they jounced along the track toward Tagounite. "We're safe." Shaking Gypsy, she hugged him until he was awake with her.

"You know what I think?" she said to Polo. "I think the farther we get, the safer we are. I mean, the soldiers'll assume we've already been searched and quit hassling us."

"Brilliant fucking deduction."

"Hey, what's with you?" asked Gypsy.

"We've got a hell of a drive ahead of us. It's crazy to say we're safe."

"Maybe, but I don't like you talking to Puff that way."

"Tough shit. Somebody has to tell it like it is. That's

what's fouled us up all along—this fantasy tripping, pretending everything's okay because that hill-ape says it is. Look at the goddamn map. There's Tagounite and Mhamid, then miles of nothing but sand dunes. Even in Algeria we . . ."

"Oh, shut up," said Puff. "You sound like you don't want to make it."

"It's not that."

"I don't care what it is. Stay on your bummer. Don't drag us down."

Soon Puff and Gypsy were murmuring again, imagining after all their troubles that they were halfway home. For them, returning to the States would be a new beginning. But for Polo nothing would have changed, nothing would have been accomplished. He couldn't go back at all unless he was willing to serve a long stretch in jail, and he wasn't.

Even if they got to Algeria, that wasn't his idea of Eldorado. Though he hadn't mentioned it to the others, he wondered whether they'd be granted political asylum. He'd read that the regime was holding the Black Panthers under virtual house arrest. Why should they welcome The Gravy Train? Morocco was certain to demand their extradition, and the United States would just as surely support the demand. What if the Algerians gave in to the pressure?

And who wanted to be stuck in Algeria anyway? Eventually he'd have to leave it too. Then what? As they thundered along the washboard track, Polo could conceive of the rest of his life as a road full of barricades and detours, with him scrambling madly to save his own skin and accomplishing nothing else. He'd lived like that for two years and was sick of it. Just once he longed to do something that mattered and break his record as a small-time loser.

They crossed the Jbel Bani by a low, crooked pass and

coasted from the spur of hills onto a hard plain. Once more the wind was droning, laden with dust that lashed the cars. The *piste*, veering west of the Dra Valley, was a path of crushed pebbles marked by an occasional white milestone or signpost. Tamarisk trees, twisted and spectral, rattled their limbs like bones.

Narrow causeways of concrete spanned the sandy bottoms of the dry washes and across one particularly broad *oued* a single lane had been built several feet above the ground for more than fifty yards. At either end, in startling contrast to the darkness, hulked huge, pale dunes tufted by grass. As the tires of the Land-Rover drummed on the cement, Polo took it slow. A strong cross-wind was pushing him toward the edge of the causeway and good-sized pebbles pinged at his fenders.

Ted had shortened the distance between them and dimmed everything except his parking lights when suddenly a bright flash blinded Polo. He thought it was Ted signaling him, but the flash came from in front. High beams had burst on as a jeep drove from behind a dune and onto the pavement. Polo flicked his own lights off and on, demanding the right of way, and when the other driver didn't slow down or switch to his low beams, he slapped the horn. But the jeep kept coming.

"Hey, he's not stopping," said Puff. "Must be a roadblock."

There was a second flash behind him. This had to be the signal. But in the mirror he saw another car sweep onto the causeway, blocking it in that direction. Army jeeps had boxed them in and were bearing down on them.

Gypsy leaned forward. "We better stop."

"What the hell, there's no way off. Wait till we're on the other side."

Speeding up, Polo switched his lights off and on again

and sounded the horn to attract Ted's attention and intimidate the Moroccans. But the jeep sped up and blew its horn too, as if daring him to try and knock it into the ditch. Polo wouldn't give ground first.

"What are you doing?" Gypsy grabbed his arm.

"Get back."

The windshield cracked. Gypsy groaned and fell to the floor.

"He's shot," screamed Puff. "He's bleeding."

Polo didn't wait another second for the signal. Jamming both feet to the floor, he brought on the high beams and a strangled noise from the accelerator. The engine coughed, sputtered, then caught, and the Land-Rover roared head on at the jeep. Another shot nicked through the glass, ripping away the rearview mirror. "Down," he shouted. "Get the hell down."

Loosening his seat belt, he bent low, steering blind, the wheel in his left hand while his right clawed for the rifle behind the dashboard. Bullets banged into the hood and block and chewed the windshield to bits. Stinging slivers peppered his bare neck. Gypsy had stopped screaming; Puff started. For an instant there was no shooting, but the jeep's horn was honking, then its tires squealed. He was aware of two distinct explosions—one as the Land-Rover rammed the jeep, another as his head smashed into the dashboard. Then Polo heard nothing.

He revived on the floor, bleeding heavily from a gash in his forehead. All around him hysterical voices were crying and cursing in English and Arabic, yet Polo made no noise. With the M-16 for support, he sat up and waited while his vision quit swimming. When it did, he watched his left wrist flap like an oiled hinge where the bones had sliced through the skin. His blood looked blue in the dark, his bones a beautiful ivory, and he felt no pain. Perhaps the nerve had been crushed. But even as he observed the wound abstractly, he knew he had to act before nausea and weakness and fear overpowered him.

Raising himself on the strength of his good arm, he stared over the dashboard and discovered a soldier on the hood of the Land-Rover. The man had sailed through the jeep's windshield, shredding his face and shoulders. He probably felt nothing when Polo poked the M-16 against his head and finished him. The fact was, Polo didn't feel much either. His first kill had come too late to matter.

But that didn't stop him. Propping the rifle on the jagged window sill, he squeezed off a clip, and the soldiers in the jeep didn't have a chance to take cover. One man was hung up on the door to the left. The driver, impaled on the steering column, couldn't be budged. So they scrambled frantically to the rear, tumbling headlong onto the concrete. Polo thought he'd hit a few of them.

He sagged to the floor, his back to the bottom of the seat. He gripped the empty rifle between his knees and fought against his dizziness. Though he wouldn't look now at the blood and bones of his broken wrist, he couldn't help thinking, My hand. I'm going to lose my hand. And that seemed like losing everything.

A bilge of weakness welled up in his stomach, and he nearly vomited. Polo had to swallow several times, then blink to clear the blood from his eyes. Bullets whined overhead. He was conscious of a lot of firing from the Renault, but couldn't tell whether there was any shooting in front of him.

"Puff? Gypsy, are you there?" he whispered.

Someone was breathing heavily but didn't answer. The weakness in his stomach had gotten worse, and for the first time he was afraid and wanted to stay where he was until this ended. But he thought there was only one way it could end, and so he loaded the automatic.

Crawling across the floor, he came up on the passenger's side, backlit by the lights of the other jeep. A little orange flame spurted, singeing his left shoulder. A splinter of glass had gone into him, he thought. No more than that. Wrestling the rifle, he aimed at the flame, which flickered again. It spat twice more before he sprayed all around it and snuffed it out.

Polo slumped to the floor, dazed and bewildered. Now pain stabbed him in the shoulder, neck, ear, and wrist. The left side of his body wouldn't work. He couldn't even wink the blood from that eye. Against his will, he watched the arm swinging limp, the hand dangling by threads of flesh, and almost blacked out. But as his brain blurred, the sharpness of his anger kept him partially alert, listening to his blood bubble from him at half a dozen places. Gradually he no longer felt the separate pains. There was just one agonizing ache.

All sounds—gunshots, as well as screams—crashed toward Polo from the rear, cascading over the car like tidal waves. With his legs and the rifle, he levered himself onto the seat and looked at Puff and Gypsy on the back floor.

"You okay? You hear me?" he asked. Or believed he had. He couldn't be sure he'd spoken, the noise of his blood was so loud in his ears.

Balancing the M-16 on the back of the seat, he aimed toward the other jeep. It took all his strength to yank the trigger. He fired until his jaw went slack, his lips were wet, and he was swallowing pieces of teeth. Before he fell, he heard Ants scream, then someone else, and Polo tried to answer. But his mouth was full of sharp chips and a salty fluid that muffled his voice.

He rolled onto his back, lifting his right hand to test the numb spot at the center of his face. His fingers were twisted in the trigger guard, and the rifle smacked him in the head. As Polo was sucked under, he thought he'd been overwhelmed by one of the immense waves and tried desperately to scream in his last outburst of anger for Ants or Kuyler or anyone to save him.

Ted had recognized the ripping, staccato action of the M-16, and the instant Ants's head snapped forward, spilling blood onto Bert, who was flat on the back floor, he knew what had happened. One of Polo's shots had hit the boy. "Stop!" he shouted. "For chrissake, Polo, stop shooting." But Ants was dead, with a neat hole at the base of his skull.

Ducking under the dashboard, Ted was uttering an abject, bleating sound as he reloaded the pistol. His fingers shook, and he started swearing. Empty shells clinked to the floor, then he dropped a few good cartridges. Christ, get a grip on yourself. You can't give in to it. But the boy's death destroyed something inside him.

They'd been doing beautifully, picking off the Moroccans one at a time. Ants had never got rattled. He'd sent out a steady stream of fire as Ted loaded, then had crouched down to reload while Ted fired. Every time Ted had seen a soldier fall, he'd thought they were going to scrape through this. If they kept calm, unlike the Moroccans who jumped from the jeep and charged wildly, they'd get away. But then Polo had cut loose with the M-16.

"Polo," he called. "Come up and cover me." There was no answer.

"Are you all right?" Bert whimpered.

"Yes. Stay down."

"Where's Ants?"

"Don't talk. They'll hear you."

Ted listened for footsteps. He didn't know how many soldiers were alive and was afraid they might rush him. Without Polo to cover his flanks, they could easily surround him.

Reaching over Ants, he pushed open the door on the passenger's side. A bulb brightened in the ceiling, and he crushed it with the pistol butt, while a volley of bullets slammed into the upholstered panel, rocking it back on its hinges. It sounded as if all the shots came from the same weapon and the same direction, the right rear fender of the jeep behind the Renault. He'd noticed four soldiers fall during the early shooting. That left two, and he believed he'd wounded one of them. But he wondered why no one had fired from in front of the Land-Rover.

"Don't move," he whispered to Bert. "Don't make any noise no matter what."

He flung wide the driver's door. Nothing. If there were soldiers on that side in back or front, he was sure they'd have seen it and wouldn't have held their fire. But to double-check and draw their attention, he stuck out his hand, wriggling it, casting a shadow on the door panel. Still nothing.

When a single stray shot whipped through the rear window, Ted eased out of the car on his hands and knees. He climbed off the causeway into the sand, crawled a few yards, then knelt up.

The Renault and the jeep were less than ten feet apart, the space between them brightly lit by the jeep's one remaining headlight. A shot ricocheted off the roof of the Renault, leaving a stripe of raw metal. Yes, there was just one guy behind the right rear fender. Sooner or later, when no one returned his fire, he'd come out of hiding to have a look.

Ted glanced past the Land-Rover to the other jeep, where there was no sound, no movement, no sign of life. Had Polo killed his half dozen before they got him? And what about Gypsy and Puff? No, don't think of them. Don't think about anyone, not even Bert. Just hold tight and hope for a clean shot.

Crawling farther to his right, he had command of the entire area between the cars. At this range he couldn't miss. But let it be quick and don't blame yourself. It was that big-jawed bastard in Agdz who'd finally caught on. That had to be it. Ted wanted to believe this wasn't an insane, suicidal play on Polo's part. No, the game was over once the officer took their names and license numbers. He must have learned the truth, then telephoned the barracks in Tagounite.

Still, Ted wouldn't have shot first or, like Polo, tried to ram his way through. They might have bribed the soldiers. Or, if nothing else, the Moroccans would have made better targets as they came to the cars to ask for their papers. But that was over. He had to hurry the hell away from here before reinforcements arrived.

The jeep bobbed slightly, as the soldier stood on the bumper to look over the roof. Then his boots scuffed the concrete as he stepped down and inched along, out of sight, on the passenger's side. If he's got a brain, he'll bust the headlight, thought Ted. But he hoped he was dealing with a dope, for he'd have a perfect shot as the man crossed the bright spot between the cars.

Ted braced the butt of the big .357 against the causeway, steadying it in both hands, his eye not far from the hammer. The boots scraped the pavement again, then paused behind the front fender. The soldier hadn't switched off the lights. Instead, he fired a few harmless shots, revealing his position. When Ted didn't answer his fire, didn't stir, barely breathed, the soldier stood up.

He had a good shot now, but didn't rush himself. He relaxed his arms, then his fingers, so he wouldn't jerk the trigger and have the gun jump. Don't be too careful, he thought. In the chest. Catch a piece of him and pop him again.

The Moroccan stepped into the light and foolishly paused. When a moth blundered from the darkness, he cringed, his face taut and sleek with sweat. An ordinary foot soldier. Too bad. He'd expected an officer. He didn't want to kill this guy, so he waited. But then the Moroccan moved toward the Renault and Bert. Ted had no choice and the soldier didn't have a chance.

The first shot doubled him over. The second, striking high on the shoulder, straightened him up and stripped the rifle from his hands. It flew from his chest, as if he'd thrown it, and landed in the *oued* behind Ted, who leaped onto the causeway, firing a third time, tumbling him backward. Without breaking stride, he sprinted around the jeep to be sure there were no survivors. In the dark he stumbled through bodies, none of which moved or moaned when he kicked them. Ted forced himself to crouch down and take a closer look. They were all dead.

In front of the jeep, the soldier was on his stomach, struggling to rise. With appalling effort, he had managed to bring himself to his hands and knees, bleeding in three separate streams from his wounds, and when a fourth stream started at his mouth, Ted knew what he had to do. It was a thing he hated, but the man would soon die anyway and it was cruel to let him suffer through this.

Placing the pistol at the back of his neck, Ted pulled the trigger, and it was as if he'd hurled down an enormous weight. The man's arms and legs went out from under him in an awful sprawl, his forehead thudding against the concrete. Then Ted smashed the headlight on the jeep, and waited while his heartbeat slowed and his eyes adjusted to the dark.

Bert was sobbing on the floor of the Renault. He raced to the car and dragged her onto the seat. She didn't appear to be hurt.

"Where's everyone?" she gasped. "Where are they?"

"I'm here. It's okay."

"But the others, how about them?"

"You sit still and get a hold of yourself. I'll see."

He should have done this first, he realized as he skirted around the Land-Rover. Someone could have been alive in the other jeep and had the juice for one last shot. But though Ted was trembling, he felt dead inside. Not weak or scared or sick, just used up, empty. Anxious as he was to save Bert, he couldn't care very much about himself and had to make himself go slower, to recall all he'd learned from too many moments like this.

The radiator, block, and tires of each car had been shot. They'd be no good to him, but he wouldn't have driven on to Tagounite anyway. Someone was bound to be waiting there. They had to get away from the road.

Near the jeep he listened to the seeping of water, oil, and blood. One soldier was still dangling from the door; the driver was still skewered on the steering wheel. In back, the soldiers had fallen in a heap, and Ted pawed through their bodies. They were dead.

Before looking in the Land-Rover, he called loudly, "It's me, Ted." As he opened the door, a bulb in the ceiling blinked on and one of Polo's legs flopped off the seat. His body had been chewed up by bullets and flying glass, and a shell fragment had clipped his moustache and upper lip, widening his toothless mouth. He'd pressed the M-16 to the deep gash, as if to slow the bleeding or give the rifle a hideous kiss. His other arm was wrenched around at an odd angle and when Ted saw the wrist where the shattered bones had burst through, he had to turn aside. Somehow that seemed worse than the bulletholes.

But he couldn't hide his eyes forever. He needed the M-16. Grabbing the barrel and the stock, he tugged sharply, snapping Polo's finger from the trigger guard, and set the rifle outside the Land-Rover. On the floor he found three full clips of ammunition and wedged them into his back pocket.

Puff and Gypsy looked like they were locked in a loving embrace, but blood was the bond that glued them together. Puff's broad back was perforated in four places. Ted put a hand to it, then to her bare wrist, and felt nothing.

Gypsy was pinned beneath her. Stuffing the pistol under his belt, Ted used both hands to pry Puff off of him and onto the seat, taking pains not to look at her face. Gypsy's head, neck, and shoulders were shiny with blood, and he had decided not to flip him over when he thought he noticed the boy shudder. A death spasm? Then he groaned. As Ted grabbed his arm, Gypsy screamed.

Ted lost his grip and let him fall. If he'd had the gun in his hand, he might have fired on reflex. But just as suddenly as the pain had brought Gypsy to consciousness, it pulled him under again, and he breathed like a leather-lunged old man. Most of the blood on him was Puff's. He had only one wound in the chest, about two inches below the collarbone. The bullet hadn't come out the other side.

This time in cold-blooded clarity, not shock, Ted decided he should kill him. He'd seen men recover from worse wounds than this, but they'd had quick medical attention and Gypsy wouldn't get any. Though Ted knew a bit about first aid, he had no supplies, and they were more than thirty miles from the border. He couldn't carry him to Algeria. What was the sense of nursing him through the night and having him die tomorrow or the day after from hemorrhaging or gangrene? He'd only slow them down so that they'd die too.

Gently he placed the gun barrel at Gypsy's temple and closed his eyes. He'd have liked to shut his ears and freeze his feelings too. But if it was the right thing to do, why was he afraid to watch?

He gazed at Gypsy, who was so skinny he could see almost every vital sign in his body. The tense pounding vein at his temple, the rapid fluttering of his eyes under the red lids, his Adam's apple working drily in his throat, the weak rise and fall of his chest. No, Ted couldn't do it while he was watching. So why do it when he wasn't? After all he'd gone through, after the high price so many people had paid for this boy's freedom, he couldn't bear to finish him while there was the slightest chance he'd survive.

Gathering Gypsy to his chest, he lifted him from the Land-Rover. A bundle of damp skin and bones, the boy didn't weigh much. His teeth chattered as he shivered, and Ted held tighter, trying to warm him. Then Gypsy revived abruptly, looking around in alarm.

"It's me," said Ted.

"What? Where? Put me down." He squirmed.

"Don't worry. I've got you."

"No," Gypsy said distinctly. "Really, I'm all right."

Ted set him on his feet, but kept an arm around his waist. He was still squirming and swiveling his neck, as if to shake the effects of a long sleep. Ted kicked the door of the

Land-Rover shut, extinguishing the light that gleamed on Polo and Puff, picked up the M-16, and helped the boy to the Renault.

"I think I better sit down," Gypsy said when they got there. Though his legs were steady, it sounded like he was smothering.

Ted lowered him to the ground, leaning him against the front fender, and stood the rifle beside him. "Come on, climb out," he said to Bert, who hadn't stopped sobbing.

"It's no good. Don't you see? Look at Ants."

"Please, I need your help. Gypsy's hurt."

When she didn't answer, he went to the trunk to collect whatever was worth carrying. Dozens of slugs had torn through the metal, ripping apart their suitcases and popping the goatskin water bags. The uncanned food was soaked and ruined. The rest was too heavy to lug with them. Ted took the army blanket, a poplin windbreaker and several undershirts from Phil's grip, and a roll of tar tape from the tool box.

Gypsy's eyelids had drooped and he'd slumped onto his side.

"You okay?" asked Ted.

He nodded. "Is there anyone but you and Bert?"

"No."

Again he nodded.

"Quick, get that shirt off." As Gypsy began pawing at the buttons, Ted said, "Let me," and peeled the blood-soaked denim from his shoulders. With one of Phil's undershirts, he blotted and cleaned the bullethole, working mostly by touch in the dark, muttering, "Okay, okay. Almost finished," whenever Gypsy moaned. He folded two other tee shirts to form a compress and wadded them over the wound and bound the makeshift bandage tight with tar tape. Then he shoved Gypsy's arms into the sleeves of the poplin jacket and zipped it up to his chin.

After fastening the roll of tape around the barrel of the M-16, he wrapped the rifle in the army blanket. "Be right back," he said to the boy, who was panting harshly.

"Come on, baby, we gotta go," he begged Bert as he scooped his money and the Michelin map from the glove compartment. A few dirhams and dollars fluttered from his fingers, but he didn't bother chasing them. He put the bills into his pocket with the bullets.

Easing Ants onto the floor, he reached for Bert, his hands bloody. Sobbing, she resisted. "No. Everybody's dead."

"Gypsy's alive."

She looked up. "And the others?"

There was no time to waste. Ted dragged Bert from the Renault, doing his best not to hurt her. But when he let go, she collapsed and he had to grab her arms and shake her. "Don't do this. Please, don't make me."

Her eyes were shut, her mouth wide and wailing. The way sound traveled in the desert, anyone might have heard her. So Ted slapped the flat of his hand across her face, and felt almost as bad as he would if he'd shot Gypsy.

Her eyes opened in amazement, her mouth closed with the sound of suddenly clenched teeth. Her tiny hand tried to cover the print of his much larger palm on her cheek, and she stared at him like she couldn't believe what he'd done and feared much worse.

Ted kissed her hand, then kissed the spot he had hit. "I had to," he mumbled. "Please, baby, hurry."

She nodded absently and seemed semiconscious. But at least she wasn't screaming and would walk when he told her to.

Ted led them from the causeway into the *oued*. He had

an arm around Gypsy's waist, and could hear and feel his hard breathing. In his other hand he had the rifle rolled in the army blanket. Bert stumbled on ahead until the night nearly swallowed her. "Wait," he whispered, and she dropped back beside him, hooking her fingers through his belt loop. As they walked into the wind with the sand stinging their faces, he refused to think of the things he might have forgotten, of all that he'd left.

VII

THERE WAS only one way to go. From the map, Ted knew the dry washes flowed west to the Oued Dra. When they reached the river, they could follow it south to Tagounite and from there to Mhamid. But these were remote objectives, for much as Bert and Gypsy had trouble keeping up the pace, it was more important to put miles between the road and them. Soon he was half-carrying him and dragging her, yet he didn't slow down.

Automatically he calculated their chances, and though the odds were against them, they had a few advantages. The wind chased dust around their feet, covering their tracks. It was after the midnight curfew, and no more civilian traffic would be traveling south. Even if the army sent someone to check on the jeeps, it would take time to make sense of that bloody collision on the causeway. Maybe they'd assume everyone was dead and call off the alert. Or if they'd been in contact with the officer in Agdz and realized the body count was short, they might not search for survivors until dawn. By then Ted intended to be far from here.

As the *chergui* whistled and wheezed at them, they rasped back, their throats and nostrils raw with grit. Ted was reminded of last night's snowstorm, but this was much worse. Nearly as cold as a blizzard, the sandstorm choked them, blinded them, and flayed them with sharp grains of quartz.

"Let's go higher," he said, guiding them to level, solid ground where the walking was easier and the wind squandered its strength over a broad plain.

Still Gypsy sounded like he was strangling. His wasted body had become one huffing lung, and Ted felt his chest inflate and collapse, weaker at each gasp.

"It's no good. I can't catch my breath," he said.

"Is the tape too tight?" asked Ted.

"No. It's like there's air inside burning me. I've gotta stop."

"In a minute."

"No, man. Now." His legs folded, and he fell down.

"Okay, we'll rest." But Ted stayed on his feet, prowling about, squinting into the darkness, listening to Gypsy pant louder like he was on the last mile of a marathon. Had the bullet nicked his lung? Ted seemed to remember men who were lung-shot spat up buckets of blood.

"He's shivering," said Bert, kneeling beside the boy.

"It'll be better when we're moving."

"I'm thirsty," croaked Gypsy.

"We'll be at the river soon." As he bent down, Ted saw how badly he was trembling and unwrapped the blanket from the rifle to drape it around his shoulders. "Just a little further. Then we'll drink."

By a combination of bullying, coaxing, and deafness to their demands, Ted managed to march them two miles,

maybe more, then thought he sensed the plateau slanting
toward the Dra. Gypsy's gasping was a monotonous whine
broken only occasionally as he coughed on the dusty air.
But when his legs folded a second time, Ted held tight and
wouldn't let him fall.

"He's choking," said Bert.

"No use stopping. The sooner he gets water the better."

"But look, he can't walk."

"I'll carry him. You take this." He handed her the M-16.

When Ted picked up Gypsy, his respiration improved.
Though he couldn't call on enough energy to speak, he
nodded his gratitude, then faded into a fitful doze, his head
hanging back, his jaw slack.

In spite of his own pain, Ted set a dogged pace, focusing
on the dark line of the Oued Dra hundreds of yards ahead.
He'd found the best position, bent forward at the waist, and
simply shoved one foot in front of the other. But his arms
ached, the strain told in his shoulders and thighs, his calves
had knotted, and now he couldn't catch his breath. Rock
hard under his heels, the ground sent its punishment jolt-
ing up his legs along his spine to his head, and a jagged
pain sliced deeply at his sides as he made progress in desperate lunges, pitching forward, then recovering his balance.

"Ted." Bert yanked his belt loop. "Stop. Please, stop."

"Not here. Down there. See it?"

He leaned into every step, as he'd watched workhorses
do, but the going got tougher when the land flattened.
They crossed a field of scrub bushes and coarse cutting
weeds. Through a palm grove, they staggered the last yards
on a path that brought them to the bank of the *oued*.

Behind a barrier of date palms, Ted said, "Here," and
Bert pitched aside the rifle and curled up in the grass,

hugging her knees to her chest and crying quietly. Her tears lashed at him, terrible as any tirade, but Gypsy had greater need of his attention.

The boy was unconscious. Ted stretched him out on his back, elevating his feet against a tree trunk. He didn't awaken even when Ted tested the bandage to be sure no blood had seeped through. His face looked unnaturally pale, his lips purple and cracked, and something whirred in his throat, as if he were dredging air through matted straw.

"I'm going to get water," said Ted.

"What?" asked Bert.

"I'm going to the river."

"No. Don't leave me."

"It's not far. Look." He pointed to the flat banks of the *oued*. "You can watch."

Beyond the shelter of the palm fronds, the night was brighter, and he half-expected to cast a shadow on the sand, but was grateful that he didn't. If Bert could see him, so could anyone else. He dashed to the Dra, switched the pistol from the front to the back of his belt, flung himself on the ground, and drank. The water quickly quenched his thirst, but he kept guzzling until his belly ached with its fullness. Since they didn't have canteens, this was the best way to carry it—inside him, like a camel.

Then, taking off his shirt, he threw it into the river, clinging to one cuff, unfurling the faded denim like a flag. As the material soaked up moisture, it started to sink. Ted reeled it in, filled his mouth with water, and sprinted to the palm grove, lugging the wet ball of cloth and breathing through his nose.

When he got to Bert, he pressed his mouth to hers and jetted the water between her lips. "Now suck on this," he said, showing her how to twist a drink from his shirt.

When she was satisfied, he squeezed a trickle into Gypsy's mouth. The boy swallowed painfully, his sharp knuckle of an Adam's apple grating in his throat. Though he didn't answer when Ted spoke to him, he strained for the water and obviously wanted more.

Ted mopped his clammy cheeks, his high forehead, his thickening lips. Something smelled foul. Rotten flesh already? More likely it was the odor of his own exertion. Again Ted thought, the smartest thing is to leave him. He couldn't live much longer. Just long enough to louse them up. But he'd been through this. Now Bert would know, and since he'd found it hard to drag her away from her dead friends, he hated to think how she'd react if he ditched Gypsy.

"Okay, babe, time to go." He lifted the boy .

"Does he hear us? Can't he talk?" asked Bert.

"I think he's asleep."

But Gypsy was far beyond sleep. His thin body had gone limp, his lungs pumped a little less air. Ted started up the trail with Bert tagging along behind him, cradling the rifle like a baby.

At most they had five more hours of darkness, and at the first light of dawn they'd have to hide. Sleeping during the day, they'd head south again that night. Now he concentrated on what he could see of the oasis—the plots of grain, the palms weighted with dates, the mud walls that blocked the wind, the murmuring river, the smelly irrigation ditch that paralleled the path. I'll get to those trees, he told himself, then rest. And when he reached the trees, he thought, Fifteen minutes and we'll make that wall. It's a better place to stop. But as they approached the wall, he said to himself, Just to that stand of bushes. You can do it.

Yet, near the shrubs, he noticed they were too sparse and thought, At the next palm grove, we'll be safe.

They trudged on for two hours like this until Bert's legs wobbled and she tripped over her feet. "Ted, Ted," was all she said as she tugged at him.

"Not far. Hold on."

Releasing his belt loop and the rifle, she slapped face-down in the sand.

He heard her fall, yet in his stupor he stumbled a few more steps. Too tired to turn, he backed up until he stood over her. She looked small and wretched, lying there like a toy soldier that had tumbled with its toy gun. Her body quivered, but he couldn't tell whether she was crying, fighting for air, or both. At this rate, she might not last any longer than Gypsy, and that sent a chill of clarity through him. Bert was the one who counted. Without her the rest of this was ridiculous.

"Just a second. I'm coming."

He spoke like he had a long distance to travel and in a sense he did. Slowly, in several excruciating stages, he low-ered himself to his knees and bowed so his arms were outstretched with Gypsy pinning them to the ground. Leaning back, he yanked his hands free, scraping off skin. As his joints popped into place, Ted was paralyzed until a tingling feeling returned. "You're all right. Rest a minute," he said.

Though he wanted to lie down beside her to soothe Bert and accept the comfort of her closeness, he was afraid he'd fall asleep and never wake up. So he murmured and passed his hand along her flank. Yet she still seemed dis-tant, and it wasn't only that she didn't answer. It was as if he were losing her, as if she were dissolving into the dust, even as Ted touched her. They were separated by an exhaustion and pain so profound nothing, especially not his pathetic attempt at tenderness, could bridge the gap between them.

"We have to go," he said sooner than necessary.

Clumsily he climbed to his feet, hauling Bert to her hands and knees, and was reminded of the Moroccan he'd hit three times, then dispatched with a pointblank shot in the neck. More gently then, Ted urged her up.

Since he couldn't hold Gypsy in his arms any longer, he forced him upright and took the body across his back in a fireman's carry. But suddenly something in the boy snapped, and he writhed and screamed, shattering the silence of the oasis.

"Stop him," said Ted, spreading his legs for balance. "Shut his mouth."

"He'll smother."

"I said shut it."

She clamped her hand to his face, and after a brief struggle Gypsy was quiet, his breathing much weaker. Bert must have noticed this, but neither of them mentioned it.

"Walk next to me," he said, arranging the load so that he had one arm free. "Lean on me."

As the stars disappeared, the sky grew ash grey in the east, and while the riverbed widened, the *oued* itself diminished to a thread purling over smooth sand. The wind was blowing harder, gathering up dust and driving it into dunes that barricaded the path and poured tendrils through the fields. The palms stood in stunted clusters, and some had died and turned brown. Two or three had had their fronds torn off and the trunks tilted against the morning light like shabby columns.

Then they wandered out of the oasis altogether, where

the dunes combed higher and were scooped hollow on the leeward side. With Bert clasped to his hip, Ted had trouble keeping his feet. Wading through sand, they sank ankle deep, and powder grated in their noses, eyes, and throats. It was torture to breathe or swallow. Ted's one thought was not to drop Bert or Gypsy as they battled these dunes and each other like drowning swimmers.

At last they gained the cover of a palm grove and limped from the trail into a lush field of grain. Bert fell like a stone and lay stunned on the soft bed of green. Crouching, Ted shrugged Gypsy from his shoulders, but the burden seemed a permanent part of him and he felt he was peeling loose layers of his own flesh. His strength failed, and he spilled the body in front of him. Though Gypsy hit square on his bad side and shriveled like a burnt spider, he didn't make a sound. It was Ted who cried out, first at his blunder, then at the pain which exploded through his upper torso. Clutching his chest, he rolled onto his back and let the loamy earth shape itself to his aching muscles.

This was a mistake. Even through the distortion of weariness and pain he recognized they were too close to the path. Anyone on it would have spotted them. But he couldn't move. The most he could do was leave his eyes open so he wouldn't sleep. That'd be the end, he thought.

When Ted finally did move, he made another mistake. Dragging himself to the irrigation ditch, he splashed the putrid water over his face, neck, and head, and dipped some into his mouth, meaning only to rinse it out. But he couldn't help himself and swallowed. What was it Phil had said? Schisto-something-or-other. These ditches were diseased, yet he didn't quit slurping it down until he'd drunk his fill.

As he drew back, Bert was on her belly beside him, lap-

ping at the stream. Now she'd tasted it too. One sip was all
it took, he guessed, so she might as well satisfy her thirst.
But Ted pounded his fists at his thighs. Fatigue turned
any man into an idiot. That's what he had to guard against.
He could cope with his fear and force it to work for him,
but this punchiness could wreck them.

When Bert was finished, he steered her far from the path
and didn't mention the polluted water. Then he hauled
Gypsy to the hidden spot in the grass and settled him on
his back with his feet in Ted's lap.

"Are we staying here?" asked Bert.

"A few minutes."

"I'm exhausted."

"We can't stop."

"Then let's leave now before I faint."

"Soon as I catch my breath."

What a waste, he thought, elevating the boy's feet, when
he couldn't last. Still, you had to hope . . . No, he wasn't
hoping, just going through the motions, while his mind
groped for an angle, an escape from this noose they'd stuck
their necks into. And that brought him back to abandoning
Gypsy.

Jesus, it was just like this whole job. He'd overlooked
everything he'd learned, anything that was logical, and
before long it had him thinking and acting like a fool.
Though nothing could excuse what he'd already done, how
many more allowances could he make for that? He might
delay it, but if he wanted to survive, circumstances, not his
squeamishness, had to start dictating what he did.

Bert touched her hand to Gypsy's forehead. "He's sweating."

"Could be shock."

"That's bad, isn't it?"

"Yes."

"He must be heavy for you."

Ted didn't answer. What if she suggested it? Would he do it then?

"Will he live?" she whispered.

Though Ted wasn't sure whether Gypsy heard them, he said, "I doubt it."

Bert pulled away, as if afraid the wound was contagious. It is, Ted was tempted to tell her. They'd catch it, too, walking under this slowly dying corpse.

"It's time," he said.

He offered her a hand, but she ignored it, perhaps believing that as long as she could stand on her own, they didn't have to leave Gypsy.

Bert was wrong. Now, while they had the strength, was the time to do it. Not sloppily, at the last second, when it wouldn't matter. They had to kill him and bury the body. Unless they did that they might as well be stuck with him till the end.

Ted hoisted Gypsy, stooping to accept the weight across his shoulders, and felt as though a harness had been hung on him. There was an overall ache and also barbed points of pain where his joints jammed together and the bones jabbed at his skin.

Bert went first. Slope-shouldered and somehow hulking despite her size, she moved like a man, walking on the outside edges of her sore feet. She seemed older, much older, and if she'd aged in the last few hours, Ted didn't like to imagine how he looked. He felt ancient and sway-backed as a mule. Maybe this was the night his body would begin paying off its bad debts and he'd skip middle age and become an old man.

On the trail, Ted took the lead. Visibility was better

about two hours before daybreak, and he pushed on rapidly, anxious to get near Tagounite before the town woke.
But Bert clung to his belt loop and at times he believed
she'd tripped and he was towing her like a sled of stones.

When his shoulders became damp and sticky, and something oozed down his spine, he assumed it was sweat and
said nothing until Bert murmured, "He's bleeding."

"Where?"

"His shoulder. Through the bandage and jacket."

"How about his mouth? His ears?"

"No. Just his shoulder. It's pretty bad. All over your
back."

"On the ground?"

"Yes. There too."

Ted stopped. "Turn and look. Is there a lot on the
path?" He stayed bent forward, facing southeast where the
sky had brightened above the hills.

"Yes, big gobs of it."

"Is he alive?"

"Can't you tell?"

"No. Reach your hand near his nose and mouth."

"Ted, you do it. I . . ."

"I don't want to put him down. I don't know that I could
pick him up."

"Yes, he's breathing." Bert sounded resigned rather
than relieved.

"Okay, hurry back and cover the blood."

"How far?"

"As far as it goes." He pivoted so he could watch. "I'll
wait here. Snap it up."

As Bert kicked dirt over the blood and ground it in with
her heel, each step appeared to be an agony. Cringing as
if the trail was scorching hot, she resembled one of those

wizened old women from the villages. While Ted watched her, he heard the *plop-plop-plop* of more blood dripping from Gypsy into a pool at his feet.

By the time she returned, her spine seemed to have hardened into a permanent curve and the hollows which he had always admired in her cheeks had drawn tight over the frame of bone. Ted yearned to caress her, kiss her, somehow erase the haggard expression from her face, but he could barely speak. "Get this stuff around my feet."

She squatted to spread sand over it, and he scuffed his shoes to help her.

"Walk behind me," he said, "and wipe up our tracks and the blood."

"Shouldn't we do something? I mean, he's . . ."

"I'll see to it once we stop."

An hour later, when he spotted several mud huts not far from Tagounite, he detoured from the main trail onto one that bridged the irrigation ditch and cut diagonally through cultivated plots which were less and less lush as he got away from the *oued.* For a few acres the farmers had fought the desert to a standstill, but then tongues of sand began to lap at the borders, reclaiming the land. The fields had a baked crust, as though they'd been fired in furnaces, and only weeds sprouted in the cracks. Sand dunes had surrounded the surviving palm trees.

Clambering over one high dune, which was concave at its center like a bomb crater, Ted settled Gypsy at the base of a squat palm. The circular wall of sand concealed them, and the slanting fronds would provide shade when the sun rose. Bert floundered down after him, obliterating the trail of blood.

"Gimme your shirt," he said. "I have to get water. I'll

soak yours and mine now, so you and Gypsy'll have something to drink. It'll be too dangerous once it's light."

He helped her with the buttons, starting at the bottom, and their dry, rough hands met in the middle at her chest and stayed together an instant. When she slipped off the shirt, her body looked pink and tender. Her breasts had a youthful lift. She wasn't old and beaten no matter how badly her face showed the strain. A little girl, Ted thought. Just a baby. He kissed her cheek—her skin tasting of salt and sand—took the shirt, and left.

At the irrigation ditch, Ted darted a glance up and down the main trail. Beyond it and a line of low scrub bushes, the banks of the Dra dipped abruptly to a depth of six feet or more. A lemony light had flared from behind the hills, and the sun, hovering just below the horizon, would soon soar over the top. If he risked running to the *oued*, Ted was afraid he'd be seen, so he stuck his face into the foul ditch water, which was refreshing once he'd shut out the septic smell. Then he drenched his shirt and Bert's, rolled them up, and returned to the sand-encircled palm tree.

Half-naked, Bert slept next to Gypsy on the floor of the dune. It might have been a shallow grave containing two bodies about to be buried. The familiarity of the scene sent a shudder up Ted's spine. Christ, how many times had he been through this? For years, all over the world, it seemed the earth had widened its maw and he'd thrown meat into it.

Ted went down and woke Bert. Propping herself on an elbow, she had sand beaded on her bare flesh. He brushed it off and passed her the shirt, which she bit into as if he'd brought her a piece of fruit. Then throwing back her head, she twisted the cloth till water streamed into her mouth, over her lips, her chin, and chest.

Bert shivered. "Beautiful. Delicious," she panted. "I was dreaming of water."

"Good. Drink it before it dries."

Ted sponged Gypsy with the cuff of the other shirt, cleaning his eyelids and moistening his chapped lips. As the boy's mouth opened, he squeezed a trickle of water into it. The first swallow sounded scratchy, like there was gravel in his throat. The second was smoother and, after that, the tight lines around his lips and eyes loosened. But when Ted asked, "Do you hear me? Don't try to talk. Just nod," the boy didn't respond.

Blood seeped through the jacket and blanket, spreading a stain on the sand. The sun was high enough now to glisten on the rust-colored granules. Gypsy's bandage had to be changed, but Ted decided to wait until Bert was asleep.

She had bunched up the damp shirt and buried her face in it, still thirstily gnawing.

"Here, baby, lemme have that. You lie down."

He prodded her onto her side away from Gypsy. As she shivered, he drew the denim over her shoulders, although that couldn't have warmed her much. He thought of bundling Bert in Gypsy's blanket, but knew the boy needed it more.

When she was asleep, he folded back the cover and unzipped the jacket to tug at the bandage he'd taped to Gypsy's chest. The tape came off easily, but the wadded undershirt had stuck to something. He yanked harder and it tore away with the sound of rotting adhesive. Gypsy groaned, then was quiet.

Though the wound wouldn't close, a little less blood dribbled out at every breath. Ted cleaned it with his wet shirttail, then ripped a square from the blanket, doubled the wool over twice and clamped it to Gypsy's chest. Since the roll of tape had fallen off the rifle barrel, he slit one of the sleeves from his shirt and used it to tie the compress around the boy's shoulder.

After burying the bloody tape and bandage, he went to the crest of the dune where he could watch the path. The lemony light intensified to a hot, hard-edged orange as the sun sailed over the hills. The *oued* had carved a deep notch in this range, and while sluggish water from the Dra leaked through the ravine toward the desert, heat and sand blew in from the Sahara, arid and odorless as bone meal. That was the route they'd follow tonight.

Pulling the Michelin map from his pocket, Ted placed them in an oasis north of Tagounite. From here, the Dra Valley veered southeast to Mhamid, but once beyond that, they'd have to head directly south where there were no towns, no *oueds*, no oases, and the tracks deteriorated into sketchy dots across an enormous expanse of white. Though the border wasn't marked, highway N50, skirting the Grand Erg Occidental, was on the Algerian side. Their one hope was to reach that road and flag down a truck transporting ore from the mines in Tindouf to the railhead at Béchar.

But Ted's belly went hollow as he added up the miles. It was at least forty, the last fifteen through open desert. As a youngster in boot camp he'd carried a sixty-pound pack on a fifty-mile hike. Gypsy must have weighed more than twice that. How long would it take to cover the distance with the boy on his back? And without food or water, why even consider it?

He creased the map, tucking the empty, uncharted section out of sight. First they'd get through this day, he thought, then the night. Their immediate goal was Mhamid. Make that before worrying about Algeria. Dividing the distance into a day and a night and a new town at a time, Ted could face it.

Fetching the rifle, he ripped the other sleeve from his shirt and snapped a slender limb from the palm. Once he'd knocked off the unripened dates, the branch was hard and smooth, and he wrapped his shirt-sleeve around it. Then, standing the M-16 between his knees, he used the branch as a rod to stroke out the barrel. When he was satisfied with the bore, he pulled the clip and cleaned the action, wiping it as best he could.

The familiar ritual soothed and reassured Ted. Stacking the clips in his lap, he shucked the cartridges onto his shirttail and rolled them between his fingers, polishing them before he popped the bullets back in one at a time. When he slid a clip into the M-16, he heard it click home securely. There was only one place to put the rifle and the spare clips where they wouldn't get dusty again, and that was inside the blanket with Gypsy.

After stowing them safely beside the boy, Ted started on the .357 magnum. Emptying its chambers, he poked four spent shells into the sand and slipped the live ones into his pockets with the others. He had maybe a dozen and a half altogether, and as he pressed the pistol to his lips and blew through the barrel, he wondered whether he shouldn't save three bullets. One for each of them. He hadn't come this far at such a great cost only to be captured. After all that had happened, it wasn't hard to imagine what the Moroccans would do to them.

The metal tasted oily and awful, and he took it off his tongue. No, the hell with that. He wouldn't do it. He'd sworn to Bert they wouldn't be caught, but he wasn't about to shoot her or himself. Not when he wouldn't kill Gypsy. What kind of sense was that?

Ted had the barrel in his mouth once more when Bert shouted, "Don't."

Startled, he banged his front teeth.

"No, please don't."

"Quiet. It's okay," he said. "I'm just cleaning it."

"Oh." She sighed and sat up.

"No more yelling. You'll have the whole village down on us."

"God, gimme a minute to think." She raked a hand through her matted hair and after glancing around frantically, as if she'd forgotten where she was and how they'd gotten there, she fixed her eyes on Gypsy. "How is he?"

"The same."

"He hasn't talked?"

"No."

Bert dug nervously at the sand, building a little pyramid. "It's hopeless, isn't it?"

"He might pull through. I've known men that . . ."

"Not just for Gypsy. Us."

"Hell, no. We'll make it."

After a moment she said, as though thinking aloud, "It'd be easier without him, wouldn't it?"

"It'll be tough no matter what."

"But easier without Gypsy?"

"I'd rather not discuss it, okay?"

"Why not?"

"It doesn't do any good."

"What does? We have to do something. If he had a doctor . . ."

"He doesn't. I'm sorry, baby."

"But we could sneak into town tonight and leave Gypsy where they'd find him. There must be an army doctor in Zagora or Mhamid."

"Maybe, but if he lived, they'd execute him anyway. So

what's the sense? And they might grab us. They'd sure as hell know we're in the neighborhood."

"Ted, we can't just abandon him."

"I didn't say we would."

"What then?" She threw down the sand, demolishing the pyramid.

He realized he hadn't fooled her, not for a second. Bert understood that carrying Gypsy they couldn't make it. Buzzard-like, she'd circled the same subject, but, like him, was reluctant to swoop in for the kill.

"We'll push on and pray we get to Algeria before it's too late," he said. "We have a long walk tonight. Why not sleep?"

"What about you? Aren't you tired?"

"I'll rest later. That's it, lie down and shut your eyes. Tomorrow we'll be out of this," he crooned, and knew he wasn't lying. In a day or two they'd be out of it one way or another.

At the crest of the sand dune, Ted struggled to stay awake and stand guard. But as the sun brightened, it bleached the land, distorting his vision and stinging his eyelids. When he shut them, they seemed translucent. The red he saw might have been his own blood, the wavering blue lines, his veins. Strangely he started to shiver and again thought of a blizzard, of being snowblind, and of how extreme heat and cold were much the same.

As the shadow of the palm shifted, he crawled after it to keep his bare arms and face from burning. But open or closed, his eyes ached constantly now, and the glare caused a dizzy sickness at his stomach. He barely had the strength to duck when two men, holding hands, appeared on the main path. They emerged from a shimmering mirage, their sandals scuffing up clouds that hung in the hot air long after they had vanished. Their laughing voices lingered, too, rattling in the dry pan of Ted's brain.

Later a Berber drove a donkey loaded with lumber in the opposite direction, and while the animal ambled on, he crouched at the ditch and urinated. Ted felt sicker still, and knew it wasn't just the sun and lack of sleep. The scummy ditch water had done this to him. While the man chased after the donkey, his djellabah dancing in the dust, Ted nibbled a cluster of green dates, trying to clean the rancid taste from his mouth. But the fruit was bland and waxy, and he might as well have been munching a candle.

By noon the sun had become molten, pouring through the palm fronds, scalding the sand and the seat of his pants. The heat pursued him, and so did the fat, droning flies. Drunk on sweat, they crawled to their favorite spots at the corners of his eyes, lips, and nose, and preferred to die there rather than buzz off when he slapped at them.

Then the sun was spinning and the shade shifted faster, leaving more of the dune exposed to the harsh light. Below him, Gypsy and Bert stirred in their sleep, twitching like insects under a magnifying glass. Ted scurried woozily around the rim of the crater, but couldn't escape. His face fell against the cinders of sand, and he retched yellow bile and bits of date pulp, and buried his vomit like a dog.

Finally he went down to wake Bert.

"I'm sick."

"What is it?"

"My stomach. You stand guard and lemme rest. Watch the path. You notice anyone headed this way, call me."

"Will you be all right?"

"Yes. I just need sleep."

The pistol was pressing at his belly, and he packed it

inside Gypsy's blanket with the M-16 and rolled over, clutching his knees to his chest, as he'd seen Bert do. The palm tree arched over him like an umbrella, but swords of light slashed through the fronds, and it seemed he was trapped at the bottom of a raffia basket where the heat was thick, the air achingly thin. Breathing in burned his throat; breathing out singed his lips. The sun had a pulse and panted, too, through a sour mouth with a dead-leaf tongue that murmured in his ear. Or was that Gypsy gasping?

The boy's skeletal face bore the scalloped contours of the countryside—all jutting ridges and dark crags. His skin had boiled and shrunk like rawhide, drawing his upper lip above discolored teeth and revealing bristles on his chin like whiskers on a dead man.

Still clasping his arms around his knees, Ted cushioned his belly and rocked back and forth, wrestling the illness. Yet he sensed that he was losing, sinking, that this time the earth had opened its maw for him and parts of him were dropping off and he couldn't retrieve them. For a moment his mind glowed like an ember in the sand. He had to be better by evening. They couldn't stay here. But gagging, he brought up more bile and felt worse. His thoughts crackled, then flickered out.

2

FROM THE peak of the dune, Bert gazed at Gypsy and Ted, who looked dwarfed and pitiful, like figures examined through the wrong end of a telescope. She'd often watched herself this way, especially after her months in jail when she'd first mixed with people, mechanically smiling, laughing, talking, yet had felt that she—her real self, at any rate —was standing off to one side, observing intently, aware of everything, understanding nothing. Only in the last few days with Ted had she broken the habit of abstracting herself. Now the situation had gone beyond her again.

Though she wanted to take Ted in her arms, she didn't dare touch him. Her hands were hot and gritty, and she feared he'd cringe at the gentlest caress, not simply because of his sunburn, but because her affection would act as another demand on him, and he already had too much to worry about.

Near Bert, a black beetle the size of a silver dollar strode up the dune on bent-twig legs, leaving tracks like a long zipper. As the steepness increased, sand slid from under the bug and it scrambled madly to stay in place, but tumbled to the bottom in an avalanche of dust.

Immediately it dug itself free and started up a second time, tireless and undeterred. Toward what? It made her sick and weary to watch. She turned back to Ted and wondered how she could help.

Gypsy and she were a bigger burden than he suspected. He wasn't going to get his money. Would that knowledge make Gypsy heavier for him? And what about her? They were both dead weight, and there was just one way to solve that. Be totally dead so Ted could save himself.

Silently Bert slid down to Gypsy. Wrapped in the woolly green blanket, the boy resembled a gnarled stick that had grown moss, but when she extended her hand above his mouth, his breathing warmed her palm. A few inches lower and, weak as he was, he'd smother without a whimper. Ted wouldn't do it, not with her around. It was up to her.

When she pressed her palm to his nose and mouth, Gypsy did nothing for an instant, then his eyes fluttered behind inflamed lids that had been sealed shut with gum. His lips parted and his teeth were like live coals against her skin. Bert drew back as if she'd been burned, and Gypsy went on wheezing diligently, dying at his own speed.

Bert was breathless, too. Once he was dead, there would be no justification, not even a reason—bad or good—for what they'd done. The whole scheme had been senseless from the start, she saw now, and maybe it was fitting to end it in absurdity by killing the person so many people had died to free. But she couldn't do it.

As she smoothed the blanket around his shoulders, she felt the barrel of the pistol. Checking to be sure Ted wasn't awake, Bert carried the gun up the dune, trembling, trying to calm down and decide how to do this. Though she couldn't kill Gypsy, she thought she could take care of herself. Then Ted could do whatever he had to. That was the one gift she could give him—a release from the web of entanglements she'd woven.

Her hands shook as she shoved the .357 to her temple. She'd expected the barrel to be cold, but it was very hot, and she moved it a fraction of an inch from her skull. This is going to make a hell of a noise, she thought. I won't hear it or see the mess. He will. Ted would wake in time to watch her fall. Then what? He'd have to run for it before anyone rushed out from the village. But first he'd finish Gypsy. He wouldn't have a chance unless he did that.

But was it that simple? Why did she count on his killing Gypsy when she couldn't do it? She made him sound like a savage.

Bert knew how she'd have reacted if he'd committed suicide. When she woke and found him with the gun in his mouth, she'd screamed at once, not caring who heard. Now if she went ahead, he was bound to believe it was his fault and see her suicide as a kind of accusation—an unfair one, since she and the others, not Ted, were to blame.

No matter how she turned it in her mind, it seemed she'd cause him more trouble than she would herself. In an instant she'd be out of it, but he'd have to pick up the pieces. No, she wouldn't be releasing Ted, just dumping everything in his lap when the least she could do was lend him what little strength she had, share the responsibility for all that had gone wrong, and die with him if it came to that.

Bert's hand was numb from gripping the gun. She lowered it to her leg.

The beetle was still bustling on the treadmill of sand, its antennae bent, its shell speckled with grime. As Bert nudged it toward the top, she thought, I won't take the easy way. The bug tried to nip her, but then it was over the edge, skidding down the far slope, striding purposefully, as though there were something out there other than a universe of dunes.

As Bert watched the heat-warped countryside, she noticed a cloud of dust to the north. It couldn't have been a car; the path wasn't that wide. Someone on foot, she figured, and didn't call Ted.

When the cloud was closer, she saw inside it what appeared to be smaller clouds of different colors. They were sheep, marching in a woolly mass, their coats powdered brown, red, and orange. A boy flung pebbles at the flock, and a dog trotted briskly beside him, yapping at the stragglers. They were jammed together so compactly, they looked like a single animal with several dozen heads and four times as many hooves.

At the trail that turned toward their dune, the dog lifted its leg at a clump of weeds. It lapped a drink from the irrigation ditch, then raised its snout sharply, sniffing and barking. The dog sprang across the canal and, nosing along the narrower path, picked up their scent.

Bert was afraid to call Ted now, afraid to make any noise. Though the boy shouted, the dog ignored him and loped nearer. When Ted groaned, it barked steadily, waving its plume of a tail. Bert had the pistol, but couldn't use it. That would bring the boy and everyone else, and so would this barking, she feared.

But the boy tossed a stone and dashed after the sheep, which had wandered into the thorn bushes at the bank of the *oued*. After baring its fangs for a final growl, the dog raced to catch him.

Ted had his head up, his eyes filmy with fatigue and confusion. "What's that?"

"Nothing. A dog. It's gone now."

Nodding, he nestled in the sand. He'd known it was a dog. When the barking had bothered his sleep, he'd begun to dream about the hounds they had back home, and remembered how dangerous a dog could be. Though they'd buried their tracks and Gypsy's blood, a hound could have sniffed them out. Did the Moroccans have dogs?

The question almost woke him, but before he had an answer, Bert's voice had lulled him to sleep and he was dreaming again, this time about the German shepherds that prowled the army bases in Vietnam. Big and vicious, they were like the sharks that swam after garbage scows in the Caribbean. Their lean snouts lifted to show fierce teeth, their malicious snarling . . .

Bert shook him awake. "Something's coming."

There was a great grinding noise, and he knew it wasn't a car. Not a jeep either. Snorting and backfiring, it roared through the dry wash, louder than any truck. A tank, Ted thought, head reeling, his guts wrenched by spasms. Jesus

Christ, a tank. Snatching the revolver from Bert, he hurled
himself up the dune.

The ground shuddered as the noise got nearer. Sand
slithered from under him. In the *oued* a cyclone of dust
boiled behind a large, lumbering vehicle that appeared to
be part truck, part tank, and was packed with troops. Next
to the driver a soldier manned a machine gun mounted on
the cab.

"What is it?" asked Bert.

"A halftrack."

Despite its size, it drummed effortlessly over the soft
riverbed, carving its own path. It had truck tires in front and
metal treads, like a tank's, in back, and these cleats cut the
oued into deep double furrows, spraying sand on the six
soldiers who huddled on the flatbed.

As the halftrack thundered north toward Zagora, Ted
trembled long after the ground quit shaking. He had
counted on jeeps and trucks and troops on foot, and
though he feared them, he'd learned ways to elude them.
But the halftrack threw him into turmoil. It could take almost any terrain, and once it had harried them from their
hiding place it would be hopeless to run. Firing over hundreds of yards of desert flats, the .50-calibre machine gun
would chop them down.

He tried to tell himself it was a routine maneuver. Maybe
the army patrolled this area every afternoon. But it was
much more likely the Moroccans had discovered they
hadn't gotten everybody last night and were combing the
countryside for survivors.

Bert slid down the dune and slumped against the palm
trunk, her sunburned face twisted with pain. "Is that thing
after us?" she asked.

"I'm not sure."

"So big and ugly." Her lips had pressed into a thin, white line.

"What's the matter?"

"My stomach. Cramps."

"Christ, it's that damn ditch water. You better lie back and rest. We have to be ready to shove off soon as it's dark."

"Oh hell, what's the use?"

Ted moved beside her. "Don't talk like that. Don't give up."

"Look, be honest. We don't have a chance. Why don't you go on alone?"

"You're talking crazy. You're not that sick."

"You won't make it carrying Gypsy. Or me."

"Lemme worry about that. You'll feel fine after you've slept."

"Oh Jesus, don't you see?" She seized his wrists. "You're not going to get paid."

"Who the hell said anything about . . ."

"There's no money. There never was. Polo and Phil lied to you."

He started to pull away, but Bert still had his wrists. "They tricked you. They didn't have the second two thousand. They were going to tell you when we got to Algeria. Believe me, Ted, I didn't know anything about it until yesterday. Nobody did but Polo and Phil."

"It doesn't matter," he mumbled.

"Yes, it does. I'll pay you. Soon as we're in the States, I'll find a job."

"Shh." He retrieved his hands. "Shut your eyes. I want you to stop thinking about this. It's all right."

"But Ted, it's not."

"I swear to you it is. It doesn't change anything. Now sleep."

When she was quiet, he crawled up the dune and sagged against the sand, as much to stop staring in bewilderment at Bert as to stand guard. The sun was spilling its color on the countryside like the bloodstain on Gypsy's blanket. The flat plains glowed a burnt orange, the chiseled hills a brilliant red. The sky, which had been bone white for hours, became blue at the horizon, then purple, then mother-of-pearl. From the east the wind returned, riffling the palm fronds and spreading fingers of sand. The dunes resembled ocean rollers, with blowing dust like foam at their crests and zigzagging rivulets on their sides. It looked like the sea at evening after a feathering breeze had passed.

Trapped here, they might have been marooned on one of those islands in a cartoon—a spit of sand, a solitary palm, and three survivors. That's what he'd told her, wasn't it? That he'd take her to a desert island. But where was the clever caption that could account for the bad joke that had been played on him?

Ted hadn't been lying when he assured Bert the money didn't matter. At least not at the moment. Two thousand bucks, ten thousand, twenty wouldn't save them from this jam. But if they managed to squeak through, he knew now they wouldn't be going to that other island. He'd arrive in the States with a little loose change left over from his advance, then have to start hustling for another connection, a quick score.

No, you two aren't going anywhere together. Probably you never were. Guys like you don't get out, he thought. And it wasn't that he feared he'd die here. It was just that he couldn't believe he'd ever go from this to anything better or different. He'd been doing it for decades. How did he expect to stop? Very likely there'd be another job, then another and another, always in some desolate spot, always for some desperate and self-defeating purpose, until finally he became the old man he felt like.

You had fun fooling yourself for a few days, he thought. He couldn't work up much anger at Polo and Phil. What good would it do? They lied to you; you lied to yourself. His mistake had been believing he'd caught a bluebird, that he'd leave the business by going in for one last big job, for a killing.

To keep his mind occupied and postpone more thinking, Ted turned to Gypsy, although there was nothing much he could do for the boy. His sleep was fitful; his lungs pumped out more air than they sucked in. The bandage had a spot of blood on it, drying into a scab of sorts, but since he had no water, Ted didn't bother to peel it off and dab at the wound. He got a whiff of the odor of unwashed flesh, filthy clothing. The onset of gangrene? He had to get away.

When he returned to the top of the dune, the sun seemed to balance on its own reflected brilliance, and as it sank, Ted shivered. He was hungry and had a headache. His tongue tasted foul and was swollen with thirst. Then his teeth were chattering, his body shook, and he heard a grumbling noise.

Ted ducked just before a blade of light slashed him in two. He rolled down to Gypsy and Bert as the halftrack pounded through the oasis, and he grabbed Bert when she tried to sit up. "Stay down," he shouted in her ear.

Drawing the .357, he flipped onto his back. The searchlight butchered the darkness above him, and he expected the metal treads to smash through the sand dune and trample them. But then the ground throbbed a little less beneath their heads. The clanging cut to the right, around the dune, and the noise faded until it wasn't much louder than the beat of their hearts. Ted hauled himself up to watch the halftrack trundle south toward Tagounite, the barrel of its machine gun paralleling the sweep of the searchlight.

He waited till he was calm before asking Bert, "You okay?"

"Yes. Was it the same one?"

"I don't know. I didn't notice a light on the other."

"God, that scared me. They must be after us."

"We'll be gone if they double back. Can you sit up?"

"Sure." And she did, but teetered groggily and had to lean on him.

"How's your stomach?"

"Not bad. I'm thirsty."

"We'll walk in the *oued* near the water. You can have a long drink before we set out."

"Is it time to start?"

"I'll tell you when."

Removing his belt, he fashioned a shoulder strap for the M-16, hooking the buckle over the barrel and fastening the other end to the trigger guard so it would be easier for Bert to carry. Now his trousers, loaded with money, cartridges for the pistol, and clips for the rifle, hung low on his hips, and he had to roll the cuffs twice. Grabbing his belly, he got a meagre fistful of flesh. His love handles had dissolved. Some way to lose weight, he thought.

When the halftrack had an hour's head start, he handed Bert the rifle. "I don't want you worrying. This won't be hard."

She was unconvinced. "If there's trouble, tell me what to do. I'll do whatever you say."

"Fine, but there's not going to be any trouble. Only a hell

of a hike. You can do that, can't you?"

She nodded, brushing her hair, which was salted with sand, away from her face. "But I meant what I said. I'd understand if you went on alone."

"Well, I'm not. So forget it." Then he gave her a light kiss on the forehead, much like the one that had started everything five nights ago.

3

THEY slipped through the oasis from palm tree to palm tree, up the path, over the irrigation ditch, and across the main trail. Thorn bushes snagged at their clothing as they crept along the steep bank of the *oued*, looking for a low spot. Finally, Ted had to wriggle over the edge on his belly and reach back to lift down Bert and Gypsy.

Beyond the shadow of the embankment, he dreaded he'd hear the heavy drumming of the halftrack. But with Gypsy slung across his shoulders, he couldn't hurry. It was hard enough to stay upright and stagger through the fine sand.

Near the stream, the ground was firm and he told Bert to drink first, while he stretched Gypsy out and trickled a little moisture into his mouth. The boy wouldn't take much.

When she was finished, he lowered his own lips to the water and thought he'd never tasted anything—not beer, wine, or whiskey—that was better. But every time he swallowed, he went momentarily deaf and experienced an unreasonable fear until he'd raised his head and reassured himself no one was around. He began to drink in a rocking motion. Dipping forward dizzily, he'd swig at the *oued*, then pause before lapping another mouthful. He'd seen skittish wild animals act like this. Afterward he was sick rather than satisfied.

*　　　*　　　*

At first, as they walked beside the sandstone wall, Gypsy felt lighter, maybe because of dehydration. But with every mile he seemed to gain weight, and Ted started counting to himself, as if calling cadence. He didn't repeat the numbers. They mounted steadily, and he thought of them as bricks he was stacking, a trench he was digging, a straight highway he was driving. Entering the monotony, he shut off parts of his mind and won some relief from the pain. When he hit two thousand, he figured that had to be a mile. Do that fifteen times and you'll be in Mhamid before morning.

But in a few hours he was too exhausted to count past ten, and so he did repeat himself, mumbling half-aloud and finally just grunting. Though his feet and ankles were wooden, his thighs were on fire, burning fiercely as they stabbed at his groin. Even wrapped in the blanket, Gypsy's wasted body was all barbs, sharp edges, and blades, like something hung on Ted's back with grappling hooks.

Yet he wouldn't stop. He hobbled on until they were beyond the oasis around Tagounite, and there were no more lights or palm trees lining the *oued*. The Dra had entered a deep canyon through the hills, and the riverbed was narrow and winding, blocked here and there by big boulders that had been buffed smooth by blowing sand. Steep, tapering gullies ran from this ravine to a plateau above, and down them whistled crosscurrents of wind.

The gorge they were going through was totally dark, the shadow of one wall extending to the base of the other. Overhead the desert sky looked depthless, brightened by stars and a wedge of moon. But the light didn't touch them, and though this darkness, the wind, and the rocks underfoot made walking difficult, Ted was glad they were hidden. Then he heard a familiar, frightening racket and ahead of them, where the canyon curved right, he saw what appeared to be an immense insect with a single eye. Probing the rugged terrain, this beam preceded the halftrack as its metal cleats clanked through the rubble. The light sliced across Bert, Gypsy, and Ted, silvering them for a second, and swung away. But before Ted had time to speak, it swept back to Bert, who froze like a doe that had been spotlighted. When a burst of machine-gun fire buzzed over their heads, she turned to run, and he had to shove her behind a boulder. Dumping Gypsy with her, he ducked for cover, too, while the searchlight wavered, then focused on the boulder. Bullets beat slivers and sparks from it.

Bert squirmed, and Ted held her by the belt, afraid she'd stand up.

"Jesus, they're going to get us," she said.

"Quiet. Be still."

"What'll we do? They saw us."

"The rifle. Gimme the goddamn rifle." Ripping the M-16 from her shoulder, he forced her farther behind the rock.

The halftrack had halted about twenty yards in front of them, its engine snarling in neutral, and someone squawked through a microphone—first in Arabic, then French and garbled English—for them to come out and identify themselves. The English gave the Moroccans away. They knew who they were after.

To the left and behind him lay an open field, but Ted didn't dare try to outdistance the spotlight and the machine gun. To make a break, they had to move forward, closing the angle of fire. Ten feet to the right rose the canyon wall and, running his eyes along the rim, Ted located the next gully about twenty-five yards ahead, just beyond the halftrack.

"When I say go," he told Bert, "you take the rifle and don't stop."

"Where?" She darted a glance behind them.

"The other direction. To that first gully. We gotta get to the top where the halftrack can't follow us."

The man with the microphone was speaking Arabic again. Flat against the ground, Ted craned his neck around the rock. None of the soldiers had hopped down from the flatbed. Obviously they'd stay put behind the armor plating unless ordered out. He knew and they knew he couldn't wreck the metal treads or puncture the front tires which were full of foam, but he had a target.

Ted aimed the M-16 along the slant of light, and the instant he touched the trigger, the bulb exploded and the talk stopped. Sending a second burst at the same spot, he must have hit the machine gunner, for no one answered his fire. Then he drew the .357 and drilled a few armor-piercing slugs at the grille of the halftrack, hoping to crack the block.

"Now! Run!" He clamped a fresh clip on the rifle, gave it to Bert, and pushed her toward the wall. Slinging Gypsy over his shoulders, he lumbered after her.

In the halftrack, someone punched on the high beams, but they weren't as bright as the spotlight had been and didn't illuminate much on either side. Whoever had come to man the machine gun was chopping the gravel around the big boulder, then laying down a line of fire across the ravine, raising puffs of dust and splitting rocks. But Bert and Ted were passing in the opposite direction. The soldiers heard them and shot wildly in the dark. Several ricochets slapped at the wall, showering them with chunks of sandstone.

When they got to the gully, the halftrack was just trucking around, and Ted cursed himself for not hitting the block. Still he thought they'd be safe once they were out of the *oued*. But this gully was broad and smooth, and he realized at once it wouldn't hold back the halftrack. It was too late to run for the next one. The high beams were on him. The .50 calibre rattled, then was cut off by the corner of the wall as he started to climb.

Though Bert was far up the incline, he screamed, "Faster." Tumbling forward, collared by Gypsy's limp weight, Ted flung out a hand to keep from falling and continued to scramble. His fingernails split and his palm was bloody from clawing at the shale which slid from under his feet. For a second he had a nightmarish sense he was stuck in place.

Letting his head hang loose, he looked back between his legs. The halftrack had heeled around to enter the alleyway, and the machine gunner was firing, but the jerky maneuvering threw off his aim. Bullets cracked the pebbles behind Ted.

"Cover me," he cried to Bert, who was already at the top.

She didn't understand. Maybe she couldn't hear. The halftrack was rumbling up the ramp, the gunner stitching a seam along its center. He'd rivet Ted as soon as he reset his sights.

"Cover me," he begged her.

This time she understood, yet still hesitated, holding the rifle far from her body as if it were alive and poisonous. Ted was about to ditch Gypsy and run for it when she stepped to one side, shouldered the M-16, and squeezed off a burst that banged into the armor and shattered the left headlight. Then the barrel was jumping and her shots flew wide, but she had slowed down the driver and made the machine gunner duck.

At the top, Ted rolled Gypsy off his back and took the rifle. He and Bert raced along the gully to a point directly above the halftrack. Without the spotlight, the gunner had to guess where they were and had trouble turning and tilting the gun. The other soldiers had just shifted to the far side of the flatbed when Ted fired down at them. He got the machine gunner first, before mauling the crowd of them. Finishing the clip, he switched to the pistol and shot through the hood into the engine. Then he reloaded the rifle and raked the soldiers a second time.

No one shot back, and the halftrack was huffing and chugging downhill. He could tell by the way it bucked that it wasn't in reverse. The driver was dead and so was the motor, but he kept shooting till it smashed into the bank of the gully.

Ted waited and listened. For a moment nothing moved. Then a wounded Moroccan leaped off the flatbed, clutching his chest, and broke for the *oued*. Ted hit him, and he plunged face first, his arms outstretched, sledding along the gravel.

Again there was nothing except a splashing sound. Ted emptied the last clip into the bodies and reloaded the pistol. "Stay here," he said.

"Where are you going?"

"To see whether there's anything we can use."

"No, don't." Bert had his arm.

"We need food and water." He pried her fingers loose. "You look after Gypsy."

Digging in his heels, the .357 in his hand, Ted cautiously approached the halftrack. The dry air was full of fumes, the shale around the halftrack slippery with gasoline, oil, and other fluids. One spark, he thought, and they'd all be fried. What would happen if he fired a shot?

Awkwardly he climbed over the armor-plated panels and, without putting down the pistol, groped through the mess. But there was no food that he could find, not even when he ripped the dead soldiers' pockets inside out. Under the stack of bodies, there were, however, a few ten-gallon water cans, all of them punctured. Ted carried one leaking drum back to Bert and held it high so they could drink as water spurted from the bullet holes. It had a salty taste—of blood, he suspected—but he said nothing about this to her. Most of it splashed on their chins or chests or the ground anyway.

The tin rang hollowly when he tossed it into the gully. He threw the empty M-16 after it.

"Are they all dead?" asked Bert.

"Yes," he said, going to Gypsy, who lay crumpled, but alive, inside the blanket. Ted brought the boy onto his back.

"Do you think I hit anyone?" she asked.

"I don't know, but you saved my life."

Bert didn't look up from the gully until he said, "We have to go."

"I don't think I want to. All those men dead and . . ."

"Come on." He tugged her away from the edge. "There's no time to talk."

VIII

THEY MADE the oasis near Mhamid an hour before dawn, delirious with thirst, heads throbbing from hunger. Moaning in hoarse monotones, they floundered through the cultivated fields, searching for the Dra. Twice Ted had to tear Bert away as she tried to drink from irrigation ditches. The wind was cold and cutting, and carried seeds of sand that rooted among the grain stalks, spreading thread-like vines and sprouting new dunes in the palm groves. Every day the farmers had to beat back the desert with shovels and buckets.

When they reached the *oued,* which had been reduced to a muddy gurgle, they dropped onto their bellies and drank. Ted funneled water into Gypsy's mouth, but it drooled from his lips, and the boy coughed feebly to clear his throat.

Because there was no protection next to the stream, they retreated to a patch of mint, fenced in by fat date palms. Lying there was like floating on a cool, green lake. Ted bit into the succulent leaves, releasing a sweet scent that soothed his throat and nostrils. Rooting around on her hands and knees, Bert nibbled the plants before falling asleep next to Gypsy, leaving Ted to watch over them.

The camels came at daybreak, advancing from the eastern desert out of an orange disc of sun, rising, disappearing, then rising again from dark troughs in the dunes. At first Ted believed he was dreaming, but he couldn't shake the sight from his eyes. They kept coming in great herds, hundreds of them. The drovers wore loose cotton caftans dyed a deep indigo, and the cloth snapped and luffed like sails. Most of the men were perched on wooden saddles padded with fleecy sheepskin, swaying and creaking on the one-hump, *mehari* camels. Some owned ornate, hammerlock muskets and carried them cocked against their thighs. Parts of their turbans had been twisted mask-like across their noses and mouths, and the skin that showed on their foreheads and hands had been blue-tinted by dye.

The women, too, wore billowing blue robes, and their lower faces were covered by a corner of the garment, which they clenched in their teeth. Only their eyes, stained with antimony on the lids and brows, were exposed. As they got nearer, there was the jangle of jewelry. They had silver bracelets on their wrists, rings on their fingers and in their braided hair, and large, triangular breast plates suspended from their necks.

As the Blue Men moved toward Mhamid for the weekly market, several camels stopped at the mint patch to crop the tender shoots. Flat on his back, shielded by a screen of palm fronds, Ted held himself rigid, the pistol in his hand, and heard them spitting, burping, and blubbering as they ruminated. Then at a harsh command from the drovers, they clomped back onto the path.

He realized they couldn't stay where they were and woke Bert. Stuffing their pockets with mint, they stole through the mauve morning light to the farthest edge of the oasis, where they hid in an empty irrigation ditch at the base of a mud wall. Behind it sand whined and seethed like sea-waves lashing a bulkhead.

Ted woke much later to find Gypsy moustached with dried blood, and believed the boy had hemorrhaged and died. But he was still breathing—just barely, but breathing nevertheless. Licking his thumb, Ted was erasing the brown handlebar when Bert looked over and let out a muffled cry.

Her nose had also bled and, judging by her startled eyes, his must have too. But in her exhaustion, very close to hysteria, she couldn't make sense of what she saw. Did she think he was dying? Or that the blood belonged to the dead soldiers in the gully? It did give them all a ghoulish look, and he knew she hadn't recovered from that clash with the halftrack.

Before she could cry again, he said, "Just a nosebleed, baby. The dryness did it. Here, lemme help." Steadying her head, he flaked the blood from her upper lip.

She sagged against the warm bricks, her eyes shut, her mouth open. When she ran a hand through her hair, split strands of it clung to her fingers, crackling with static electricity. There was no shade, no escape from the sun. Though the air weighed a ton, it didn't contain an ounce of moisture. The heat might have been bearable, if it hadn't been for this deadening dryness, the wind, and the dust that turned every breath into torture.

"What are we waiting for?" she asked.

"Dark. We can't travel till tonight."

"Jesus, after a day here I won't be able to walk. Is there any water? Where's the *oued?*"

"Across the fields." He pushed her back when she started to stand up. "Stay here. Somebody'd sure as hell see you. Chew on the mint before it loses its juice."

Gnawing a leafy stalk, she muttered once more, "What are we waiting for?"

Though he knew, he didn't answer. At first he'd been waiting for Gypsy to die. Now that that wouldn't make much difference, he was waiting for them to die.

The border wasn't far from Mhamid, but as he remembered from the map, there were no oases or towns on the other side, only the road, N50, a straight red line like a streak of blood through the emptiness. He didn't bother adding up the miles again. He had very little strength left, and was losing that fast. They'd never get there, not walking, not without food and water.

There has to be another way to reach that road, he told himself. There's always a way when you're wide awake to recognize it and not afraid to try. The time had come to take bigger chances before he was too weak. No risk could be greater than remaining here or leaving empty-handed.

Ted was trying to figure how to sneak into the town that night and steal a car, when he saw a man leading a camel toward them. The Moroccan held a rope of braided hemp which had been hooked through the animal's nostril by a brass ring. They passed on the path about ten feet away, but never noticed the three of them huddled in the ditch. Nor did Bert, who was dozing, know that anyone was near.

The camel looked fat and flush, its hump hard under a saddle which had a sleek water bag and a bulky canvas sack tied to it. The man was a Haratin, a black descendant of slaves from the Sudan. His caftan was spotted with wet patches, for he had just come from the *oued* where he'd washed his turban, which bled dye-stained tears over his face. Blotting them with his sleeve, he adjusted the large pouch that swung from his shoulder by a leather strap.

He was headed for the market, Ted thought, to sell the camel. But, not far along the path, the man stopped next to a few palms and hobbled the camel by folding its right front hoof underneath it and strapping it to its leg. After unloading the supplies from the saddle, he turned east, knelt, and prayed, repeatedly bowing and pressing his face to the ground. He ended up with sand embedded in his broad black forehead.

Still hidden in the ditch, Ted crawled away from Bert and Gypsy and concentrated on the goatskin water bag, its belly bulging and taut, its legs erect. Glistening beads of dampness dotted the bald patches where the hair had worn through to the hide. The sight affected him strangely. Afraid he'd do something stupid, he stared at the ground a second.

The Haratin had unrolled a ragged scrap of carpet, loosened a drawstring on the canvas sack, and unpacked half a dozen oranges, several overripe bananas, an oval loaf of Berber bread, and a soft ball of white cheese. Breaking off a crust of bread, he scooped at the cheese and lifted a lump of it to his mouth. His fingers made moist, popping sounds as he sucked each one clean.

Ted experienced the same strange feeling, but this time didn't turn aside. Tense and quiet, torn by conflicting urges, he watched the man savor every bite as if teasing him. Slowly he chewed a banana which Ted could have swallowed whole. Peeling an orange, he casually tossed scraps of rind very near the ditch. Ted didn't believe it was possible, but he began to have hunger pangs for one piece of orange peel which was within his reach. His belly rumbled and though he would have thought that fear and the last two days had drained every drop of moisture, his tongue was suddenly slick with saliva.

When the Haratin hoisted the water bag, unplugged one leg, and let a clear stream spurt between his lips, Ted couldn't stand it any longer. What if I beg for food and something to drink? We're dying. How could he say no? Hell, I'll pay. I'd give a hundred dollars for the oranges alone. Twice that if he'd throw in the water bag.

But Ted waited till he'd calmed himself, and knew it was the camel they needed most. Buy that, then the water bag. The food you can bargain for afterward. The man might have wandered in from the desert, might not have been warned about them. He couldn't pass up this opportunity. With the camel and the water bag and maybe a few oranges they could set out at once.

He glanced to the right where Bert had Gypsy's head in her lap and was leaning forward to shade his face. She was still asleep, and he decided not to wake her. No use worrying her, and he didn't want to argue. He knew what he had to do.

Tucking his shirttail around the revolver, he slapped the dust from his trousers and stood up. For an instant the ground tilted crazily and grainy dots spun before his eyes. Yet he strolled from the ditch as though there was nothing unusual about his being here. A sunblistered American in a tattered shirt.

Although the Haratin eyed him curiously, he didn't act shocked or frightened. But Ted's heart thumped, his empty belly echoed its beat, and his mouth was parched again, as were his palms. Smiling, he said, *"Bonjour, Monsieur."*

"Boanzour."

"You have a handsome camel." The sentence might have been from an elementary French grammar book, but he judged by the black man's expression that he hadn't understood. Since Ted's Arabic consisted of several stock phrases, they'd have to bargain in sign language.

"*La bès.*" Ted gave his hand a firm shake.

"*La bès,*" he answered with a puzzled grin, getting to his feet.

The man's skin, though weatherbeaten, was unscarred except near the left nostril where the flange had been torn, as if he, like the camel, had once worn a brass ring through it. But both his eyes were good, which meant he couldn't have been too old, and beneath the robes his body looked solid and sinewy.

Nodding and clucking his tongue like a connoisseur, Ted patted the camel's neck, and heard it burble deep in its bent throat. I must be out of my goddamm mind, he thought. This was the truest measure of his desperation—to take this kind of chance for a misshapen creature with a harelip, yellow teeth, and raw saddle sores. How the hell did you ride it? Circling it, trying not to stagger, he inspected the broad, cloven hooves and swatted its flanks. The animal switched its tail, exposing a colony of ticks at its anus.

Returning to the Moroccan, who had waited in bewilderment, Ted nodded more emphatically, gestured to the camel, then to himself. After he'd done this twice, the man smiled, shook his head, and tapped his chest. It was his, and he wasn't selling. Or hadn't he understood? When Ted repeated the bartering motion, the man stopped smiling, jiggled his hand, and said, "*Makach.*"

There was no time for the usual Byzantine bargaining. Ted had no idea what a camel cost and didn't care. He didn't even care whether this one was for sale. He just knew he had to have it and the water bag, quick.

When he pulled the wad of dirhams and dollars from his pocket, a bullet, its brass hull gleaming, came with them and clinked to the path. Though Ted ground the shell into the dirt with his shoe, the man must have noticed it. Yet he had his eyes on the fat sheaf of bills, eager, alert, and at the same time wary.

Counting out the equivalent of two hundred dollars in dirhams, Ted touched the camel, then held them toward the man, who side-stepped the offer, grasping the braided halter in both hands, as if it required monumental effort to control himself.

Ted's head was whirling. Spreading his legs for balance, he shelled out another two hundred to sweeten the pot, thinking, That oughta do it. But he'd overdone it. The amount exceeded the man's comprehension. If he hadn't suspected something before, he did now and was afraid. Frowning and murmuring to himself, he refused to look at the money.

A mistake, thought Ted. The whole move. Too late to back down. He'd played his last card. The man would report them, and they couldn't get away without the camel, the water—without a goddamn chance.

Ted ripped the lead rope from his fists. Angry and frightened, the man didn't fight back. Instead he assumed a sort of formalized begging stance and spoke rapidly in words which needed no interpretation. Cupping his palms at his chest, he demanded his animal.

Ted slapped the four hundred dollars into his hands, but the Moroccan let the bills fall at their feet. As Ted watched his money being whipped away on the wind, the Haratin snatched at the halter, and Ted had to knock him back. The camel, precarious on three legs, began to buck and spit, and the ring in its nose was tarnished with blood. Ted's arm socket popped, but he had a good grip on the rope and didn't let go.

More furious than afraid now, the man screamed and cursed and beat at his blue robes. When Ted pointed to the dirhams, he kicked them, then rushed in, his hands clutching Ted's throat, the sharp nails digging deep. Ted didn't have the strength to break his chokehold, and while the camel dragged him in one direction, the man yanked him in another. Ducking forward abruptly, Ted butted him in the face with his forehead, mashing his nose and lips. As the Moroccan staggered back, spitting blood, the wet turban uncoiled from his shaved skull and slithered to the ground.

Ted was wobbly, too. He'd nearly knocked himself unconscious, and as he struggled for air, his throat gave a strangled sound. The black man brought a curved knife from the folds of his caftan, and Ted barely had time to dodge the blade. Drawing the .357, he tried to ward him off, but the Haratin lunged a second time and Ted pistol-whipped the side of his head.

Dropping the knife, the man caved in to his knees, bleeding badly, then almost at once was on his feet, screaming as he fled for the village. Ted aimed at his spine, but realized if he fired, everyone in the oasis would hear it. Releasing the rope, he grabbed the knife, caught up to the dazed Moroccan, and bashed his head with the gun barrel. But when the man went down, Ted knew he wouldn't stay there. Already he was writhing, laboring to stand up. Ted struck him again, straddled his chest, and stabbed him just under the Adam's apple. Pain revived the man for a last moment, and he thrashed and tried to call for help. But blood, not a scream, burst from his mouth, bathing Ted's hands. As the chords of his neck snapped like catgut, Ted felt sick at his stomach, yet didn't stop until the man was motionless.

Then someone did scream. It was Bert, who had awakened in time to watch Ted murder the Moroccan. Tottering toward him, she shouted wildly, and when he went to quiet her, she wheeled around and ran. He still had the knife in one hand, the pistol in the other, and she seemed to think he intended to kill her too. But before she'd gone five yards, she fell in a heap, her eyes electric with panic.

"Don't. They'll hear."

"Why? Why did you do it?" she asked. "I saw you. I saw everything."

"I had to."

"But why?"

"The camel and the water bag. We had to have them. He wouldn't sell. He pulled a knife."

"I don't care. I don't care," she cried, shaking her head. "Why?"

Heaving the knife far into the palm grove and pushing the pistol under his belt, he dragged Bert to a sitting position. She fell against his legs, feebly clawing at his trousers. "Why?"

"That's enough. We have to go."

He hauled Bert to her feet. Even she was horribly heavy for him now, and for a moment he allowed himself the luxury of leaning on her. Over her shoulder, he saw the camel chomping at weeds, waiting for its owner. Though Bert had stopped crying, she kept asking, "Why? Why?"

"Please," he said, "pull yourself together."

"Oh Ted, I'm so tired."

"Go to Gypsy. Wait there till I call you." He nudged her toward the wall.

When she was out of sight, Ted tore off his shirt and

stuffed it in the man's slashed throat to slow the bleeding while he stripped the body of its clothing and few belongings. Under the loose caftan, the Haratin had on a sleeveless tunic and baggy cotton trousers, and in his pockets were a pack of matches, several dirhams, an English pound, a penknife, and a stack of letters bound with string.

The first one, written in spidery, purple ink, read, "Assiz was our guide on a most fascinating and enjoyable afternoon in Mhamid. He didn't speak English or French, but we found him cheerful and courteous. We highly recommend him. Mr. and Mrs. Jeffrey Longworth, Akron, Ohio."

Another bore an embossed letterhead from the Department of Anthropology, the University of Chicago. "During our study of the oasis, Assiz Larbi Abbazi was a willing and capable worker. He was, also, more than eager to explain the local customs and folklore, but I fear that most of his information was apocryphal. Perhaps he serves best as an indication of the extent to which the French, and now the tourists, have infiltrated this once isolated community and debased its culture. Dr. A. J. Winters."

Ted didn't read the rest. Leaving the dead man his letters, he dropped the other things into his own pocket and set aside the turban and caftan. Then he gripped the Haratin's bare ankles and towed him up the path, his head rolling this way and that, as though it were attached by a single thread. Already blood had seeped through the shirt at his neck, streaking the sand.

As he dragged the dead weight behind him, Ted tried to convince himself that he'd had no choice. You couldn't have carried Gypsy. Not for a mile, much less to Algeria. He might not make it to the mud wall. But Bert's question echoed in his ears. Why?

He no longer saw anything so crucial about survival. No,

he thought, it wasn't worth it. This was the worst yet—to touch the damp black body, to have blood up to his elbows, to watch the man's head dangle and the wound yawn gruesomely.

He shouldered the body over the wall. His mind no longer dictated what he did. Raw instinct urged him on. Swiftly he dug a shallow grave, shoved in the body, and buried it, scraping and kicking at the sand that thirstily drank blood. Wind helped him fill the hole. Once covered by a layer of dust, the man resembled a statue rounding into rough shape. Then he lost his humanity a limb at a time. Feet, legs, arms, face, they all went under, as Ted scrabbled at the earth like a dog.

He knelt there panting afterward, his stomach wracked by cramps, but he'd been emptied even of bile. Heaving drily, he stumbled down from the dune and smoothed dirt over the blood on the path. He put on the caftan, cleaned his face with the turban, then untwisted it and draped it over his head, tying it like a kerchief under his chin.

At the carpet, he collected all the food, including the smallest crumbs, and packed it into the canvas sack. Eager to get away, he didn't take time to eat, but he did drink, unplugging the water bag and sipping from a hollow hoof. The water was warm and tarry-tasting.

In the black man's shoulder pouch, he found odds and ends of cloth and a spare caftan. Calling Bert, he said, "Wear this. It'll keep the sun off you. Here's the food and water." But their eyes didn't meet and their hands never touched as he gave it to her.

When he started after the camel, the strange, overstuffed animal limped off ponderously on three legs. Not wanting to scare it away, Ted spoke as he would have to a horse, "There, there, big fellow. Take it easy." The four hundred

dollars worth of dirhams flittered around like bright butter-
flies, but he didn't bother to stoop down and gather them.

He snatched the lead rope, and the camel tossed its head,
snapping Ted's arm, but he held tight, murmuring, "Easy.
Easy now." As he stroked the sickle-shaped neck, the camel
batted its long eyelashes with an expression of absolute
superiority, as if unaware of its ugliness. Between the flaps
of its hare lip stuck a pink tongue, glistening like some
internal organ it had burped up.

Ted passed the braided halter to Bert, and they still
didn't look at one another. While he went for Gypsy, she
stared at her feet, and the camel gazed haughtily over her
head, across the desert. Sunbaked and immobile, she and
the animal formed an improbable frieze of mismatched
parts.

Lifting the boy's head by the frayed hem of the blanket,
Ted dragged him out of the ditch and onto the path.
Plumes of chalky powder wavered at Gypsy's lips, as if the
air was freezing cold. No other part of him moved. Since
he had no idea how to make the camel kneel on its calloused knees, Ted unhobbled it, stooped over, and said to
Bert, "Step on my back and up onto this thing."

"Are you sure?"

"Yes. Do it quick."

Planting her sandal on his spine, she seized the wooden
pommel and swung herself into the padded saddle.

"Is there room for him?" asked Ted.

"Yes. In front of me."

"We'll have to stretch him across."

Ted levered the boy upright and said, "Grab hold," and
while Bert grasped the blanket, he squatted and looped his
arms around Gypsy's pipestem legs. When he said, "Pull,"
they heaved the body up over the saddle. Drab wool hid his

feet and head at either end, and he looked like a bulky rug rolled in front of Bert.

"Can he breathe?" she asked.

"I think so."

"But isn't it bad for him to . . ." Her voice trailed off. At this point everything was bad for Gypsy, and not much better for them.

2

BEYOND Mhamid the Oued Dra dried up altogether, dissolving into the Debaia, a boundless, sandy plain, and as they abandoned the riverbed, the camel picked its own path. Ted held the rope loosely and limped along beside it. He glanced back only once. The oasis appeared verdant, cool, and inviting, the sharp geometrical shadows of its casbahs shimmering like dark pools. Several houses had elaborate designs on their sides—glittering stones and sticks and palm fronds embedded in the mud, each ornament like a last protest against the desert which extended from here to Egypt.

They ate as they walked, wolfing the fruit and washing bread and cheese down with water. Then Bert, like the Haratin women, fixed a corner of the caftan across her head and clenched the cloth in her teeth, so that her whole face was hidden except for one weary eye. Gripping the pommel, she slouched in the saddle, half-asleep. When she breathed in, the blue material matted against her nose and mouth; as she exhaled, it bubbled out.

Staggering deeper into the Sahara, Ted couldn't stand the emptiness and focused his aching eyes on his feet. The wind, sweeping in from the east, was sterile, with nothing on it to smell or taste except the stench of his flesh, the bitterness of his sweat. He steered by the falling sun; feeling its fire on his back, he knew he was still going east. Lizards and insects skittered away from him, and it seemed that whatever had managed to survive here was trivial and terror-stricken. Ted didn't exclude himself.

That afternoon they passed outcroppings of primary rock encrusted with marine fossils. Seeing these petrified seashells, he thought he was hallucinating, but touching them to be sure they were real, he bloodied his hands on the jagged spines.

Later they reached other rocks, on which prehistoric people had scratched stick figures of men and animals. These carvings also reminded him of marine fossils dredged from the deepest ocean trenches. The size and perspective struck him as correct. That's what it meant to be human here—to have pinhole eyes, nostrils, and ears, and a mouth that might have been fashioned by an inverted fingernail.

Ted didn't attempt to fight his feeling of insignificance. Waves of horror and exhaustion washed over him, and wandering in this immensity, he was willing to concede that nothing mattered, neither he nor anything he'd ever wanted. His thoughts had the lunar dryness and indifference of the landscape, and he knew no words and no reason to express them.

So Bert and he stayed silent, leaving footprints that vanished, bleeding beads of perspiration that evaporated before they struck the ground. Once he blacked out for a second and woke to see the camel step over him. The fat, furry belly passed, then the padded knees and the rag of tail. Springing to his feet, he caught the camel before Bert realized what was wrong, but after that he tied the rope to his wrist and was pulled along like a prisoner, unable to hope his suffering would end soon, much less express his greatest fear that it would go on forever.

Then darkness sheltered them from the desolation, from each other and all that remained unspoken. Ted navigated by the North Star, eating and drinking on the move. He had become a hollow reed, a length of bad plumbing whose sole function, it seemed, was walking, panting hoarsely, ignoring the pain, and passing gas like the flatulent camel.

Although they had long since crossed the border, Ted didn't stop that night, and morning crashed over his weariness with a dizzying crescendo of mirages. Mountains, towns, palm trees, and people appeared to float in front of him on brimming blue lakes. The sky became bright orange in the east and a semicircle of sun, totally distinct in spite of the dust and the air inversion, rested on the horizon. Ted hurried as if expecting this helium-filled globe to lift them with it when it rose.

Preoccupied by his race for the sun, Ted felt the pavement before he saw it. Its solidity sent a jolt up his legs. Running north-south, the road snaked away to obscurity in either direction. He scuffed his feet on the asphalt a second time to make sure there was no mistake. Then they walked north no more than a mile and encountered a broad, concrete kilometer stone. *N50. Béchar 330 K.*

Beside the stone, the camel crouched of its own accord, grumbling contentedly like a purring cat. Bert climbed off and hobbled around on her swollen feet. The corner of the caftan had blown back from her face, and her hair was a nest of filthy wires.

Ted stretched Gypsy on the ground, but didn't fold the blanket away from his head. Squatting on his haunches, he stared south at the distant pinpoint where the road disappeared toward Tindouf.

"What now?" asked Bert, sitting beside him.

"Wait." After so many hours of silence, his voice sounded rusty and remote.

"How long?"

"As long as it takes. Someone'll show up sooner or later. We'll make it." But he spoke almost as if their escape were a punishment, and when she looked into his eyes, he turned away. He didn't want her pity, which he took as another proof of how poorly he'd done. He'd pulled them through as he'd promised, but he couldn't forget how they'd gotten here and how far it was from where he longed to be.

"I'm sorry," she said, wondering how many times she'd had to repeat herself. For days she'd done nothing but apologize, and yet she doubted anything she said would ever be enough. Still, she tried. "I mean it. I'm sorry for everything."

In answer, he could only tell her the truth. "So am I. For everything."

Nervously, Bert began fumbling with the blanket at Gypsy's face. "Don't fool with that," he said, but she extended her hand over the boy's mouth, as though testing the heat of a flame. After baring the underside of her wrist, she suddenly shivered, and drawing back, wrapped her head and face and hands in the blue cotton.

"He's dead," she said.

Ted nodded.

"I said Gypsy's dead." She was crying soundlessly inside the caftan, wetting the cloth at her lips.

"Yes, I know. I'll bury him soon as I have some strength."

Then they sat in silence beside the camel and the dead body, bundled against the blowing sand, keeping a careful space between them.

About the Author

MICHAEL MEWSHAW was born in Washington, D.C., in 1943 and was graduated from the University of Maryland (A.B.) and the University of Virginia (Ph.D.). His first novel, *Man in Motion,* was published in 1970. He spent eighteen months abroad on a Fulbright Fellowship in Creative Writing, then returned to the United States, where he finished his second novel, *Waking Slow.* He and his wife, Linda, have lived and traveled extensively in Europe, the Middle East, and North Africa. Since September of 1973 Mr. Mewshaw has been a member of the English department at the University of Texas.